A NEW DAWN OVER MULBERRY LANE

ROSIE CLARKE

WITHDRAWN FROM LIBRARY

B

Boldwood

First published in Great Britain in 2022 by Boldwood Books Ltd.

Copyright © Rosie Clarke, 2022

Cover Design by Colin Thomas

Cover Photography: Colin Thomas

The moral right of Rosie Clarke to be identified as the author of this work has been asserted in accordance with the Copyright, Designs and Patents Act 1988.

All rights reserved. No part of this book may be reproduced in any form or by any electronic or mechanical means, including information storage and retrieval systems, without written permission from the author, except for the use of brief quotations in a book review.

This book is a work of fiction and, except in the case of historical fact, any resemblance to actual persons, living or dead, is purely coincidental.

Every effort has been made to obtain the necessary permissions with reference to copyright material, both illustrative and quoted. We apologise for any omissions in this respect and will be pleased to make the appropriate acknowledgements in any future edition.

A CIP catalogue record for this book is available from the British Library.

Paperback ISBN 978-1-80162-243-1

Large Print ISBN 978-1-80162-244-8

Hardback ISBN 978-1-80162-242-4

Ebook ISBN 978-1-80162-245-5

Kindle ISBN 978-1-80162-246-2

Audio CD ISBN 978-1-80162-237-0

MP3 CD ISBN 978-1-80162-238-7

Digital audio download ISBN 978-1-80162-240-0

Boldwood Books Ltd
23 Bowerdean Street
London SW6 3TN
www.boldwoodbooks.com

1

JUNE 1958

The Pig & Whistle bar smelled of lavender polish and everything sparkled as Peggy Ronoscki walked in that sunny morning in June. Mrs Mags, her new cleaning lady, was working out well and her daughter Julie was brilliant behind the bar. Both the Pig & Whistle and Peggy's boarding house were doing well, and business was steady for her husband Able and Tom Barton. She thought that Able would have liked to be in an even better position with the building firm he and Tom Barton ran. Tom was slow and careful and, although that frustrated Able at times, his friend and partner was reliable and the firm was growing all the time. Peggy was pleased that Tom took his time about making decisions, because Able could sometimes be a bit reckless and plunge in without thinking it all through, though he was a good businessman and didn't make many mistakes.

Tom had been born in Mulberry Lane and was a good friend of the family long before he had met Able and eventually decided to start the building business. He'd built up his reputation as a lad by always being ready to help anyone and could repair just about anything in the building line.

Able was younger than Peggy by a few years and an American she'd met during the war when he was in London on special assignment with his general. Peggy's first marriage had been going through a rocky patch at the time and she'd fallen in love with the handsome young soldier. Later, after their twins were born in 1942 and, when the war was nearly over in 1945 Able returned, having lost an arm while on active service. Peggy's first husband had died of an illness discovered when he was recovering from a knife wound inflicted during his heroic intervention during an attack on Peggy's best friend, Maureen. It left Peggy free to marry the man she loved after a period of mourning. Since then, things had got much better for her and her family.

For a while after their marriage, Able and Peggy had moved to the Devon coast and run a small café near the seafront. However, her daughter Fay's ambition to be a famous ice skater had brought them back to London. Peggy's eldest son had wanted to move down to the Devon area for his work in the aviation industry and so he'd bought their cottage and she had taken over the Pig & Whistle again. It was the place she was happiest in and it suited everyone.

All in all, life looked good these days to Peggy, even though she'd begun to notice a few lines at the corners of her eyes and she'd put on weight this past winter. Able said he liked her the way she was, but Peggy had always been slim and she hated the idea of developing a middle-aged spread, even though at her age she ought to be grateful to be fit and healthy. Well into her fifties now, she still felt full of energy and enjoyed her cooking as much as ever, never ceasing to experiment with her recipes. Though, she knew that the most popular dishes were the tried and trusted ones that she'd cooked for years.

Peggy picked up a glass from behind the bar that she'd noticed had a tiny smear on it and began to polish it with a cloth. The one thing she couldn't abide was a smeared glass and this one had escaped the cleaner's notice.

However, everything else looked to be spotless and Peggy was about to head for the kitchen to begin cooking for the day when the door burst open and her best friend, Maureen rushed in. She looked flustered and upset and Peggy sensed instantly that something awful had happened.

'It's Gordon—' Maureen began and gasped for breath. 'He got up this morning and said his chest felt a bit tight and then suddenly collapsed on the kitchen floor. I rang the ambulance and they took him straight into hospital.'

'Oh, Maureen love,' Peggy said, moving to hug her, instantly concerned for her friend. She could imagine how distressed Maureen must be by her husband's collapse. 'Why aren't you with him?'

'They wouldn't let me; I'd just be in the way. Besides, I had Gordy's breakfast to get and I needed to open the shop. They told me it would be best to go in later as I would just be sitting around waiting while the doctors examine him. He'll need X-rays and all sorts so...' She choked back a sob, but her eyes were filled with tears. 'He was unconscious by then so I just kissed him and told him I would be in later. I've seen Gordy off to school and I'm on my way to the hospital now. I just wanted to tell you I won't be in today...' Gordon ran their grocery shop on the corner of Mulberry Lane. It had been left to Maureen by her grandmother, but Gordon had expanded and improved it, making it the profitable business it now was, but Maureen helped Peggy to make cakes for their little cake shop, next door but one to the Pig & Whistle.

'Of course, you won't,' Peggy said. 'Are you all right for transport?'

'Yes, I've got the car,' Maureen replied. 'We have some deliveries to go out, so I couldn't take my van...'

Peggy nodded. She understood that Maureen didn't much like driving her husband's car, which was a large second-hand Daimler and heavy on the steerage for her. Her van was smaller and lighter and she was used to it, but since their assistant needed it for delivering groceries, she had no choice.

The shop at the corner of Mulberry Lane was now two properties turned into one and always busy. Gordon worked from eight in the morning until six-thirty or later in the evenings and often went back in on a Sunday morning to do stocktaking or refill his shelves. Their deliveries were done by a young artist named James, who struggled to make a living from his work and was glad of a few shillings a week to pay his rent. Maureen took him food regularly because, as she said, he would forget to eat if she didn't.

'Go, go,' Peggy urged her as she saw her distress. 'I can hold the fort here. I have plenty of help these days. Let me know how things are when you can – and remember, if you need help, I am here for you any time, day or night.'

Maureen nodded, but she was too tense and strained to smile, barely holding back her tears. 'I'll ring,' she promised and dashed out again.

Peggy sighed. Her feeling of well-being had vanished with her friend's news. As she knew only too well, happiness could vanish like a puff of smoke. She'd experienced the grief of loss herself when Able had disappeared for years during the war, and she felt for her friend.

Maureen had been through a fair amount of trauma at one time or another. Her father had been a bit of a tyrant and then she'd fallen for a rogue and been left with a child on the way. Her luck had changed when Gordon Hart asked her to marry him and she'd found happiness in her life with her husband, her stepdaughter Shirley and her first child, Robin. Unfortunately, Robin had died after a severe case of a chickenpox. Maureen and Gordon had been blessed, though, with their son, Gordy, who was not quite fourteen now and in the lower class of senior school, and was adored by the whole family. Shirley, Gordon's daughter by his first marriage, was working at a hospital in Durham, where she'd learned to be a doctor. Her friend would cope but Peggy hated to think of her unhappiness.

* * *

Peggy shook her head as she made her way to the kitchen. She had a busy morning. She needed to bake cakes for the little shop she and Maureen ran with occasional help from Rose Barton and a permanent assistant, who served behind the counter. Peggy also liked to supervise the running of the boarding house, though she had help there, thank goodness, and hardly needed to do more than prepare the evening meal for those guests who required it. Her manageress was more than capable of doing almost everything else.

'I can cook the breakfasts,' Pearl had told her a few months back. 'You really don't need to come in every morning that early, Peggy. I know how you like things and with Mum and my daughter too, I can manage.'

Peggy rolled up her sleeves and got started, baking a batch of madeira cakes and lemon-drizzle loaves, before switching to madeleines and apple pies. She had just put the last of the pies into the oven when Rose Barton entered the kitchen.

'I came as soon as I could, Peggy,' she said. 'I knew you'd be wanting help when Tom told me that Gordon had been taken to hospital.'

'I need to make a large shepherd's pie and a couple of cheese and onion flans for the bar,' Peggy told her. 'Could you start on the shepherd's pie please?'

'Yes, of course,' Rose agreed. 'Gosh, those lemon-drizzle cakes look good – I'll buy one of those for Tom later. I shan't have time to bake for him today – I have to attend a school meeting later this afternoon. My Jenny brought the letter home with her yesterday. I'm not sure, but I think she may be in some kind of trouble...'

'Surely not?' Peggy said. 'I know she can be a little bit lively, Rose – but she isn't a naughty girl, is she?'

'I thought she was doing well at school,' Rose admitted with a worried frown. 'But at the moment my problems are nothing compared to Maureen's – have you any idea what is the matter with Gordon?'

'Maureen said he complained of a tight chest and then just collapsed.'

Rose nodded. 'Tom said it was something like that... Do you think it is his heart?'

'Might be,' Peggy replied as she pounded expertly on the pastry she was making. 'He works such long hours, Rose. That shop was just a little corner shop when he took it over. Maureen's father seldom made much of a profit, but Gordon has expanded it and taken on Mrs Tandy's old shop and I know he was talking of taking on another shop a couple of streets away – Maureen didn't want to, because she said it was too much work for him and it looks as though she might be right.'

'She will be devastated if anything happens to him...' Rose said. 'I don't know how she would manage it all.'

'Oh, don't,' Peggy begged. 'I know it doesn't look good, but they can do things these days, can't they?'

'I don't know...' Rose looked up from peeling the onions for the shepherd's pie, tears trickling down her cheeks. 'Tom's father just died last Christmas. He suddenly collapsed and died on the way to hospital – they couldn't do anything for him...'

'I know – and I was so sorry,' Peggy said. 'I really liked Jack Barton. I know he spent that time in prison before the war, but he was a good friend to me and he had a rotten time with that wife of his – she was a cold fish...'

'Yes, Tom told me about her. I know she always blamed him for his brother's death on that bomb site in the war, but he still cared about her and it was awful the way her mind went... and then his father. That really upset him last Christmas... Oh, he tried to make it a happy time for the kids' sake, but I knew his heart wasn't in it.'

'Is he feeling any better now?' Peggy asked. She was fond of Tom Barton, whom she'd watched growing up into a fine young man with a lovely family. Rose's daughter Jenny and their son Jackie were the pride of his life and he loved them both. He'd built up his business from nothing by sheer hard work and she'd been so pleased when he and Able set up the building firm together. Tom was one person she really trusted and he deserved some good luck as much as the next man and more than most in her opinion.

'He's still brooding a bit, though he makes out he's all right,' Rose told her. 'I don't know what to say to him, Peggy. His father wasn't old – not much older than you.'

'I know. We were good friends,' Peggy said. 'Is Tom worried that he might have inherited a problem, do you think?'

'I'm not sure – the doctors said Jack's heart just gave out...' Rose wrinkled her smooth brow. She was a very attractive woman with dark auburn hair and Tom had fallen for her hard when she first came to the lanes, though at the time she hadn't been interested in him. 'Tom's as healthy as anything – why would he worry about something happening to him?'

'Because he has you and the children and he wouldn't want you to be left a widow and struggling,' Peggy told her. 'If Tom is wondering if he'll make old bones, it is you and the children he's thinking of, believe me.'

'Yes, I suppose so.' Rose looked thoughtful. 'He shouldn't worry. I am certain nothing will happen to him for years and years.'

'I am sure you're right,' Peggy agreed, but she knew Tom well and was certain that his father's sudden death at the age of fifty-six had been a terrible blow to him. As it had been a sudden heart attack it might well have given Tom reason to worry that the same thing could happen to him.

She shook her head. 'Let's think about something else, Rose. Did I tell you that Fay won her skating competition yesterday?'

'No! Did she?' Rose looked at her and smiled. 'You know I never thought she would keep on with it this long. I told Tom I thought she would get tired of all the training and hard work – but now she's winning competitions...'

'Yes.' Peggy smiled proudly. 'I thought the same as you – and Janet was sure that Fay wouldn't stick to it, but she has. We're all so pleased that she is enjoying it the way she does. Freddie quite enjoys playing ice hockey, but football is his first love. Able says if it's what he wants to do when he leaves school in a couple of years, he will encourage him to do it.'

Peggy had had Able's twins later in life when she was in her thirties, after her first marriage had begun to fall apart. Janet was her firstborn and Pip her second. Janet now lived in Scotland with her husband, daughter and young son, and visited perhaps three times a year. Pip lived in the cottage in Devon that had been Peggy and Able's. He had a wonderful job with an aviation firm, was earning a lot of money and could commute more easily from there than London. He and his wife Sheila had two children, Chris and Sarah, and their family was unlikely to grow as Sheila had almost died when her first child had been born. The second one had been easier, but the doctors were still of the opinion that she should not have another and she'd promised her husband she wouldn't think of it, because they'd come so close to losing each other and neither of them could contemplate a future without the other.

Peggy smiled as she thought of the family holiday they were planning when the schools broke up. Pip had invited the whole family down and Peggy was hoping they could all get away. She'd made arrangements for extra help in the pub and Able would surely arrange things with Tom, and Janet had promised she would come too if she could.

'Have you heard from your Janet lately?' Rose asked almost reading Peggy's mind. 'She hasn't said anything about any more babies?'

'No, they have Maggie and their eight-year-old son, Jon,' Peggy said. 'I think that's all they want – it's just right for them, so Ryan says and Janet doesn't argue. She is quite content with her life as it is now.'

Rose nodded. 'That's what Tom says too. I thought he might like another child. We were talking about it before Christmas – one more before there is too big a gap, but since then he won't consider it.'

Peggy looked at her thoughtfully. 'There you are then,' she said. 'It is obvious that Tom is concerned that you shouldn't be left with too many young children to care for if something were to happen to him.'

'But it won't,' Rose wailed. 'And I'd like another baby before I get too old – remember I'm older than Tom.'

'And still a young woman,' Peggy said with a smile. 'You've plenty of time left yet, Rose – look at me, thirty-eight when I had the twins and now, I'm nearly fifty-four.'

'You don't look it,' Rose replied, looking her up and down. 'I think those extra few pounds suit you, Peggy. If you go too thin when you're getting older it can make you look haggard. You still look young.'

Peggy laughed. 'Have you been talking to Able – he says it suits me. He thinks I had got too thin and he's pleased I've put on a few pounds – but I shall have to be careful. The last thing I want is not to be able to get into my clothes.'

Rose shook her head. 'You're still a long way off that, Peggy. If I look half as good when I get to my fifties, I'll be over the moon.'

Peggy smiled as she took a tray of ham rolls through to the bar. The music was playing quite loudly. It was the Everly Brothers singing 'All I have to do is dream'. She liked that one, but it was too loud. Peggy would have to remind the barmaid to turn it down a little. She tended to turn the music up a bit too much, which was fine when the younger customers were in, but the regulars weren't as keen.

Peggy set the rolls down, turned down the transistor and returned to the kitchen. She wondered how Maureen was getting on – and Gordon. Pray to God he was all right! She wasn't sure what her friend would do if her husband was really ill.

2

Oh God, let him be all right! Maureen sat in the waiting room at the London Hospital and prayed for all she was worth. She'd been sitting here for a couple of hours now and her mind was going round and round in circles. If anything happened to Gordon – if he died or was mentally impaired by this seizure, or whatever it was, she would blame herself. She should have forced him to slow down. Some years back, Gordon had planned on them having more time together as a family and for a while they had, but then the business had started to build and he'd got drawn into it more and more, spending hours at the shop – hours when she would have preferred him to be at home. She should have told him so!

Yes, it was wonderful that Gordon had made such a success of her father's small shop, turning it into something far more modern and prosperous and expanding with lots of shelves and a self-service area so that people just took what they wanted. Some people had thought he was mad, laughing and saying that folk would just help themselves and clear off without paying, but they hadn't done that. Everyone put their things in a basket and took it to the counters. Of course, there was some pilfering, but that happened in every shop and they didn't find it did them much damage.

'I do know that old Mrs Jenkins picks up a box of matches and slips it in her pocket without paying,' Gordon had told Maureen once when they were discussing the progress of the business. 'But I can't find it in myself to say a word to her. Tell the truth, I often slip her an extra bit of cheese or bacon in her groceries without charging her.'

'You're too soft, love,' Maureen had chided with a smile, but she didn't care what he did. Gordon was in charge of the shop and it was a good job for him. After he'd been severely wounded in the war, she'd wondered if he could ever work again, but he'd gradually got himself fit and his limp was only noticeable if he walked too far. He enjoyed being in the shop and had a young lad to help him fill the shelves and keep an eye on things – and another man who came in twice a week to do deliveries for them. He worked as a landscape artist and his name was James Morgan. Maureen had seen some of his work and it was good, but he couldn't earn enough money painting and selling his pictures to make a living.

Maureen liked James, because he was a bit forgetful and dreamy, his gaze always seeming to peer into the distance, as if he were searching for something elusive. She'd taken him a dinner round to his studio a few times, because he was far too thin and she thought he probably forgot to eat when he was working. The smell of paint and oils had been strong in the large open room, which was where James ate, slept and worked. He had a sink at one end and a toilet outside in the yard, as well as a shed where he kept things, and that was it. His bed was a mattress on the floor and he either ate standing up or sitting cross-legged on his mattress while he contemplated the easel and his latest work.

Her mind had wandered! Maureen brought her thoughts back to her husband. Why hadn't anyone told her anything? How was Gordon? Had he come to his senses or was he still unconscious? She felt sick with worry and her head was pounding. At least she didn't need to worry about Gordy until half-past three, when she picked him up from school; her son was a quiet, sensitive lad who never caused her any bother anyway – but goodness knows how Ginger Murray was doing in the grocery shop! He was only fifteen and she wasn't sure he could cope with the customers, let alone count up their change properly, but there'd been no one she could ask to go in except for him, because both Rose and Tom Barton were busy with their own lives and, goodness knows Peggy had enough to do. Unfortunately, there had been no one else Maureen knew well enough to trust – and she couldn't leave this place until she knew how Gordon was. Her head came up sharply as a nurse walked towards her.

'Mrs Gordon Hart?' she asked and Maureen's breath exhaled in a gasp as she tensed for bad news.

'Yes, how is he?' she asked, her hands gripping so tightly in front of her, the knuckles turned white. 'Is he conscious again?'

'Yes, I'm pleased to say your husband is awake and asking for you. You can go in for a few minutes, Mrs Hart.'

'Thank you – but how is he? What caused him to collapse like that? Can I speak to a doctor?'

'The doctors are still running tests and they will discuss your husband's case and let you know in due course.' The nurse looked at her disapprovingly.

Maureen bit her lip. She'd been a nurse herself in the war, but she would have found something to comfort an anxious wife rather than make cutting remarks. All that mattered though was that Gordon was awake, so Maureen followed the nurse into the ward.

Gordon's bed was at the far end, which meant they were not treating him as an urgent case. She drew a deep breath of relief and yet couldn't help worrying. Were they taking his illness seriously or had they just dismissed it as a mere faint? Maureen had been a nurse long enough to be concerned, even though it was some years since she gave up her career. She had really only joined the military nurses because of the war and to escape her father's domination.

Gordon smiled at her tiredly as she reached his bed. 'Still here, love? Knew you would be. You should go home. You've things to do and I'll be all right.'

'I was worried about you,' Maureen told him and reached for his hand. 'You just collapsed in the kitchen and I had to call the doctor. He rang for an ambulance and they brought you straight in. I came as soon as I'd seen to things.'

'I know.' He squeezed her hand gently. 'I'm glad you came, but go home now, Maureen love. I shall worry if you don't. You've got Gordy to think of and the shop. I'm not sure how soon they will let me out – the doctor spoke of X-rays and tests. He seems to think it may be a bit of a problem with my heart.'

'Oh, Gordon...' Maureen caught her breath. She'd feared as much but prayed she was wrong. 'You've been doing too much. We should take on another assistant – one we can leave in charge...'

'While I sit at home and twiddle my thumbs?' Gordon frowned. 'I might cut back on my hours a bit, but I'm not giving up whatever they say. Life isn't worth living if you don't have work or an ambition to do better, and I'm only forty-six, too young to retire yet.'

'Don't say that! What about me and the children?' Maureen cried. 'Don't you want to see Shirley get married?'

'Of course I do, when she is ready,' he said. 'I'm proud of her – of all of you – but I can't just pack up and live like an invalid, Maureen. I'd hate that, you know I would. I thought I might be done for after the war, but you trusted me with the shop and that made me feel good. I wanted to build it up for you and the children.'

'And you have,' Maureen replied with a smile that spoke of her love. 'I'm proud of what you've done, Gordon, of course I am – but I don't want you to kill yourself for money. We could afford an assistant so that you get more time off – you'd still need to keep an eye on things.'

Gordon sighed and relaxed against the pillows, clearly exhausted. 'Let's see what the doctor says. I shan't be sitting at home every day with my feet up, Maureen. I'd die of boredom.'

'I know.' Maureen smiled at him. 'I'd feel the same way, love – but maybe just a few less hours, for me and the kids?'

Gordon smiled and touched her hand, but he was too exhausted to squeeze it. 'I know I'll have to cut down; I've been feeling a bit tired – just don't try to wrap me in cotton wool.'

'As if I would.' Maureen gave him a direct look. 'Though, we don't need that new shop you were talking about opening, Gordon. It would mean a lot of extra work – and for what? We've got all we need.'

He frowned and then nodded. 'Perhaps you're right about that, Maureen. I'll invest the money I'd put aside into a house to let instead. It isn't as good an investment as another shop would be, but it is something to safeguard you and Gordy. Shirley will be fine once she's settled back here. She'll have a good job for life, you know how dedicated she is.'

'Or until she marries and gives up work to have a family.'

Gordon shook his head. 'I doubt it will be just yet. Shirley has too much sense to do that for a few years. She's finished her training and she'll be back soon to take up a position as a GP.' His look of satisfaction had banished the worry lines in his forehead. 'She'll be coming home to live, Maureen, and living locally.'

'Yes, I know,' Maureen smiled as she agreed, knowing how proud Gordon was of his daughter. Shirley had done so well at her studies, passing all her exams as she went from student to junior doctor, and she'd been offered a permanent job at the hospital, where she'd worked the past three years, but she'd stuck to her guns and believed she might have secured a post as a junior partner in a local surgery.

'I want to help people like us,' she'd told her parents when she'd come home the previous Christmas. 'I like visiting people in their homes and looking after them when they most need it.'

'You've always been such a caring girl,' Maureen had said and kissed her. 'I hope you know how proud we are of you.' And now Shirley was making plans to leave the teaching hospital, where she'd felt obliged to work for a few years after qualifying, and come back to her roots. She could have worked in any hospital and gone on perhaps to become a highly paid consultant – she'd been told as much by her tutor – but she'd wanted to return to her home and work locally.

'You taught me that,' Shirley had told Maureen. 'You loved me despite the way I'd behaved to you when Dad brought me round that first time – and you got me home when I was so unhappy on that farm and cared for me. I owe what I am to you, Dad and Gran – you all helped me achieve my ambition.' As a young child Shirley had been difficult but after her experience on the farm, where she'd been harshly treated, she'd appreciated Maureen's loving care.

Maureen sometimes wondered about Shirley's love life – or the absence of one. She'd had a puppy love for a boy name Richard Kent, whom she'd known since she was very small, but he'd let her down and she'd broken it off with him. She'd met someone else round at Peggy's. Keith was in the Army at the time, but as far as Maureen was aware, he'd left a few years back and was working for a charity abroad, helping to build homes for the poor of Africa.

His brother had started out working for a charity amongst the ruins in Germany after the war and Keith had joined him, but that project had finished and the brothers had moved on to another charity and another location in Africa. Maureen believed that her stepdaughter still wrote to Keith, but she had no idea whether there was any more than friendship between them. As far as Maureen knew, she'd had no real boyfriends at college, because, as she'd said, 'I'm too busy, Mum. I've got plenty of time for all that.' Yet she was twenty-five and Maureen sometimes worried that she might never find love.

'You look thoughtful...' Gordon said and reached for her hand.

'I was thinking about Shirley. She'll be home soon and it will be lovely to have her back.'

'I know you missed her when she went off to college, so did I – but we had to let her go, love.'

'Of course we did – and she's done us proud, Gordon.'

'She certainly has,' he agreed and looked at her. 'Now go home and stop worrying. I'm in the best place and the doctors will soon sort me out.'

* * *

Shirley read the latest letter from Keith and smiled. He was coming home in July, after some years when he'd only come back for one brief visit, because of the difficulty of the journey, and had written that he would see her in London. As yet, he hadn't got his flight from Johannesburg booked but would let her know as soon as he had. The building work they'd been commissioned for was now done and he'd decided to live in London for a while. Shirley wondered how much of that was to do with his desire to see her. She wasn't quite sure how she felt. Keith had become a firm friend over the years – but was that all he was?

After Keith had joined his brother in his charity work, he'd only been home to visit once and that was before he'd gone out to Africa. Understandably he couldn't just come home for a few days. He'd seemed reluctant to leave her then.

'I really care for you, Shirley,' he'd told her. 'I know you're busy with your studies – but when you've passed all your exams and you're a doctor, would you consider getting married?'

'Are you asking me to marry you, Keith?' Shirley had asked, feeling pleased but also apprehensive. She liked him a lot but was nervous of falling in love again because it hurt too much when the person you loved let you down.

'Not yet – but one day when you've qualified...'

'We don't really know each other well enough,' Shirley had told him seriously. 'I know I like being with you. We have fun when you visit and it gives me a nice warm feeling when I see you – but is that enough? I'd need to know you much better first.'

'Yes, of course,' Keith had said and held her hands, looking into her eyes. 'I know that I love you, Shirley. For me it just happened the first time you smiled at me. I know you were getting over a break-up – but you're over that now, aren't you?'

He'd looked at her so anxiously that Shirley had laughed and reached for him, giving him a hug. 'Yes, I am, long ago, dearest Keith. Richard is no longer in the picture – and I think perhaps I might like to marry you one day, but I need to get to know you first please.'

'Then I'll come back to London to work,' he'd promised, and now, more than three years later, he was. He would be there when she was back home and settling into her new job as a family doctor.

Shirley was glad he was coming home, excited. She'd enjoyed writing to him all these years. At first, his letters had been brief, just to say where he was and if the accommodation was okay, but then they became longer and he began to chat to her, just as if he was with her in the room. He told her all about the jobs he was doing; the hard grind of the building work, digging trenches and wells was all worth it because of the people.

They are so friendly and so grateful, Shirley. Whatever small thing you do for them is like a minor miracle and they bring us gifts of food or necklaces made of bone or teeth. I have a very pretty one for you. The chil-

dren run around with no shoes and some of them have very little in the
way of clothes. They don't know what a proper toy is and if you give
them something special, they are too overwhelmed to play with it. Either
it goes on a shelf, or their parents sell it to buy food.

There were descriptions of the huts the people of the villages lived in
and the scenery, of the hot dusty environment and the need for clean water.

Before we dug the well, the women had to walk nearly two miles to fetch
the water in pots they carry on their heads or shoulder and they're very
heavy. Some of the women are very thin and look old before their time.
    Ralph isn't returning to England permanently, only to secure another
commission to build wells at other villages in the province and perhaps a
hospital. The charity is doing all it can, but they need funds and I've
promised I'll do what I can to raise money for them.
    Ralph wants me to continue working with him, but I've told him I
can't – at least for a while...

Shirley pondered over that bit – did it mean that Keith wanted to return
to Africa to continue his charity work one day? She knew that the wage that
he and his brother received was very small and wouldn't support a family –
at least, not here in England. Perhaps out there it was enough? She didn't
know and hadn't asked. Shirley had worked hard at her studies for years
and, as a junior doctor, sometimes for hours longer than she was meant to,
and she was looking forward to being a GP, and although she knew there
was always work for her where Keith had been stationed, it wasn't what
she'd planned or envisioned.

Did Keith have a calling to do the work, as his brother so obviously did?
Or had he just gone out there to be with him for a while and help with
certain projects? He'd gained experience and skills that would stand him in
good stead when he came home. He could lay bricks and turn his hand to
most building work, even electrics and plumbing. Out there, he'd needed
to be able to fix anything, and over the past few years he'd learned how to.
Once back in England, he might have to take some exams to get the qualifications needed to be an electrician, but most builders would be glad to get

him and he could quite easily go to a technical college one day a week to get the certificates required.

Her father's friend Able Ronoscki had a building firm with Tom Barton and Shirley knew they were always looking for reliable men to work for them. If Keith wanted to settle in the area, he shouldn't have much difficulty finding work – but would he?

Shirley didn't want to set her heart on a life with Keith if he was planning to take off every so often to work abroad for months on end. Perhaps that was selfish of her – because he and his brother did wonderful, worthwhile work – but she wanted a home in London near her family and a job she understood and loved. If she had to be prepared to uproot and move all the time, well, she didn't think she wanted that kind of life.

3

Peggy was in the bar serving a pint of bitter when she saw her youngest son in the doorway beckoning her urgently. Freddie looked worried and he was such a responsible youth that she knew it was important. She handed over the glass and motioned to Carla to take the money, excusing herself.

'Is something wrong, Freddie?' she asked as she went out into the hall.

'It's Fay,' he told her. 'She is ill, Mum. She was at the rink skating and smiling, waving at me and then, five minutes later, I saw her doubled over. I went straight to her and she said she had pain in her side. It was bad, Mum. She was moaning and crying, so I called the supervisor over and she arranged an ambulance. She went with Fay and I came home to tell you—'

'Did the ambulance man say what was wrong?' Peggy felt a dart of fear. 'Had she fallen? Or was it sudden?'

'She said she'd had niggling pains there before but ignored it because she wanted to prepare for her next competition.' Freddie looked at her and she could see he was scared. 'One of the ambulance men said it might be acute appendicitis – that's why they took her straight to the London Hospital, because they could operate immediately if need be. If it bursts—'

'No! Not my little girl,' Peggy exclaimed and her heart raced with fright. If that happened, it could mean serious illness or even death. 'Why didn't she tell me? I hadn't noticed. Did she say how long she'd been having the pains?'

Freddie shook his head. 'I'm sorry, Mum. She was in too much pain to talk much.'

'I'm going to the hospital now – they did say it was definitely the London?'

'Yes,' Freddie confirmed. 'I asked particularly. Can I come with you?'

'Would you go along to Tom Barton's yard and tell your father what has happened please?' Peggy said. 'They wouldn't let you into the hospital, Freddie love. As soon as she's better I'll take you up – even if we have to lie about your age and say you're eighteen.'

Freddie grinned, because he was tall and strong for his sixteen years and could easily have passed as an older lad. He'd managed to get into a horror film they'd both wanted to see that way with his cousin, Maggie, when she was visiting last Christmas. 'Thanks, Mum. I'll go and tell Dad now.'

As Freddie set off at a run, Peggy returned to the bar and explained to her regular help, Carla, who was coping admirably with the lunchtime rush before she went to take over at the cake shop. Then she went through to the kitchen and told Mrs Maggs where she was going.

'Don't you worry about a thing here, Peggy love,' her cheerful cleaning lady told her. 'If needed, I can pull a pint and I can take stuff through to the bar.'

'I think Julie and Carla can manage the bar, but if you could watch those cakes for me?' Peggy motioned to two trays of cakes. 'If you put them in now, they need twenty-five minutes.' Julie was Mrs Maggs' daughter and Carla had been working part-time for her in the pub as well as several hours a week in the cake shop.

Mrs Mags smiled at her confidently. 'You just leave it to me, love – and Carla will take them with her later in the boxes, same as usual.'

'Thank you.' Peggy thanked her lucky stars for her present staff who were all so reliable and good at their jobs. If this had happened a while back, Able would have been left holding the fort and that wasn't fair on him. He had his own work to see to without helping to run the bar, though he would never have complained. 'I'll catch a bus straight away if I hurry.'

She grabbed her coat and purse and rushed out into the lane. There was a bus stop at the corner of Mulberry Lane and the bus arrived there just as she did, panting and anxious not to miss it and have to wait.

'Is there a fire somewhere, love?' the bus conductor asked cheekily and then looked at her face. 'Sorry, missus – didn't mean to upset you.'

'You haven't,' Peggy assured him, 'but I need to get to the London Hospital quickly and I didn't want to wait another ten minutes or so for the next one.'

'Trouble, is it?' he said and accepted her fare. 'Life has a habit of bitin' yer on the bum, doesn't it, missus?'

Peggy nodded but didn't answer as he moved further down the bus. She wasn't in the mood for a long conversation, even though the man meant no harm and was just being friendly. Worry was making her feel a bit sick. If anything happened to Fay... but it wouldn't. She was a young girl with all her life ahead of her. She couldn't die over a silly thing like this – but why had she neglected to tell anyone about her pain?

Peggy closed her eyes against the tears. It was bad enough having Maureen walking around with that stark look of fear on her face, let alone the threat of a burst appendix. She didn't know for certain that was what it was, of course, but the ambulance men often knew the signs and... No! She wouldn't allow herself to think that way. Peggy had always considered herself a lucky person. Her luck wasn't going to change now. She crossed her fingers and prayed in her head and heart.

Would God listen? Did he think people were selfish when they prayed every time they needed something? Peggy wasn't a regular churchgoer, though she would call herself as good a Christian as some that did – but could she expect her prayers to be answered just like that? She shook her head. You got up in the morning, did the work you needed to do, treated everyone decently and helped your friends and neighbours – strangers too sometimes. Surely that was all anyone could do?

Dashing away a tear from her cheek, Peggy scolded herself. She couldn't go to pieces. Her family and friends needed her. Maureen was suffering dreadfully with worry over Gordon, because the doctors still weren't saying much, even though he'd been in the London a few days now and they'd done a lot of tests. Peggy needed to be there for her. Yet for the moment all she could think about was her beloved daughter. Freddie had looked pretty miserable too. The twins often argued, but they were close and he would feel it dreadfully and Able would be devastated if he lost his lovely daughter.

No! Peggy wasn't going to think that way. Fay would get better, come home and plague them all with her tantrums and her demands once more. She'd never been the easiest of Peggy's children. Fay had been seriously ill once before and it had resulted in her having slight hearing difficulties. For a time she'd been a difficult, awkward child but then she'd changed as she grew older and took an interest in her skating.

Please, let her come home and be healthy and happy again...

* * *

Fay's appendicitis hadn't quite reached the stage where it had become dangerously infected, but it was causing her pain and the doctors had decided to take it out. She'd been sedated and was being prepped for surgery when Peggy got to the hospital. She was allowed to see her for five minutes, during which Fay fell asleep.

'You can ring this evening, Mrs Ronoscki,' the nurse told her. 'If she is awake and well enough, you may visit then – from seven until eight p.m.'

'Yes, thank you. We shall,' Peggy said.

It was made clear to her that she couldn't hang around in the hospital and it was as she was on her way out that she met Able. He'd driven here as soon as Freddie told him the news and looked worried.

'How is she, Peggy?'

'They've given her a sedative and she is sleeping – they're operating to take it out but it hasn't burst.'

'Thank God for that,' Able said and sighed with relief. 'I thought for a while we might lose her.'

'I think she should be all right now,' Peggy said. 'Apparently, she's been suffering for some time – why didn't she tell us?'

'I expect she didn't want to give in. Probably wants to keep on with her skating,' Able said thoughtfully. 'She has to practise all the time if she wants to get anywhere and this will set her back, because she won't be able to skate for weeks – perhaps months. She's very like me, Peggy. Won't give in to things if she can help it.'

'Yes, I know.' Peggy smiled at her husband. She knew that sometimes he got pains where the arm he'd lost during the war should be. It was strange, because Able felt pain just as if his arm was still there, but he usually ignored it and only occasionally swallowed an aspirin.

'We shall have to be strict over the skating until she's fit again,' he said, frowning.

'That won't please her,' Peggy replied with a sigh.

'She's old enough to understand that she will have to rest and build up her strength again gradually,' Able said. 'Besides, she will have to think about her other studies now for a few months. Has she said anything to you about what she wants to do when she leaves school?'

'All she ever tells me is that she wants to go on with her skating. I asked if she wanted to work in an office or teach and she gave me a resounding "no". She said in a very languid tone that if she had to work, she would prefer to be a model for clothes or an actress.'

Able chuckled and nodded, amused by his daughter's answer. 'That sounds like our Fay, but I'm not sure what her chances are of getting a job like that, hon.'

'Very slim I should think,' Peggy said with a smile. 'Both of those jobs involve far more work than Fay imagines and both are precarious. She can actually cook well when she wants to, so if the worst comes to the worst, she could always help me. Not that I want her to. I should prefer her to branch out and do something exciting – a job she would really love, but I can't imagine what that would be as yet. Her skating has been everything to her – but whether she has a future in that direction I don't know.'

'Have you asked Sara what she thinks?'

'No, I haven't spoken to her for weeks. The last time I did so was just after last Christmas. She was pleased with Fay's progress then but...' Peggy nodded, thinking of her last conversation with Fay's skating instructor. 'Perhaps I should, Able. We ought to know what the opportunities are for her. I mean, amateur competitions are fine while she's still young, but she does need a career or a life beyond school. If it could be in skating it might suit her.'

'I should think you need to win a few important competitions to get taken on for an ice panto,' Able said. Every year they bought tickets for one of the ice shows that were put on a few weeks before Christmas. It was a pleasant family outing and they all enjoyed it, but Peggy had always expected her daughter to outgrow her love of skating and want to move on, go to college perhaps. Freddie was already making plans for university. He wanted to study physical training and become either a sports teacher or a professional footballer.

In February that year, both he and Able had been upset by the news of the terrible plane crash involving the Manchester United team. The team had been flying back from a European cup tie in Belgrade when the plane crashed on take-off just after stopping to refuel at Munich Airport in West Germany. Twenty-one of the people on board were killed, seven of them Manchester United players – and another had died of his injuries some days later. It was a terrible, shocking tragedy and had rocked the world of football, distressing many people whether they were fans or not. Freddie had been in tears over it when he saw the news on TV.

'It's awful, Mum – all those people dead...'

'I know,' she'd said. 'It is very sad – and a lot of them were talented young men, too.'

Freddie was a Manchester United supporter, never missing a good match on the radio or TV and going to local matches whenever he could. Twice, for a special occasion, Able had taken him to watch Manchester United. They'd travelled on the train, stopping overnight at a small hotel. He loved playing as much as watching, though.

'If I'm good enough I might get taken on by one of the big clubs as a junior player. They train you up and then, when you're ready, you get a try-out for the first team.' He'd grinned at his parents. 'If I'm not good enough I wouldn't mind being a sports instructor.'

'You're really good at all sport,' his father had told him. 'Don't underrate yourself, Freddie. You can do whatever you want to do.'

'Yeah, I know, Dad,' Freddie had said easily. 'I dare say I could get in with a smaller club, but it has to be the best for me – or I'd rather instruct others and teach them the skills they need.' Freddie was the quiet one in the family, but he didn't lack for either ambition or determination.

* * *

As they drove home, Peggy thought that Fay's twin would take it all in his stride. He'd always been the easiest of her children to please and was like his father in the way he cared for others. His ambition was there, but he would put it aside if his twin needed him. So many times, Freddie had missed football practice to take his sister to the rink, because his parents were busy and didn't like her travelling alone on dark evenings.

Freddie was waiting at home, listening to country music on his radio that Saturday, and jumped up as soon as his parents walked into the kitchen.

'I thought you had football this afternoon?' his father said.

'I did,' Freddie replied, but I wasn't playing – just a reserve – so I rang and told them I couldn't make it this week. Mr Miller was fine. He said it would give me time to get over my injury.'

'What injury?' Peggy said, startled. 'You didn't tell me?'

'It was just a slight sprain on the practice field the other day,' Freddie shrugged his shoulders. 'Nothing to worry about, Mum. My ankle swelled a bit but it is okay now – but just as well I didn't play today... Anyway, how is Fay? She is what matters now.' He looked and sounded so grown-up that Peggy's heart caught. Freddie wouldn't be her little boy much longer.

'She is having an operation, but it isn't as bad as you feared, love. It's just to be on the safe side they told me.'

'Thank goodness for that,' Freddie said and smiled in relief. 'I've never seen Fay like that and I thought she might die.'

'I don't think so,' Peggy replied and touched his cheek. 'Don't worry, darling. The hospital will look after her.'

Freddie nodded. 'Sometimes they can't though. Maureen rang while you were out. She wants to talk to you. I think she is upset again... her husband must be very ill.'

'In that case, I'll go round and see her,' Peggy said. 'Was she at home?'

'Yes, she said so.' Freddie looked at her sadly. 'Do you think Uncle Gordon will die? He's not my uncle, I know – but I really like him and he told me to call him that.'

'Yes, I know you like him.' Freddie sometimes went round and played football with Gordy. The younger boy adored him and Maureen often gave him his tea on a Sunday so that he would stay longer. 'I hope he won't, Freddie. I'm praying it's just that he's been doing too much.'

'He's been looking tired for a while,' Freddie said. 'I've seen him rubbing at his chest, as if it hurt.'

Peggy looked lovingly at her son. He was such a caring, intelligent lad, observant too. He'd seen more than she had – or Maureen. 'We'll just have to hope he gets better and comes home again soon.'

4

'I was going to ask you if you could have Gordy for me,' Maureen said when Peggy arrived. 'But Freddie told me that Fay is in hospital, so... I mean is she all right? Has she had the operation?'

'Fay is going to be fine and I can still have Gordy,' Peggy assured her. 'If I go into the hospital during visiting hours this evening, I'll get someone to look after him for that time. I know it's serious, Maureen, or you wouldn't look like that.'

'They've asked me to go up and discuss Gordon's condition,' Maureen explained and caught her breath. 'I think it is more serious than I'd hoped, Peggy. I was praying it was just tiredness and overdoing it, but they said we need to discuss his illness.'

'Oh, Maureen love.' Peggy looked at her with sympathy. 'I shall pray for you and him. I hope there's something they can do to help.'

'Yes, I hope so too,' Maureen replied. 'If it's his heart – well, sometimes they can't do that much, Peggy. I know medicine is improving all the time, but when a heart wears out.'

Peggy nodded but took her friend's hand. 'You don't know what it is yet, love. Don't start imagining things. I did that this morning and it doesn't help!'

'I know—' Maureen caught back a sob. 'I can't bear the thought of losing him, Peggy – and I just don't know what Shirley would do. She thinks the world of her father. You know how she was when Robin died. It took us ages to convince her that it wasn't her fault that she'd given him chickenpox. Most children have it and are fine – but Robin was just unlucky. He might have had an underlying condition that meant he couldn't fight it the way some do...' She took a shaky breath because her firstborn still held a big place in her heart and it still hurt to remember his loss.

'I thought life was so good a few days ago,' Peggy admitted. 'I believed we'd come through the storms and were in for some nice peaceful years, growing old gracefully...'

Maureen gave her a wry smile. 'Us grow old gracefully? We'd both be bored, Peggy. You especially. You never stop working.'

'Well, I shall in the school holidays. We're all going down to stay with Pip and Sheila, and I've been told that I am going to be forced to relax and enjoy myself. Pip says I shan't be allowed to as much as pick up a tea cloth.'

'A likely scenario,' Maureen said, disbelieving. 'You'll be baking them cakes and washing up – or running the local rock 'n' roll party for the Youth Club.'

Peggy laughed at the idea. Rock 'n' roll was the latest sensation to come over from America and was taking the country by storm. Young girls and boys had gone mad for it and some of the lads were wearing special suits with drainpipe trousers and long jackets with velvet collars. Their ties were just thin black strips and their shoes had thick soles, and they wore their hair in a certain style that marked them as Teddy Boys. However, some of them had caused a lot of damage to property, which gave the music a bad name. It wasn't the music that caused the trouble, but quite a few of the older folk believed it incited the youths to riot.

'It depends on whether or not we spend long days at the sea. Able wants a day out to see how the café is doing; he's still in touch with April. She was doing well, but last summer it wasn't so good. Able says she probably needs to spruce the place up again. I know that's why we did well there, because he was always thinking of something different to bring the customers in.' April had taken over the lease of their café when they returned to London, but still kept in touch with them now and then. 'We're looking forward to the break.'

'I'd like to get away, too, but with Gordon ill...' Maureen sighed and shook her head, before glancing anxiously at her watch.

'You'd better get off then,' Peggy said. She noticed that Gordy had come in from the garden and was looking at them with wide eyes. At thirteen years old, he seemed a quiet, shy lad and much younger than Freddie, who had developed into a young man early. Gordy was still an uncertain boy and thin with freckles across his nose and a soft mouth. She knew the bullies picked on him after school was out, because Freddie had stood up for him a couple of times and that was why Maureen didn't like leaving him to play alone on the streets. 'You're coming to have tea with me, love. Is that all right?'

'Yes, thank you, Aunty Peggy.' Gordy's face lit up in a big smile. 'Freddie said he would show me his collection of cigarette cards next time I came round.'

'You could play football in the back yard, I expect.'

Gordy nodded and then looked at his mum, his eyes reflecting his anxiety. 'Tell Dad I love him and I hope he is soon better...'

'Yes, darling, I shall,' Maureen said. She kissed the top of his head and Peggy could see her fighting her tears. She hugged her son and then nodded to Peggy, who took him away before his mother broke down. Maureen was clearly trying to keep her fears from him. Had she told Shirley yet? If so, she hadn't mentioned that to Peggy. She ought to let her stepdaughter know and quickly, because if anything happened to Gordon and Shirley hadn't had the chance to come home and see him... well, it could lead to bad feeling. Peggy decided that she would mention it to Maureen later when she took Gordy back home.

* * *

Maureen's heart was racing as she entered the hospital and made her way up to the ward. Sister Raynard saw her coming and stopped her entering.

'Will you step into my office please, Mrs Hart.'

Maureen followed her in, feeling sick. She'd seen that look on a nurse's face before and knew it meant bad news.

'Please sit down,' Sister Raynard indicated the spare chair. 'Doctor will be with us in a few minutes. He asked me to bring you in here so that he could talk to you privately before you speak with your husband.'

'Gordon is worse than we thought then?' Maureen drew a deep breath. 'How bad is it?'

'I am not the right person—' The nurse looked up as a shadow loomed and then the doctor entered. He was a tall, thin man with grey hair and he smiled grimly.

'Mrs Hart?' He extended his hand. 'I'm glad you could come. We need to discuss your husband's treatment. I believe you were once a nurse?'

'Yes, for a short time during the war...'

'Then you may have learned enough to understand what I have to tell you.' He paused and looked at her with sympathy. 'Unless things improve with your husband's heart, I estimate that he has a year at most – and that is if he stops working and takes sensible exercise.'

'An operation...' Maureen seized on the slight hope. 'Is there any chance of anything like that, sir?'

'If we could, I'd take it out and replace it with a new one,' he said. 'I think his war experiences probably took a greater toll than anyone realised at the time, Mrs Hart. However, since an operation to relieve his problem is not yet possible – I want to do some repair to a valve and see if we can remove a small blockage.'

'See if you can remove it?' Maureen picked up on the hesitation.

'It rather depends on what is causing it – whether it is just fatty tissue or something more serious.'

'And you're not sure from the X-rays and tests?'

'No, they were inconclusive.' He nodded. 'The operation might be straightforward, but if it is something unpleasant, shall we say, I might not be able to take it away – and your husband is refusing to have anything done at the moment.' He frowned. 'In my opinion, he is probably working too hard, taking too little exercise and eating the wrong foods.'

Maureen felt the sting of criticism. Had she contributed to his illness by indulging his love of good food? He wasn't fat but had put on a few pounds around his waist. Yet it was Gordon's refusal to have the operation that made her look at the doctor anxiously. 'Gordon doesn't want to have the operation?'

'He demanded the truth, Mrs Hart, and I had to tell him that I didn't think he could have too much longer even if we were successful in removing the blockage and repairing the valve. He said it wasn't worth the risk – apparently, his uncle once had an operation and died under the anaesthetic and he doesn't fancy risking it. Gordon tells me he had local anaesthetics when he was wounded in the war because the doctors believed he might not react well to a general one.'

Maureen nodded. 'Gordon told me he didn't like being put out and had refused it when he was badly wounded. They just gave him gas and air, pain relief and local anaesthetics when he needed stitching.'

'He would need to be put under for what I have in mind,' the doctor told her. 'So, we have a dilemma, Mrs Hart. If I operate, your husband may have a few decent years, though I can't guarantee that, but if I don't...'

'What are the risks of having the operation?' Maureen asked anxiously.

'Well, heart surgery is only in its infancy,' he admitted. 'And there are risks – to all operations. You must know that from your own experience?'

'Yes, I do,' Maureen admitted. 'I've seen patients die on the operating table while being worked on and it is always dreadful for the nurses and doctors, as well as the families. It does happen, but many more operations are successful and save lives.'

The doctor nodded. 'So will you advise Mr Hart to have the operation?'

'I'll talk to him and hear what he has to say about it,' Maureen told him. 'I won't put pressure on him if he is set against it.'

'You understand that he will have a limited time to live without it?'

Maureen blinked hard to hold back the tears. 'Yes, I do, and I don't want to lose him – but it has to be his choice.'

'Sometimes, people are not in any fit state to make that decision when they're ill, Mrs Hart. I was hoping that you might help me to persuade him...'

'No, I can't do that,' she replied, gripping her hands tightly to stop them shaking. 'Gordon has the right to decide and I want to support him, not bully him into something he doesn't want.'

Maureen could see that her answer had not pleased the doctor but she knew better than to try to convince Gordon to have treatment he had already said he did not want, even though she desperately longed for him to be better again.

* * *

Gordon's expression warned her as soon as she was shown into the small private room he'd been moved to after the results of his tests. 'Don't ask me to have the operation, Maureen. I know there's a chance it could help me, but there's also a chance it will kill me. If I don't have long anyway, I want to spend my time with you and the kids.'

'I know,' Maureen said, refusing to let her tears fall, because she knew he would hate to see her cry. 'It's what I want, too, Gordon. If I thought it was an easy option, I'd say go for it, but I don't know – perhaps we could see someone else. They might have got it wrong—'

'Too damned right they have,' Gordon said in a cheery tone that she didn't believe. 'I'm just tired – been overdoing it for a while. I'll be fine if I take it a bit easier.'

'Of course you will,' Maureen agreed. If that was the way he wanted to treat his illness, she was ready to go along with it. The last thing she wanted was for her husband to feel that he was being pitied or fussed over. It wasn't in his nature to feel sorry for himself and she could only help by agreeing with whatever he wanted. When he was ready to accept his illness, she would talk to him about it, but she knew very little herself. One day perhaps heart surgery would be possible, but Maureen knew even small operations could cause problems and she couldn't push Gordon into taking that risk if he didn't fancy his chances. Besides, miracles sometimes happened and things got better without medical intervention. If Gordon wanted to believe he was just tired, then she would accept his decision.

'You haven't spoken to Shirley I hope?' Gordon said suddenly, making her flush with guilt, because of course she had and Shirley was coming home that weekend.

'I told her you were a bit overtired and had gone into hospital for a rest. She is coming home this weekend.'

'Maureen – you shouldn't have worried her.'

'She said all her exams are long over and it's just routine work. Besides, she said she intended to come home for a few days anyway. She'll go back to finish her contract out, of course, but she wants to see someone about a job. Apparently, she has been offered an interview at that big practice on the Commercial Road. She thinks the job is probably hers if she wants it, but she is coming down for the interview to confirm it anyway.'

Gordon nodded, looking relieved. 'That's all right then. She's worked hard, Maureen love. I don't want her missing out on anything because of me – and I'm asking you now not to tell her what that doctor told you.'

'All right, I won't,' Maureen said, knowing that it was easy to give her promise but it would be very hard to keep it. Shirley would ask all sorts of questions if she saw her father getting weaker and she would expect Maureen to be honest with her, but she couldn't go against Gordon's wishes, however bad she felt, so she promised and he smiled.

'I know you'll keep your word however hard it is,' he said. 'I love you – you do know that?'

'Yes, of course I do,' Maureen replied, choking back her tears. 'I hope you know how much *I* love you?'

He nodded, a quiet look of acceptance in his eyes. 'I've been lucky,' he told her. 'I knew that it was almost curtains for me a couple of times during my time in hospital in the war. When that wound wouldn't heal... and then you helped me to get well again. We had Gordy and life has been good – and, if the worst should happen, there is money in the bank and a decent business for you and the kids.'

'Please don't,' she choked, because it was too much. 'We'd all rather have you...'

'And you will. I'll beat this – just like I did when they wrote me off in the hospital.'

Maureen nodded and blinked hard. It was different this time; she knew it and so did Gordon, but he would never admit defeat.

* * *

Maureen's tears fell freely when she was walking out of the hospital. She saw a taxi and flagged it down, not wanting to cry on public transport. At least in the back of a taxi, she could cry as much as she liked. London cabbies were used to all kinds of things and they'd seen folk crying after they left the hospital many times before.

She went to Peggy's to collect Gordy and her friend said nothing, just throwing her arms around her and holding her while she wept.

Maureen told her what the doctor had said and Gordon's reaction. 'He wants to spend what time he has with us...'

'I don't blame him,' Peggy replied. 'Yes, he could go for the treatment and perhaps gain himself a few months or perhaps longer, but he might not come back to you. At least this way, you can have some time together and then if he changes his mind, perhaps he can still try the treatment.'

'Yes, I suppose.' Maureen looked at her, misery in her eyes. 'He thinks he is lucky to have had more than ten good years with us – but it isn't long enough, Peggy.'

'Of course it isn't,' Peggy agreed. 'I know how you feel, love, but Gordon wants to grab what he can of life while there is still time.'

'I know. I shan't try to talk him into the surgery. If it was risk-free, he wouldn't need persuading – but anything to do with the heart is always risky.'

'Yes, I'm sure. If he wanted to try it, that would be fine, but if he doesn't...' Peggy hugged her tighter. 'Whatever you need, I'm always here for you and Gordy. Would you like to stay here tonight? There's plenty of room.'

'Better not in case the hospital rings,' Maureen said but felt wistful. She really wanted to be with Peggy that evening.

'We can ring the reception there and give them this number,' Peggy suggested. 'I'll ask Able, he'll do it for you. It isn't a good idea to be alone tonight, love.'

'Yes, all right then, I'll stay,' Maureen agreed, feeling relieved. 'Where is Gordy?'

'He's in Freddie's room. There's a camp bed and he's curled up on it, fast asleep. They've been playing football and then darts all afternoon and evening.'

'Freddie is so good with him,' Maureen said. 'It's what he should do – be a sports teacher. He'd be wasted as a footballer. I know that's more glamorous, but he could do such wonderful work with children once he's qualified.'

'That's what Freddie says too,' Peggy agreed. 'He will try to get a trial with a big club, but if that doesn't materialise, he's going for a scholarship in sports so that he can teach.' Peggy went to the cupboard and took out a bottle of brandy. 'I'm going to make us both a coffee and put a good dollop of brandy in it, do us both good.'

Maureen drew a shaky breath. 'I didn't even think to ask about Fay!'

'She was still in the recovery room when I last rang. I've been told I can go and visit in the morning but not until then.'

'Poor girl,' Maureen sympathised. 'We both seem to get our troubles, Peggy. Why does life have to be so hard?'

Peggy shook her head. 'Things happen, Maureen. I've always thought myself pretty lucky, despite what has happened over the years. My life hasn't been without storms, but I've weathered them and come out the other end. At the moment, you can't see any blue sky at the end of the tunnel, but one day you will.'

'It's always darkest before the dawn.' Maureen bit her lip. 'I know you're right, Peggy – but just now it all looks bleak...'

5

Maureen woke to Peggy pulling back the curtains. She sat up in alarm, her heart thumping with fear. Was it Gordon? Had something happened? 'Has the hospital rang?'

'No, but Shirley arrived last night and found your house in darkness, so she went to the boarding house and Pearl gave her a bed for the night. She told her she thought you were staying here overnight and so she came round – she was worried. I told her just what you said Gordon wanted you to tell her.'

'Good – not that it will satisfy Shirley. She's done her five years studying and another two getting hospital experience as a young doctor, and she's going to be a GP pretty soon. I can't see her just accepting what we tell her – and the hospital will tell her the truth if she asks.' Maureen sighed. 'Gordon wants to save her pain, so she can enjoy her last few weeks at work and her new job when she starts, if she gets it, of course – but she'll soon pick up that he isn't his usual self.'

'Naturally she will – and then she'll blame you for not telling her,' Peggy warned. 'Gordon should never have asked you to give that promise.'

'Well, I'll keep it for as long as I am able,' Maureen said with a wry look. She saw that Peggy had brought her a tray with tea and toast. 'What's all this? I'm not the invalid.'

'But it's nice to have breakfast in bed sometimes,' Peggy said. 'I was up and I thought it might do you good to rest a bit longer, prepare yourself for Shirley's questions.' Peggy nodded to her and left her alone.

Maureen sighed and closed her eyes. It was a real luxury to have breakfast in bed. She hadn't done that for years. In the early days of their marriage, Gordon had brought her tea and toast a couple of times when she'd been under the weather, but mostly, she was up first and getting tea and breakfast for everyone else, ready to go to work. It was her life and she'd enjoyed it, spending her evenings with Gordon in quiet comfort, apart from the occasional visit to the cinema or the pub. She realised that they'd settled into the kind of life that suited middle-aged couples, but she was still only in her late thirties. True, she would be forty next year, but that was still young these days, wasn't it? Gordon had talked of them doing new things together once, but then he'd become more and more involved with the business and seemed to forget the trips to the zoo and the rides out into the country. They did it now and then, but not enough if she was honest.

Did they still have time to enjoy a few treats together? The thought that they might not struck Maureen like a knife to the heart. She'd been so content with her life – her work and her friends – had she shut Gordon out? Had he felt that he wasn't needed? Was that why he'd become so immersed in his work – or was it just life? He'd wanted to make a success for her sake and the children's.

Maureen drank her tea and ate a round of toast, but she wasn't hungry and she pushed the tray aside. It was stupid to let the doubts take over now. She wasn't sure what the future held. The doctor's prognosis hadn't been encouraging, but he'd been trying to persuade them that Gordon must have the treatment. Sometimes, it wasn't as bad as they said and patients given a few months to live had a few years instead. Gordon was several years older than Maureen. She'd known that when they married, but it hadn't seemed to matter then – now all of a sudden, she had a sick sense of fear that she was going to lose him too soon.

Throwing back the bedclothes, Maureen got up and went to the bathroom. She didn't want to stay in bed and think because it would drive her mad. She needed to see Shirley and then get on with her life, because feeling sorry for herself wouldn't help anyone. She had to stay strong for Gordon and the children.

* * *

Shirley knew as soon as she spoke to Maureen that she was lying about her father's health. She looked uncomfortable and, even though she tried to make light of things, Shirley knew her too well. She'd thought as much when she discovered that Maureen was staying overnight at Peggy's. Why would she do that if she wasn't upset?

She waited until Maureen had finished, looked her straight in the eyes and said, 'So now why don't you tell me the truth, Mum? I expect Dad told you to lie to me, but I'm no longer a little girl and I know you both very well. You're upset and trying to fight it. Tell me, please. I promise I shan't let him know you did...'

Maureen shook her head. 'I can't, Shirley. You're right, he did make me promise and I am anxious – but a promise is a promise.'

'Right, well, I'll speak to his doctor later today,' Shirley said and frowned. 'He shouldn't have put that burden on you, but I know what Dad is like – as stubborn as can be.' She smiled, moved forward and gave Maureen a hug. 'I guessed straight away that something serious was wrong as soon as I found the house in darkness. I know you always keep a little light in the hall upstairs.'

'Yes, that's a giveaway,' Maureen said and hugged her back. Shirley was no longer a girl and she had a very direct and confident manner these days, but underneath she was still the loving, caring girl she'd always been. 'I'm glad you're back, Shirley, and speak to the doctor if you want – but don't argue with your father when you know the truth.'

'I'm not going to promise anything,' Shirley said, 'but if he's ill, I shan't make him worse, Mum. You know he means the world to me.'

'Yes, I do know – and you lost your mother much too soon...'

'But I got another one.' Shirley smiled at her. 'I hope you're pleased to see me home?'

'Yes, I am, darling. I know it is only for a few days, but it's lovely to have you here.'

'I'll be back for good soon,' Shirley said. 'I wanted to see you and Dad – but I've also got that interview, though I'm fairly sure the job is mine. I shall be working three days a week in the practice and three in a clinic that specialises in looking after the old, poor and needy – children too, sometimes, if they are from the streets. Though it is up to me if I want to finish early on Saturdays.'

Maureen looked at her. 'And that's what you want, dearest?'

'Yes, it is, Mum. With the NHS these days, most people are pretty well cared for and I'll do my part in my three days a week at the practice, but there are still people who don't fit in. They don't have a regular GP and they wouldn't dream of presenting at a hospital. Most of them just suffer in silence until they collapse on the street and are taken in by an ambulance. Many of those are too far gone to treat and they die – but if we can treat them sooner, then they may have a better life. Not necessarily much longer, but more comfortable.'

'Oh, Shirley, you make me feel ashamed,' Maureen said, tears in her eyes. 'I was a nurse but I gave up when I had Robin and then Gordy – and I've been busy and content. I could have given a few hours a week to a clinic like that – even if it was just changing bandages.'

'You've had enough to do, cooking, cleaning and looking after Dad,' Shirley said, 'but one day, when Gordy no longer needs you so much, you might do some voluntary work, Mum.'

Maureen nodded her head in assent. 'Perhaps I shall one day – but not just yet...'

'No – not while Dad needs you,' Shirley agreed. 'If he is very ill, it won't be easy. Dad doesn't like to be fussed over.'

'No, he doesn't – he needs straight talking,' Maureen said. 'But I don't think he'll change his mind about anything. We'll talk again when you've been to the hospital.'

'Have you rung them this morning?'

'Not yet. I was told to ring at eleven. The nurse said that if there was a change, she would let us know.'

'If it is his heart, it could happen any time,' Shirley said, looking serious. 'Yes, I'm guessing, Mum, but it is an educated guess. Grandfather died young of a heart problem and so did his father. It only seems to affect the men, which means that Gordy might be at risk one day.'

'Shirley, don't!' Maureen was horrified. 'Why didn't anyone ever tell me?'

'Because Dad wouldn't talk about it. I didn't know until last year when I looked up my family's medical history and the reason given for death on the certificates. I was curious why I'd never had grandparents as a child and I discovered that my grandmother died in childbirth in her thirties and Grandfather died of heart failure in his fifties. My mother's family was different – I haven't been able to trace them at all. Dad would never talk about her after she died and although I have her name from my birth certificate, I know nothing more about her. I don't think she came from London – so I'm going to ask Dad about her parents.'

'Perhaps he won't know,' Maureen said. 'If she came from away, she might not have known her parents either. It happened in the wars. She could have lost them in the first war.'

'Yes, that's a possibility,' Shirley agreed. 'But I'm right, aren't I – it is something to do with Dad's heart?'

'You'll have to speak to the doctor,' Maureen said. 'I was too upset to take it in really.'

'Oh, I shall,' Shirley replied determinedly. 'I want to know what Dad's hiding from.'

* * *

'You're saying his arteries are blocked?' Shirley asked and frowned at the doctor. 'Surely there isn't any surgery for that, is there?'

'I discussed it with a brilliant young surgeon who has been working on heart medicines and he said from the X-rays it is only one small section that is blocked. If we could divert the blood flow around it, that might give your father several more years of life.'

'It's experimental then,' Shirley said thoughtfully. The doctor had years more experience than her but seemed to have set his mind in one direction and she wanted to explore all avenues. 'Surely, if he stops smoking and cuts down on his fatty foods and perhaps takes up exercise, it should help his condition.' She looked at him hopefully.

'Yes, and that would normally be my advice,' the doctor told her. 'It's just that we thought there might be a chance to improve Mr Hart's quality of life as well as prolong it.'

'And how long do you think he can survive if he doesn't want this treatment?' Shirley pressed him, because she needed to know the truth. 'Please tell me, sir.'

The doctor gave her a straight look. 'If he is extremely lucky and looks after himself, perhaps five years. However, there is no guarantee. He could just go to sleep one night and not wake up if his heart stops.'

'And he might be much better if he follows the proper diet and exercise routine that I shall set for him.'

'Mr Hart hasn't been very responsive to anything we've suggested thus far.'

'He will do it for me,' Shirley said and smiled confidently. 'Thank you for telling me the truth, sir. My mother is devastated. She thinks we're going to lose him any day, any hour...'

'I had to make her aware that it could happen – and it could, Miss Hart. Yes, it is possible that a new regime will improve his health, but it isn't cast in stone.'

'I'm sure I can make him listen to sense.'

He smiled at her determination. 'Well, you clearly care for your father a great deal and I hope you can make him listen and that your father improves. I can offer a tablet that may help ease his chest pain.'

Shirley thanked him. 'Perhaps you will talk to his GP about that,' she said. He assured her he would do all he could and she left, making her way to the ward, where her father lay with his eyes closed. The doctor she'd just spoken to seemed to have given her father little chance, but she knew from her studies that people with similar conditions could and did live several years if they followed the doctor's advice: cutting down on stressful work, following proper exercise and diet – and no smoking. She'd seen damaged hearts and lungs in her time at the hospital and there was a theory now that much of the damage was from smoking. That was another theory in its infancy but one that she definitely believed in.

* * *

'Hi, Dad,' Shirley said cheerfully as she entered his ward. 'So how are you feeling? Are you ready to come home yet? I've been told they will let you out tomorrow.'

'Shirley!' her father's eyes jerked open. 'Did your mother send for you?'

'No, I came home for a visit and an interview for a great job – and I heard you were in hospital. I came straight up and spoke to the doctors and I know all about it. I think you were right to refuse the surgery, even though it might have worked – but that doesn't mean I'm letting you off the hook. You're going on a strict routine of diet and exercise and less work – and that should give you a few years yet.'

Shirley saw a flicker of hope in his eyes and knew that he'd been thinking the same way as Maureen – that he didn't have long to live. 'The doctor said if I didn't have the surgery, I might only have a few months...'

'It's true, you might,' Shirley admitted, 'but we can fight it. You have a blocked artery, Dad, but it isn't as bad a case as some I've seen. A new regime could make you healthier and give you longer. I want you to try it – will you, for my sake and for Gordy's and Maureen's?'

'Yes, if you think it will help.' He sat up and smiled at her and she saw the immediate change in him. He'd gone from thinking imminent death was inevitable to believing he had the chance of a few more years.

Shirley smiled and leaned down to kiss his cheek. 'Thanks, Dad. Let's beat this thing – at least for a while. You don't have to be like Grandad and just give in to it.'

'My grandmother said he did,' her father told her. Shirley nodded; she'd heard that before, though she'd never met her great-grandmother. 'When they told him, he had a heart problem, he just sat in his chair and let it take him. I suppose he didn't have much to live for after his wife died.'

'You won't do that,' Shirley replied. 'I'll be home for good very soon and I'll expect an improvement when I get back.'

'Will you be living with us then?'

'Yes, if you'll have me?'

'You know the answer to that one,' he said and looked pleased. 'We've both missed you – your mum and me, and Gordy too.'

'Gordy looks a bit too thin and pale,' Shirley commented. 'Now that you're going to be spending more time with the family and less at work, you can perhaps find out why he isn't as confident and full of life as he should be at his age.'

Her father nodded. 'I'll get another assistant in to take over the day-to-day work at the shop and just pop in now and then.'

'Or Mum will,' Shirley said. 'After all, she ran it for years and she is quite capable of doing it for a while. I'll help her at home.'

'What about your life, Shirley?' her father asked seriously. 'I know you're coming home to work in a local practice – but you need to go out with friends and you might want to get married.'

'That can wait,' Shirley said firmly. 'I had lots of friends at uni, Dad, and I had lots of fun there, too, but now I want to get down to work. It's what I trained for and I'm not going to throw it away to get married as soon as I've qualified. Besides, I care about my family – all of you. You gave me what I wanted and now it's time for me to give back.'

'You're a good girl,' her father said. 'If... when anything happens to me, you'll make sure your mum is all right?'

'You know I will,' Shirley replied. 'Maureen was wonderful to me and I love her as much as I would if she'd been my birth mother. She is a special person, Dad, and I'll be there for her when she needs me – but that won't be yet. Believe me, I'm sure nothing is going to happen to you that quickly.'

Shirley could see the trust and love in her father's eyes and she mentally crossed her fingers. It was true that the proper diet and exercise could help his condition, but that still didn't mean he wouldn't collapse and die suddenly – hearts were like that and sometimes just gave up with little or no warning – but he needed to have hope and so did Maureen and Gordy. She knew that for many patients, hope was important, because without it they just tended to give up. That wasn't going to happen to her father if a little support from her and his family could prevent it.

6

'Is Uncle Gordon all right?' Fay asked when Freddie told her that he was in the hospital on another ward. 'I like him a lot... he always remembers to ask me how I got on in my competition and seems really interested.'

'I like him too,' Freddie said seriously. 'I haven't been told much, but they were all looking very serious until Shirley came home for a visit, but now they seem happier. He's going home today.'

'I wish I could,' Fay remarked and looked sulky. 'I shall miss my competition next week.'

'You couldn't compete yet,' Freddie said sensibly. 'You have to be careful for a while, because you mustn't split your stitches and you need to heal properly inside.' He frowned at her. 'If it had got any worse, you might have died. Why didn't you tell Mum you were ill?'

'Because I wanted to practise,' Fay replied.

'Is it worth dying for? When you think of all the sick people who have no choice – people dying of starvation and terrible diseases – you're so lucky, Fay. We're both lucky. Don't throw your life away for skating – and don't worry Mum and Dad like that again.'

'Oh, don't scold me,' Fay said, her gaze dropping. 'I know I was daft. Mum and Dad are coming in now. You have to go and wait in the corridor.'

'I know. I was lucky I could get in at all. Mum told them I was nearly eighteen so they let me visit.'

Fay gave a little gurgle of delight, because she loved a little bit of mischief. 'Mum is super like that,' she said and touched his hand. 'Thanks for coming. I know I was an idiot, Freddie.'

'You always have been, but you're my twin and I'd kill anyone that hurt you,' he replied, grinned and walked off just as his parents approached. He went into the corridor and sat down, picking up an evening paper someone had left and reading the sports page. It had cricket scores and horse racing, but he most liked the articles on football. He found a small one on the second-from-last page. It said that Manchester United was looking for young players to train for the under-eighteen squad with a view to playing in the first team when they were older and ready. He supposed they needed to replenish their team after the terrible accident that had devastated them. Some players might feel they didn't want to play for a team that had been so tragically depleted, but Freddie thought he might like it – they'd been a fantastic team before the accident, though it might take a while to get back to normal after what had happened at Munich.

He stared at it for a moment and then tore the advert out. There was a phone number to ring and if he was lucky enough to get a trial, it might mean wonderful things for his future. He wanted to play for one of the big teams or not at all – or only as a hobby. Freddie didn't know why he would only be satisfied by the best, but it was a part of his nature. If he had the trial and they said he wasn't good enough, he would know then what to do next. He was at the age where he would soon have to make his decision, because the best players were always those that got taken on early. Some players did get picked from university teams, so it might not be his only chance, but in his heart he would know if he had a trial, whether he was good enough or not.

* * *

The doctors had said that Fay could come home in a few days and would then need another week off school, but when asked if she could return to her skating training, the answer was no.

'I would personally advise that she doesn't take part in any kind of strenuous games for a couple of months,' the doctor told them. 'If she had a fall or overstretched herself, it could lead to complications that might cause considerable pain and stress – so it's best just to leave it for a while.'

'If I do that it will take me ages to catch up again,' Fay grumbled when she was told the news. 'He doesn't understand, Mum. It takes hours of practice to perfect a jump and if you let it slide – well, I might never get it back...'

'Of course you will,' Peggy told her. 'It will put you back a bit but—'

'No, it isn't that simple,' Fay frowned at her. 'Sara told us that it's easier when you're young and you first start, but if you neglect your training when you get older, it is much harder to get that peak fitness back... and there's only a couple of years to go until the next Winter Olympics. I thought that was my chance. It's in California and if I'd been picked...' Her eyes brimmed with tears. 'It won't happen now and I won't get another opportunity.'

'You're only sixteen,' Peggy replied. 'Not exactly in your dotage yet, love.'

Fay didn't argue further, but she looked thoughtful and a bit sad and Peggy thought it best to let the idea just simmer for a while. Surprisingly, Fay didn't bring it up again and Peggy worried that she would simply ignore the doctor's advice and carry on with what she wanted to do regardless. They could forbid her from going to the rink, but that would cause tantrums. Fay had to accept what was best for her and make the right choices. She was no longer a small child, but a girl who would soon be a young lady and ready to think about her future.

* * *

At home, Peggy was working harder than ever. Maureen understandably could only manage an hour or two now and then to help with the cooking. She had the shop to manage now, which meant all the ordering and popping in two or three times a day to see how things were going. She'd advertised for a manager but so far no one had applied – at least no one suitable. She had Gordon at home and although he was happy to rest for a while, it would not be long before he started fretting over the shop.

Maureen had stuck a notice in the window of the shop and Peggy followed her example and advertised for a part-time cook to help with the cake making. She found a woman of her own age fairly quickly, who could make good plain cakes that helped to fill the shelves – madeira, jam sponges and seed cakes were her speciality, which left the fancy stuff to Peggy.

It was fine for a time, but Peggy wondered if they should think about giving up the cake shop. It did very nicely and she sold a lot of her home-made jams and marmalades now that she could buy the sugar off ration. Able had encouraged her to try it as soon as sugar rationing ended in the early 1950s and she'd found they sold almost as many jars of jam as they did cakes these days. It had been started when there were three of them, but Sheila had given up her share when she moved to the country and that had made it harder for Peggy and Maureen. She'd had various helpers. Carla was very good, but she liked serving in the bar or the shop and divided her day between the two. Rose could bake good cakes, but with her children growing up and Tom expanding his business, she needed to be at home most of the time and only helped out now and then.

Peggy was busy in the kitchen the morning Able fetched Fay home from the hospital. Fay entered the room walking a little gingerly and Peggy knew she'd finally realised that she would feel the soreness for perhaps longer than she'd first thought. She smiled at her mother and settled on a chair at the table, watching as Peggy whisked the mixture for a coconut cake.

'Can I lick the bowl please?' she asked as Peggy scraped the mixture into the tin.

Peggy handed it to her. Both the twins liked to run their finger round the bowl and lick the mixture from it. Freddie was at school that day, but had he been home he would have asked too.

'Can I help you a bit?' Fay asked, surprising Peggy. 'As I'm not going to be able to train for a while – can I help you with the cakes? I don't want to do boring old lunches for the pub.' Fay was decisive on that point. 'But I should like to make cakes – fancy ones, too.'

Peggy looked at her for a moment and then smiled. 'If it's what you'd like, I'd be glad to teach you, darling. I know you've made simple things – but it gets harder the fancier you get.'

'Yes, it does,' Fay agreed in a very grown-up manner. 'It's like skating in a way – you have to practise to perfect your cakes. I'd like to start with the kind of thing you do, Mum – but then I'd like to make wedding cakes and special occasion cakes. Several tiers with lots of icing and stuff.'

'Are you sure?' Peggy couldn't quite believe what she was hearing. 'That isn't just a hobby, Fay – it's a career...'

'Yes, well, I think it's what I want to do when I leave school,' Fay said, looking at her directly. 'You and Dad have both asked me what I want to do and I've been thinking about it. I read about it in the booklets they bring to school for future careers and I saw that you can go on courses. I saw one advertised at a chateau in France. They do all kinds of special cooking there – Cordon Bleu I think it is called.'

'Yes, I shouldn't be surprised,' Peggy said. 'You realise I've never done anything like that – what I know I've taught myself.'

Fay nodded, looking serious. 'You're what they call a good *plain* cook, Mum. I know you can make lovely things and you did well in that competition, getting through to cook at the Savoy – but you don't do the kinds of things I'd like to cook. For that you have to be taught.'

'Yes, I expect so,' Peggy said, smiling inside at her daughter's opinion of her cooking. One day Fay might experience some less than good food and then she might realise how good her mother was, but, as always, her head was filled with dreams. 'Well, I'm sure we can arrange for you to do a high-class cooking course, Fay. Perhaps you can graduate to this special one in France when you're older.'

'You can teach me the basics,' Fay said in a lordly manner. 'I'll need those, Mum, before I can think of doing one of those advanced courses – but I believe there is a scholarship to the French chateau. If I entered for it, I might win...'

'Well, you might,' Peggy agreed. 'Just when were you thinking of entering for this scholarship?'

'Oh... next year sometime. I think I'd need to be at least seventeen, perhaps eighteen – but I've got a lot to learn yet. I can look for a course I could do in the evenings in the meantime.'

'Yes, you could,' Peggy replied and hesitated, but the question had to be asked. 'What about your skating, love? Won't you want to get back to it when the doctor says it is all right?'

'I might,' Fay conceded, 'but if I'm behind all the others and I can't be the best, what is the point? If I am going to be a chef, I have to practise and learn and that takes a lot of time.'

'Yes, it does,' Peggy conceded. 'I was planning to make some almond fancies. Would you like to try your hand at them?'

'They're Dad's favourites,' Fay said and smiled at her. 'I bet I can make them as good as you...'

'Come on then, show me,' Peggy invited and gave her the list of ingredients. 'Let's see what you can do.'

* * *

'I was hard put not to laugh,' Peggy told her husband later that day when the twins had gone up to read in their rooms before they went to sleep. 'She told me that I was what people call "a good plain cook" but she wants to be the best...'

Able's eyes twinkled with amusement. 'Well, hon, our young lady is going to get a shock when she gets out in the world. Do you think we should let her try school dinners for a while?'

'But she is right in a way – that's exactly what I've always been. How often do I make fancy sauces that take hours to perfect? My cakes are delicious, but they are just what most women who can cook are capable of making. Yes, now and then I do something fancy but not the kind of thing Fay has in mind.'

'Do you think she'd be any good at it?'

Peggy looked at him thoughtfully. 'Yes, I do, Able. Look how good she was at skating almost from the start. If she puts her mind to it, I think she can achieve what she wants – and there is certainly more of a future in it for her...'

'I sense a *but*?' Able raised his eyebrows. 'What are you concerned about, hon?'

'If she gives up her skating just like that, will she look back and regret it? I'd love her to be a cook, Able – I mean a real cook, capable of working at a big hotel like the Savoy, but I don't want to push her into it. She loved her skating and was so good.'

'Yes, she did and she was,' Able agreed, 'but she was very disappointed that she didn't win two of the bigger competitions she was entered for. I think Sara told her that she had no chance of getting into the Olympics unless she improved.'

'She didn't tell me that...' Peggy frowned, but suddenly it made sense. Fay had ignored the pain in her side because she was desperately trying to improve in time to be picked for the next Olympics – but in her heart she'd known that with the time she would be forced to take off to recover, she'd never get there. Even if she worked hard for years, she might not reach that standard of excellence.

'Well, Sara told me when I fetched Fay one Saturday when you were working.' Able smiled gently. 'Maybe it is best if we just let her make up her own mind. She will probably change it if she doesn't like cooking.'

'What did you think of the almond macaroons this afternoon?' Peggy asked. Able had eaten three at teatime.

'Some of the best you've ever made,' he replied.

'Then you should tell your daughter, because she made them.'

He looked surprised. 'Truly? She didn't say...'

'No, and that is unusual. I think she's uncertain and wanted to hear what you really thought. She knew you would praise them if she told you she'd made them.'

'Yes,' Able chuckled. 'Fay knows me too well. I suppose I tend to spoil her a bit.'

'Just a bit,' Peggy said. 'We'll find out what we can about these cooking courses then? Can we afford them? I'm certain they will be expensive.'

'Of course we can. We're both doing well – and, besides, if Fay has something like that to work for, she'll be secure for life.'

'Yes. There's always work for a cook – but I'm not sure that she realises how hard she'll have to work yet.'

* * *

'I'm going to visit the London Planetarium next month, when the school summer holidays start,' Freddie told his sister when he visited her in her bedroom on her return from hospital. 'I've wanted to ever since the Duke of

Edinburgh opened it in March, but I haven't had time – would you like to come with me?'

'I might – depends on how busy I am,' Fay told him. 'I think it would be fun, though. Especially with you because you know stuff and can tell me what it all is.'

'I'm glad you're better,' Freddie said to his twin as he sat on the bottom of her bed and she lay propped up against a pile of pillows. In the background, they could hear Andy Williams singing a sentimental song on the wireless downstairs. 'I thought I might lose you for a while, Fay.'

Fay looked at him, the light of mischief in her eyes. 'As if you'd care. You wouldn't have to give up your football to cart me around everywhere – and there would be more of Mum's apple pie for you,' she teased. Like his father, Freddie was very partial to a large slice of apple pie with cream.

'I mean it,' he said seriously. 'Oh, you're a pain in the backside at times, Fay, but you're my twin – and I feel as if we're joined. When they were operating on you, I felt fear and then relief – as if you stopped feeling anything.'

'That's what happened,' Fay said, awestruck. 'Do you remember when you fell off your bike and sprained your wrist, and cut your knee open?' He nodded. 'I felt your pain then and I was frightened. We're special, aren't we, Freddie? Us two – we'll always have a special bond.'

'Yes, I believe we shall, even when we're older and marry – not that I plan to marry for years. I want to have adventures and train to do something worthwhile. I hope I'll get a trial for a big club – don't tell Mum or Dad yet, but I've applied to an advert I saw for young players to join the junior team at Manchester United.'

'Would you have to leave London?'

'Yes, but I may have to do that if I want to go to university anyway. I was hoping for Cambridge. I thought I might get into the rowing team or the football team, perhaps both. If I train as a sports teacher, it will be a good career and if I'm lucky enough to get into a big team then that will be special.'

'You're like me,' Fay said and laughed. 'I only want the best... I think I was rude to Mum today without meaning to be. I told her she was a good plain cook, but I wanted to learn to be special.'

'Mum is better than that,' Freddie replied. 'She's a smashing cook – why do you think she's so busy all the time. What did she say?'

'She just smiled the way she does and asked me if I was willing to give up my skating for it.'

'And are you?' Freddie asked. 'It's meant the world to you for ages.'

'I still love it and I shall skate sometimes when I can, but for pleasure – I'm not good enough, Freddie. I want to do something I can excel at and my ankles aren't strong enough to stand all the practice. I'd been wondering if I should tell Sara I was going to give up for a while...' She sighed deeply. 'I get pain in my ankles if I practise too much, so I don't always and then I'm not quite good enough to win.'

Freddie nodded. 'I noticed you weren't so keen a while back – and then when you were ill, I thought that was the reason, but you really have had enough, haven't you?'

'Sara said I had no chance of making the next Olympics unless I practised more and if I had to wait for the one after that – well, I think it would go on too long. I have to do something that will earn me a living. I can't live with Mum and Dad forever, though I know they'd have me.'

'You've grown up,' Freddie said, nodding his approval. 'You wouldn't be keen on a boyfriend just yet then?'

'No,' Fay replied and threw a pillow at him. 'Don't be daft. I'm sixteen and I've got things to do – I don't want to be married at seventeen and have a baby before I'm twenty.'

'Good!' Freddie threw the pillow back at her, grinning as she ducked. 'We both have things to do and we have each other – we don't need complications yet.'

'I know. Cooking properly is hard work – as hard as figure skating – but you don't need strong ankles, just good comfortable shoes to be on your feet for hours at a time.'

'You know what you're in for then?'

'I've seen Mum cooking for years and I know how hard she works. Dad sometimes tells her to do less, but she keeps going. I suppose she wants to provide a good life for us. Once we have our own careers, perhaps then she'll retire and go back to the sea...'

'I can't see Mum leaving the Pig & Whistle for a few years yet,' Freddie said. 'She loves it – and her friends. At the seaside, she worked just as hard, but she didn't have many friends. Here, she has lots of them and the time she spends in the bar is like having fun for her.'

'It has made more work for Mum with Auntie Maureen being so busy with the shop,' Fay commented. 'I know she has some help, but she still has to do all the fancy stuff. When school breaks up for the summer, I'm going to help her for a while. It will give me a good idea of the basics and then I can find a course to do when I leave school next year.'

'Aren't you staying on until you're eighteen?'

Fay gave a shake of her head, her fine, straight, blonde hair flying. 'I don't want to go to university like you – if I can get into a decent cooking course next year that's what I want to do.'

'If Dad will let you leave school before you're eighteen...'

'He usually lets me have what I want,' Fay replied airily. 'Mum is the one that you have to convince – and you can do that for me. She listens to you, Freddie.'

'Why do you think I'm going to help you get round her?'

'Well, you will,' Fay said and blew him a kiss. 'You always do...'

Freddie looked at her for a moment and then laughed. 'You little minx, Fay. One of these days you'll meet someone who won't give into you – and then what will you do?'

'I'll come running home to my big kind brother,' Fay said cheekily. 'I know where I'm well off, don't worry.'

Freddie laughed. No doubt his sister would get just what she wanted. He'd never known his parents to refuse her anything within reason – and their mother loved cooking. She would probably think how nice it would be to have her daughter working with her in the kitchen... or maybe not. 'Just don't drive her mad with your tantrums,' he advised. 'Or she might just insist you stay on at school and finish your education, as they always intended you should.'

7

Shirley smiled as she left the interview. The job at the Hurst Surgery was hers and she would start at the end of July. She only had to return to hospital for a few days to say goodbye to her colleagues and friends and then she could move back home with her parents and start her new job.

It felt good to know that the years of training had paid off. The Hurst Surgery partners were impressed with her results and the letters from various tutors. Especially the one from the consultant, Mr Anderson, that said she would be missed and they'd hoped she would stay on at the Dryburn Hospital in Durham, close to where she'd trained to become a doctor. She'd chosen to work there as a junior, because it felt right to give something back and she'd made friends in the area.

Shirley knew that she was capable of specialising in children's medicine and she had been tempted by the offer to join Mr Anderson's team, because he was a very respected paediatrician who not only worked at the hospital but also gave lectures at the nearby university. She'd spent some restless nights trying to decide, because it was such a worthwhile job – but then she remembered her little brother, Robin, and the way he'd died of a childhood illness that really should have been curable. She felt the local doctors had neglected him. The outbreak had affected a lot of children that year and

Robin wasn't the only one to die – but surely, they should have been admitted to hospital when it was seen how ill they were?

Shirley wanted to make sure there were no unnecessary deaths in her practice. Some illnesses you couldn't fight even now with all the improvements that were happening in the medical profession, but those that were survivable should be and would be overcome if she had anything to do with it. She'd paid particular attention to those childhood illnesses and had proved good at looking after children in the ward – that was why the consultant, Mr Raymond Anderson, who specialised in surgery on children, had asked her to join his team. He'd been quite put out when she declined.

Mr Anderson was in his late thirties. A good-looking dynamic man who got his own way most of the time. He wasn't yet married and quite a few of the nurses were potty about him. They seemed to fall into a daze when he was around and Sister had had to speak sharply to a couple of young nurses.

Shirley wasn't that impressed. She thought Raymond Anderson was arrogant, too sure of himself and uncaring of others' feelings. He was, of course, a wonderful doctor, and she admired his work very much. Had she not been set on what she wanted to do, she would have enjoyed working with him – despite his arrogance and his bad temper. She'd witnessed him throw a piece of chalk at one medical student who hadn't been paying attention to his lecture. His aim had been accurate and the chalk had hit the student on the cheek. The young man had been humiliated verbally and asked to leave the class if he couldn't stop dreaming. However, the punishment worked because that particular student never let his mind wander in Mr Anderson's class again.

No, Shirley didn't much like Mr Anderson, even if he was one of the leading experts of the day in children's surgery... He'd been a part of her life for the past few years, but he meant nothing to her. She made a determined effort to put him from her mind. There was a whole new future waiting for her now.

Shirley brought her thoughts back to her plans for the future and then to Keith. His last letter had said he would be home in late July or early August. He couldn't be more precise, because he had to travel by train to

Johannesburg where he could get a flight. Now that it was possible to fly to Africa, it had cut weeks off the journey that would always have been by ship until the first commercial flight by a land plane in 1952. However, Africa was a big country and the journey to get to Johannesburg was long and hot and dusty according to Keith's letter. She was looking forward to seeing him and they had a good friendship through their letters, but would it be more when they met again? Shirley wasn't sure. She had been unhappy when they first met and his friendship had meant a lot to her but seven years was a long time and she was a different person now.

She smiled as she thought how pleased Maureen would be when she told her the good news. It would be lovely to live at home again, and she could keep an eye on her father, though she was bound to miss her friends and colleagues from the hospital.

* * *

'I wanted to apologise for letting you down recently, especially when Fay was so ill,' Maureen said when she popped into Peggy's kitchen the next morning. 'I hope she is feeling better now?'

'No need, love. Yes, Fay seems fine. You'd hardly know she'd been ill. They bounce back quickly at her age.' Peggy looked at her friend. 'But how is Gordon?'

'He is feeling a bit better and he told me to come round after I'd been to the shop – and I wanted to tell you our news. Shirley is delighted because she got that job she was after.'

'You said she was confident it was hers,' Peggy replied, looking up from the sponge she was mixing to smile. 'That's wonderful, Maureen – and has she gone back to university?'

'Yes, she went yesterday afternoon. She wants to enjoy the last few days at her hospital and she's done all she needs to do here for a while. I've no idea what she said to Gordon, but he is sticking to the diet and the exercises she's set him.'

'You look easier,' Peggy noted. 'Shirley's visit has done you both good. You'll enjoy having her home again.'

'She's like a breath of fresh air,' Maureen agreed and started to whip some fresh cream ready for the sponge Peggy was making. 'I'm not sure I can come back to spending a full morning here cooking, Peggy – so what did you want to do about the cake shop?'

'I've got some help with the plain cakes and I can manage a few fancies – and Fay has decided she wants to learn to cook, so she'll be helping me in the school holidays. We should keep it going for a while, Maureen. You might want to do it again once Gordon is better.'

'If he ever is – but I think we should keep it going if you can manage for now,' Maureen said wistfully. 'I do feel bad about not pulling my weight though...'

'Daft!' Peggy raised her eyebrows. 'You'd do the same for me, wouldn't you?'

Maureen inclined her head and Peggy laughed.

'There you are then. Come when you want and do as much as you feel like and I'll manage.'

'You always do,' Maureen said, 'but you must say if it starts to get too much? I don't want you to be ill.'

'Me? I'm as tough as old boots,' Peggy said confidently. 'Able sometimes asks me where I get my energy from.'

That made Maureen laugh, because Peggy's husband was a few years younger than she was but he sometimes complained he couldn't keep up with her. Like many other young men, Able had lost a limb to the war. He'd never made anything of it and coped with most tasks without help. Sometimes a small button would need a little attention or a tie, but he rarely wore ties and preferred pull-on shirts that he could get into without her assistance. It was a casual way of dressing, although, occasionally, a suit and a shirt with a tie was needed, but not often. Able's style was his own and Peggy told him he looked like an American lumberjack, which made him laugh.

'That's probably what I'd be if I lived back home,' he'd said to her recently when she'd teased him. 'If you hadn't rescued me and taught me how to be happy, I'd be a woodsman and a recluse.'

'Don't be daft, you're a good businessman,' Peggy had replied and he'd grinned, but she'd had the feeling that he'd meant it.

'Yes, I am – but I have to be, because I have you and the twins – I want them to have the best, Peggy. A better life than I had as a child and I'll make sure that happens.'

Peggy knew that Able had had his troubles as a youngster, with his father and his brother – it was his brother who had caused him to have an accident and there was a scar on his hip to prove it. He walked with a slight limp at times, though he corrected it as soon as he realised. She'd often wondered if it caused him any pain, but if it did, he never spoke of it.

Peggy and Maureen worked in harmony for a while and then Maureen glanced at the clock. 'I need to go and see if Gordon is all right,' she said. 'I'll get him a cup of coffee and a salad sandwich. It was always a slice of cake for his elevenses, but Shirley says if he's hungry, he has to have a piece of lightly buttered toast and marmalade or a salad sandwich. I'm trying to do the same. I could do with losing a bit of weight...'

'Me too,' Peggy agreed. 'I went into a size thirty-eight last time I bought a new dress in the winter, but I'm working on it and I've nearly managed to get into my thirty-six summer skirts and dresses again.'

'You're just right,' Maureen remarked. 'I need a thirty-eight and if I'm not careful I'll be heading for a size forty hip.'

'Just as well Shirley has put Gordon on a strict regime then – but what about Gordy? If you're not making cakes, he's missing out and he's a growing lad.'

'I've been buying him cakes and things from the shop,' Maureen admitted. 'He loves your rock cakes and your madeleines, Peggy and the coconut tarts and almond macaroons. I'm buying small things because if I bought a fresh cream sponge, neither Gordon or I could resist – and I won't put temptation in his way.'

'I know how you feel,' Peggy agreed sympathetically. 'It is so hard to cut down – but you have to help Gordon stick to his routine.'

'I know – we have to give Shirley's idea a good trial, although...' Maureen sighed. 'What if I'm simply depriving him of the things he enjoys and it does no good?'

'No one said there was a cast-iron guarantee,' Peggy replied stoutly. 'Gordon obviously believes in her theory and is willing to give it a go – if he didn't, he would just refuse to go along with it.'

'I know...' Maureen's frown disappeared. 'That's just me being negative.

I think he seems better, less tired, and he is genuinely happy to be home with us.'.

'Then you shouldn't worry. For years you've indulged him,' Peggy said. 'He wanted the good, filling food you prepared and enjoyed every mouthful. It was his choice then and it's his choice now. No one can make us eat if we don't want to – and no one can force us to diet. We have to want to do it.'

'That reminds me. I have to check on James – my starving artist – and make sure he has eaten recently. He tends to forget about food if I don't take him a few meals now and then.'

Peggy laughed. 'You look after him as if he were another son.' She thought for a moment. 'Why don't you ask him to do more at the shop? He does your deliveries but surely he could open up for you in the mornings and work an hour or two. You trust him, I know.'

'Yes, I do, but he is working frantically to get enough stuff together for an exhibition this summer. I shall have to look for a manager, but James isn't planning on shop work as a career. He is clever and talented, Peggy. One of his paintings sold for a thousand pounds to an American...'

'That is a lot of money. I didn't realise he was famous.'

'He isn't yet – but sometimes he does something commercial and it sells, though lots of his stuff just sits there for ages.'

'Still, I see what you mean about not working full-time in the shop... pity, though, it would make things easier for you.'

'It would be a waste of his talent,' Maureen said. 'His family are country people and his father has a minor title, I think, but they don't have much to do with him, because of his lifestyle. He was meant to take over running the estate and they cut him off without a penny when he said he wanted to paint.'

'That wasn't very nice. I'd never do it to one of mine.'

'No, I'm sure you wouldn't,' Maureen agreed. 'Gordon supported Shirley all the way – and I'll make sure Gordy does whatever he wants to.'

'You'd better go, love – once we get talking, we never stop...' Peggy said.

Maureen laughed, popped her last batch of almond tarts in the oven and went. Gordon had been right to tell her to spend some time with Peggy, because she felt better now. Their friendship had survived the war and all the trials and tribulations that came after. She knew that Peggy would always be there for her and it gave her comfort to have such a friend – and yet the shadow of Gordon's illness still hung over her. She just couldn't imagine life without him...

* * *

'You're back then – did they turn you down?'

Shirley turned as she heard the sarcastic voice behind her and glared at the man who had spoken. He might be a brilliant doctor, but he was certainly a second-class human being in her book.

'As a matter of fact, they were pleased to get me,' Shirley said coldly and then saw the light mockery in his eyes. She decided to give him a bit of cheek back. 'Since I studied under you for much of the time, who would be to blame if I wasn't good enough for a GP's surgery?'

For a moment he looked taken aback and then he laughed. 'Of course they jumped at the chance,' he said. 'It's a damned waste in my opinion, Shirley Hart – but I suppose you know what you want?'

'Yes, it's why I trained to be a doctor because I want to treat sick people who need me,' she said defiantly. 'You get your pick of all the students to join your team, Mr Anderson. My practice is in a poor area where a lot of doctors don't want to go. I'm going to be working in a clinic for the down-and-outs a couple of days a week – and they do need volunteers so badly. I know it isn't everyone's choice. Many of the patients smell, they're dirty and they have lice and fleas when they arrive. They just won't go to the hospital, because they're frightened, and they don't have a regular doctor. Now they will have – because I am hoping they will get used to seeing Doctor Shirley.'

He looked at her hard for a few moments, then inclined his head. 'That is worth doing, Doctor Shirley. Will you come to the end-of-term party as my guest?'

The question came out of the blue and she answered without thinking, 'I've arranged to go with a group of friends. I'm sorry. I can't let them down.'

He nodded. 'Of course, you would have...'

As he walked off without another word, Shirley felt a pang of regret. Her arrangement with her friends was a loose one and she could easily have gone with him instead – but she was a newly qualified doctor and he was a consultant and years older.

Shirley frowned. She wouldn't have dreamed of him asking her to the party and didn't know why he had – why would he? The age gap was so wide and so was the social one. She came from the East End and had chosen to live and work there. He was from a good family, had gone to private schools, probably – she had no idea where he'd grown up – and his life was here, working and living in his own circle. It wasn't a comfortable mix and it was best that she'd turned him down... and yet there was still that faint regret she didn't quite understand.

8

Freddie thought he must have done something wrong as the master in charge of the game, Mr Matthews, called him over after the game that Saturday afternoon. 'Ah, Master Hart,' he said. 'There is someone here who wants to talk to you, young man.'

'Have I done something wrong, sir?'

'Quite the contrary. You had a very good game – we only won because of your brilliant tackling. It isn't just the goalscorers that win matches. You saved us from losing a couple of times... Ah, here he is. His name is Michael Smith and he is a football scout.'

Freddie did a double take as he looked at the small man in a thick jacket with a cap pulled down tight over his head. His trousers were tucked into long boots – sensible attire for a football field that was wet after a few days of rain, but not a look he would associate with a football scout.

He looked Freddie up and down and then nodded. 'I'm Mike and I'm looking for young players to train up for our team – the Sheffield Rangers.' He offered his hand.

Freddie hesitated a fraction of a second and then took it. He almost recoiled. The man's touch was moist and sweaty and there was something about him that made Freddie want to run away.

'How do you do, sir?' he said politely.

'How would you like a trial for our team?'

'I'm sorry, but I've applied to Manchester United for a trial,' Freddie said. 'It was very nice of you to consider me – but I have already asked about a young players' team with them.'

There was shock and then anger in the man's eyes and Freddie was glad he'd followed his instincts. 'You don't know what you're missing,' he muttered furiously. 'You're not bad – but nowhere near good enough for Manchester United.' He stalked off to talk to another boy who was standing with his father; they shook hands and got chatting, smiling and nodding.

'Why did you refuse the offer?' the sports master asked Freddie with a frown. 'He asked about you first and I thought that was what you wanted?'

'I *have* written to Manchester United and asked for a trial,' Freddie said. 'I got the address from a newspaper. I want to play for one of the best teams, sir – if I can't, I'd rather be a sports teacher like you.'

Mr Matthews smiled and nodded. 'You've got a good head on your shoulders,' he replied. 'I don't agree with Mr Smith – I think you have the potential to be very good indeed, if you're given the right chance. Well, done, Freddie.'

'Thank you, sir.' Freddie smiled to himself. He hadn't liked the football scout and he wouldn't regret turning him down, though it seemed his friend, Bob Travers, had accepted the offer and was grinning like a cat that got the cream as he came towards him.

'What do you think?' he asked Freddie. 'I've got a try-out for the Sheffield Rangers and they're top in the second division. Mr Smith says there's a chance that they will go up next season. In a couple of years, I could be playing in the first division!'

'That's great, Bob,' Freddie said. 'You deserve it after those goals you scored – two out of the three.'

'If it hadn't been for you at the other end, we might have been three down by half time.' Bob frowned. 'Why did you turn the chance down? We could have been playing together...'

'Not sure,' Freddie said hesitantly and then made up his mind. 'Just be careful of him, Bob. I don't know why, but I don't trust him – and his hands were sweaty.' He didn't know why that last bit mattered, but it did.

'Yes,' Bob agreed. 'They were.' He glanced to where the football scout was chatting with his father. 'We're mates, Freddie, and I'll take notice of what you said – though he must be all right. Dad wouldn't let me go if he thought it was dodgy.'

'No, of course he wouldn't – but he might not realise.' Freddie shook his head. 'Take no notice of me. It's great you've got a trial and I'll bet you'll be playing for the first team in no time.'

'Thanks.' his friend smiled at him. 'Can I come back to tea with you this evening? Your mum is a smashing cook and mine's in hospital.'

'I didn't know that,' Freddie said. 'Of course you can. Mum is bound to have something nice for tea. She always does and she never minds me bringing someone home. Let's ask your dad.'

'Oh, he'll be glad to get me out of the way for a bit,' Bob replied. 'He can't think straight at the moment. He's worried to death about Mum. She's had an operation to take out her womb.' He shook his head. 'I'm not supposed to talk about it, but I think she had something serious and they said they had no choice. Dad says they've told him they caught it in time, but he's still worrying himself sick over her.'

'I should worry about my mum if something like that happened,' Freddie said seriously. He touched his friend's arm lightly. 'You come round ours as much as you like, Bob. Mum always has enough food for everyone and she'll make you feel better.'

'Thanks, Freddie. I like your mum – and Fay. Don't tell her, but I think she's a smasher, very pretty. I know she wouldn't look at me, but I can look at her, can't I?'

'As long as you treat her with respect,' Freddie replied and grinned to show they were still friends. 'Besides, she knows just what she wants in life. She is going to be a famous chef now and learn to cook wonderful cakes and desserts. She says dinners are boring but desserts are what everyone wants.'

'Cor, I'd like to marry her when I'm a famous footballer,' Bob said and grinned. 'We wouldn't bother with boring meat and vegetables we'd go straight to the cake...'

'Yeah, sounds good,' Freddie agreed, 'but don't let on you like her – I warn you, Fay has sharp claws. She is great when she wants to be, but she can be a bit cruel if you let her. She doesn't do it with me much because I'm her twin, but she might just break your heart.'

Bob nodded. 'You're a good mate, Freddie. I hope one day we end up playing on the same team.'

'Yeah, that would be good,' Freddie agreed, 'but I think I'm going to finish school and do my university course – unless Manchester United take me on, of course.'

'Oh yeah? Pigs might fly,' Bob teased and Freddie aimed a blow at his ear, which missed by a mile. They pushed each other in a friendly way and ran to join Bob's father to ask if he could come to tea.

'Of course, you can, lad,' his father said. 'Be home by eight-thirty. Will Freddie's father take you to the bus stop?'

'I'm all right catching a bus alone, Dad. Can you give me sixpence for the fare?'

'Here.' His father handed him half a crown. 'Take that and buy yourselves an ice cream each.'

'Thank you, Dad.'

'Thanks, Mr Travers. That is very kind of you.'

'Not at all, Freddie. I always know Bob is all right with you.'

* * *

'Why did you turn the chance down?' Able asked his son when they'd taken Bob home that evening. He'd insisted on getting the car out and driving Freddie's friend to his house once he knew that his father was at the hospital. 'We'll see you safe inside, lad. It's no trouble to me – and if anything worries you at any time, you come to me. I'll always be here and ready to help you, Bob.'

'Thanks, Mr Ronoscki,' Bob had said and his face lit up. 'I like coming to your house – Mrs Ronoscki is a smashing cook.'

'Yes, she is,' Able had replied and smiled. 'There's always room for another at our table and don't you forget it.'

Freddie looked at his father thoughtfully now that they were alone and his friend was safely home. 'You remember we had a talk when I was fourteen, Dad? You told me there are some men I shouldn't trust too much, men who might try to take advantage of me and do nasty things?'

'Yes, I remember that talk very well,' Able said and looked at him expectantly.

'I think that maybe that football scout was one of those,' Freddie said. 'I didn't tell the sports master what I thought – but I warned Bob to be careful of him. I expect his dad has told him to be careful about things like that, don't you?'

'Perhaps – not all parents feel able to talk about those things,' Able commented. 'Maybe we might mention it next time he comes round?'

'I'll tell him at school,' Freddie said. 'Bob likes Fay. He thinks he wants to marry her one day – I told him not to waste his time. She is set on becoming a famous cook now she's finished skating and she won't let anything stand in her way until she gets there.'

'Has she really finished with the skating?' Able asked. 'She's told you so?'

'Yes. She has made up her mind she'll never be good enough to win the Olympics. She's like me, Dad. She only wants the best – I want to play for the first division not the second. If I can't...' He shrugged and his father smiled.

'You'll do what you can make a success of.' He touched his son's hand lightly. 'We're the same – you and me. I do what I can as best as I can and I'm content – but then, I've got your mother.'

'Yes. I want someone like Mum when I get married – but it won't be for years and years. I want to do things first – go to uni, train for whatever I can, and then travel the world a bit.'

Able raised his brows. 'Where were you thinking of going?'

'America for a start – and then places like India and China. Perhaps Japan and Europe, of course, but I want to spend a year exploring and then come home and settle down in a good job.'

'Well, I shan't stand in your way – once you're old enough. Shall we say twenty or twenty-one?'

Freddie nodded. 'I should be finished whatever training I do by then, perhaps even have a year or two in a job. Of course, if I get a place with

Manchester United, I will have to wait until my career there ends... or just go for short holidays abroad.'

'Got it all planned, haven't you, son?'

'Yes, mostly,' Freddie said happily. 'But if it doesn't happen, I'm fine at home.'

Able laughed. 'No, don't settle for second best, Freddie. You go for it – I'm behind you all the way.' He smiled and ruffled his hair as the car came to a halt in the back yard of the Pig & Whistle. 'You're a good lad and I want you to have a wonderful life.' He paused for a moment, then, 'I'm glad you had the sense to turn down that offer – always say no, Freddie. Whatever someone offers, if you think there's anything dodgy, just say no.'

'You bet!' Freddie ran on ahead. 'We're back, Mum – is there any apple pie left?'

* * *

'Do you think you should have a word with Bob's father?' Peggy asked that evening when they were preparing for bed and Able had told her of his conversation with their son. 'Freddie's instincts are good and if he thought... perhaps Bob shouldn't go...'

'Freddie is going to tell Bob what we talked about when he was fourteen,' Able said. 'It may be better coming from him – I'm not the lad's father and it might seem wrong if I told him. But if I get the chance, I might just have a word in John Travers' ear.'

'Yes, I think that would be the best way,' Peggy agreed. 'We're lucky to have such sensible children, aren't we?'

'We have wonderful kids,' Able told her with a smile. 'But it helps if you bring them up right. I can understand Bob's father being distracted right now, but there was plenty of time in the past to warn him. You spoke to Fay and I spoke to Freddie. If they understand the things that can harm them, it helps them to stop and think first.'

'Our children have always been too busy enjoying themselves to think about straying. Freddie with his football and Fay with her skating...' Peggy paused, then, 'Do you think Freddie will get a trial with Manchester United?'

'Who knows? Life is filled with little miracles, hon. Yet, I don't think it matters. He'll be disappointed for a while if it comes to nothing and then he'll pick himself up and be the best sports teacher ever.'

She nodded. 'I think I'd almost rather that he was a teacher – if there are men like that in the professional sport...'

'Not all football scouts are that way, but it happens – and it could happen at college just the same,' Able said reasonably, 'All you can do is warn them of the perils of too much drink, drugs and bad influences and then you have to let go, hon.'

'Yes, I know.' She went into his arms, lifting her face for his kiss. 'I love you so much, Able. You've given me such happiness – and the twins too. They've grown up in a happy house and they're both decent kids.'

'Good kids who have to grow up and find their own lives, hon. We may find they do things we don't like as the years pass, but we'll still love them and that's all that really matters.' He smiled into her eyes. 'Are you tired?'

'Not a bit.' Peggy's eyes sparkled with mischief. 'Are you?'

'Would you like me to show you?'

'Yes, please,' she said and so he did...

9

Peggy answered the phone the next morning. It was her eldest daughter and she was delighted when Janet said she was coming down from Scotland to stay for a few days at the end of term. She'd been living there with her husband, her daughter, Maggie, and son, Jon, for some years now so they didn't get to see each other as much as she would have liked.

'I know you're going down to stay with Pip in the second week of August,' she said. 'I'd like to come, too, if we may. Pip says he doesn't have room to put us up in the cottage, but he's going to fix something up for us so we can all spend time together.'

'That's wonderful, Janet,' Peggy said, 'but what about Ryan?'

'He might be able to come to Pip's one weekend, drive down – a long weekend – so he will if he can. It will make things easier once they get some of these new motorways, they're talking about, built. Ryan has been very busy again lately, so he could do with a break.'

'Are things okay between the two of you?' Peggy asked, sensing something in her daughter's tone. She knew they'd been through a rough patch some years earlier, but after the birth of Ryan's son, Jon, they'd seemed to settle down.

'Yes, absolutely fine,' Janet said. 'Don't worry, Mum. I'm perfectly happy with my life and I'm busy a lot of the time. I have two small jobs and I go for lots of walks – and horse riding, too, sometimes.'

'I didn't know you'd started riding?' Peggy questioned. 'I didn't think you were keen on horses.'

'I wasn't particularly, but Maggie wanted me to ride with her sometimes and so I decided to learn – and I wanted to get fitter as well. I've lost a stone since last summer and I feel better for it.'

'Good for you,' Peggy said. 'Well, that all sounds wonderful, darling. We shall look forward to your visit. It seems ages since you were down.'

'Yes, I know. We couldn't make it last Christmas because Maggie got that dreadful cold – it was more like flu really.' Maggie was just over two years older than Peggy's twins, born of Janet's first marriage. At eighteen, she must be seriously considering what she wanted to do with her life, Peggy thought but didn't ask, because she knew Janet would tell her when she was ready.

'The thing is, Mum—' Janet hesitated. 'After the holiday when I go back to Scotland, Maggie wants to stay with you for a while. She leaves school at the end of this term and she's refusing to go to college. She says she isn't interested. I asked her what she wants to do and she said she wants to talk to you about it.'

'Talk to me?' Peggy was surprised. 'But I've never done anything – what do I know about careers for young women?'

'Come off it, Mum. You're one of the most successful businesswomen I have met. I mean, I know some women who run hotels and guesthouses up here with their husbands, but they don't hold a candle to you. I've no idea how you manage it.'

'Because I genuinely love what I do,' Peggy told her. 'You've never had a job that you truly love, Janet. You never really had time to think about it. Once you left school you went to work at that canteen and then you were married and Maggie was born. You've only ever done part-time jobs since then...'

'I know.' Janet sighed down the line. 'I don't take after my mother, do I?' She laughed. 'Ryan says he wouldn't want me any different. He doesn't care if I go to work at all – I only do it to fill in the time while he's away and

Maggie is out at school or with her friends. She is never at home these days. I swear the only time I see her is when Jason takes us riding.'

'And who is Jason?' Peggy inquired, hearing a new name.

'Oh, he is a sort of local squire, has a wonderful big old house but not much money – but he runs the riding stable we use and he taught me to ride.'

'And how old is he?'

'I've no idea, Mum, though I suppose he is in his late twenties. He inherited the estate when his father died, but estate duties nearly ruined him. He has hung on to some decent paintings and most of the land, but he had to start the riding school to keep the wolf from the door – as he says.'

'Good-looking?'

'Why do you ask? There's nothing going on.'

'I was thinking about Maggie,' Peggy said. 'She is a pretty young woman now and might be fascinated by the local laird.'

'He's not actually a laird,' Janet said, 'but I suppose he is very attractive to a young girl. I hadn't thought about that possibility, Mum, because she was more interested in her horse than him or it seemed that way to me. I tend to think of her as still a schoolgirl.'

'She is a young girl but she's a similar age to the age Shirley Hart was when she thought herself in love with a far from suitable young man. Richard treated her so badly – but she's happy enough now. She qualified a couple of years back and did the last few years in the hospital as a junior doctor, but now she is coming back to work in the East End – not too far from us actually.'

'Maggie will be pleased to see her. I think they got to know one another last time we were down. Shirley was on holiday and they went out together a couple of times.'

'That will be nice for them both then, though I think Shirley expects to be kept pretty busy at the practice and the clinic where she has volunteered.'

'I think Maggie hopes to be busy too,' Janet said. 'I'm not supposed to say because she wants to ask you herself, but she thinks she wants to work with you, cooking and serving in the bar.'

'Goodness!' Peggy was astonished. 'Fay has just decided she wants to make fancy cakes.'

'Maggie is more interested in the kind of cooking you do every day, but perhaps a bit more upmarket,' Janet said. 'Don't let on I told you, will you?'

'Of course not, but I'm glad you did. I was thinking I might have to take on more staff soon, because Maureen doesn't look as if she will be back for some time. I did tell you about Gordon when I last rang?'

'Yes, you did and I know how distressed she must be. She lost Robin and if she loses Gordon as well...'

'She's had enough sorrow to last her one way and another,' Peggy agreed. 'Fay is getting over her operation, but she isn't interested in her skating at all. I've had to tell Sara she's given up. In fact, she spends most of her time with her nose in cookery books – cakes and desserts that is, nothing remotely like what we serve here at the Pig & Whistle.'

'So she won't be taking over from you then, Mum?'

'No, I can't see Fay ever settling for running a pub or a café like Able and I did – it will be head pastry chef at the Savoy for her or something similar. She wanted to go on a cooking course in France this summer.'

'You won't let her?' Janet sounded startled.

'No, of course not. She says next year will be better – but we'll have to see. Able is trying to find somewhere in this country where she can take a course – in London preferably.'

'Well, he'll find something – let's hope it suits madam.'

'Don't call her that, Janet. She is headstrong at times but she's a lovely girl and can be really sweet.'

'When she wants to.' Janet was always a little harsh when it came to Fay in Peggy's opinion. 'After all that money you spent on her skating lessons and the costumes.'

'Able paid most of it,' Peggy reminded her. 'He likes to give the twins as much as he can and he's their father so I don't interfere.'

'You do as much for me and Maggie. I'm not green over it, Mum. I just think she's spoiled, that's all...'

'Perhaps she is a little, but Able thinks the world of both of them – and he does put his foot down sometimes. Personally, I think his attitude and the security he provides has made both of them independent and ready to go out and do what they want in life.'

'Maybe I am a bit green,' Janet admitted. 'I'm the one that didn't do anything with my life. Pip has a fabulous job and relishes his perfect life down there on the coast – and Sheila is working part-time in a cake shop, which she loves. I'm the one who doesn't know what to do with myself.'

Peggy caught the note of slight discontent. 'Are you sure you and Ryan are all right?' she asked again and Janet sighed.

'Yes, we are, Mum. I told you – but I am feeling bored, to be honest. I've had enough of just messing around with part-time jobs. I'd like to do something more worthwhile, but Ryan thinks I should be content as we are.'

'You've stopped in Scotland far longer than you expected,' Peggy said tentatively. 'His job was supposed to last for five years...'

'And then they promoted him, because they didn't want him to leave, and gave him loads more work, so I hardly see him,' Janet said. 'Oh, I love it up here, Mum. I'm just a bit scared, that's all – life seems to be slipping by and I'm not sure I've done anything with it.'

'You have two beautiful children, Janet. That must count for something?'

'Yes, it does,' Janet agreed. 'I love them and I love Ryan – but I need more. Maggie wants to move down to London and Jon is always out with his friends playing – Ryan is working most days until seven at night. What do I do? I cook a few scones and serve cream teas to the tourists.' She sighed. 'We're so out of things up here. If I'd been in London, I'd have joined the march to protest for nuclear disarmament.'

'I considered it, but I was just too busy.' Peggy replied. 'A lot of people disagreed with it, but I think the situation is getting dangerous and it would be a good thing if the whole world could agree to abolish those awful weapons.'

'We don't want a nuclear war next time, Mum.'

'Perish the thought there will be another. We're only now getting over the last one.' Peggy frowned. 'So you're pretty fed up then, love?'

'I don't know. I just want more, Mum. Perhaps I'm unreasonable, but I do.'

'Janet, you're not having an affair, are you?' Peggy asked with her usual directness.

There was a pause, then, 'No, I'm not, but I've thought about it...'

'With Jason?' Her instincts were working overtime and she'd sensed something – an unease in her daughter that told her she was bothered over something or someone.

'Can you read me so well?' Janet laughed. 'Yes, I was interested but I didn't trust him, because he flirted with Maggie as well as me, although, as I told you, she didn't seem to notice – and I knew it was foolish.'

'You're my daughter. I know you, Janet. I know your mood swings. Please don't be an idiot. This man may be attractive, but Ryan is a good husband and you'd hate yourself afterwards.'

'I know – and I haven't given in,' Janet said firmly. 'I want to get away for the summer if you'll have me. If I stay with you as well as Maggie, Ryan won't question it. He'll just get on with his work and come down when he can and I'll be out of temptation's way.'

'Yes, of course you can stay. Pearl is very busy at the boarding house, Janet. You can help her for a few weeks if you want – after we come back from Pip's.'

'Okay, fine,' Janet agreed. 'I'm going to ring off now, Mum. Love to Able and the twins.'

Peggy sighed as she replaced the receiver. She'd been so pleased with the idea that Janet was coming down for a while, but now that she knew why, she felt sad. Janet's life never seemed enough for her. Her first marriage had started badly, because of the estrangement from her father when she became pregnant before marriage, and ended tragically when her husband's war wounds robbed him of life. After she'd married Ryan, Peggy had thought Janet would be happy – and she was, in a way, but every now and then she got fed up and put her marriage at risk. Why couldn't she be happy?

Peggy had never had time to become restless. Besides, Able was the only man for her and she wouldn't change him even if she could – but Janet just couldn't find that elusive peace of mind. Perhaps if Pearl gave her plenty of work to do this summer, she would settle down at last. What she needed was more than a job, she needed to find something that she really wanted to do – the way that Fay had wanted her skating and now her fancy cake making – but Able was Fay's father and Janet's father had been similar – restless and never quite content with what he had. Thankfully, Pip took after her, but Janet was like Laurie.

Shaking her head, Peggy went back to her work. Janet spent too much time alone. Didn't Ryan understand what his long hours at work were doing to his family – or didn't he care?

* * *

Janet was annoyed with herself after she put down the receiver. Why had she told her mother that she fancied Jason? She'd never even admitted it to herself until her mother got it out of her. Yes, Jason was strong, handsome and had something about him that most women would find attractive, but he was younger by a few years, though not enough to matter, if she really wanted him.

No! Janet shook her head. She was being stupid. She did like Jason and she did fancy him, especially in his riding clothes when he often wore just a shirt that showed the strength of his muscles, his tight-fitting jodhpurs that clung to strong thighs and those sexy long boots. He was like one of the heroes out of a Mills & Boon romance, the kind that Maggie was reading all the time now – a dashing earl from some historical adventure. He'd given her a few looks and his hands lingered when he helped her into the saddle, though he hadn't said anything suggestive – but he didn't need to with those eyes!

Janet wasn't sure how Maggie felt about the man who gave her riding lessons and schooled her over the jumps at his stables. She was eighteen and confident in most ways, but she'd never had a boyfriend, or none that she would admit to. One of the lads from the local school had tagged along after her for the past three years, carrying her satchel, running errands for her and buying her ice creams on a hot day, but Maggie treated him just as she did her cousins at home, with a mild detachment and the odd, brilliant smile. Janet had felt sorry for poor Kev, as his friends called him. He had freckles in the summer, gingery red hair and greenish eyes and they gazed on Maggie with doglike devotion, following her every time she moved.

There was no doubt in Janet's mind that Kev adored Maggie, but she hardly noticed – except now and then when she would thank him for some service and give him that smile.

Ryan said that Maggie had her mother's smile. He thought they were alike, but Janet saw a lot of Mike in her daughter these days and it had brought back painful memories, making her long for her youth again and the short time of happiness she'd had with Mike.

It wasn't that she didn't love Ryan, she did, but it had always been different from the first time. Janet wasn't sure how, but at times she felt there was something missing – a closeness and joining of minds she'd felt with Mike that she didn't quite have with Ryan. It made her feel guilty and when he spent long hours at work, she questioned if they were growing apart.

No, she mustn't let it happen! Maggie might not be Ryan's daughter, but she thought of him as a father and was more affectionate towards him than she was to her mother. Maggie and Ryan did love each other, but they also struck sparks off one another and that led to tantrums. In her early teens, Maggie had been difficult to discipline and they'd argued often, over what she should wear, when she should be home at night after going out with friends and her school results. Maggie's exam results had fallen short in those years, though of late they had been a little better. She did very well in literature, history, English and domestic science, but nothing else seemed to appeal to her. She did not wish to study at university and had only stayed at school this long because Ryan had had a long talk to her and asked her to do it for his sake.

'I'll stay on to please you, Dad,' she'd told him. 'But it is a waste of time. I don't want to do any of the jobs they keep telling us about at school.'

'What do you want to do, Maggie – have you any idea?' he'd asked gently.

'Yes, I know just what I want to do – but I don't want to talk about it yet in case it doesn't happen.'

'Perhaps I could help to make it happen, Maggie.'

'It depends on Granny Peggy,' Maggie had replied. 'I want to work with her – and to take over the Pig & Whistle one day.'

'You want to be a publican?'

'Yes, in a way,' Maggie had agreed, 'but I shan't run it the way Granny does. I want to do lunches, evening meals, too, in time – special meals, like some of the places you've taken me to, Dad. There is plenty of room there if it was renovated and extended out the back… perhaps with a conservatory-type room that could have nice green plants and oak tables and chairs with bright cloths and little vases of flowers on the tables. We'd have a good wine list and people would visit from all over, because we'd be different.'

'You've thought this all out, haven't you?'

'Yes – but it depends on Granny,' Maggie had said seriously. 'It would cost money to make it nice enough to attract the right customers and she might not want to spend that money – or to have me working with her. I should want us to work together until she decides to retire and she will one day.'

'Yes, she will – and perhaps I can help with the money to bring all these grand ideas to fruition?' Ryan had smiled.

'Would you do that for me?' Maggie had asked. 'I know I'm not really your daughter – not the way Jon is your son.'

'You are every bit the same to me,' Ryan had said firmly. 'I love both of you and whatever I have is for both of you, equally.'

'You're so kind,' Maggie had told him. 'I'm glad Mum married you – and I'm happy you didn't split up a few years ago.'

'What do you know about that, miss?'

'I know you were both unhappy and you quarrelled a lot – but it's better now, isn't it?'

'Yes, much better up here,' Ryan had agreed. 'I'm happy, you're happy, Jon is fine, as far as I know, and I think your mum is all right.'

'Yes, Mum is all right,' Maggie had nodded her agreement. 'She ought to be because you're the best.'

Remembering that conversation, which she'd overheard, Janet felt ashamed of herself. Ryan was the best and she should never give him reason to leave her, either in spirit or physically, which she knew would happen if she had an affair. He might not divorce her, but he would certainly give her the cold shoulder and their marriage would be over.

Was Jason's masculine appeal worth the risk? The sensible answer was no. Janet gave herself a mental shake. It was a good thing she was going away for several weeks this summer. She would visit her family – and Pip would set her straight. They understood each other so well and he would give her some straight talking. Janet could stay down in London for a while and see that Maggie was settled before she returned.

She could even suggest to Ryan that they moved back down to London. After all, if it was agreed that they should invest in the pub to turn it into the special place Maggie had in mind, it made sense to live there for a while – and it would be much better if she was removed from temptation altogether.

10

Shirley glanced at herself in the mirror as she prepared for the party that was being given before the summer break for the medical students and the doctors from the hospital who were their guests. It wasn't so long ago that she'd been a student herself and she'd enjoyed her years as a junior doctor at the hospital, mixing with both students and doctors, but the time had come to return home, just as she'd always promised herself. So why did she feel a little regretful this evening? She could have been attending in the company of the man whose work she most admired and might have done if he hadn't been such a beast to his students.

She shook her head. It was stupid to feel like this on a night she'd looked forward to, a night of celebration with her friends – but the regret still lingered as she finished dressing in a full-skirted dress with a big white stand-up collar. It had been expensive, a birthday present from her father, it was perhaps too much for the party and yet if she didn't wear it now, she probably never would. She applied a dusting of powder to her nose and a shimmer of pale pink lipstick. Glancing in the mirror, she knew the dress suited her and sighed. As she realised that she was wishing she'd agreed to go to the party with Mr Anderson, Shirley was furious with herself. She'd always thought she disliked him, but now she was a little mixed up, unsure of her feelings about leaving all her friends behind when she went home, especially a certain person who despite his arrogance had a smile that lit up his eyes.

Supposing she had gone to the party with him? The whole idea was idiotic and if she'd agreed, he would have regretted his impulse to ask her – of course it was an impulse. He was too old for her and they were too far apart in every way to enjoy each other's company. She'd always believed him arrogant and he was impossible to be with for any longer than it took for his lectures to take place. Remembering what a fool he made his students feel at times, she dismissed him from her mind. She was going to the party with friends she liked and it would be fun...

It was fun, of course, the minute she met her friends and they all trooped into the Albany Hotel, where the party was being held. It was an old-fashioned place with a lot of shining mahogany and big, elegant mirrors with subdued lighting. However, the students had transformed the large reception room with balloons, glitter and streamers and quite a few of them had dressed up in fancy costumes. Particularly the male, newly qualified junior doctors, who seemed desperate to let off steam after so many years of study.

Shirley had always been popular, both in her years as a student and as a junior doctor. She was always willing to help anyone struggling with homework or to explain something if she understood it and a friend didn't and yet she'd never broken hearts or had a steady boyfriend. Consequently, she was considered a bit of a mystery and that evening she found herself inundated with requests to dance. Drinks were in ready supply, but Shirley stuck to orange juice, because she'd seen what drinking a bit too much did to some of the other students, a few of whom had lost their chance of a wonderful life because they'd let it take hold. She was too happy that evening to need alcohol to make her laugh and her eyes shine. Her laughter rang out again and again, and wherever Shirley was that evening, a little crowd surrounded her.

'You look very lively and happy this evening, Doctor Shirley.' the voice made her whirl around in surprise. 'Do you have time to spare a few moments for me?'

'Mr Anderson...' Shirley faltered. Her little court of junior doctors had melted away, scared off by the lion now in their midst – a man they admired and disliked in equal measure. Admired for his undoubted skill and disliked for his astringent tongue and his biting sarcasm when they did something wrong. 'Yes, of course – do you jive?' The music was Bill Haley and the Comets and fast and her scepticism must have shown in her face.

'I'm not that old or decrepit,' he said acidly. 'I don't mind a bit of rock 'n' roll – but actually, I want to talk to you. I thought a quiet drink in the lounge?'

'Yes – if you wish...' Shirley was surprised but allowed him to lead the way to a secluded table apart from the fun and laughter in the big reception room where the students and junior doctors were having a great time by the sound of the shrieks and giggles.

A waiter appeared instantly, something that hadn't happened when Shirley queued with others for drinks earlier. It was as if the great man snapped his fingers and everyone jumped to attention.

'What would you like, Doctor Shirley?'

'Orange juice please. I prefer to stick to non-alcoholic drinks when I'm at a party.'

'Of course. Very sensible. I would expect no less from my star pupil...'

Shirley's pulses raced as he looked at her. Was that sarcasm or did he genuinely mean it? His dark blue eyes were unfathomable and a little shiver ran down from her nape to the middle of her spine. He did have a mesmerising look that held your attention – it was the reason that all the students hung on to his every word. His good looks might have had something to do with it as far as the females were concerned, she thought wryly. If you allowed yourself to think about it, he looked like one of those suave film stars that were so popular – a finer-featured Rhett Butler, perhaps. *Gone with the Wind* was one of Shirley's all-time favourite films and she'd seen it four times – Mr Anderson didn't look like the star of that film, but he had the dominance of the character and the charm when he chose to.

'You wanted to talk to me, sir?' she asked as the waiter went off with their order – orange juice and a malt whisky.

'Do you think you could bring yourself to call me Ray – or Raymond?' he asked and there was an odd note in his voice. 'I'm not quite in my dotage, you know, Shirley.'

'Of course not, s— Ray...' she said and then felt ridiculously shy. 'That doesn't seem right. May I call you Mr Anderson please? I'm still in awe of you... as are all your students.'

'You are no longer my student and as of today you no longer work with me,' he said with a little frown. 'You know that I really did try to keep you here at the University Hospital? I thought you would make an excellent addition to my team – and I don't do that lightly, doctor.'

'I know – and I'm grateful for the compliment,' Shirley assured him. 'If I hadn't always had a dream of what I wanted to do, I should have been honoured to accept, Mr Anderson.'

'Thank you.' The waiter returned. Mr Anderson gave him a note and waved him away. 'I'm glad you feel that way – and I admire you for sticking to your guns, Doctor Shirley. You clearly know exactly what you want from life and that is something I always applaud. I just wanted to make sure that you understood there is *always* a place here for you with me – should you not be happy in your first choice.'

Shirley was too surprised to answer for a moment. She hadn't imagined he would offer a second chance. 'I— thank you,' she stammered. 'That is very kind of you.'

'I am never kind – at least only to puppies, kittens and little children,' he said and she saw the twinkle of laughter in his eyes and laughed, for the first time at ease with him. 'Had you accepted, I would have worked you harder than all the rest with no mercy.'

'I know,' she replied with a smile and saw that he was the one surprised this time. 'I should have expected and wanted it.'

'Yes – and that's why I want you, Doctor Shirley. I know I can't persuade you to change your mind – and it wouldn't be fair – but you won't forget me, I hope, or my offer?'

'No, I shan't forget you, Mr Anderson,' Shirley smiled warmly. 'I owe what I am mostly to your lectures. I'm grateful for the education I received here – and to you most of all.'

'Gratitude?' He gave her an odd, deep look. 'Well, I suppose it is a start – I thought for a while you disliked me intensely?'

'Perhaps a bit – when I was on the end of your sarcasm,' she said and met his eyes boldly in a way she would never have dared while still working with him.

He gave a shout of laughter and raised his glass to her. 'I'm going to miss you, Doctor Shirley – but I wish you a happy life and give you leave to return to your friends.'

Shirley hesitated, then, 'I think I shall fetch my coat and go home.'

'Then you must allow me to take you in my car,' he said and put down his half-finished whisky. 'No, I insist – you will be quite safe. I shall not take unfair advantage, Doctor Shirley.'

She hesitated, then inclined her head. 'I never thought you would – and I gratefully accept. Thank you.'

* * *

Later, as she prepared for bed, Shirley reviewed that drive home with pleasure. Mr Anderson had gently pumped her for information about her family and her reasons for what she was doing. She'd told him everything, about Robin's death, her unhappy time at the farm and the good fortune she'd had when Maureen took her home.

'She has been better than any mother to me,' she'd said. 'I love her – and I love my father very much—' Her voice had faltered a little. 'He isn't well now... a problem with his arteries. I've put him on a diet and exercise routine.'

'And will he stick to the programme?'

'Maureen and I will see to it that he does. It is another reason why I need to go home.'

'Of course. I am sorry your father is ill and I hope his health improves.' He'd hesitated, then, 'I think we're not too far from the kind of surgery and medicine that will save patients with that sort of problem, but unfortunately there is nothing yet, or if there is, it is only experimental.'

'I know. I researched it as soon as I found out.' Shirley had sighed. 'I believe the right surgery will be available soon, but for now it is still too difficult, so we just have the diet and the better way of living.'

'With you to care for him – and your stepmother – he stands more chance of a longer life than many.'

'Yes.' Shirley had held back another sigh that might have been a sob. 'This is where I live... until tomorrow... and then I'm off.'

'Yes, of course.' He'd stopped the car outside the accommodation block, switched off the engine and turned to her, offering her his hand. 'Good luck, Doctor Shirley – and if there is ever anything I can do to help, please get in touch.'

She'd smiled. 'Yes, I shall – and thank you.'

She'd taken his hand and he'd held hers firmly for a moment. 'Good-night,' he'd said simply. 'Get some sleep. You have a busy life ahead of you.'

'Yes, I know,' she'd replied and got out of the car. Just as she did, he'd leaned forward and she'd had the oddest feeling that he wanted to kiss her, but he didn't, and she'd continued to get out, gave him a little wave before closing the door.

Lying in bed, she was torn between excitement at the thought of going home and starting her new life and a feeling of loss.

* * *

'I'm so glad you're home, Shirley,' Maureen greeted her with a hug. 'Your dad is no worse – in fact, if they hadn't told us what his problem is I'd probably have agreed he should return to work – but so far, I've managed to stop him.'

'Good.' Shirley hugged her back. 'It feels nice to be home again, Mum. I've missed you and Gordy and Dad, our friends – and these streets.' She laughed. 'Does that sound nuts?'

'A bit, because I know you've enjoyed all the fun and new things you've seen up there in Durham – and it was a lovely place to study and get your qualifications, Shirley. I wasn't sure if you might decide to stay there at the hospital. You were offered a good job, weren't you?'

'I could have joined the team of a very clever children's doctor,' Shirley admitted. 'Mr Anderson is a surgeon and performs some wonderful operations that save lives. I was tempted in a way, but the reason I trained was to help folk around here – where that help is often desperately needed.'

'Yes, I understand – you always felt that Robin's death could have been prevented, didn't you?'

'Yes, Mum, I did,' Shirley agreed. 'It wasn't your fault and it wasn't mine – but perhaps if the doctor had understood how ill he was, he could have admitted him into hospital and there he would have received the treatment he needed.'

'Perhaps – but sometimes these things just happen. There were so many children ill with the chickenpox that year and it can take lives.'

'In children with underlying problems, sick children, undernourished or neglected, yes – but Robin was loved, well fed and cared for, with all the attention we could give. It should not have happened – the doctor missed something.' Shirley sounded angry, because she was. Robin's death had haunted her down the years; the grief and pain of losing a small child was too much and if she could save a few – save their parents from feeling as her family had – then she would be doing something worthwhile.

'I miss him too every day,' Maureen said and looked sad.

Shirley reached for her hand and squeezed it. 'I know you do, Mum. It never goes away, does it?'

'No. There will always be a little part of me missing – but I'm lucky to have you, Gordy and your father,' Maureen said and smiled at her. 'You go on and you make life happy for those you have, Shirley. I miscarried a baby after that and I never fell for another – your father was too worried that I might die next time, so we stopped, but I have lots of friends and a busy life.'

'I know and I'm glad,' Shirley agreed. 'But I want to do what I can to stop it happening again, Mum. I know children will still die – no doctor is a miracle worker – but I may save a few.'

Maureen nodded. 'I understand – and the need to practise around here, Shirley, but one day you might regret not taking that job in Durham – do you think?'

'No. I may miss people,' Shirley admitted. 'I made a lot of friends up there, Mum...'

'I know.' Maureen nodded. 'I don't think there was anyone special, though – was there?'

'I was too busy to bother with all that,' Shirley replied. 'I wanted to be the best I could be. Not to be top of the class or better than others for the sake of it – but just as good as I could be.'

'You got good qualifications two years ago,' Maureen said, looking at her carefully. 'Gordon thought you might come back then?'

'I wanted more hospital experience – and I continued to attend Mr Anderson's lectures whenever I could spare the time. You can never know too much, Mum, because one day someone's life may depend on you knowing one tiny detail that you might not have seen had you not read that extra paragraph or treatise.'

Maureen nodded. 'I never completely finished my time as a nurse because I had Robin. I liked nursing for several reasons and I might have continued if that hadn't happened, but I don't think I was ever as dedicated as you've been, Shirley.'

'It was different for you. You went into nursing because of the war. You had to care for men who were so injured that a lot of them were dying or would never recover – and you had Robin. You never regretted that, did you?'

'No – how could I?' Maureen smiled at her. 'He was a gift from God. Had it not been for Gordon, I might have struggled, though, but he was wonderful to me, always has been. He never once acted or spoke as anything but Robin's father.'

'He loves you, that's why.' Shirley gripped her hand. 'Don't worry, Mum. We'll look after him.'

'Yes, I know.' Maureen smiled. 'He already seems better.'

'And you – you're not overdoing it? Not still trying to bake cakes for the shop as well as look after our shop?'

'No, Peggy won't let me do much. She has employed helpers – and Fay is learning to make cakes too. She is rather good at it. I was dubious when Peggy told me – but I ate a lovely lemon-drizzle cake of hers the other day and thought it was Peggy's own.'

Shirley laughed. 'Are you telling me Fay made it?'

'Yes. I could hardly believe it, but Peggy says that it's only the start for her. Fay is bent on doing stuff we would never have attempted.'

'She doesn't expect to sell them in the shop?'

'I wouldn't think so.' Maureen laughed. 'Peggy says she'll probably end up as the pastry chef for the Savoy Hotel or something...'

'Wonders never cease,' Shirley said. 'When I last spoke to her, she was still mad on her skating and talking of winning the Olympics at figure skating.'

'She had an accident and realised that her ankles aren't strong enough to stand up to all the training she needs to do and then she had to have time resting when she was rushed into hospital with appendicitis.' Maureen frowned. 'I think Fay always needs to be the best and if she can't do it one way, she'll try another.'

Shirley smiled. 'I can't argue with that and I think it's rather nice – though if she'd been content to help Peggy...'

'She may be getting help from another direction,' Maureen replied. 'Maggie is coming down for the summer and it seems she's interested in helping out for a while, at least that is what Janet told Peggy.'

'Now Maggie always sticks to what she wants,' Shirley said, not feeling surprised. 'She told me that though she loves Scotland and will always want to spend holidays there, she likes London best – and I knew she liked cooking, but all kinds of things, not just cakes.'

'She told you then,' Maureen said and looked thoughtful. 'I wasn't sure whether she would stick to it – Janet never seemed to be much interested in the pub or the café when they had it. She has always had her own life...'

'Maggie thinks her mother never got over losing her father. She says it is sad because Ryan thinks the world of Janet and Maggie, and she does him – she can't remember her real father much.' Shirley frowned as she tried to remember. 'I didn't see him a lot, but I think he was good-looking – Janet's first husband?'

'Yes, he was – very,' Maureen agreed. 'She was mad about him when they married.'

'I know he died – what happened? Why doesn't Maggie remember him?'

'Mike was at war when she was born and he hardly saw her. He died terribly and Janet woke to find him with blood on his pillow and face, lying next to her. He had a nasty haemorrhage because of the metal in his head moving, I suppose. It would have been shocking to a young wife to see that and I think that may have left its mark on her – though we all thought she would be happy when she married again. Ryan lost his wife and first family, but he's always been good to Janet and to Maggie – and he adores Jon.'

'Yes, I know. Maggie always says he's wonderful to her. I think she is a bit wary of her mother – as if she doesn't quite trust her not to walk out on them.'

'I don't think Janet would do that,' Maureen said and shook her head. 'It would be stupid and she isn't – restless perhaps, but not cruel or thoughtless.'

'But is she happy, Mum?' Shirley asked. 'I've always known you and dad were happy together, because you loved each other, but Maggie has always been afraid her parents will split up. I suppose because they used to argue a lot.'

'But surely that is over?'

Shirley shrugged. 'We'll know when Maggie comes for the summer. She usually tells me what she is thinking.'

'I think Peggy is a bit worried.' Maureen shook her head. 'I need to start getting our meal ready. Why don't you pop round and see Peggy for a while?'

'Why don't I help you and pop round later?' Shirley smiled at her. 'What are we having this evening?'

11

'Maggie, darling!' Peggy exclaimed as the tall and rather beautiful young woman walked into her kitchen that evening at the beginning of August. 'I wasn't expecting you for another week – is your mother with you?'

'She's coming down in a couple of days,' Maggie said. 'I left school a few days early, Granny. I was supposed to go in for the end-of-term prize-giving, but I haven't won any certificates that matter to me, so I skipped it and came down on the train. I'm more interested in seeing you – you know I've got something to ask you, because Mum told you, didn't she?' There was a tiny note of accusation in Maggie's voice.

'Yes, she did. I suppose she wanted to prepare me, but it doesn't matter either way. I should love having you work with me, Maggie, if you're sure it's what you want to do?'

'Oh, so much!' Maggie said enthusiastically and flung her arms around her. 'I've always loved this place – the smell of it and the laughter and voices. You know what I'd like to do with it in time?' Maggie looked at her anxiously. 'I don't mean right this minute...'

'Why don't we let you settle in for a few months and see how it goes?' Peggy suggested. 'If by next spring you're still of the same opinion, we'll look into doing the work we should need and research it a bit.'

'You don't need to do much research, Granny, I've already done my homework and I believe I know the kind of place that will do well round here.' Maggie beamed at her. 'I know you have your regulars and there is no need to change the bar too much; it is already perfect – but we'll have the restaurant bit separate. However, I'll bet that after a short time, your regulars will be wanting you to serve them our food in the bar as well.'

'You're very sure and full of enthusiasm,' Peggy said, smiling at Maggie's pleasure. 'I have to warn you that it is very hard work, Maggie. I've always kept bar meals simple because I never had time to cook anything too fancy.'

'It doesn't have to be that fancy,' Maggie responded. 'We'll always do your wonderful shepherd's pie and your other favourites, of course we shall – but we could do steak and gammon steaks with pineapple and a lot more variety of sweets. Home-made soups too and nice crusty bread.'

'You'll need an army of helpers,' Peggy said, but Maggie only smiled. Peggy could see she had it all planned in her head and if she had the energy and drive, well, why not?

'We can give it a try, hon,' Able had told her when she'd explained what Maggie wanted to do. 'You've always been happy the way you are, doing most of the cooking yourself and employing part-time people to assist you – but with Maggie's help and energy, you could open the business up and do something different, make it a bit special.'

'Do you think it will catch on round here?' Peggy asked Maggie now. 'I mean we're in the East End not the West...'

Maggie tossed back her long, shining, dark hair, which fell in a straight curtain about her shoulders and over her face. 'We'll be modern, Granny – trendy. We're nearly into the sixties now and you don't have food rationing to bother you any longer. What you did during the war and after was tremendous, but life is different now. We have rock 'n' roll and flying abroad for holidays is going to be all the rage soon. People have more money in their pockets and they want places to spend it.'

'Yes, I know, that's just what Able said.' Peggy smiled at her. 'You're a breath of fresh air, Maggie. I shan't know whether I'm coming or going, but I think it will be fun.' She hesitated, then, 'Fay will be with us some of the time, because she is learning to bake. Some of her cakes are good enough for the shop and we eat all the others – it saves me baking for us.'

'Yes, Mum said Fay had some new idea of being a top pastry chef – I think it is great. She can try making things for the restaurant when she starts her course and see how she gets on...'

'It's all going to be rather exciting,' Peggy murmured, wondering how long the two girls would continue to agree in the same kitchen. Fay did like to spread out when making her cakes and desserts, which was fine with Peggy, but Maggie was different. She would be up early and expect to be busy all morning preparing lunches for the bar.

* * *

However, the next morning when she started work, Peggy found that Maggie had already divided the kitchen into three stations. 'I shall use this one for the lunches; that's yours, Granny, and that is Fay's. If we all stick to our own areas, we can't go wrong.'

'I'm not certain we'll have enough oven space,' Peggy said thoughtfully.

'Maggie and I discussed that last night,' Fay said, entering the kitchen. 'I thought we could put a small kitchen on at the back of the cake shop. I'll move in there then and be out of your way.'

'You're not in my way, darling,' Peggy replied. 'There's plenty of room for us all here.'

'Yes, for the moment, but once I get up and running there won't be.' Fay looked at her. 'I've been thinking about the future – not just yet, but when I'm fully trained.'

'Oh, I expect you'll work for a big hotel then,' Peggy suggested, but Fay shook her head.

'Maggie and I thought of something better,' Fay said and looked at her consideringly. 'I mean, you don't really need the cake shop now, do you?'

'Not really. It was your Auntie Sheila's idea and Maureen and I sort of inherited it – but you wouldn't have the scope for the kind of cakes and stuff you want to make here in Mulberry Lane, Fay.'

'Well, I might sell a few, but I'm not thinking of having it as a shop like you do – it will be my base, my headquarters. I want to do private catering for big parties and weddings, things like that.' Fay looked at Maggie and grinned. 'I told Maggie what I wanted to do and she agreed the money is in private catering rather than slaving away in the kitchens of a big hotel.

They get the credit and the money then – but if I set up my own catering company, I do.'

'But they want more than cakes and fancy sweets.' Peggy was slightly bewildered by the change of tack and the speed in which her family were taking over.

'That is where I come in,' Maggie said. 'The Pig & Whistle is only the first stop on my plan, Granny. Once we get it up and running as I'd like it, I'll have time to help Fay with the mains and starters for her parties and weddings. Besides, Fay can manage canapés and fancy bites – or she will be able to by the time she's finished her course. As she said, this is all for the future. We both have to learn a lot yet.'

'Well, you two must have had a long chat last night in your room,' Peggy replied. 'You will have to give me a little time to catch my breath and I should have to discuss the cake shop with Maureen – it isn't just mine, you know.'

'Auntie Maureen doesn't have time to help now,' Fay said. 'You've had to employ someone to bake with you, but you won't need much help for a while now we're here.'

'Have you spoken to your father about all this, Fay?'

'Not yet – but he will say yes if you do, Mum. He always does.'

'Not always,' Peggy said, but it was likely he would agree. 'And when would you want to take over the cake shop?'

'Oh, not yet. We can run it as it is for the moment – but a new kitchen would be a big help. A professional one with a lot of stainless steel.'

'I think I could do with a cup of tea,' Peggy said, feeling as if she'd stepped onto a merry-go-round. Maggie seemed full of ideas and together with Fay they were a whirlwind. 'I really do need time to think about all this.'

'I'll make it,' Maggie offered. 'Sit down for a few minutes and then we'll start. I've got a new menu for the bar to discuss...'

* * *

'You could have knocked me down with a feather,' Peggy told Maureen when she popped in later that day. Peggy was in the bar, having left the kitchen to her helpers after making the cakes she needed for the shop that day. She'd enjoyed the banter as they worked and felt happy to leave the preparation of the bar menu to her granddaughter. 'They've got together and worked out this grand scheme – mostly Maggie, I believe. I'm not sure what to think.'

'To be honest, I'd be glad if Fay and Maggie took over the cake shop,' Maureen admitted. 'I have more than enough to keep me busy with the grocery shop and Gordon to look after. It won't stop me popping in and we can chat over a cup of tea as easily as over the mixer.'

'Of course, we can.' Peggy laughed. 'I feel a bit like the songbird that has been tipped out of its nest by the cuckoo, except that it is wonderful to have them around and see them so happy together.'

'Don't think of retiring too soon,' Maureen said. 'You know it didn't work before. Just take it a little easier and there's always the bar and the regulars.'

'Yes, I think that's what the girls have in mind for me,' Peggy replied. 'I'm going to be pushed out front to sell the project while they do the hard graft in the kitchens. Maggie said they still need my experience – and neither of them have much knowledge of how to balance the books.'

Maureen chuckled. 'Does it make you feel old? I know when I remember Shirley as a little girl and then see her as the confident doctor she now is, I feel ancient.'

'You're younger than me,' Peggy reminded her.

'Yes, but we've never noticed the age gap, have we?'

Peggy shook her head. 'We've been friends for so long, Maureen. I never think of age, just that you've always been there for me.'

'And you for me.' They smiled at each other. 'You let them take the shop over, Peggy. Keep a guiding hand on the reins for a while, but let them get on with it. We never made much out of the cakes, did we? It was just for fun and companionship. Now we have the new generation to take over – let them.'

'You really don't mind?'

'Not one bit. Gordon said I should let it go a couple of years back, but I wouldn't. Now I'm glad we kept it for Fay and Maggie.'

'I've had a word with Carla. Maggie wants her to stay for a bit longer –

they're planning to have a desk in there to take orders and someone to answer the phone in time, but that is for the future, when Fay has finished her training and Maggie is ready. For now, it stays as it is – but with them doing most of the work.'

Maureen nodded. 'Sounds exciting to me, Peggy. Are you thrilled – or nervous?'

'A bit of both,' Peggy admitted. 'I can see the possibility and Able is all for them having a go. He has said for a long time that I was doing too much. We can take more holidays. Julie is capable in the bar and her mother is an excellent cleaner. We're well set up for extra staff now.'

'You're going down to stay with Pip in a couple of weeks, aren't you?'

'Janet arrives soon and then we'll all go down together and stay for two weeks – but not Maggie. She's just coming for a few days because she wants to get on with things. Fay isn't sure; she says she may come for a while and go back with Maggie.' Peggy shook her head in wonderment. 'Suddenly, they aren't children any more, Maureen. They are young women and they have minds of their own.'

'Yes, I know,' Maureen smiled. 'Gordy is still young enough to be more interested in playing football with Freddie than what he'll do when he leaves school, but then, girls usually grow up fastest, don't they?'

'It's in our nature, I suppose.' Peggy sighed. 'How is Shirley's new job going, I wonder.'

'It's her first day.' Maureen pulled a face. 'I'm not sure it will be much fun for her. They've thrown her in at the deep end – she's at the clinic today.'

'Oh, well, it will show her what to expect,' Peggy said and frowned. 'It's fine for Maggie to talk about the new trends and everything being modern – but there is still too much poverty and suffering in our city, Maureen. I was in the market the other day and I saw this poor old woman pushing a pram with a rickety wheel. It looked as if she had all her worldly goods in it and I felt so sorry for her. I would have liked to give her a good hot meal, but a man tried to help her up the pavement and she turned on him, swearing and hitting at him.'

'I suppose it is pride – and fear,' Maureen said, looking sad. 'She is most likely homeless and used to fending for herself. Perhaps she thought he wanted to steal her pram – or put her in a home for the elderly...'

'I think that is what some of them fear,' Peggy said. 'You see them wandering the streets in dirty clothes and you want to help, but they only accept a cup of tea or a few coins if they trust you.'

'The Sally Army tries to help, but they don't like charity and they hate being told they should seek a job or a shelter – unless it is freezing cold and then some of them go to one of the missions for a bed for the night.'

'I suppose they trust those they know.' Maureen looked thoughtful. 'I saw one of the churches distributing hot soup the other night as I walked home from shopping down the market.'

The two friends looked at each other sadly. London's East End had changed a great deal since the war, which had destroyed some of the worst slums during the Blitz, but some problems remained the same and there wasn't much anyone could do about it, except help those they could when they could.

'Ah, well,' Peggy sighed. 'We shan't change things sitting here, Maureen. So we're agreed then – the youngsters can take over the cake shop?'

'Yes, of course.' Maureen laughed. 'It's a relief really, though I'd never have suggested it.' She got up to leave. 'Oh, I went to see my artist the other day and he has manged to get a show. He was thrilled and it could make all the difference to his career if he sells a few of his pictures. It takes such a long time to build a reputation as an artist.'

'Who is an artist?' Maggie asked, entering the pub with a dish of warm sausage rolls, which she placed in the cabinet.

Maureen told her about James Morgan and Maggie looked interested.

'So he just works for you part-time to help pay the rent on his studio then?'

'Yes. He didn't have much money or a place to stay when he first came to London. We told him about the top floor of a house that was being rented out cheaply. It had big skylights and was ideal for his painting – and he asked if he could deliver our groceries. We took him on straight away.' Maureen smiled. 'He's a nice lad, dreamy and forgetful, but he does our job and helps out whenever we need him. I think he paints a lot early mornings – and sometimes down by the Docks. He likes the light early in the day and he is fascinated by London – especially what is left of the old city. Some of his pictures are very stark and I'm not sure saleable, but he paints portraits and landscapes, too, and they're lovely.'

'He sounds interesting,' Maggie said. 'And you take him food you've cooked sometimes?'

'Yes – when I have time,' Maureen answered and smiled. 'I'm not sure he eats in-between – perhaps a roll if he thinks to buy one when he is out.'

'I'll take him something for you sometimes,' Maggie offered, surprising her. 'I want to try lots of different things and there's usually plenty of food left over. What does he like?'

'I think he eats whatever he gets,' Maureen said and laughed. 'He always seems grateful whatever I take – though he does like a spicy stew I used to make. I don't make them now because they seemed to upset Gordon.'

'I'll make him a curry then,' Maggie said. 'Granny often uses different spices in her cooking and that made me think about spicy food. I found a book on Indian cooking in the library last time we were in London and I asked Dad to buy me a copy. It had some wonderful recipes and I'm experimenting with them. Would it be all right if I took one round tomorrow?'

'I'm sure he'd be delighted.' Maureen took a receipt book from the bar and tore off a page, turning it over to write the address. 'I was going to visit him tomorrow if I had time so that is just right.'

'I'll go then.' Maggie laughed. 'I love looking at art – it's one of the reasons I want to be in London. There are so many galleries here.' She looked pleased with herself. 'I might ask if he'd like to display some of his pictures here – if I think they are good enough.'

Maureen looked at Peggy and raised her brows. There were certainly changes ahead for the folk of Mulberry Lane, just let Maggie get going and she would turn them all upside down.

12

'Well, I hope you enjoyed your first day in your new job?' Maureen said when Shirley came in that evening for her supper. 'You've had a long day, love?'

Shirley glanced at the clock. It was a quarter to seven. 'I worked longer hours than this at the hospital, Mum, but it was tiring. We had a huge queue at the clinic and some of the cases really needed hospital treatment, but if I'd suggested it, they would have disappeared faster than they came in. We had ulcers and suppurating wounds to treat, as well as coughs and skin problems and a broken ankle.'

'But worthwhile? No regrets?'

'None at all,' Shirley said and sat down to drink the cup of tea Maureen had poured for her. 'This is really good – hospital tea was often stewed, unless we made it ourselves in the rest room. They have so many patients to get round that you're lucky if you get a decent one.'

'We've got a pork chop with jacket potato and vegetables this evening,' Maureen said. 'Is that all right for you?'

'Fine – but don't give Dad too much fat on his – cut it off if it is fatty.'

'That's the best bit, though,' Maureen said, 'but I asked for nice lean ones, so hopefully they are.' Shirley nodded as she looked at them on the plate ready for cooking. The jacket potatoes were in the oven and smelled good, but of course, they needed butter to make them taste really nice with salt and pepper. 'I'm going to put just a small knob of butter on all our potatoes so we all have the same.'

'It will keep us all healthy,' Shirley agreed, 'but you don't have to suffer, Mum. You don't have any health problems and you're not overweight.'

'I've actually lost a few pounds since Gordon was ill,' Maureen agreed. 'But I'll eat the same as your dad, Shirley. It isn't fair to expect him to give up the things he enjoys if I sit and eat them in front of him.'

'You love him very much, don't you?'

'Yes, I do,' Maureen agreed.

'Good. I'm glad you're both happy.'

'You don't still hanker after Richard?' Maureen asked, because she knew Shirley had felt very let down by the young man she'd been in love with in her early teens, right through to just before university.

'Richard? No, not at all. I saw him now and then at the university and in the hospital. He still works there and I dare say he will be a registrar before long and then a consultant. It's what he wants above all else.'

'And you don't? It's still GP work for you?'

'Well, I'll know when I've been working here for a while. The clinic was a bit like the Accident and Emergency at the hospital. They sent us there sometimes to let us see what it is like to deal with the rough end of the stick – it's the worst duty of the lot for a young doctor. You get drunks and people being sick, who don't need us at all – they need to go home and sober up, but they clog up the beds and make it hard to find space for the real emergencies, and that can be hectic, especially when there's no consultant around, and you have to make quick decisions you're unsure of.'

'That must have been frightening at times?' Maureen suggested.

'It can be a bit nerve-wracking in your first year as a junior doctor, but you just have to take it step by step and deal with whatever presents itself.' Shirley laughed. 'Let's stop talking about me and my work, Mum. What have you and Gordy been doing today?'

'He took part in his sports day cricket match. As you know, he prefers football, but it's the wrong time of year – and he'll be in his school's football team this winter, so he is pleased about that.'

Shirley nodded, prodding her. 'What about you then? What do you do for fun?'

'For fun?' Maureen stared at her a moment and then laughed. 'It's a long time since I've thought about having fun, love. I've always enjoyed my mornings working with Peggy and your dad and I go out now and then – to the cinema or occasionally for a nice meal.'

Shirley nodded. 'Now that I'm here you could have more evenings out if you want, Mum. Go somewhere with Peggy or Rose Barton – or anyone else you like. I'll be here for Gordy and Dad, and he might like to go to the cinema sometimes.'

'I might now and then,' Maureen conceded. 'But you're young – you should be out to dances and the theatre, wherever you fancy. I'm content here listening to the wireless and knitting.'

'You're not old, Mum, but that makes you sound old – why not join a keep-fit club or do an evening class? Isn't there something you'd like to learn just for you?'

Maureen thought about it. 'I'm not sure. I like all handicrafts, so there might be something I could learn at night school. I could look into it – but if I do, then you must too. I don't want you slaving away all day and sitting at home all night.'

'Oh, I shan't do that,' Shirley said. 'Keith will be home soon and we shall go out sometimes – it's nice to walk in the park on a Sunday and have tea. That would do you and Dad good too.'

'Yes, it would. We used to do it when Gordy was younger, but we haven't for a while now. I'll suggest it to him when we get a nice afternoon on a Sunday.'

Shirley nodded. She sat watching as Maureen grilled the chops and then dished up their meal. Her father came in from the garden at the back where he'd been kicking a ball about with Gordy.

He smiled and nodded to her. 'Had a good day, love?"

'Yes,' she replied. 'It was interesting and rewarding.'

'You can't ask for more than that,' he said and drew his chair to the table. 'That smells good, Maureen. I like a nice pork chop now and then.' He glanced at his plate and frowned. 'No fat on these chops? The rind with a bit of crisp fat is the best bit.'

'I know. I'm sorry.' Maureen gave him a look of apology. 'The fat is bad for you, love – for all of us.'

Gordon nodded, but although he ate the tender greens and the jacket potato, he left most of the pork, pushing his plate away with a sigh. 'Sorry, I don't fancy it that way, love. Grilling a pork chop with no fat makes it a bit tough.'

'I'll get fish for tea tomorrow,' Maureen said. 'A nice piece of yellow cod or salmon is tasty without a lot of fat – and much better for us.'

He nodded but didn't answer. 'I could do with a cup of tea – and I want proper milk and sugar in it. I refuse to cut them out.'

'I know.' Maureen kept her thoughts to herself. She'd known it would be hard for him to stick to this regime, because he liked the fat on chops and the skin on the chicken and a good meat pie with thick pastry soaked in delicious gravy. It was going to take all his willpower and hers to keep him happy with a diet like this.

* * *

'He has to stick to it, Mum,' Shirley told her later as they were washing up together in the scullery. 'If he continues to eat the things he always liked, his condition will just get worse and there's nothing else we can do – one day soon perhaps, but not yet.'

'I know – they told us,' Maureen said. 'I don't like to see him leave his food like that, though. He always ate well.'

'And look where it has got him,' Shirley frowned. 'It's hard, Mum. Sticking to a diet with very little fat is difficult and it's boring – you have to be careful what you buy. Fish is good because it is so low in fat, but you can't eat it all the time. Just look for the kind of things he liked – but lower in fat, if you can.'

'I know, but I gave him salad three nights last week and he refused to eat the last lot – said he wasn't a rabbit and he wanted roast beef and Yorkshire pudding with roast potatoes and gravy.'

'Poor Dad,' Shirley said and looked sad. 'Poor you, too, Mum. You like cooking and it must be hard for you trying to find something tasty that will suit him.'

'Chicken and new potatoes and broccoli for Sunday,' Maureen replied, 'but if I don't give him any of the crispy skin, he'll pinch a bit from somewhere.'

'Can you get a tin that roasts it without the addition of fat?' Shirley asked. 'I'm sure I saw something like that advertised. You just let it cook in its own juices – they're bringing out all sorts of new things these days. I'll have a look in my lunch break tomorrow. I'm at the surgery and I get an hour to myself. There's a big hardware store just round the corner. I'll pop in there and see if I can find something.'

'Yes, we can try,' Maureen agreed, but in her heart, she knew it was only a matter of time before Gordon refused to stick to the strict diet. Could she force him to if he didn't wish it? In life there were always choices and you had to make them yourself. Gordon wanted to prolong his life and he was trying, but there came a point when perhaps life might seem dull and pointless if forced to go without everything you enjoyed.

* * *

Shirley was thoughtful as she walked to work the next morning. She'd had high hopes that a diet and exercise regime might give her father some respite – a few years longer with his family. He'd been keen at the start, but his enthusiasm had waned as everything he'd loved to eat was denied him. Maureen was trying hard to please him, walking a middle way, but they needed to make a complete break from the kind of meals they'd had before. Perhaps she could find a recipe book as well as the roasting tin that claimed it would cook meat without most of the fat normally added.

'You look pensive...' the voice that hailed her made Shirley whirl around and she broke into a little run to meet the young woman coming up behind her.

'Maggie! Lovely to see you. I was going to pop round last night, but Mum said you and Fay had gone to some conference somewhere.'

'Yes, it was a confectionary conference.' Maggie gave a delightful giggle. 'A grand name for a taste-and-buy really. They had some wonderful treats on offer and we stuffed ourselves silly – and bought far too much. I'll bring some round for you.'

'Please don't,' Shirley said quickly. 'Poor Dad is suffering enough as it is – he couldn't resist chocolates and sweet cakes.'

Maggie clapped a hand to her mouth. 'So sorry, Shirley. I forgot for a moment – how is he?'

'He seems a bit better in himself, but he is hating his diet. Mum cut off all the fat from his pork chop last night and he pushed it away.'

Maggie nodded. 'A chop is no good without crisped rind and fat – but she could cut it into thin strips and do a low-fat sweet and sour sauce to make it tasty. Put pineapple and onions and peppers in with a little honey and various other ingredients.'

'That sounds tasty,' Shirley said. 'And it is definitely low in fat?'

'It is the way I do it – and you have rice with it, which is good for the kind of diet you're talking about. I've got a few recipes that might help – light sauces that make all kinds of things taste good... I'll write some down for you and bring them round.'

'Thank you. I was thinking of looking for a book with those kinds of recipes.'

'You won't find many,' Maggie said. 'Most people aren't willing to try something different. It's one of the reasons I want to cook. I know we can make food healthier as well as tasty.'

'I go in here,' Shirley said as she came to her GP practice.

'I'll pop round to you,' Maggie said and reached out to hug her. 'Don't worry, Shirley. We'll sort him out between us.' She giggled and showed Shirley the basket she was carrying. 'I'm taking a curry to a starving artist – at least your mum says he's starving. I wonder if he'll like my latest creation.'

'If he's starving, he'll eat it so fast he won't taste it,' Shirley said and left her friend as she entered her new place of work. Maggie was filled with enthusiasm for her chosen career, but whether she could find things that would make Shirley's father eat sensibly and also enjoy was another matter.

'Ah, Doctor Shirley,' the receptionist boomed at her across the crowded waiting room, bringing her thoughts to the present. 'We have a long list of patients for you to get through this morning. The news that we have a lady doctor has brought our female patients flocking in.'

* * *

Shirley hardly stopped all day. She grabbed a salad sandwich and a glass of orange juice at a small café across the road, feeling pleased that somewhere so nice had set up in the area and could offer the kind of food she wanted. Maureen had offered to pack a lunch for her, but she'd said she wanted to see what was available and she was pleased she had, because the food was fresh and tasty. Maureen's lunch would have been nice, too, but sandwiches always went soggy if left in their greaseproof paper too long.

At the end of the day, just as she was writing up her last records, her boss, Doctor Mike Reynolds, tapped at her door and then entered. He smiled as she stood up.

'No need for that, Doctor Shirley. I just wanted to ask how you got on – did you have any bother or was everyone welcoming?'

'They all seemed pleased to see me – and all my patients were women,' Shirley said. 'Oh, and one little boy who had cut his knees quite badly in a fall from his bike.'

'Good. Most of the women asked for you. I'm not sure how we'll get on when we need to pass some of the men over – we've always been a male-dominated practice. Female nurses, but you're our first female doctor – but then, there aren't that many of you about yet.' He smiled at her in a friendly way. 'We're glad to have you on board – you had some glowing references from your tutors. Apparently, we're lucky to get you, because they wanted to keep you on at the hospital?'

'I was offered a job there,' Shirley agreed. 'I went into medicine because I hoped to practice here in my home area – and I'm very grateful for the chance.'

'Well, keep up the good work. I'd ask you for a drink and a chat, but my wife has guests this evening. You must come to dinner – I'll ask my wife to invite all the staff so we can have a social get-together.' He beamed at her and went out, leaving Shirley to finish up and put on her jacket.

* * *

Shirley left the surgery and began to walk to the bus stop, but as she did so, a small car pulled up beside her and she heard someone call her name.

'I was told you might be leaving about now...'

Shirley looked round and gave a little gasp of surprise and pleasure as she saw Keith in the driving seat. She walked towards him with a smile on her face.

'You're home then – why didn't you let me know you were coming? I didn't expect you just yet.'

'I was offered a seat to Johannesburg on a private plane, where I got the commercial flight home,' Keith replied with a grin. 'That sort of thing doesn't happen every day, Shirley. I grabbed the chance and saved myself the price of a long journey home by train.'

'Golly! That sounds very posh. I didn't even know you knew anyone with a private plane?'

'Oh, he's a very rich man and it was just a small plane that he flies himself – he was in the Air Force during the war. He came out to look at our project because he has something similar that he wants to set up, and I told him I was travelling home as soon as I could get a train. He insisted that he take me to Johannesburg.'

Shirley looked at him curiously. 'What was it like to fly?'

'A bit hair-raising at times.' He opened the passenger seat for her. 'Get in and I'll tell you on the way.'

Shirley slid into the seat beside him. 'How did you manage to get a car?'

'I hired it from Mr Shelby's company. He is the man who flew us to Johannesburg – and that's one of the things he does. I got special rates.'

'How long have you been driving?' Shirley asked.

'Since the Army, but I didn't have a vehicle myself – and I couldn't afford one now, to be honest. I've only got this because I was given such a special price.'

'That was very kind of... Mr Shelby, did you say?'

'Yes, it was kind – but he does have his reasons.' Keith signalled as he moved off. 'He wants me to help set up his new project in Africa. I haven't given him an answer yet...'

'Are you thinking about it?' Shirley frowned. 'I thought you'd decided to come back to England and look for a job here?'

'I had... I have,' Keith told her and shot a quick glance at her face. 'I suppose it all depends on you, Shirley – whether you want me to stay?'

'I think that is something you need to make up your own mind about,' Shirley told him. 'I know that I've looked forward to seeing you, but if you've had a good job offered...' She left it open, feeling a bit unsure of how to take this sudden reversal of intentions.

'I want to be with you,' he said simply and his smile made her feel better. 'You know I care about you, Shirley. We've had an odd sort of relationship so far – me committed to helping my brother get his project up and running and he and I have had our troubles these past years.' For a moment Keith looked serious, but then he shook his head. 'Things are better there now and I felt able to leave him. I'm hoping to find a decent job here and to spend as much time as possible with you. I thought we might go out for dinner this evening?'

'That would be lovely,' Shirley agreed. 'What kind of a job are you looking for?'

'Well, I have a lot of experience with charity projects, so perhaps I could find a job with one here – there must be jobs for people like me with registered charities in this country.'

'Yes, I suppose so—' Shirley hesitated. 'Is there anything else you would consider?'

'Well, I'm a good bricklayer and I can do most things in the building trade.'

'I know of someone who is hiring bricklayers,' she said thoughtfully. 'You would like Tom Barton, I'm sure.'

Keith nodded. 'I think I met him once. It would do until I found something else anyway.'

Shirley looked at him doubtfully. Keith didn't sound as if he had settled to staying around in London permanently.

13

Maggie put her starched white apron on the next morning and prepared to start work in the pub kitchen. She wanted to try something different that morning but wasn't quite sure what to cook – 'not another curry' was what Fay had said when Maggie mentioned to her that Maureen's starving artist had eaten the whole dishful whilst talking to her the previous day. So she'd thought about making another for him.

'Make him something different – it makes the kitchen smell and affects the taste of my cakes,' Fay said, pulling a face.

Maggie continued as if Fay hadn't spoken. 'He just ate and ate and said it was the best food he'd had in ages,' she told Fay. 'I hope it doesn't give him tummy trouble – I thought it would last him a couple of days.'

'He was probably so hungry he didn't notice what he was eating.' Fay wrinkled her nose. 'I don't much like the smell of curry. I prefer a nice beef pie with kidney and beer, the way Mum makes it.'

'Maybe I'll try that,' Maggie said with a nod. 'I'll make one for the pub the way Granny does – and another slightly different for us. I can take whatever is left over round to James.'

'I thought you weren't interested in men?' Fay accused. 'You've got too much to do before you settle down.'

'I have and I'm not,' Maggie said, but she smiled, because she'd liked the forgetful young man who had eaten her curry and told her he desperately wanted to paint her – but not yet, because he was up to his eyes in work for his exhibition.

'You have a wonderful bone structure,' he'd said, turning her face one way and the other. 'Arresting, that's the word. As soon as you enter a room, you are noticed.' He'd gone into a dream then, eating his curry as fast as he could get it down and looking at her so oddly that she wanted to laugh. 'Yes, I'll paint you when I get this other stuff done.' He'd waved his hand airily and Maggie had seen that he had five easels set up and seemed to have an unfinished picture on each one. 'It depends what mood I'm in,' he'd said, seeing the question in her eyes.

'Do you ever finish anything?' Maggie had asked, amused.

James had waved a hand at a pile of canvases with their backs turned to the room. 'There are some there – I don't like many of them.'

Investigating, Maggie had found some landscapes of the sea and others of open countryside that she liked, but there were many more of London's dockyards and of cranes, stark against the sky. Some she didn't like at all, because they were too dark.

'I like the seascapes and some of the London ones,' she'd said. 'When you've finished your exhibition work, would you paint something for the pub?'

'If you feed me,' he'd grinned at her. 'Please will you take your dish and go now? I can't work with you around – but you can bring me some food another day if you want.'

'I might,' she'd said and picked up the empty dish. 'You're not very polite, are you?'

'No – but I'm busy...'

Maggie had laughed and departed. He was certainly different from the other young men she'd met and, because of it, had made an impression on her.

She brought her mind back to her work as Peggy walked in.

'What are you making for the pub lunches today, Maggie?'

'I thought your beef and ale pie, Granny – and a cheese flan, also another vegetarian dish.' She focused on her grandmother. 'Will you tell me how you make your pie the way Fay likes?

'You can have my recipe books, Maggie,' Peggy said taking them from a shelf. 'I don't know what is of use to you, but they are all my own and could come in useful.'

'Oh, thank you,' Maggie cried and seized on them with alacrity. 'I collect people's recipes and try them out and sometimes change them a little. I've got quite a few from Scotland. When people know you're interested in cooking they give them to you.'

'I don't have any proper cookbooks, only my own,' Peggy said doubtfully. 'I'm not sure they will be any use to you as I imagine you'll need some special ones for what you're setting up – you and Fay...'

'Oh, I think they will be very handy,' Maggie replied with a smile. 'You need to be able to cater for all tastes, Granny – besides, Fay wants to bake and she doesn't like the smell of my curries.'

'I do,' Peggy said and smiled. 'Look, this is the beef and ale pie – you'll need to visit the butcher, Maggie. We don't have what we need. If I were you, I'd get off and do it now. I'll make a start on the pastry for the sausage rolls. We can't forget them. Some of my regulars come in every day just for their sausage roll.'

* * *

Maggie met Rose on the way back from the butcher. She liked Rose Barton and they stopped and talked for some minutes, making Maggie hurry on the way back to the Pig & Whistle because she didn't want to be late. Rose hadn't been into the pub for a week or two, because she'd been busy.

'I used to come most days,' she'd said wistfully. 'But I am always so busy these days. Tom likes me to look after the phone calls for him – he says the customers like talking to me rather than him or any of the lads.'

'Yes, I'm sure they do,' Maggie had agreed. 'But you must come and have lunch with us one day. Let me experiment on you and see what you think of my cooking. I can't always do the things I want to for the pub – not yet. Not until I get it going as a trendy restaurant.'

'That will be nice, Maggie. Brighten the place up a bit.'

'Yes.' Maggie had smiled and they'd parted. She'd hurried on, because the pie was going to take a while to make and the customers wouldn't wait for their lunch. It had to be ready and waiting when they arrived.

As she reached the pub, she saw someone walk under the arch and frowned. It looked like her mother was here. She hadn't expected her to come for another day or so yet – was something wrong? Had she and Ryan had another argument? Maggie hesitated, deliberately letting her mother get in and greet the others before she joined them.

* * *

'Mum, it's lovely to see you,' Janet said and hugged Peggy. 'I'm sorry I couldn't get down when Maggie did, but she was impatient to come and I had something arranged for a couple of days – I didn't want to let my friend down, because she had guests staying and I'd promised I'd help out with the cooking.'

'Of course, it didn't matter,' Peggy replied and smiled. 'Maggie is welcome to come and go as she pleases – she is a young woman now not a child.' Although, the law said that a young adult under the age of twenty-one still had to obey their parents' wishes, Maggie had a mind of her own and to keep her on a tight leash would only cause problems.

'Ryan says she is sensible enough now to trust her to do what she thinks right,' Janet said and sighed. 'It only seems a few minutes ago that she was playing with dolls and running in and out of the house, asking for biscuits and drinks – now she makes her own cakes and a coffee whenever she feels like it.'

'She has grown up,' Peggy said and laughed. 'It happens to us all – I've had it twice; with you and Pip and now the twins. They're talking about leaving school and what they'll do with their lives.'

'But they're only just sixteen, Mum. I thought Able wanted them to stay at school until they're eighteen?'

'Well, I think Freddie will – unless he gets a trial for this big team he's written to.' Peggy looked round. 'But where is Jon? I thought you might bring him down?'

'He is staying with his father for the time being. He had some sports events on at school.' Janet frowned. 'He's a funny kid, Mum. I'm never quite sure what he really wants.'

'I expected he would come down to Pip's with us...'

'His father will bring him – he said this cricket match was important, so I didn't make a fuss. He's a bit like Freddie in that respect – he likes his sport.' She was fonder of Freddie than of Fay, though she wouldn't dream of saying as much to her mother, who would have told her that she should love them equally. Janet wasn't sure why she didn't get on so well with Fay as she did with Fay's twin brother. She had withdrawn a little from her half-sister. Perhaps it was a jealousy thing – her mother was prepared to do so much for her youngest daughter – and yet she knew that was stupid really. Peggy never did anything for Fay that she wouldn't have done for any of her children. 'And what about madam?' Janet asked now. 'Is she still insisting she wants to bake fancy cakes?'

'Oh, I think so, but they've expanded their ideas now and are talking of going into business together,' Peggy said, laughing. 'I shall be redundant in a couple of years and those two will take over.'

'Maggie and Fay?' Janet asked and Peggy nodded. 'Really? Only a few years ago they were jealous of each other.'

'Not any more,' Peggy replied. 'It's a pleasure to watch them together, discussing the merits of this and that – and Maggie is helping me teach Fay the basics. Your daughter is a decent little cook, Janet.'

'Yes, she is,' Janet agreed and smiled. 'I expect she takes after you – we all do.'

'I never expected it,' Peggy told her. 'I saw them both as doing something more glamorous. It was a big surprise that Fay wanted to bake and even more so when Maggie told me her ideas.'

'Yes, it surprised us, too,' Janet said, 'But Ryan thinks she should be given her chance to do something she likes – and who am I to disagree?'

'You are her mother, your opinion matters, you know it does,' Peggy said sharply. 'But why should you disagree?'

'No reason – I don't,' Janet spoke thoughtfully. 'I suppose it was just a surprise.'

'It may pass for both of them, but I don't think so,' Peggy went on, smiling. 'I'm inclined to think our daughters will make a success of things.'

'Ryan told me that if you agree to altering things here, he is happy to invest money in the business for her.'

'Yes, well, we'll see – it may be needed sooner than he thinks, because they have all sorts of expensive ideas, but Fay still has a long way to go. Maggie will work with me and learn as she goes – though she may do some night-school classes.' Peggy looked thoughtful. 'This course they've talked about – well, I suppose I'd feel more comfortable about letting Fay go if Maggie was with her.'

'Yes, Maggie is sensible despite her grand ideas,' Janet agreed. 'She would keep Fay from doing something daft – if she could—'

'Fay isn't that bad,' Peggy defended her youngest. 'I know you always disagreed with her skating, but it made her happy and did her no harm. I was sorry she gave it up in a way, but she decided that she could never achieve the heights she wanted and that was it.'

Janet nodded. 'Maybe I'm a little jealous, Mum. They're so young and yet they know what they want.'

Peggy frowned. 'What is wrong, Janet? I'm always ready to listen, you know that – don't you?'

'Yes, I do, Mum,' Janet laughed. 'I'm just being stupid. Is it the mid-life crisis, do you think?'

'You're not old enough,' Peggy said. 'Janet, look at yourself in the mirror. You are a beautiful woman and young enough to do exactly what you want in life. You could do anything – learn to do whatever you wanted – don't feel sorry for yourself. If you're bored, then find something exciting you want to do and do it, love.'

'Supposing I wanted to travel, see something of the world?'

'I'm not the one to ask,' Peggy said. 'You should talk to Ryan – maybe he'd like to do something different too.'

'He's so wrapped up in his work.'

'Men get like that at times, but if you told him you feel restless, he might change his ways.'

'And if he didn't?'

'That's something you have to sort out between you – but if you're truly unhappy, you always have a home here with us.'

Janet nodded and sighed. 'I know. I'm not unhappy. I think I'm just bored. I don't know what I want to do. I wish I did...' She broke off as Maggie and Fay entered the kitchen together.

'Hi, Mum,' Maggie said and went to kiss her cheek. 'Is Dad all right?'

'He is at a conference today and tomorrow,' Janet explained. 'He says he'll try to get a few days off when we're at Uncle Pip's and come down. He'll bring Jon then, too.'

'He promised me he would, so he will,' Maggie said confidently and smiled at Fay. 'Fay found some wonderful second-hand cookery books on the market, Granny. Can we use the kitchen to make some of the recipes this afternoon?'

'Yes, of course you can,' Peggy agreed. 'Have you got all the ingredients you need?'

'Yes, thanks,' Fay replied. 'I bought everything on the market. Most of it was cheaper and, as long as you insist on the fruit and veg you want and don't accept anything from the back, it is fresher.'

'Yes.' Peggy laughed. 'They all know better than to try that one on me. One young man tried to give me peaches from the back of his stall once. I opened the bag and handed them right back and told him I wanted the fresh ones or I'd buy elsewhere. He called me a rude name and I walked away. One of the other stallholders went over and told him to mind his manners and threatened to clip his ear. The next time I paused to look at his fruit, he handed me a paper bag and invited me to pick my own.'

'No one was rude to me – they all seemed eager to serve me.'

'I'm not surprised,' Peggy said. 'I imagine they fell over themselves to serve you.'

'Well, one or two of them were a bit soppy.' Fay shook her head, dismissive of the market lads. 'Mum, we've found out about a cookery course we'd both like to take,' she said. 'Not the one in France – I'd like to do that next year, but it's a high-class hotel down in Devon. We could go there from Pip's house and take it together – but it costs money...'

'It would be good experience, because they teach us in the kitchens and we help to prepare the meals for the clients,' Maggie said. 'Mornings, we help with lunches and in the afternoons, they give us lessons – in the evenings, we can help out with dinner if we want, but that is optional.' She was looking at her mother. 'Dad told me he would pay if I wanted to take a course this summer. I'd like Fay to come with me.'

'What does it cost?' Peggy asked.

'Fifty pounds – but we get our rooms and board as well.'

'Fifty pounds each?' Peggy was shocked. 'How long is this course then?'

'Three weeks.' Maggie looked hesitant. 'I know it sounds an awful lot of money, but it's the kind of thing we need to see first-hand...'

'I suppose it is,' Peggy agreed, 'but with all the other things you need, Maggie, it is rather a lot. Isn't there a cheaper one?'

'I don't know. We saw that and thought it looked just right.' Maggie looked disappointed. 'Will Dad think it is too much?' she asked her mother.

'I don't know,' Janet said. 'I could telephone him this evening and ask if you like?'

'Yes, please. We have to book it by Saturday or it will be too late, so the girl in the office says. She says it always sells out every year and we're lucky to get the chance because it has normally all gone by now. Someone cancelled recently and it's the only reason they have spaces.'

'I'll ring Ryan this evening,' Janet promised and looked at Peggy.

'I'll speak to your father,' Peggy promised Fay. 'You'll both have to be patient.'

* * *

'Of course, she can have the money if it's what she needs,' Ryan said when Janet spoke to him later. 'If Peggy doesn't want to fork out for Fay's course, I'll pay, call it an early birthday present. It would be better for them to be together – keep them out of mischief.'

'Are you sure?'

'Of course. When have I ever said no to anything either of you wanted?' Janet thought she heard a note of reproach.

'You haven't. It just seems a lot of money to pay out for something like that.'

'I can manage,' Ryan said. 'I may be coming down sooner than I thought, Janet. I have something I want to talk to you about.'

'Anything serious? It's not Jon, is it? He isn't ill?' She felt a moment of panic. Jon was spending his days alone, in the company of friends, but his father didn't get home until seven some nights. He was still a child. She should never have left him!

'It isn't Jon. He's fine, Janet. I think he's enjoying this cricket tournament – his team are winning apparently.'

'Then tell me,' she sounded impatient and knew it.

'I'd rather talk face to face,' he said. 'Don't worry, love. It isn't anything terrible, at least I don't think you will mind too much – so, tell the girls I'll pay.'

Janet stared at the phone as it went down at the other end. He'd finished the call abruptly, as if he didn't want to say more now. What was Ryan not telling her?

Once before he'd acted a bit oddly with her and she'd believed he was having an affair, but she'd worried for nothing.

Janet shook her head. Whatever it was, Ryan would let her in, in his own time...

* * *

Janet looked at herself in the full-length mirror in her bedroom as she was undressing that evening. Peggy's mirror was a lovely antique that Janet envied her, bought during the war when it had been impossible to buy anything new, and it always flattered a little.

Her mother had told her that she was a beautiful woman and could do anything she wanted with her life. Was that true? Her hair fell to her shoulders and was expertly cut so that it brushed over her brow. She'd had a permanent wave months ago and let it grow out, preferring it straighter these days. It did suit her and she'd kept her figure. Was that why Jason had looked at her as if he wanted to devour her the day before she left Scotland? He'd hinted that he didn't want her to go, stroking the back of her hand with one finger as he took the reins from her after their ride.

She closed her eyes, recalling the way his hands lingered about her waist as he'd helped her dismount and the smouldering looks he'd given her as he'd said he'd hoped they would ride together more often now that Maggie had gone to London.

Had she delayed coming down for that last ride out alone with him? Would she have given in if he'd actually asked her to have an affair with him? So far it had only been a touch of the hand, warm breath on the back of her neck as he prepared to help her mount up and those eyes... the way he'd told her she was beautiful... or was she just imagining it, because she needed some romance?

Janet remembered how her heart had raced when she went out to meet him and how his smile had lit up his handsome face. He'd helped her to mount her horse, exactly as he'd helped both her and Maggie each time they rode with him, but there had been something different – as though they'd both relaxed their guard and she'd had to fight against leaning in to kiss him as he took the leading reins back at the end of their ride, and told her he would be thinking of her while she was away.

No, it was all wrong! She wouldn't give into these thoughts! Janet was angry with herself for being tempted by the young Adonis. He was too young and she was married with children. She would be mad to throw all that away just for a quick fling, because that was all it could ever be.

Why was she such a mess? Why couldn't she be enthusiastic about something like both Fay and Maggie? Why wasn't she happier? What did she want out of life?

Janet let her thoughts drift back over her life, but they came to an abrupt halt when a memory flashed into her mind – Mike lying in bed beside her, blood soaking the pillow and smeared around his mouth. Her fear that he'd died in agony needing her while she slept had haunted her for years. She felt a sharp twist of pain and tried to push the memory away, but it stuck. Why had he died while she slept at his side – why hadn't she woken to hold and comfort him in his last moments? She felt a pang of grief. Perhaps she ought not to have married again? Did Mike resent it – was that why she was so restless?

Janet decided she would take flowers to his grave. It was years since she had. She'd lived away from London so long, but now she would visit it and talk to him as she had after he died. Perhaps then this spirit of loneliness would leave her...

14

Peggy always felt a bit uneasy when she left the pub for a holiday, but once she was on her way, she settled down and forgot about everything that could go wrong.

'That place has been there more than a hundred years,' Able had told her once. 'It isn't going to fall down just because you're not there, hon.'

She'd laughed, because he was right and as he was often reminding her – he always kept the insurance up to date.

His big American car was full of people and suitcases and both Janet and Peggy shared the driving with him on the way down to Pip's. Freddie was itching to learn but had a while to go yet before he could get a provisional licence. Maggie hadn't passed her test yet, though she'd had a few lessons. Fay, like her twin, was too young and as yet had shown no interest.

They stopped a couple of times for drinks and meals and arrived at the cottage in Devon, which was situated at the edge of a pretty village and only a few miles from the nearest beach, at around four in the afternoon. Pip came out to greet them, hugging his mother first and then his sister. He looked at Janet and made a face.

'You're too thin,' he said. 'What's wrong?'

'Nothing. I've been horse riding and it keeps you fit – you should try it.' She poked him in the chest. 'You're getting fat.'

'Good. I'm happy,' Pip replied and grinned, refusing to let her teasing affect him. 'Sheila has cooked enough for the British Army, so she'll feed you up.' He turned his attention to Able and then the girls. 'What's this I hear – we have two famous chefs in the family now or is that three?' He glanced at his mother.

'Just two,' Peggy said, laughing as she went to greet Sheila, who had come out to see them. 'Those two will achieve more than I ever did.'

'You're a wonderful cook, Peggy,' Sheila said. 'You taught me and people are always complimenting me.'

They went on ahead into the cottage, which hadn't changed much, apart from an extension at the back, since Peggy's days, talking happily together and leaving the others to follow. Inside, the hall smelled of lavender and roses and the wood block floor shone where Sheila had polished it. The oak furniture gleamed with all the loving care she lavished on it and in the sitting room, the chintz covers and curtains were fresh and bright.

'Pip has the caravan out in the back for the girls,' Sheila said. 'He bought it last year for us to tour in and we thought it would suit Maggie and Fay down to the ground – save Janet having to get a hotel room.'

'What about Freddie? He would probably enjoy the caravan too,' Peggy said. 'I thought you said it sleeps four?'

'Yes, it does – but I thought he might like to share Chris' room. He's been as pleased as Punch getting it ready for him.'

Peggy nodded. She knew Freddie would have found it fun in the caravan but wouldn't interfere with Sheila's arrangements. The cottage was bigger now than it had been when she lived in it with Able. Pip had had the kitchen extended out at the back and built another bedroom so that he could have Sheila's family and his own to stay. He'd put a lot of windows in the kitchen extension, which made it a very pleasant room to sit in and talk these days.

* * *

The talking went on for ages, everyone following each other around as cases were unpacked, food eaten and all the family gossip caught up on. Pip wanted to know more about Janet's riding and she told him she'd started it to keep Maggie company sometimes, but then discovered she enjoyed it a lot herself.

'There is a stable not too far away,' Pip told her. 'You can both take a horse out there if you fancy it.'

'We might do that,' Janet replied, not looking at him.

'Mum can. I want to spend some time in the kitchen with Aunty Sheila,' Maggie said. 'Can I help with the cooking while we're here please?'

'Of course, if you want,' Sheila agreed and smiled, 'but you're here for a holiday – days at the sea and picnics in beauty spots.'

'We're taking a cookery course,' Fay informed her. 'We'll only be here a few days – we have to start then at a hotel called Seaview in Torquay. It is on the seafront and a big expensive place.'

Sheila nodded. 'I know it – up on the cliff tops, where the path winds round the coast. Someone did tell me they run cookery courses up there in the summer. She said they make their students work very hard. It won't be much of a holiday for you.'

'We want to do it,' Fay said. 'We're both looking forward to it.'

Sheila nodded. 'When I was your age, I had to help my mother in the pub she ran. I did some cooking for her and cleaning – and when I was eighteen, I started to serve customers with drinks.'

'Did you enjoy it?' Maggie asked, interested.

'Not particularly at first. It was just something I was expected to do as a sense of duty. Peggy and Maureen showed me the fun side. We enjoyed ourselves making cakes together and I learned to make a lot of different things my mother never taught me.'

'How is she now?' Peggy asked and saw a shadow pass across her daughter-in-law's face.

'Not so well,' Sheila said. Her parents had recently given up their pub that had been their life, because her mother had had a stroke and been ill for some months. She was back at home now, the hospital having done all they could, and they were coping, but life had become more difficult for her and Sheila's father. 'I go and visit once a fortnight. My father is feeling a bit down, but Mum seems to have accepted it and tells him he'll marry again when she's gone.'

'Oh, that must be upsetting for him?'

'Yes, he feels that he's doing all he can to make her happy, but nothing he does is enough. It's sad because he's always been a good husband to her.'

'Yes.' Peggy sighed. 'I expect it is a result of the illness, Sheila. She probably doesn't realise what she's saying or how it hurts.'

'Dad told me he hasn't even thought about another wife. He's just trying his best – some folk don't realise when they're well off.' Sheila's mother had always been difficult and Sheila had told Peggy several times that she wished her mother was more like her.

Glancing at her eldest daughter at that moment, Peggy saw a flicker of something in her eyes. Did she realise that Sheila's words could also relate to her? Janet was not an easy person to understand. Peggy was still worried about her eldest daughter and she resolved to ask Pip to have a word with her. See if he could get to what was troubling Janet.

* * *

'You know Janet,' Pip said when Peggy tried to broach the subject later. They were in the garden and he was showing her a rose she'd planted years ago that had now spread right up the side of the garage wall and was shedding pink petals everywhere. 'She's never content unless she has a problem.'

'That's harsh, love,' Peggy said. 'I worry that she isn't really happy.'

'If she isn't happy with Ryan, she needs her head examining. He worships the ground she walks on.'

'That's what I thought, but it isn't necessarily what she wants to make her happy.'

Pip nodded. 'I know – I don't think she ever got over seeing Mike like that... perhaps she does need to see a doctor, Mum. Just to talk it through and get it out of her system. She went through quite a bit back then, what with the cottage being flattened by a crashed plane and then Mike being wounded and losing his memory. They were just getting used to each other again when he died.'

'It was so sad,' Peggy said.

'Janet needs to be busy,' Pip replied thoughtfully. 'I will talk to her, Mum – see if I can get her to open up to me.'

'Good.' Peggy gave him a hug. 'At least I don't need to worry about you – I can see you're fine.' An accident a few years earlier had given them all a fright and left Pip susceptible to chills in the winter. He could suffer with breathing difficulties if he caught colds, but now in the summer he was clearly thriving. 'It seems to suit you down here?'

'It does, very much – best move we could make,' Pip said. 'Sheila was a bit restless to begin with, but she soon made friends – and it is closer to her mother, so that makes it easier for her to visit.'

'It must be difficult for her father?'

'Sheila worries about him,' Pip admitted. 'She doesn't know what he will do if anything happens to her mother – and the hospital said it could at any time.'

'That is sad,' Peggy replied. 'I worried about your father when he was very ill – even though we were estranged. You can't help it.'

Pip nodded. 'I've told her we'll look for a little place close to us if he's left alone. I'm doing very well here, Mum. I've been involved in De Havilland's success with their new plane; they gave me a rise a few months back and I can afford to get another small house or cottage for Sheila's father. They've been living in rented accommodation since they had to give the pub up. He never bought a house because they liked living where they were and it was a tied pub.'

'I know how he feels,' Peggy said. 'The Pig & Whistle is my home. If Maggie takes it over eventually, I'll have to look for somewhere else.'

'Will you come back to the country?' Pip asked, looking a bit anxious, because his cottage had been hers and Able's before he'd bought it from them.

'No, I don't think so.' Peggy reassured him she didn't want him to sell her the cottage back. 'I'm not sure what we shall do – I think Able might like a trip to America. Just to visit people and places – and we might settle elsewhere in London after that.'

Pip looked at her quizzically. 'You're not ready to retire yet, are you?'

'Not quite – and Maggie doesn't want me to just yet. She's very young and she has a lot to learn, but she will one day. She is thinking of doing things so differently, Pip. I'm not sure if it will work for her – and Fay has her own ideas, too.'

'Able could build you a lovely new house somewhere.'

'Yes, he could and would if I asked, but I don't know where I'd like to be and nor does he. We both enjoy living in Mulberry Lane.'

Pip nodded. 'I liked it fine when I was at school – but I moved on, Mum. You should give it some thought, or it will happen that you need to move but have no idea where.'

* * *

'You wouldn't want to live in the country again, would you?' Peggy asked Able when they were lying side by side in bed that night. 'If we do give up the pub in time, we'll have to think about where we want to move.'

'There are plenty of new houses going up in London,' Able said. 'We might find a plot and build our own – or move out somewhere, perhaps to the suburbs. Somewhere you could get into town easily by tube or bus if you didn't want to drive.'

'Yes, that might be an idea,' Peggy agreed. 'I'd still have the boarding house and you'd still have your building firm with Tom.'

'We could travel for a while – take some time to make up our minds.'

'It's funny but Janet was talking about travelling.'

'You're worried about her,' Able said and frowned. 'I've had a bit of an idea, but I don't want to say until after the holiday – and then I'll discuss it with you both.'

'Tell me now,' Peggy said, intrigued and tickled him but he shook his head.

'I'm not sure yet, hon. Give me a while to think about it and I'll be certain, rather than disappointing you both...'

15

The phone call came the following evening as they were all settling down to their evening meal. Pip went to answer it and returned looking serious. He paused for a moment and Sheila rose to her feet as he went to put his arms around her.

'Is it Mum?' she asked and her bottom lip wobbled.

'Yes, they've just taken her into hospital again. She's had another stroke; they don't have much hope for her, love.'

'Oh no!' Sheila exclaimed and looked at Peggy. 'I'm so sorry, but I'll have to go. Dad can't cope alone.'

'He told me to say he can manage,' Pip said, 'but I told him we'd be there as soon as we could.' He met his mother's concerned gaze. 'Will you look after everything here, Mum – the kids and all of it?'

'Of course, love,' Peggy replied instantly. She glanced at their son, Chris, a leggy teenager now, so serious and anxious for his other granny. Sheila and Pip's daughter, not quite eight, looked on in silence. Peggy reached for her hand. 'It's all right, Sarah darling. Granny and Grandpa will be here and Aunty Janet.'

Sarah got off her chair and went to stand close to her grandmother. Tears were in her eyes as she looked at her mother and saw her distress.

'It's all right, darling,' Sheila said. 'I'm just going to visit Granny and Grandad in Torquay. You'll be all right with Granny Peggy, won't you?'

'Yes, Mum,' Chris spoke strongly despite the anxious look in his eyes. 'We shall be fine. We're all right. You go with Dad.'

'Thanks, son.' Pip threw him a grateful look. 'We'll telephone you as soon as we can and let you know how things are.'

Sheila hugged her daughter and then her son, before running upstairs to pack a small suitcase for her and Pip. A stunned silence had fallen over the family as the couple departed with white faces and anxious looks.

'Poor Sheila,' Janet said after they'd left. 'Well, that's put a bit of a dampener on things, hasn't it?' Their lovely family party had been abruptly cut short.

'It is very unfortunate,' Peggy said. 'It's bad enough that her mother has been so ill, but to be called away when she has visitors makes it more difficult for her. Never mind, we'll have a good holiday anyway. You, and the twins and Maggie can still go to the sea tomorrow. If Chris and Sarah want to go, too, they can.'

'What about you?' Janet asked. 'It is supposed to be your holiday as well, Mum.'

'I'm fine here. I'll just potter about, sit in the garden and listen for the phone – just until we know how things are.'

'I'll drive you all to the beach,' Janet said. 'There's no point in us all sitting round and doing nothing. Sheila wouldn't want that.'

* * *

There was no call the remainder of that evening or the next morning. Peggy was just making a cup of tea after lunch when the phone rang and Able took the call. It sounded very serious and when Peggy brought their tea into the sitting room, she saw from his face that it was bad.

'Sheila's mother died an hour ago,' he told her. 'Pip said her father is very upset. Sheila is staying with him until after the funeral – but he is coming back this evening. He said she insisted and he'll go back the evening before her mother is buried.'

'Oh, what a shame for her,' Peggy replied. 'Do you think we ought to go back to London, Able? Come for a holiday another time?'

'Pip said that is the last thing Sheila wants. She is just very sorry that she's spoiled things.'

'Of course, she hasn't – it isn't her fault and I know she was so worried about her mum. Her mother wasn't always as good to her as she might have been, but she still loved her.'

Able nodded. 'It's a pity to go back when everyone has looked forward to this, Peggy, but we'll do what you think right, hon.'

'I'll talk to Pip this evening. If he is just coming back because he thinks he owes it to us, I shall tell him we're going home, but otherwise, we'll stay.'

'I think Janet wants to stay on – and the girls had arranged to travel on from here to Torquay so they'd be better to stay put.'

'Yes, I know.' Peggy sighed. 'It just makes things sad when it should have been a happy time. I'm not sure what Chris and Sarah will make of it – they're a bit young for a funeral, especially Sarah, but it's up to their parents, of course.'

* * *

Pip asked them to stay when he got home that evening. 'I've just come back because I have a work meeting tomorrow,' he said. 'I shouldn't be too long, but then I'll probably go back to Sheila the next day. She told me to stay with you and go down for the funeral, but I know you won't mind staying on and taking care of things for us, Mum.'

'If you're sure you wouldn't prefer that we took the kids to London? I thought it might take their mind off it all.' Death was hard to cope with for young children and Peggy was thinking a change of scene might help.

'No, because Chris wants to come to the funeral and Sarah will be weepy and frightened if we take her. She's better off here with you and Able and the others, but I want you to stay.'

'Maggie and Fay leave for their course next week anyway,' Peggy said, 'so it will be us, Freddie and Janet, that's all – but I do feel bad that we're intruding at a time like this.'

'I feel better with you here. There have been a few burglaries of empty properties recently – when the owners are away for a weekend or just out in the evening. I've done all I can to make the place safe, but I'm glad you're here.'

'Oh, well, if we're of use.' Peggy smiled, her mind at ease. 'Will you bring Sheila's father back with you?'

'If he will come, but he's very independent. He may refuse to leave his home – I am hoping to persuade him if I can find a nice little place to purchase close by.'

'I noticed an end-terrace house for sale just down the road from here,' Able said. 'I thought it looked quite nice – pretty front garden and roses growing up the wall, though it may need a bit of attention inside.'

'I saw that too,' Janet said. 'Would you like me to have a look, Pip? I'm quite good at doing things up a bit. If it needs tradesmen, I could get estimates for you – and I could help if it is just decoration.' Janet always did the decorating at her home herself and was good at it, though she'd had no professional training.

'Could you? I know you did your own cottage up. Sheila loved what you'd done when we came up for a visit. So, yes, please,' Pip said and smiled at her. 'If it is all ready for him, I might get him here. He likes a nice garden and if he lived in one of those terraced cottages it would suit Sheila. She could visit most days then, make sure he's all right.'

'You'd need to buy it at the right price,' Able said. 'I'll have a look myself – see what they want for it and try to get it for you at a sensible figure.'

'Supposing he doesn't want to leave his home?' Peggy put in. 'You'll be stuck with a house you don't need.'

'It's easy to let places here,' Pip told her. 'I've been thinking of buying something anyway. I've got money in the bank just sitting there, so I thought I'd invest it in property – perhaps more than one.'

'If you do, let me know,' Janet said suddenly, her eyes lighting up. 'Especially if they need renovating. I'd like to invest in that... not that I have much to put in.'

'I'd let you be my property manager, pay you sixpence a week,' Pip said and laughed as she pulled a face at him. 'Let's see what this first one is like before we jump in feet first – and Ryan might have something to say if you were down here too often.'

Janet didn't answer.

Pip frowned but didn't quiz her further. Peggy realised he hadn't yet got round to having that little talk with his sister.

* * *

Pip had departed for his meeting when Janet walked down the road, peering in the windows of the terraced house. It looked to be in sound condition, though clearly needed work to smarten it up, so she took the telephone number of the estate agent and went back to the cottage to ring and make an appointment.

It was arranged for two that afternoon, and after eating a solitary lunch, she returned to the empty property and met the rather young man that turned up on a bicycle. He spent an hour showing her round and by the time she'd seen the whole cottage and done some calculations in her head, Janet was convinced it was a good buy and told him that her brother was interested and would telephone him the next day.

'We do have another interested party—'

'We saw it first and we want it,' Janet said decisively. 'You won't let anyone else have it, will you?' She gave him a brilliant smile and, to her surprise, his cheeks went pink.

'No – not if you want it.'

'I'm going to do it up,' Janet said decisively. 'When it's finished, you won't know it.'

'That's lovely,' the agent replied and looked almost shy. 'I do hope you'll be happy here.'

He got on his bike and pedalled away furiously, leaving Janet softly chuckling to herself.

As she returned to her brother's home, she was singing. She'd never thought about it before, but the one thing she was truly good at was home-making. It had started when she was first married to Mike and couldn't afford anything new in the old cottage they'd rented. She'd done the decorating there herself, making cushion covers and curtains, all the little things that made a place come alive – and she could turn this forlorn little house into a comfortable home.

* * *

Pip was as keen as Janet and they discussed local tradesmen and prices over the phone. Janet was eager to do most of the work herself.

'I'll get on to my lawyer and tell them I want it bought quickly so you can get on with it, Janet. There's no need for it to take months if they pull their finger out.'

'They might let us start work as soon as the first contract is signed,' Janet said.

'Good idea. I know the owners, so I'll ask if they will. I'd like it done as soon as possible for Sheila's father's sake. If he can see it being worked on, perhaps he'll let us bring him home with us.' Pip sounded thrilled.

'I can strip the bathroom and kitchen, but I'll need a plumber, electrician and carpenter. I'll do the decorating myself. Trust me, Pip. I'll make your house beautiful for you, and Sheila's father will want to come and live in it.'

'I do trust you,' he said, 'but if you do all that you'll be down here for some weeks – the whole summer and well into autumn. Are you prepared to give it so much time?'

Janet didn't hesitate. 'I was going to spend most of the summer at Mum's, but I'd probably get in Maggie's way if I did that, so yes, I'm fine with it, Pip. I can always find a room somewhere.'

'Don't be daft,' he said and she could imagine the face he was making at the other end of the phone and laughed. 'You'll stay at the cottage with us.' Pip hesitated, then, 'Is everything all right with you and Ryan? You seemed a bit down...'

'I think I was just bored,' she said. 'Ryan is always working – every night he has paperwork to finish. I know he loves me and I love him, but I sometimes need more, Pip. I know I should be satisfied with my home and family.' She'd had a few twinges of guilt about Jon. Was her young son all right left at home without her and Maggie? He'd wanted to stay and his friends were close by. Ryan would give him his breakfast and evening meal, but at lunchtime, he would be eating with Janet's friend just down the road. She'd said he could play with her children, so he should be fine. It was his choice and Ryan had thought he was old enough to amuse himself for a few hours during the day, but Janet would be relieved when her husband brought him down. Ryan had promised to come sooner and then Jon would only have had a few days without her.

'Why should you be satisfied just to stay at home?' Pip asked, bringing her wandering thoughts back with a jolt. 'You should have an outside interest – I thought you did some cooking or something?'

She laughed. 'Yes, so boring that you can't even remember what I do!'

'Right, so that tells me you need more.' He was silent for a moment, then, 'I've saved a bit of money – more than I need for this house for Sheila's father. Why don't we go into business together? We could buy houses that need restoring and you can have the job of doing them up and we'll share the profits – what do you reckon?'

Janet felt a tingling sensation at the back of her neck. 'I think it is a wonderful idea, but do you mind where the houses are? I might not be able to spend all my time down here.' She laughed. 'Ryan might object then and Jon has to go to school.'

'I should think he jolly well would object and, as you say, Jon needs you around – pick the next house where you like and I'll make time to come up and see it and discuss budgets.'

'Perhaps we should see how this one turns out first, as you suggested,' Janet replied, feeling a spasm of nerves in her stomach. 'I love the idea, Pip – but it would be your money and we need to see if I can do it profitably. Once we've finished this, we'll see what it would sell for and if there is a profit should you wish to sell.'

'Oh, I wouldn't. If Sheila's father turns it down, I'll let it out, probably holiday lets...' Pip said something that Janet couldn't hear. 'I have to go, Fay. Do whatever needs doing and I'll give you the money to cover it when we get back.'

Janet replaced the receiver. Her worries about Jon were temporarily forgotten. She felt both excited and nervous. The current project had been begun as a favour to her brother and because she knew it would keep her mind from wandering to Jason for a couple of months or so – but to do it as a business... Could she? Did she know enough about it? Janet had done a lot of decorating for herself and friends and she had a keen eye for colour and design, but making money from a passion she indulged whenever she had the chance was different. However, she would give it a try and see what happened.

She decided to get three different prices for the work and to buy the materials herself. She could actually do the tiling in the bathroom and kitchen. She'd done it in her own home and two of her friends had admired what she'd done and asked her to do theirs.

'I like the way you've put those patterned tiles in here and there,' her friend Susan had told her. 'Where did you get them?'

'They are Spanish and old,' Janet had told her. 'I found them in a junk shop in a box in the corner. They were dusty and forgotten and I bought them for ten shillings.'

'They're lovely,' Susan had sighed. 'I've looked for something different but can't find much.'

'I think there were more,' Janet had said. 'I'll go back and look again and see what I can find.' Her tiles had been maroon, which was an unusual colour, and she'd never seen any others, but she found a mixture of blue and green tiles. Susan had loved the blue ones with a fancy pattern and so Janet had done her bathroom for her with white tiles mixed with the gorgeous, old, Spanish ones she'd bought cheaply. She still had a big box with a mixture of blue and green tiles and decided she would use them in Pip's house.

She telephoned Ryan. 'How is Jon – is he all right without me?'

'Of course, he is, Janet. He isn't a baby and he has lots of friends. Whenever I ask him what he's been doing, he says he's been playing sport with his mates.'

'Good.' She hesitated and then told him about Pip's idea.

'That's a good idea, Janet,' he said, sounding surprised but pleased. 'I'm going to be busy for a while and it will give you something to do that you enjoy.'

'I wondered if you could bring that box of wall tiles down for me? You are still coming down?'

'Yes, I know where the tiles are. I was clearing out some of the junk in the garage and wondered if you wanted them. I'm coming down next weekend for a few days – as I said I want to see you and talk to you – is that soon enough?'

'Yes, of course. I have to strip all the old stuff out first and get a plumber in,' Janet assured him. She hesitated, then, 'I'm glad you're coming, Ryan. I do love you...'

'I love you,' he said and paused. Then, 'Was there anything else, Janet? I have some work to finish this evening.'

'No, I just wanted to tell you what Pip suggested and ask you to bring the tiles, and to ask how you and Jon are.'

'Stop worrying about Jon. You need to let him be independent, Janet – he's fine. I'm sorry, I really do have work—' His tone was impatient and she bit her lip.

'He's just a young boy, Ryan. I worry about him.' Janet's voice sharpened.

'I'll let you talk to him... Jon, your mother wants a word...' Ryan handed over the receiver to his son without another word to her.

'Mum – what's wrong?' Jon asked, sounding a bit scared.

'Nothing, darling. I just wondered how you were getting on?'

'Our cricket team is leading the schools' league. I scored twenty runs today and bowled one of the other players out.'

'That's good. As long as you're all right, Jon. You can stop with us at the cottage for the rest of the holidays when you come down with your father.'

'All right – if you want. Can I go now? Dad's got tea ready – beans on toast.'

'Oh, well, bye then...'

She replaced the receiver, resisting the urge to burst into tears. Work, work, work! That was all Ryan ever did. It was no wonder she'd responded to Jason's masculine charm and the way his eyes seemed to be asking her a question all the time.

Janet bit her lip. Ryan did still care for her, she knew he did, but he didn't seem to understand that she needed more; he was more interested in his work.

Pushing her uneasy thoughts to one side, she drew a large plain pad towards her and began to draw something that was in her head. If she knocked down the wall into the little scullery, she could make a lovely, big, airy kitchen...

Her lips curved into a smile as she planned the changes she would make and then started to write down a list of materials and prices. In the morning, she would drive into town and pick up some leaflets and make a few enquiries. When she'd refurbished her own cottage in Scotland, she'd managed to get trade prices on some of the goods she'd used. Perhaps she could negotiate a deal like that down here.

16

LONDON

In the clinic in London, Shirley finished bathing and cleansing the old woman's feet. They were covered in bloody sores and her toes were twisted and misshapen. It was usually a nurse's job to do this sort of work, but Mitsy had taken a liking to Shirley and allowed her to remove the tattered boots that she'd been wearing as she hobbled into the clinic that afternoon.

'They said you're all right,' she'd commented, looking fiercely at Shirley. 'What can you give me for me feet, missy?'

'That depends on what is wrong with them,' Shirley had replied. 'May I have a look please?'

'I don't want them nurses,' Mitsy had grumbled, her eyes dark and wary under the man's felt hat she had jammed tight on her head. 'The last one I had threatened to cut them off if I let them get bad again.'

'I don't think she meant it,' Shirley had said, hard put to it not to laugh. 'Let's have a little look then, shall we?'

She'd gently removed the worn boots and peeled away the filthy socks underneath, revealing the blisters and bloody sores. Examining Mitsy's toes and heels, she saw where the boots had cut into her.

'You need some new boots,' she said. 'I think that's the cause of all this – and I can give you some ointment for them, but for now I'll wash them, put some ointment on to soothe them and bind them up for you. I want you to come in again next week so I can see how they're going on.'

'Ain't got no other boots,' Mitsy replied with a sniff. 'I found them when mine was pinched. Took while I was sleepin', they was.'

'Well, we do have some here,' Shirley said and smiled as she opened the cupboard in her room. 'I think you need a size seven – the ones you have look more like a five.' She rummaged in a box and found an almost new pair of brown boots in the right size.

Mitsy looked at them suspiciously, but when Shirley pulled on a clean pair of socks over the bandages and helped her to put on the boots, she nodded, a little gleam in her eyes.

'They feel better,' she admitted. 'They said you was all right – that things were better now you're here.'

'Oh, I'm sure that they were fine before then,' Shirley said and Mitsy sniffed harder.

'I ain't – some of them nurses have got heavy hands, missy. And they're mean about givin' things away and all.'

'Well, these things are all donated, either by members of the public or the Sally Army. So, if someone needs them, I give them what they need.'

'Yeah, you're all right,' Mitsy grinned, showing the gaps in her blackened teeth. 'I'll see yer next week then.' She got to her feet and shuffled off.

Shirley went to wash her hands at the sink before her next patient. She turned in surprise as someone entered. Mostly, she called them in herself. She frowned as she saw the nurse. 'Yes, can I help you?'

'I just saw Mitsy leaving wearing new boots. You are aware that she sells them for drink and then comes back again claiming that hers have been stolen. I refused her the last time she tried it on.'

Shirley looked at the nurse. There was no pity or compassion in her for the old woman and that made her wary. They were here to help not criticise. 'Are *you* aware that her feet are blistered and sore from wearing boots that don't fit her?' she asked, hoping to see some sympathy, but her answer was again uncaring and that made Shirley angry.

'It's her own fault,' the nurse said coldly. 'She's done it twice already, Doctor Shirley – she'll be after something else she can sell next time. I thought you should be warned. Some of these scroungers are as crafty as foxes; you'll probably find she's taken something of yours when you look.'

'Thank you for the warning, but I don't leave anything of value around,' Shirley said in a flat tone. 'I am sorry you think Mitsy an undeserving case, nurse, but I felt she needed both treatment and some new boots. She is my patient from now on and I will be responsible for her treatment.' Shirley was a little brusque, because she was annoyed at the nurse's manner, which bordered on rudeness.

The nurse shrugged. 'On your head be it,' she said and turned to leave. At the door she looked back. 'You probably won't want to know that your next patient is just out of prison and a habitual thief. Make sure your valuables aren't left lying around – and your stethoscope. He'll sell it for whisky if he gets half a chance.'

Shirley frowned as the nurse shut the door with a little bang after her. She might have upset that nurse, but the woman's attitude was all wrong. Yes, sometimes a patient would take advantage if they thought you were green, but Shirley felt that it was best to give them the benefit of the doubt. Mitsy was right to be wary of the nurses if they were like that one – though it was probably true that there were thefts from the clinic. It was bound to happen now and then, and Shirley had kept her cupboards locked. Even at the hospital you had to be careful with medicines and valuable things like the stethoscope she wore hanging around her neck, because drugs and equipment had been known to disappear if staff were careless.

Shirley glanced at her desk. The only thing that mattered was a nice pen her father had given her. She picked it up and tucked it into the top pocket of her white coat, leaving a cheap pen on the pad, and then went to call for her next patient. As he shuffled in, smelling of strong drink, she reflected that perhaps the nurse might be right about this one, but she wasn't going to let the nurse sour her opinions without cause.

'What can I do for you, sir?' she asked with a smile. 'What is troubling you?'

'It's me chest,' he said. 'I can't get me breath, Doctor.'

Shirley nodded. 'We'd better listen to your heart and lungs then...' she said and bent over him as he undid his jacket and shirt. She could hear the problem as soon as she applied the stethoscope. He had fluid on his lungs and it was bubbling away, his breath rasping. 'You need to go to the hospital. I think you may have a nasty chest infection, Mr Bertram.'

'Can't yer just give me a linctus or somethin'? It's what they done at the last place, and somethin' to rub on me chest?'

'Yes, I can give you those things,' Shirley said with a frown. 'But unless you let me send you to the hospital, we can't find out what is causing this problem and it won't be cured by something you rub on your chest. You might need a procedure to have the fluid drawn from your lungs.'

'Why can't you do it?' he asked warily.

'Because I don't have the equipment or the information. You need an X-ray.'

'Just give me the medicine,' he said and rose to his feet. 'I ain't goin' ter no hospital.'

Shirley sighed and wrote the prescription on her pad with her cheap pen and laid it down. 'Give that to the dispensary on your way out and they'll sort you out.' She put her hand to her top pocket as a last thought. 'I'll have my pen please, Mr Bertram. I felt you take it and it has sentimental value – my father gave it to me.'

'Must be losin' me touch,' he said with a grimace and handed her pen back to her. 'Sorry, Doc, force of habit. It won't happen again.'

'It had better not,' Shirley said and managed to keep a straight face, at least until he'd left the consulting room.

The nurse had been right about him, she had to admit. It remained to be seen if she was right about Mitsy...

* * *

'I didn't actually feel him take the pen,' Shirley told Keith later that evening. They had been to the cinema to see Charlton Heston and Janet Leigh in a *Touch of Evil* and were eating a bag of chips on the way home. 'But I'd been warned and so I checked and when it wasn't there, I knew he must have taken it as I bent over him.'

'Some of these old prison lags can't help themselves,' Keith agreed. 'He probably didn't intend to steal from you but couldn't resist it.'

'Yes...' She was thoughtful. 'If that nurse hadn't warned me, I would've lost it. I suppose I should thank her – but she seemed so cruel and uncaring.'

'I expect she's seen too much of it,' Keith said. 'She obviously knows her way around things like that – you should heed her advice, Shirley.'

She nodded, perhaps she would apologise for her abruptness. 'I hope she is wrong about Mitsy. I really do...'

'Got a soft spot for that one?' Keith smiled at her.

'Yes – well, at least, I felt a lot of sympathy for her. Her feet were in a terrible state. She'd been wearing an old pair of boots that were two sizes too small and she had some nasty blisters. Some of them were on the point of festering. She must have been in terrible pain.'

'I expect she's used to pain. People do learn to live with it when they have no choice. In Africa, the patients often came from miles away and sometimes they were half dead when they finally arrived, either walking very slowly or being carried. The poverty and sickness there makes you shudder.' He frowned. 'It's why I'm thinking of going back.' He paused, then, 'That job is still open...'

'I thought Tom Barton offered you a job?'

'He did and it was a decent wage – but not really what I want, Shirley...' He stopped walking and looked at her. 'The job I've been offered pays well – and it's worthwhile. They will need a doctor – would you consider coming out with me? We could get married and—'

'Stop right there,' Shirley said. 'Are you seriously asking me to marry you in the same breath as you've just offered me a job?' She looked into his eyes. 'Isn't a proposal of marriage supposed to be romantic?'

Keith blushed and looked uncomfortable. 'Sorry. I didn't mean it to come out that way, but it was you talking about how much sympathy you felt for those people at the clinic. A lot of the sick are children, Shirley. Their parents carry them in because they have no transport, not even a donkey. Don't you think they deserve your help?'

Shirley stared at him for a moment. His words had torn at her heart, as he intended. 'Yes, of course, they do and I'm sure you will find a dedicated doctor who will enjoy working with you, Keith – and you have decided you want to go, haven't you?'

His eyes dropped before hers. 'They offered me more money – and more money for the project. They really want me, Shirley, and I do want to go – but I also want you.' His eyes at that moment reminded her of a puppy pleading. 'I love you.'

Shirley took a deep breath. 'Do you? Do you really, Keith? I thought you did when you said you were coming home, but you haven't been here five minutes and you haven't tried to fit in with my life. Your head is full of dreams, Keith. I know what you've been doing is worthwhile and if it is what you want to do with your life, then good luck.'

'But you don't want to come with me?' He looked so disappointed that for a moment Shirley was torn with indecision. Should she give up her dream and go off with him to a life she knew nothing about?

'No,' she said at last and felt her throat constrict with tears as she realised this was probably goodbye. 'I'm sorry, Keith. Had you been able to settle here, it might have worked out for us, but I can't leave London, especially while my father is ill.' It was selfish of him to expect it. He'd known for years what she wanted, why she'd trained so hard for so many years, and now he was asking her to just up sticks and go with him.

'So you don't love me?' He sounded sulky and Shirley frowned.

'I might have if you'd given me a chance,' she said. 'I liked you a lot when we met years ago – and you helped me when I was unhappy. You promised to come home so many times, but it was always "next year" – and now you have come home and you can't wait to go back out there.'

'I was busy all the time and so were you,' he said defensively. 'Why can't you see how good it would be for us out there? I might end up with a really top job looking after a big charity in a few years. It's an opportunity for me, as well as a good cause.'

'Then take it and my good wishes for your future. My life is here in the East End of London. You've always known that.'

'Yes, I suppose that's why I didn't bother coming back before,' he said. 'It's a shame. I really thought you were the right sort – a dedicated doctor who would fit in well with my projects.' That was all he wanted really; she knew it as she listened to him, but there was no point in talking it over, because they weren't in love, but just friends and that was how it had always been, despite his words of love. Had he felt them, he would have come home to be with her long ago.

'Thank you. It's nice that you asked, Keith, but I am dedicated to the people here.'

He nodded, accepting she'd made up her mind. 'I'll be leaving in the morning then.'

'Yes, if that is what you want,' she agreed and held out her hand. 'Don't leave feeling angry, Keith. We can still be friends, can't we?'

He hesitated and then grasped her hand. 'Yes, we can be friends, Shirley. I'm very disappointed – but I still think the world of you.'

'I like you, Keith, and I'm glad you have the job you want, but I can't leave London, especially now.' And she didn't love him. If she had, it would have been far more of a wrench to stay here when he'd offered marriage.

'Yes, I do understand you don't want to leave your father.' He sighed. 'I suppose you're right. I should have come back and found a job here ages ago. Perhaps then we'd be married with a family...'

Shirley nodded but said nothing. She thought privately it would not have happened. Had the link between them been strong enough, Keith would have returned home at the end of his Army service rather than going off to work with his brother in Africa. They had liked each other and she'd thought at first it might blossom into romance, but it hadn't.

'You can still write now and then,' she said but, in her heart, she knew he wouldn't. He would find someone who wanted the same things he did and perhaps that was best.

* * *

Alone in her bedroom that evening, Shirley brushed her hair and looked at herself in the mirror. Was there something wrong with her? She never seemed to find anyone she could be truly in love with – not after Richard had let her down. Had she become too distrusting or was it just that she hadn't found the right person?

Sighing, Shirley got into bed. She had thrown back all the top covers because the night was very warm and she felt restless. The single sheet was cool and she gradually relaxed as she drifted into sleep. Just before she went to sleep, a face slipped into her mind and she smiled and settled more comfortably.

* * *

Maureen looked anxiously at her daughter as she drank her coffee and ate toast with scrambled egg the next morning.

'Keith has gone back to Africa just like that?' she asked incredulously. 'I thought he'd come home so that you could spend time together – perhaps even marry?'

'I thought so, too,' Shirley replied with a little shrug. 'It didn't work out, Mum. He wanted me to go out there – to be the doctor on site – and marry him. It was as if my being the doctor for his project was more important than the marriage bit. I said no – I'm not leaving London and he knew it before he made up his mind to take the job.'

'So it is over then?'

'It was never really on,' Shirley said and laughed as Maureen made a face of disgust. 'Don't worry, Mum. I don't have a broken heart – and to prove it I'm going to a dance this evening with friends. It's a rock 'n' roll evening and I wondered if you would iron that skirt for me – you know, the one all the net petticoats go under.'

'Of course, I will,' Maureen said. 'I didn't know you were going out this evening?'

'I didn't either, but I was asked by friends from the practice. It is a big night and in aid of charity. I bought a ticket just to be friendly, but now I've decided to go. As Mimi said, "All work and no play makes Shirley a dull girl." And I agree with her, so I'm going.'

'Mimi?' Maureen raised her brows. 'Do I know her?'

'Doctor Wren.' Shirley laughed as the penny dropped and Maureen looked surprised. Doctor Wren was older than her and a plump sensible woman. 'Yes, it is a funny name for her. She is helping to run the evening for her teenage daughters. They wanted to raise some money for victims of polio and their families, so she agreed to do it – and let them have some fun while they're at it.'

'Is it a big affair – will there be a proper band?'

'I'm not quite sure,' Shirley replied. 'Did you want a ticket if there is?'

'Me? No, I couldn't leave your dad. I do like the music, though. It's fun to listen to on the wireless. I know they say it is a bad influence – on the young lads.'

'You mean the Teddy boys?' Shirley laughed. 'They are just tearaways; fighting in the streets and damaging cinemas is so stupid. I mean, when I saw *Rock Around the Clock*, I wanted to get up and dance in the aisles. A lot of people did it, but you don't need to tear seats up.'

'No, that was stupid and Gordy likes the music, too, but he doesn't do things like that,' Maureen said. 'I've bought him a record player of his own, though he doesn't know it yet. I need to get a few records to start him off.'

'I'll buy those,' Shirley said and smiled at her. 'I know he likes Elvis Presley and Bill Haley, but I'll get a selection of the most popular.' She laughed. 'You may regret it when he plays them loud, but I know he likes music. Gordy is a bit on the quiet side, Mum. I don't think there's anything wrong with his health – he's not in any trouble at school?'

'No. I asked about that,' Maureen replied. 'I think he is just a bit shy and unsure. Your father said he was like that at his age – but he enjoyed his visit to the zoo last weekend. It was good of you to take him.'

'I'll take him to the pictures when there's a good Western on,' Shirley said. Maureen smiled. 'Well, I'm glad you're not upset over Keith and I hope you have a good time tonight.' She hesitated, then, 'You didn't turn him down because of us, did you?'

'No, Mum, though if he'd really cared for me, he would have known I couldn't leave now – but it wasn't my only, or even my main, reason. I have my work and I want to stay here anyway. Besides, if Keith had been in love with me, he might have come back years ago. He chose his project and that's fine with me. I've chosen mine.'

Maureen nodded and decided not to push the subject further. She hoped that Shirley hadn't sacrificed herself for her family, but if she said she was happy with the situation, she had to take her word for it.

* * *

Maureen told Peggy all about it later when she rang her at the cottage in Devon and her best friend agreed. 'Shirley knows her own mind, Maureen.

She is a very determined and capable young woman. If she was desperately in love with him, you'd see some sign of it.'

'Sometimes she seems very thoughtful, a bit distant, and I thought she might be in love with him – but she is going to a rock 'n' roll dance this evening so she's not much bothered.'

'Sounds fun,' Peggy said. 'I've known the time we would have had a go at that too.'

'Yes, so have I,' Maureen laughed. 'Still, it is in aid of polio victims, so fingers crossed they raise plenty of money. I gave Shirley some money for a ticket even though I shan't go.'

'If I were there I would, too,' Peggy said. 'It's the funeral in a couple of days. Pip says we're not to go. Chris wants to, but they don't want Sarah to be there, so I'll be with her. Janet and Able may go down. I shall stay here with Sarah and Jon. His father came down and dropped him off yesterday. Ryan didn't stay long, just one night, but said he'd be back shortly. An unexpected trip came up and changed his plans at the last minute and he decided Jon should be with us. I think Janet was a bit annoyed over that – she was expecting Ryan to stay a few days.' She hesitated, then, 'I told you about Janet's new project...'

'Yes, it sounds wonderful. I didn't realise she knew so much about doing a house up, did you?' Maureen asked.

'It came as a surprise to me, too – though her home is always immaculate, like something out of one of those fancy magazines. I always thought she'd had some man in to do it, but no, she does a lot of it herself. Not plumbing or electrics – but she's just knocked a wall down. She said it wasn't a load-bearing wall and it was easy. Apparently, Able checked it for her and he said it was just a single partition wall – but still. I can't imagine Janet with a hammer!'

Maureen gave a little giggle. 'It's surprising what we can do if we try. Is she happier now? You were a bit worried about her, I know.'

'She seems perfectly content, at least most of the time,' Peggy said. 'I'd better go – the children want a picnic and I have to bake some bits and pieces to take with us.'

'It was supposed to be your holiday,' Maureen reminded her and Peggy laughed.

'We do what we have to,' she said. 'Come round for lunch when we get back – all of you.' She hesitated, then, 'Any change in Gordon?'

'He's much the same. He lost a few pounds at the start, but he doesn't seem to be losing any more.'

'It takes time. I've been eating a lot of salads to get my weight down a bit and it is slow and boring. I'll make something nice that isn't fattening when you come to lunch – you will, won't you?'

'Yes, but don't cook apple pie. You know Gordon can't resist it.'

Maureen was smiling as she replaced the receiver. It always made her feel better talking to Peggy. They'd been friends for so many years and knew each other so well.

She sighed as she started to prepare the meal Shirley had suggested for her father's lunch. Maureen missed making cakes and baking pies and sausage rolls, but if salads were keeping Gordon healthy, she would stick to the regime as long as he could bear it.

17

At the funeral, Sheila clung to Pip's arm and her father's as they followed the coffin down the church aisle. Janet saw her distress and wanted to comfort her, to tell her she knew just how awful it felt to lose someone you loved, even when you weren't sure they loved you, but she'd never been really close to her brother's wife. She was sorry about that and decided she would try to make up for it while she was staying with them and working on the cottage. She liked Sheila, always had, but they hadn't seen each other often enough over the years. Perhaps now that would change.

Janet wondered about her own mother, waiting at home in the cottage with the younger children. Maggie and Fay had gone off to their course, leaving the previous day and clearly so excited that even Peggy just smiled and shrugged.

'We have to let them grow up,' she'd said. 'It is only for a short time and then they will be back and ready to take over.'

'Do you mind that they will have lots of new ideas and think yours redundant?' Janet had asked curiously.

'Not at all. I may learn something. Life goes on and it's good to do something new. I'm looking forward to it.'

Janet tried to concentrate on the words the vicar was saying, but she hadn't known Sheila's mother and she'd only come to support her brother and Sheila. She'd offered to stay and look after Jon and Sarah, but Peggy had said it was best if she did. For a moment, Janet's brow furrowed. Her son was a quiet child, so quiet that you often didn't know he was there and when you turned to see his reproachful eyes watching, it made you feel guilty that you'd neglected him. Ryan said he thought Jon was missing her and then he'd had to go on a trip for his firm so hadn't been able to stay with his family in Devon.

Janet felt really cross about that and told him. 'I thought you were going to try to have some time with us here this summer?'

'I am – I will but I have to do this first, Janet. Surely you can see that?' Ryan had sounded as frustrated as she was and tired and she'd relented.

'I know you have to work. I'm sorry. It's just disappointing.'

'I'll make it up to you,' he'd promised.

'You wanted to talk to me about something? Is anything wrong, Ryan?'

'Yes and no,' he'd replied with a wry smile. 'I've almost made up my mind, but I'd rather wait until I'm sure. Be a bit patient with me, love – and I truly am sorry that this is just a quick trip for Jon's sake.'

'That bit is fine,' she'd said. 'He will enjoy himself with the family – but we need you, too, Ryan – both of us...'

'I know – but be patient,' he'd reiterated and that's all he would say on the matter, leaving Janet frustrated and feeling that something was wrong, though when he'd kissed her before he left she'd felt his reluctance to go. 'I'll be down just as soon as I can,' he'd promised, 'and then we'll really talk. Just believe in me. I do love you.'

Janet recalled her wandering thoughts as she saw everyone was now going outside for the burial.

She looked at Sheila's white face as they all gathered round for the committal and then Pip drew her to him and she sobbed into his shoulder. Would Janet cry like that if anything happened to her own mother? Yes, she thought she probably would.

As they all walked away afterwards, Janet went to Sheila and pressed her hand in sympathy. 'I'm so sorry,' she said. 'Is there anything at all I can do?'

Sheila gave her a wan smile and then swallowed hard. 'Pip told me what you're doing for Dad. Thank you, Janet. I know you'll make that place comfortable and nice for him and he can't go on living where he is now, it isn't as if it was their home for years. When they finally gave up the pub, they just rented the first place they could get. It's not very nice and he'd be miserable here all alone.'

'You must persuade him to come and see it, though at the moment it is in a bit of a mess, because I'm stripping it all out, but I promise it will be lovely.' The owners were lovely, friendly people and Pip's solicitor had rushed the first contract through with the deposit. As soon as they knew it was for Sheila's father, they'd handed over the key and told Janet to get on with it, saying they trusted Pip to complete. She couldn't imagine that happening in London, but Pip had made a lot of friends and so had Sheila.

'Yes, I know it will be lovely,' Sheila replied. 'I saw the way you do things when we came to Scotland two years ago to visit. Thanks, Janet. I'll feel better with him living close by.'

'Yes, of course, you will...' Janet smiled warmly at her.

* * *

Janet was thoughtful as they all went back to the three-bedroomed house with no front garden and a patchy lawn at the back that Sheila's father was currently living in. It was a cold, soulless place that needed a lot of work and she completely understood why Sheila was so desperate to get her father away from it. Janet had prepared sandwiches and bits and pieces, but no one ate very much.

When Sheila's father came up to her, Janet was a little surprised. He offered to shake hands. 'Hello. I'm Bert. This place my Sheila is on about, does it have a decent little garden?'

'It has a small front garden with roses and lots of flowers and out the back there is a vegetable patch. It's a bit overgrown at the moment, but once it is dug over it will be lovely.'

'Ah, that sounds all right,' he said and smiled at her. 'Would you mind if I came over next week and took a look?'

'I'd love it if you did,' Janet assured him. 'If you were to stay with Sheila, we could get the garden done together while the tradesmen do their bit. I've ripped all the old stuff out already and I'll be decorating, but we need plumbers, electricians and a plasterer first and maybe a carpenter.' She laughed. 'I've got all sorts of ideas to make it nice and cosy.'

'I'm not bad with a paintbrush,' he said. 'I might give you a hand.' He looked around him sadly. 'I didn't want to leave my wife, but she's not here, is she? She hated living here.'

Janet took a deep breath. 'I don't really know what to think about the afterlife, but I've always felt that if there is a heaven, then it would be with people you love in a nice place, somewhere you knew and loved.'

'That's a good thought,' he said and gave a little chuckle. 'If that's true, my Dorrie will be back behind the bar of the Dog & Pheasant pulling pints for the regulars. She hated it when we had to give it up.'

'My mother is much the same. I'm not sure what she'll do if she ever has to give up.'

He nodded and went off to find his daughter, who Janet knew to be in the kitchen washing up. She would have offered to help but thought they might like some time alone so went over to Pip and told him that his father-in-law would probably be coming to stay after all.

'If he does, he can have my room. I'll squeeze into the caravan with the boys,' she said.

'You're a brick, Janet,' Pip replied and grinned at her. 'I'm looking forward to our new venture.'

'We'll talk about it some more when this is all over,' she said and went to Able, who was talking to Sheila and Pip's son, Chris. He looked as though he'd cried during the ceremony, but now he was nodding and smiling.

'I was just asking Chris about his music,' Able said. 'He was telling me that he has been invited to a gig – whatever that is – with a local group.'

'You know what a gig is, Grandad Able,' Chris rebuked and laughed. 'Yours was the first jukebox I ever saw when Mum and Dad brought me to your café one summer.'

'I had it sent over from America and the youngsters loved it,' Able explained, grinning, 'Just as they loved my pancakes and milkshakes.'

'Do you make them now?' Chris asked.

'Yes, sometimes, though just for the family,' Able told him. 'How about I make some this evening when we get home?'

'Yes, please,' Chris said and his young face lit up. 'I'd love a strawberry milkshake and... I'm not sure what kind of pancakes.'

'I'll make a selection.' Able smiled. 'I bought some ingredients from a shop yesterday and thought we might all have some another day.'

'You'll be leaving in a few days,' Chris said. 'Your holiday was spoiled this time.'

'These things happen,' Able replied, 'but it wasn't truly spoiled because we got to see our family all together and that's what really makes a lovely time. You don't have to do lots of fancy things to be happy to be together.'

Chris nodded. 'You always make things better. I'm glad we've got you, Grandad. You won't go away anywhere, will you?'

'I'll be around for a long time,' Able reassured him. 'But you're the one who will grow up and leave us, Chris – when you're a famous musician like Elvis Presley or Jerry Lee Lewis.'

'Don't be daft,' Chris said and punched him playfully in the arm. 'I'm good at playing my guitar, but I'll never be famous and I can't sing like they can.'

'How do you know?' Able challenged. 'It could happen – look at any of the rock 'n' roll stars and ask yourself if any of them expected to be famous. If you've been asked to play in a local group you might be spotted and get a chance to make records. And I like your singing, but your real talent is the way you make that guitar sing. I bet Elvis can't do that – he just strums and wiggles his hips around...' Able did what he fondly thought was an Elvis Presley move.

'Daft!' Chris giggled and poked him in the ribs. 'It's just a hobby I like.'

'You could do well,' Able told him. 'If you keep playing, I think you would make a lot of people happy just to listen to you.'

'Honestly?'

Able nodded and Chris stared at him.

'I'm not sure Dad would approve. He thinks I should be an accountant. I'm pretty good with maths and he thinks a nice steady job would be security for me.'

'And what do you want to do?' Able asked.

'Play guitar, eat pancakes and drink milkshakes,' Chris replied and grinned. 'I've got school for another two years at least, Grandad, and then college if Dad has his way.'

'Yes, plenty of time to make up your mind,' Able agreed. 'But the sky is there, Chris. Reach for it and you might grab a star.'

Chris burst out laughing and then stopped as his other grandfather entered the room, but he was smiling, too, and he came over to them, offering his hand to Able.

'Good to see you again. We haven't met much before this, but Sheila has told me so much about you – and you've made this lad smile again.' He ruffled Chris' hair and he hugged his arm. 'I'll be seeing more of him in future. I shall be living just around the corner.'

'That is good news,' Able said. 'If you ever feel like a trip up to London, visit us. Don't go to a hotel. We can put you up, either with us or in the boarding house, and we'd love to see you and Sheila and this one – if he can spare us the time once he's famous.'

Chris gave him another half-hearted punch. 'I told you, Dad doesn't want me to play professionally. He thinks accountancy is a better job, as I don't want to be an architect or draw planes.'

'The money those rock stars earn must be more than an accountant,' his maternal grandfather said and smiled. 'I reckon if you get a chance of a record deal one day we could change your dad's mind, don't you?'

'Perhaps,' Chris said and smiled. 'If you both persuade him.'

Janet looked at Able then, who had glanced at his watch. 'Do you want to get off?' she asked. 'Pip and Sheila are staying here this evening and will probably come back tomorrow morning.'

'Yes, I think we should,' Able said, 'or Peggy will worry. Are you coming back with us, Chris?'

'Yes, please – you promised pancakes and milkshakes.'

'So I did,' Able put a hand on his shoulder. 'Tell your mum and dad we're off then and I'll bring the car round.'

Janet went to say her goodbyes. 'I want to be home when Maggie rings if I can,' she told her brother. 'She said she would let us know how they were getting on.'

'They'll hardly know after half a day,' Pip said and smiled and then hugged her. 'Yes, I know, love. She's still your baby even if she is eighteen.'

'You wait until your turn comes,' Janet remarked and laughed. 'At least I let her go and Mum let Fay have her way – not that that is unusual...'

'Mum isn't the pushover you think,' Pip said. 'I know she moved to London because of Fay's skating, but she'd missed it – she loves being behind the bar at the Pig & Whistle, always has.'

'Do you think it has upset her – Maggie and Fay wanting to take over?'

'Not a bit, but I can't see her giving up altogether. It's good though if she can hand on some of the work. If they do most of the cooking, it gives her more time to talk to her friends in the bar.'

'That is what she said, but I wouldn't want her to feel she is being pushed out.'

'Do you really think anyone could push her out if she didn't want to go?' Pip raised his brows. 'I'm hoping she'll get more holidays and even go to America for a visit. I know Able wants to take her, but he hasn't said much because she was always so busy, but now they'll have more time. I'll get to see them more often too.'

'And me – you'll get fed up with me,' Janet teased, but he shook his head.

Everyone was getting ready to leave. Janet kissed Sheila's cheek and was hugged and then she took Chris out to the car, where Able was waiting. She was eager to get home, speak to Maggie, and then she might just walk down to the cottage and see if the plasterer had finished the ceiling, he'd been working on that day. But first of all she would ask Jon if he was okay, though she knew the answer. He'd been with his Granny Peggy, which meant he'd be fine. He always responded to her and seemed a different child when she was around.

Janet smiled. It would be so much better if they could live nearer to her mother. She would have to speak to Ryan about it and see if he was willing to move closer to London so Jon could see his Granny more.

* * *

'I'd better ring Mum,' Maggie said as Fay finished eating her slice of cake. They'd had one lesson that afternoon after settling in and were told that they needed to be in the kitchens by seven the next morning to begin their instruction. 'She will be anxious and so will Granny Peggy.'

Fay nodded and licked her fingers. 'I love coffee and walnut cake,' she said. 'Mum makes a nice one sometimes but not often enough, that one was delicious.'

The cake they'd had demonstrated and then been invited to taste was exceptionally light and moist and delicious and both girls had enjoyed it, though Maggie had stuck to one slice, while Fay had eaten two.

'Yes, it was good, but I imagine everything Francois cooks will be delicious,' Maggie said and rolled her eyes teasingly. 'He is as dreamy as his cakes...'

'I think he was in a dream.' Fay giggled. 'The way he was looking at you all through the lesson – I believe he likes you, Maggie.'

'He is French,' Maggie replied scornfully. 'They are flirts – my friend, Janice, fell in love on a skiing trip one year with a Frenchman. She said he told her she was the most beautiful girl in the world and wanted to make love to her...'

Fay gasped. 'She didn't?'

'No, she didn't but she wanted to,' Maggie said. 'She was scared to death of what her parents would do if they found out, so she resisted, but she said he made her melt inside and she would love him until her dying day.'

'That's rubbish,' Fay retorted. 'I'm never going to fall in love like that – I don't want to be tied to one man forever. I want to live and learn to be a famous cook – and, if I want to make love with a man I will... when I'm ready.'

Maggie gave her a straight look. 'You know we agreed, no serious men for years for either of us. We can flirt and have fun, but no sex, Fay. I don't want you falling for a baby and having to get married. Your mother would kill me for letting you get into trouble and it would ruin everything.'

'I told you,' Fay replied. 'I know I'm not ready yet – however dreamy a man is. I don't ever want to marry and I am determined that our business makes us rich and famous.'

'Yes, that's what we both want,' Maggie said and laughed. 'I could have had sex already if I'd wanted to...'

'Who with?' Fay asked, looking at her in surprise and delight. 'Was he wonderful?'

'Sort of – in a way,' Maggie told her. 'His name was Jason and he wears jodhpurs and shirts with rolled-up sleeves and he's tanned from being outdoors all the time. He took us riding – he taught Mum as well, because she couldn't until recently, but he was nice and very sexy. He told me I was beautiful and kept whispering things about how much he would like to take me out and to make love to me...'

'Whatever did you do?' Fay was wide-eyed.

'I just laughed at him,' Maggie said. 'Oh, he's nice enough – but when I marry, it will be to someone I can trust.' She smiled secretly. 'Now, there is someone I wouldn't mind making love with if I was ready to—'

'Tell!' Fay demanded.

'He's an artist,' Maggie said. 'I took him some food before we left London and he was so hungry – but he hardly knows I'm alive. He just said I had good bone structure and he would like to paint my face when he had time.'

'But he doesn't now?'

'No, he's too busy.' Maggie laughed. 'I much prefer him to Jason.'

'Isn't he trustworthy? Jason, I mean, not your artist."

Maggie thought for a moment and then shook her head. 'I wouldn't trust him as far as I could throw him.' She laughed. 'No, I want someone like Able – who is kind and loving and adores me.' She smiled at Fay. 'But not for years and years...'

'Good. We have to stick together and make ourselves very rich.' They smiled at each other, secure in the surety of youth and friendship that they would do just that. 'And now we'd better go and phone our mothers before they start calling the police.'

Laughing, they went off to find the pay phone and do just that.

18

LONDON

'Well, they look very much better,' Shirley said as she finished applying salve to Mitsy's feet. 'They must feel easier now, don't they?'

Mitsy tipped her head to one side. 'Well, that depends,' she replied and gave Shirley a long, hard look. 'If I can come back and see you next week anyway, they are and if I can't, they ain't.'

'Of course, you can visit me,' Shirley said and nodded to the biscuit tin she now kept on her desk. 'You can come and have a biscuit and a cup of tea with me any time – and I have some of the bourbon creams you like.'

'You're all right,' Mitsy said and helped herself to three of the biscuits, tucking them into her coat pocket for later. She got up to leave and then turned back. 'I've got this friend, Billy his name is. He lives in this derelict building by the river where several of us stay; he ain't well, Doctor Shirley, but he won't come to the clinic. He's terrified he'll be put in an old folks' home if he does and he don't want to go.' Her eyes looked directly at Shirley and she knew what she was asking.

'You want me to come and visit him there?'

Mitsy grinned at her, showing her blackened teeth. 'Would yer come?' she asked. 'I worry about him, see, but he won't let me bring him in.'

'Yes, I'll come this evening,' Shirley told her. 'But you'll need to tell me where it is.'

'I'll be here when you close and I'll take you,' Mitsy said. 'We don't say where we are in case the coppers move us on – and there's ears at doors.' She glared at the door as it opened and a nurse entered.

'You next patient is waiting, Doctor Shirley,' the nurse informed her.

'Don't forget.' Mitsy shot a darkling look at her as she left.

'I shan't,' Shirley promised. 'I shall see you this evening.'

Mitsy nodded and went off, directing a malevolent glare at the nurse as she passed her.

'I hope you haven't promised to go and visit one of the tramps alone?' the nurse said, frowning at Shirley. 'I must warn you, Doctor Shirley – it isn't safe to venture down by the docks late at night on your own. There are all sorts about and you could be attacked.'

'Thank you so much for the warning,' Shirley said and smiled at her pleasantly. 'I know you mean it for the best, nurse, and I shall be very careful, I promise you – but I shan't be alone. Mitsy will be with me and I think I'll be quite safe with her. She is a feisty, old lady and I doubt any of her companions will want to get on the wrong side of her.'

'I didn't mean them,' the nurse sniffed. 'There are gangs of Teddy boys and all sorts... There was a murder down there only a month ago. A woman... well, she was one of those, if you know what I mean, plying her trade – but she still had the right to walk the streets unmolested and she didn't deserve to die.'

'I completely agree with you,' Shirley said. 'I shall take an umbrella with me and if anyone attacks me, I'll give them a sore head.'

'Well, you know your own business best,' the nurse said and shut the door with a snap as she went out.

Shirley smiled to herself. It was fortunate that she wasn't going out this evening. She'd enjoyed her night out at the rock 'n' roll dance and she'd told Gordy all about it the following day. He'd loved her choice of records for his new player and told her that he liked music better than anything, except books.

'I like to read adventure stories,' he'd confessed. 'Freddie lent me several of his books about explorers and some war stories. He plays football with me sometimes...'

'I'm glad you like Freddie.'

Gordy had nodded. 'I'm glad you're home, Shirley. I'm frightened about Dad – he's very ill, isn't he?'

'Yes, he is ill, but we're looking after him.' Shirley sighed as she thought about the long time she'd spent talking to Gordy about their father. He was a serious boy and none of them had realised how much he'd picked up about his father's illness. She would have to try to take him out as much as possible to take his mind off it. Perhaps she would spend some time with him if he was still up when she got home after visiting her patients that evening.

Shirley hadn't dismissed the nurse's warning completely. The murder had shocked everyone and Shirley was aware that the murderer hadn't been caught yet. She wouldn't dream of venturing into some of those dark lanes down near the docks alone, but with Mitsy, she was sure she would be perfectly safe. There was a law of the streets and they protected their own. As a doctor who could be trusted, she would be protected and watched over whether she was aware of it or not.

* * *

Shirley saw Mitsy waiting for when she left the clinic that evening and she went up to greet her. 'I've brought a few things that may help,' she told the old lady, 'But if your friend is seriously ill, he may need hospital treatment—'

'Billy won't go near them,' Mitsy said. 'You do what you can, Doctor Shirley. We don't expect no miracles.'

'I'll do what I can for him,' Shirley promised her and followed close by her side as she led the way.

The last part of the journey was very dark and Shirley was lost long before they got there, which was probably deliberate so that she couldn't tell anyone where to go, but eventually they arrived at what looked like a deserted warehouse. Inside, it was dimly lit by a variety of lights: candles in jars and an oil lamp or two. Mitsy led her to what looked like a bundle of rags but turned out to be a man, older than Mitsy and suffering from what looked to be quite a bit of pain.

'I'm Doctor Shirley,' she said, kneeling down next to him. 'Where does it hurt, Billy?'

'It's me leg, Doc,' he said and pulled up the right leg. The sores were horrendous and Shirley barely held back her gasp.

She took out a thermos flask, which she had filled with warm water at the clinic and washed very carefully around the infected leg. Some of the sores were suppurating and Shirley squeezed gently at the edges to remove as much of the yellow puss as she could, before applying the same salve as she'd used for Mitsy. She then took a penicillin tablet from her bag and gave it to him.

'Swallow this, Billy. I am going to give you several of them and I want you to take three a day until they're all gone – is that all right with you?'

'Yeah, if you say so – Mitsy says you're all right...' He gave her a grin, his teeth black and yellow. 'I know I'm an old fool, but I don't want ter die in one of them places. I'd rather go 'ere wiv me friends.'

'I can understand that and I'm not going to put you in a home – or a hospital, as it turns out. I can treat your leg myself and I shall. I'll come again tomorrow, if I may – and if Mitsy will fetch me?'

'I'll fetch yer,' Mitsy promised, 'and I'll take yer back – but yer will be all right round here, Doctor Shirley. We look after our own.' She grinned at Shirley, who felt honoured to have been selected as being worthy of being called a friend.

Shirley took a quarter of a pound of tea, a packet of biscuits and a tin of condensed milk from her bag and put them beside Billy. She didn't say anything and nor did he, but she knew by the sudden gleam in his eyes that he appreciated her gesture.

After she was finished, Mitsy walked her back until they were in well lit streets, leaving Shirley to walk the rest of the way home alone, but before she went, Mitsy warned her, 'Don't linger in these parts alone, Doctor Shirley. We won't harm you – but there's others will. They won't dare when one of us is around, but there's some are bad right through.'

'Yes, I was warned there was a murder recently...'

'Doris was a nice enough girl,' Mitsy said. 'She often gave yer sixpence fer a cup of char if she had it – the bugger what done for 'er won't last long when we get 'im, don't yer worry. Until we do, it ain't safe to linger.'

'Thank you, I shan't forget,' Shirley said and smiled.

* * *

Shirley glanced over her shoulder a few times as she walked, but it all looked quite safe. A respectable man had just parked his smart car next to one of the newly installed parking meters, which had been introduced in July, and was feeding it with coins, before entering a late-night grocer's. A woman and a man were walking arm-in-arm on the other side of the road. Besides, why would anyone attack her? She wasn't carrying anything much of value. In her pocket was a purse with a few coins, because she never carried much money, but her doctor's bag was expensive and the contents were worth money. Some thieves would knock you on the head for a shilling. Shirley had never felt vulnerable walking alone at night, but she shivered a couple of times that night and had a distinct feeling that she was being followed.

However, as she approached her home, a man came towards her and she knew him at once. 'Able...' she said. 'You're back then – when did you get home?'

'Just this afternoon,' Able replied and smiled at her. 'I've just been to your house with something Peggy wanted Maureen to have – and they were a bit worried about you, because you're later than usual.'

'Yes, I know,' Shirley said and smiled at him. 'I went to see a patient at his home so I was delayed. Did you have a nice holiday – despite what happened to Sheila's mother?'

'Yes, we did,' Able said and smiled at her. 'I was only saying to Maureen that it was worth the journey just to see the family.'

'Yes, that is how I felt when I was in uni,' Shirley agreed. 'I'd best get home then or Dad will be on the phone to the police.'

Able laughed, waved, and she walked on past him and up to her front door. Once inside, the warmth and welcome of her home made her completely forget the uncomfortable feeling she'd had after she'd left Mitsy.

* * *

The headlines in the evening paper the following day shocked everyone. Another murder had been committed. A young woman – no more than sixteen – had been killed while soliciting custom down by the docks. On her way home, Shirley shuddered as she read the message on the newsboy's stand and walked on without buying the paper. Her father would already have it and no doubt she would hear about it when she got in.

Mitsy had fetched her from the clinic and there had been several of her friends waiting to be seen by the doctor when she got to the warehouse but afterwards Mitsy and a younger man walked her almost to her door.

'It's bad times, Doctor Shirley,' Mitsy told her, shaking her head. 'You're safe with us – we'll make sure of that, but don't you try coming out alone.'

'I wouldn't know where to come,' Shirley told her with a smile. 'I am grateful for your care, Mitsy. Thank you so much for looking after me.'

'It's us what are grateful,' Mitsy replied and grinned. 'I reckon you'll be gettin' a lot more customers soon, Doctor Shirley.'

Shirley nodded. She had enjoyed her impromptu clinic and thus far all the cases that had come to her had been treatable. What she would do when someone needed the hospital urgently, she had no idea. Billy and the others she'd seen could all have come to the clinic, but they were wary of being put away – and some of them might even have been wanted by the police – but they behaved well to her and she was happy to do what she could for them. After all, that is why she'd become a doctor and wanted to work in the East End of London, because she knew and liked these people – the people she'd grown up with.

Shirley smiled as she went into her home, to a dinner of shepherd's pie and green beans.

'There's a letter on the shelf for you,' Maureen said as she finished washing her hands and sat down. 'I don't think it is from Keith... it has a Durham postmark...'

'From the hospital,' Shirley said and got up to fetch it. 'I didn't think they had anything to send me.'

She looked at the address and the writing seemed familiar, but she wasn't sure who it belonged to until she opened it and her heart jumped with surprise and pleasure.

'Oh, it's from Mr Anderson – he is coming down to London to give a lecture next week and wants to take me out to dinner...'

'That's nice,' Maureen commented, looking at her curiously. 'Isn't he one of the consultants – you said how good he was with children, didn't you?'

'Yes. He is a brilliant doctor, Mum. I could have joined his specialist team, but I wanted to come home.'

'Yes, I recall you saying something of the sort.' Maureen smiled. 'Well, isn't that nice of him – asking you out?'

'Yes, it is lovely,' Shirley said and a warm feeling spread through her. 'I think I shall enjoy it.'

19

'He is coming down to give a lecture or something,' Maureen told Peggy the next day when she popped into the pub kitchen and made a few rock cakes as they talked. 'He's asked her out to dinner – so he must think a bit of her, don't you think?'

'Well, he must like her or he wouldn't have bothered,' Peggy agreed and then smiled. 'I know you're anxious because that chap went back to Africa and you'd thought they might marry, but don't read too much into it, Maureen. This Mr Anderson is probably just a colleague looking to kill a couple of hours.'

'You may be right,' Maureen said with a sigh. 'I tend to worry about her future – but she did look so happy when she opened the letter.'

'You'll just have to wait and see,' Peggy teased her. 'Why do you worry about her Maureen? Surely she has a wonderful future all mapped out now she's a doctor?'

'Yes, but she's got very involved with these homeless people she has been treating at the clinic, and she goes off to this derelict warehouse down near the East India Docks and it's dark and not a good area, frequented by women of a certain sort. I'm terrified something bad will happen to her one of these nights.' Maureen sighed. 'She laughs and says she's being well looked after by her patients – but there have been two murders recently.'

'Yes, there has,' Peggy agreed, suddenly serious. 'Shirley should be very careful. I know the people she's looking after won't harm her, but there are all sorts about. It isn't a good idea to be walking the streets alone after dark, particularly at the moment.'

'I've told her, and Gordon said she should stick to treating them at the clinic or take one of her colleagues with her, but she won't listen. You know what the young folk are like. They think they're invincible.'

Peggy nodded. 'Maggie and Fay have gone off on that course down in Devon. They rang the first evening and said it was all fine, but you can't help worrying – and if there was a murderer on the loose down there, I should be fretting all the time. It's a while since we had anything like that round here – do you remember when Ellie, the young woman who did hairdressing, was attacked and raped?'

'Yes, I do, and her attacker was murdered. I've always thought her husband had something to do with that, Peggy – he was a nasty sort.'

'Well, he murdered Mrs Tandy when she stopped him seeing Ellie,' Peggy said. 'He might have got away with it if you hadn't seen him running away.'

'Poor Mrs Tandy. I still think of her...' Maureen shook her head. 'She was such a good friend to me during the war, saving wool for me when I couldn't afford to buy it all at once. Where have all the years gone since then, Peggy? There's my Shirley a doctor and your twins nearly grown up.'

'Don't say nearly to Freddie,' Peggy grinned. 'He thinks he's a man now – he actually had a shave the other day. I'm sure he didn't really need it, but Able says that once he starts, he'll need to keep on.'

'They can't wait to grow up – or are we getting old, Peggy?'

'Us?' Peggy looked at her and laughed. 'Never! I refuse to be old. When I'm ninety I'm going on a round-the-world trip and then jumping out of an aeroplane – with a parachute.'

Maureen started to giggle and couldn't stop until she began to cough and Peggy gave her a glass of water. 'I thought for a minute you were going to go out with a grand gesture and jump to end it all.'

'Nah – I'll probably climb Everest the following year,' Peggy said with a wicked look.

'Don't start me off again,' Maureen begged, 'But I can just see it – you doing a parachute jump at ninety.' She shook her head. 'Just wait until I tell Gordon what you've got planned for the future.'

'He'll say, "Well, she's always been slightly nuts, hasn't she?"' Peggy laughed as Maureen shook her head.

'Gordon thinks you're a marvel, bringing up the twins and working as hard as you do.'

'Well, I must have been slightly mad to have twins at my age,' Peggy said, still in a mischievous mood. She fetched coffee cake for them and poured coffee from the pot she kept warm on the stove. Her mood had sobered as she looked at Maureen. 'Joking over, love. You ought to warn Shirley again, make sure she has some sort of weapon, a stick or a packet of pepper to throw at someone if she does get into trouble by the docks.'

'She says she has a big needle in her bag and she'll stick that in him if anyone goes for her, but she swears she's being escorted and protected, so we can't forbid her to do it. She wouldn't listen if we did.'

* * *

'Are you intending to visit those people again this evening, Doctor Shirley?' the nurse asked her as she brought her a cup of tea during a short lull in the stream of patients. 'They really should be made to visit the clinic, you know.'

'Yes, I know, nurse,' Shirley said, 'but none of them were prepared to visit us for fear of being sent to hospital or an old people's home.'

'Some of them would be much better off in the infirmary or a home,' the nurse said. 'Just be careful that you make a note of the drugs you take with you, Doctor Shirley, and don't carry morphine – some of them would kill to get their hands on it.'

'I never take anything like that with me,' Shirley said. Clearly, the nurse thought she was a novice! 'If someone was in that much pain, I would need to send for an ambulance – and I'd have to justify the use of dangerous drugs with my colleagues and my conscience.' Shirley gave her a straight look. 'I may be young, Nurse Wright, but I am fully qualified and quite sensible, you know. Most of what I've treated are wounds that have festered, coughs and chest infections. I do use penicillin, which I sign for, and simple pain relief tablets like aspirin.'

The nurse flushed at the mild rebuke and then nodded. 'I'm just concerned for your safety, Doctor Shirley. I've been working here longer than you and I know what these people can be.'

'Yes, I know and thank you for your concern.' Shirley tried a smile to reassure her. Nurse Wright tended to impose her opinions, something that some doctors would have stamped on; Shirley tried to appease her when she could.

'You've come from away and you don't know the area...' the nurse said.

'Where were you born? I don't think it was in London, was it?' Shirley asked calmly, and, as the woman stared, 'I was born not far from here, and I lived here all my life until I went to university. I think you came from somewhere down south...'

The nurse went out without another word, giving an audible sniff of disgust as she shut the door with a little snap.

Shirley sighed. She hadn't intended to make an enemy of the nurse, but she'd gone beyond her remit and Shirley wasn't prepared to have her decisions questioned. Some of the nurses tended to think they knew more than the newly qualified doctors and it had happened even at the hospital. In some cases, it did no harm to question a prescription if the nurse felt it was the wrong dose, but to try to bully her into giving up what she felt was an important part of her work just wasn't on.

Yes, it was true that Shirley had felt uncomfortable the first night after Mitsy left her, but now they were escorting her there and back, almost to her front door. The younger man never spoke to Shirley, but although clearly down on his luck and poorly dressed, he looked strong and perfectly capable of scaring off anyone who came near them.

Shirley had thought of what she might do if she were attacked one night on her way home. After all, when the dark evenings came, she would be walking back from the surgery in the light of street lamps. A needle in her bag wasn't much good, even though she'd suggested it to Maureen. So she'd bought a little box of pepper that she could just pull the top off and had decided she would throw it into the face of an attacker and she also had her bag, which she could use as a weapon if need be. A little shiver went down her back as she thought of the reason behind all the concern. It was rather horrible – two women murdered in the past three months. Both of them were ladies of the night, but Nurse Wright had a point – any woman walking alone at night in the wrong place was vulnerable.

Perhaps she should buy herself a whistle too. It wouldn't stop the attacker, but it would alert others to the fact that she was in trouble.

* * *

Shirley visited her out-of-clinic patients again that evening and returned completely unharmed to her home. She washed her hair and went to bed earlier than usual that night, because the next evening she was going out with Mr Anderson and she was really looking forward to seeing him again.

She'd been concentrating on work since Keith had gone back to Africa, and, apart from the visit to the rock 'n' roll dance, Shirley had only been out once to visit a cinema with Gordy, where she saw the musical *Oklahoma*, which had been made in 1955. Shirley had wanted to see it when it first came out but had been too busy studying for exams that year. It was making the rounds of the cinemas again and she went one Saturday with her younger brother, who hadn't seen it either, munching their way through a bag of toffees and an ice cream apiece in the interval.

They both thoroughly enjoyed it, even though the story was impossibly romantic. Since then, Shirley had spent her Saturday evenings either writing up medical notes, talking to her parents or watching the *Six-Five Special* on the television with Gordy. It was introduced by Pete Murray and its resident band was Don Lang and his Frantic Five. Maureen liked it best when Lonnie Donegan was on the show because he made her laugh.

Shirley's father had bought one of the latest televisions from Pye and they watched it in the sitting room for a couple of hours in the evenings. Her father really only liked the news and sport, but Maureen liked the same programmes as Shirley and they watched popular shows together and the occasional film, though Maureen always knitted throughout the films. She said it helped her to concentrate.

* * *

The next day, after a relatively quiet list at the practice, Shirley went home and got ready to be taken out to dinner. When her former tutor arrived, she took him into the kitchen and introduced him to her father and Maureen. She could see immediately that Maureen was a little shocked and overawed at his presence, because in his smart tailored suit, Mr Anderson had a commanding air, but her father stood up and shook hands and said all the right things. He invited their guest to sit down for a moment and they talked about the recent developments in relations between the USA and Britain with the agreement that nuclear missiles would soon be delivered to a RAF station in Feltwell, for use by them in an emergency, and the trouble that was bound to cause with the protestors. Shirley saw that her father approved of her colleague and smiled at them.

'Well, we'd better not keep you any longer – but come and see us whenever you are in London, Ray,' he said.

Mr Anderson had asked her father to call him that and Shirley felt he was relaxed and very much at home in their kitchen, which was, of course, spotless and smelled of baking as always. He smiled and said he would be delighted to call in another day, then held Shirley's coat for her. She was conscious of his hand touching her neck, even though it was brief.

'That article in *The Lancet* – about the new ultrasound for diagnostics in obstetrics...' Shirley said as they went out to the smart car standing outside. 'What did you think of it?'

'A step forward.' He smiled at her. 'As you know, I'm more of a heart and lungs man. We're making progress in that field too – and I'm sure you will be reading about it in *The Lancet* soon. I'm glad you're keeping on with your reading, Doctor Shirley.'

'You can never know too much,' she said and then saw the glimmer in his eyes. 'Stop teasing me. I know you're laughing at me.'

'Not *at* you – because you make me feel happy.'

His words made her feel breathless and for a moment she couldn't think of what to say. 'Where are we going?' Shirley managed to ask when he held the door of his car open for her to get in a few moments later.

'I'm staying at the Savoy so I booked there – I hope that is all right?' he replied. 'Is it trendy enough for you? I suppose I should have looked up where all the young things go these days?'

She heard the undertone of gentle mockery in his voice and said, 'The Savoy will be lovely, thank you. I've never been. My mother went to a grand dinner there once, but it isn't something most folks round here can afford and I wouldn't know what was trendy if you took me.'

Her companion chuckled. 'You haven't changed, Doctor Shirley.'

'Nor have you – shame on you!' She laughed. 'How are you – impossibly busy as always?'

'As always – but I made time for this little trip. They've been asking me for some time to give a lecture at the Royal Society – it is tomorrow evening at their rooms overlooking the Mall and St James's Park if you'd like to come?'

'Yes, I think I might,' Shirley replied and smiled. 'I know where it is – do I need a ticket to get in?'

'I'll give you a guest ticket,' he said. 'There will be a little drinks party afterwards, if you would care to come?'

'I'll come to the lecture,' Shirley said, 'but I'm a working girl. Too many late nights isn't good for me...'

'Ah yes, you always were one of my more sensible students,' he remarked and smiled wryly. 'Unfortunately, I can't get out of it. So I shan't see you again after tonight as I have to return to the hospital that evening... so we shall just have to make the most of this evening.'

'Yes, we will,' Shirley said. 'I'm starving. I hope there is plenty of nice food.'

'I think we can promise you that,' he replied, his eyes twinkling with humour. 'You do me good, Doctor Shirley. There I was basking in the glory of being treated like an important man, my stay at the Savoy is being paid for by the Society, and you bring me right back down to the ground.'

'You are an important man and they were lucky to get you,' she said, laughing up at him. 'However, that doesn't stop me wanting to be fed...'

'How true – it all boils down to that in the end, doesn't it? The human condition depends on a full stomach.'

'And a few other bits and pieces, like a good health service,' Shirley replied. 'A friend of mine has just returned to Africa. He has a new centre to set up for people who really are in need of both food and medicines.'

His smile disappeared. 'Were you tempted to offer your services?'

'No. I wished him luck – but this is my life. I've been very busy, too, since I came home.'

'Tell me about it,' he invited and so she did.

* * *

'I haven't enjoyed myself as much in years – and I hope to do it again one day soon,' Ray Anderson said as he dropped her at her house later that night.

'Thank you, Ray.' Shirley offered her hand, suddenly a little shy. He had insisted that she call him by his first name and so she'd given in. After all, they were no longer tutor and pupil and in the opulence of the Savoy Hotel, which had slightly overwhelmed her at first, it would have been ridiculous to keep up the barrier. So she'd let it down and was soon laughing as he entertained her with witty jokes and stories of one of his students in medical school at the university. 'It was the nicest evening I ever had and I loved it. Thank you so very much for taking me.'

'You're very welcome,' he said and took her hand, gazing down at her again. 'If I came down for a weekend, would you go to a show and dine with me again somewhere?'

'That sounds wonderful,' Shirley said and felt the pressure of his grasp as he held her hand a little longer than strictly necessary. 'Thank you – are you giving another lecture then?'

'No. Next time I come it will be purely for the pleasure of seeing you, Doctor Shirley.' He leaned forward and gave her the lightest of kisses on her lips. 'Take care of yourself. I'll write and let you know in plenty of time...'

'We are on the telephone, you know,' Shirley said and took a little notebook from her bag, scribbling it down for him. 'You can ring me if you wish.'

'Thank you, I shall.' He smiled. 'Keep doing what you want, Doctor Shirley, and don't let anyone change you...'

'I won't,' she said and then turned and went into the house, standing with her back against the front door, listening to the sound of his car engine as he drove away, back to his hotel.

Her eyes closed for a moment and she felt the sting of sudden tears. What sort of an idiot was she? Crying after she'd had such a wonderful evening? Yet she knew in her heart just why the tears had come – she'd done a stupid thing. She'd fallen in love with a man several years her senior from a world that wasn't and never could be hers. It had happened slowly over all the years she'd worked with him and learned from him, always admiring his work but never really knowing him. Now she'd seen the man beneath the stern face he showed to his students and she understood why she'd felt the wrench when she left the hospital she'd worked at after completing her medical studies.

20

'Gosh, I never knew cooking could be such hard work,' Fay exclaimed when she and Maggie reached their room and both collapsed onto their beds. 'I mean, I adored the afternoon session – those cakes were exquisite and tasted like nothing I've ever tasted before, but enough is enough!'

They had both been asked to help with the evening service for the hotel and after a hectic session at lunch, the afternoon lessons and then a very busy evening service, the two girls were nearly dead on their feet.

'I warned you it would be hard,' Maggie said and yawned. 'But when we're up and running, we'll have our own sous chefs to do the chopping and peeling. We'll just be doing the work we enjoy – me mixing sauces and cooking pies and gorgeous food and you making cakes and desserts.'

'Thank goodness for that,' Fay said. 'It's exciting though, the course, isn't it? Are you enjoying it, Maggie?'

'Yes, I enjoy the baking lessons,' Maggie agreed. 'Especially when it is Francois taking it – but I really prefer the kitchen service. I like to watch the chefs, see what they're doing and make notes in my head. Paul let me make the sauces today for the scallops. He showed me once and then let me try and when he was satisfied, he let me get on with it while he prepared the fish for another dish.'

'Was it difficult?'

'Not really – once you learn the balance. It was a light lemon flavour. Too much and it is sour, too little and it doesn't taste of anything, but get it just right and it is delicious.'

'I'm glad you enjoyed doing that,' Fay said and smiled at her. 'I'm really grateful, you know. Mum would never have let me come here if it hadn't been for you wanting to do the course too.'

'No need for gratitude, infant,' Maggie said loftily and received a pillow in the face, which she returned with twice as much power. 'I'm having fun resisting Francois' efforts to seduce me with his eyes.'

'He does look at you a lot, Maggie – you won't be tempted, will you?'

'Tempted, yes, an idiot, no,' Maggie said and laughed as she saw Fay's face. 'I'd just be another notch on his bedpost and if he thinks I'm going to fall for lines like, "You are the most beautiful girl I've ever seen..." he's got a long time to wait.'

'But you are beautiful,' Fay replied. 'I'm pretty, so Mum says – but you are truly beautiful.'

'Jason whispered those lines in my ear, but when he thought I wasn't looking, I watched him, and he used the same charm on Mum. Neither of us was daft enough to fall for it.'

'You're so practical,' Fay sighed. 'If someone said that to me, I'd melt.'

'Well, just make sure your knickers don't slip down! I don't want all my plans going to waste because you were an idiot.'

'Pig!' Fay made a rude face and then they both laughed, because they knew that all they both wanted was success in their chosen career. They were in perfect harmony and having a wonderful time. Fay might not be attracting the charming Francois' hot looks as much as her cousin, however, she was enjoying Maggie's private remarks about him. And she felt that the Frenchman might feel the wind had been taken out of his sails if he could hear them – which he never would, because although he was a hopeless flirt, he was a wonderful cake and pastry chef and they wanted to learn all they could from him

'I'm going to the bathroom,' Maggie said. 'Do you want to go or are you all right?'

'I'm fine, you go,' Fay answered sleepily. 'If I don't hear you return, see you in the morning.'

'Go to sleep, love,' Maggie said and laughed as she went through into the bathroom they shared.

Fay lay back and closed her eyes, a smile on her face. She'd thought when the doctor had told her that her ankle might never be strong enough to stand up to all the hours of practice she needed to put in to become a top-class skater that everything she loved had gone, but then she'd discovered that she enjoyed making cakes as well as eating them. When Maggie came to stay with her dreams and her ideas, Fay had known she'd found the perfect partner without even trying.

One day she might skate for pleasure again, but for the moment, all she wanted was to learn how to make the fillings for those wonderful sponges she'd been learning to bake that afternoon. They'd been so light and soft, but cut into layers with a little jam, and various fillings, so delicious. It was the kind of thing she could make simply for her mother's shop or build into a fantastic creation for a large party. Just the kind of thing that she'd wanted to learn. Her mother made lovely sponges but nothing like the one she'd tasted today... it had been of such a delicate flavour. She would show her mother how to do it when... Her thoughts came to an abrupt halt as she slid into the sleep that was so fast, she didn't wake when Maggie came back and climbed into her own bed.

* * *

'Ah, Mademoiselle Fay,' Francois spoke to her as they passed in the hallway as she was on her way down to the kitchens to help prepare the lunch service.

Fay stopped and looked at him enquiringly. Despite their jests in the privacy of their room, he was their tutor and the hotel's top pastry chef, his creations bringing the guests from miles away, even abroad so she'd heard. 'Yes, Monsieur?' She waited politely for him to speak.

'You are the cousin of Mademoiselle Maggie – oui?'

'Yes, I am,' Fay said. 'She went down to the kitchen a little earlier.'

'I wish you to give her this.' He handed her an envelope that smelled of perfume. Roses, she thought. 'You will place it on her bed, please?'

Fay had an awful desire to giggle but managed to keep a straight face as she promised she would. She pushed it into her apron pocket and nodded as she continued to the kitchens. He must be desperate to go this far, she thought, and wondered how Maggie would respond to the Frenchman's love letter. It would be best to wait until after service before giving it to her, Fay thought, though every time she glanced at her cousin throughout the busy service she wanted to laugh.

'What is up with you this morning?' Maggie asked as they went upstairs to change for the afternoon lessons. 'You looked fit to burst.'

'Francois gave me this to put on your bed.' Fay handed her the envelope. 'Paul was annoyed with me because he said I was wearing perfume and it interferes with his sense of smell when he is cooking.'

They had been told not to wear perfume in the kitchens, so Maggie nodded as she held the envelope to her nose. 'It smells as though he tipped a bottle of Evening in Paris over it,' she said. 'What did he think he was doing giving it to you on your way to the kitchen. Why not give it to me during lessons?'

'Not romantic enough. I was supposed to place it on your bed.'

Maggie gave a snort of disbelief. She opened the letter and smiled. 'He has asked me to an end-of-course party. They have drinks and lots of wonderful food and everyone gets dressed up – remember they told us about it?'

'Yes – shall you go with him?' Fay asked uncertainly.

'Only if he takes both of us – unless you've been asked by a dashing young man?'

'What dashing young man?' Fay asked. Everyone on the course was either female or years older than the two girls.

'Then we'll go together and he can escort us both,' Maggie laughed as Fay's relief showed. 'Don't worry, Fay. Even if I fancied him, I wouldn't leave you alone – and I don't. He just amuses me.'

'Do you think you'll ever fall in love?'

Maggie shrugged as the sensitive face of a young man as he'd told her she had beautiful bone structure came to her mind. James hadn't been flirting and the next moment he'd sent her home with her empty dish, no flattery or desire to see her again, merely permission to take him more food if she liked. So far she hadn't had time, but when she returned to London, she might... 'Perhaps – but with someone who won't be as obvious as Francois, that's for sure,' she said and smiled. James had hardly noticed her, other than as a potential model for one of his paintings. That might be why he'd intrigued her.

'I'm glad,' Fay replied. 'If you wanted him to take you, I'd tag along with some of the other women, but I'd rather be with you.'

'As long as we stick together, we'll be fine,' Maggie said. 'One day we'll both find men we like, but it hasn't happened yet for either of us. It's too soon, Fay. We've got far too much to do before we have time for romance.'

21

Janet was busy rubbing down some woodwork when someone walked in behind her. She turned expecting it to be Sheila's father or her brother but smiled in surprise and pleasure as she saw her husband watching her.

'Ryan! I didn't think you would be here until later this evening...'

'I got away early for once.' He looked at her thoughtfully. 'I don't think I've seen you look this content for a while. You're enjoying yourself, aren't you?'

'Yes. Yes, I am,' Janet confirmed. 'I didn't know how much I enjoyed renovating things until I started on this place. I've only done a bit of decorating and made cushions and stuff before, but this time, I ripped it all out and now I'm putting it all back together.' It was a new experience for her and she'd thoroughly immersed herself in the task.

'Sometimes that is the only way,' he said and she had the feeling he meant more than the cottage. 'Janet – there's something I have to tell you and I wasn't sure how you would take it, but now, well, you have this new idea—'

'What is it, Ryan?' Janet felt cold all over. Had her moods and her boredom got to him? Had he had enough? Was he going to tell her their marriage was over? She'd been thinking of an affair – had Ryan sensed that? She hoped not because she knew that Jason meant nothing to her.

She hadn't given him a thought since she started work on the cottage. 'Is something wrong?'

'I'm leaving my job,' he said and she gave a little start of shock, because she hadn't expected that. 'I've just had enough of it, Janet. I'm sick of working all hours, never seeing you or the children – and I want a change. I'm not sure what I'll do yet and, of course, it means leaving Scotland, leaving the home we have there. I know you love it and I'm sorry, but I have to do something or I'll go mad.'

Janet stared at him and then started to laugh. 'Oh, Ryan, that's the best news I've had in ages. We could move back this way, somewhere between here and Mum. I want to continue doing properties up with Pip and I was hoping you could help me with money, but if you can't, it won't matter. We'll manage.'

'I can let you have some – but Maggie needs some, too,' Ryan said. 'I may not have as much as I've been earning these past few years, but I think we both need a change. I've known you were fed up with me working all the time. You've been wonderful putting up with it, but it isn't fair to either of us or the kids, especially Jon.' Ryan frowned. 'I was a bit worried about him, that's why I brought him down last week. He was eating sweets and he'd got a new penknife I've never seen. I asked where it came from and he said he'd had it ages, but I don't think that was the truth—'

'You think he was lying?' Janet stared at him in dismay.

'I think he might have stolen it.' Ryan looked worried. 'I know he doesn't have enough pocket money to buy a knife like that with a silver blade and a mother-of-pearl handle. You didn't buy it for him recently?'

Janet shook her head. 'No, I didn't...' She looked at him thoughtfully, unwilling to say what was in her mind.

'What?' Ryan asked. 'I know you're thinking something.'

'I thought I might have mislaid a couple of pounds from my bag this week—' She shook her head. 'No, that's nonsense. I must have spent it – and Jon wouldn't. He just wouldn't...'

'I hope he wouldn't.' Ryan sighed. 'I would hate to think our son would do anything of the kind.' He closed his eyes for a moment. 'I love you, Janet. All of you. You do know that...? If Jon has gone astray, it's my fault for being too busy to notice.'

'Yes, I know you love us and, no, it isn't just your fault. If Jon has been stealing, I should've known. I'm his mother and see him more than you. It is just as much my fault,' she said and walked towards him. 'I love you, too, Ryan, and I haven't been patient. I've moaned sometimes and I've been bored, but I'm not now. I love what I'm doing and if you wanted to join in, I know Pip would be pleased.'

'I do have some experience with property. You know I did something similar in the war and I could advise – but it isn't what I want to do...' He sighed. 'I think I'm having a mid-life crisis or something. I'm sick of offices and business meetings. I want a complete change; I don't know what I'll do... but not building work.'

'It was just a thought,' Janet said and looked at him. 'You never really told me what you did during the war. I know that you found buildings for the Government, but that was only a part of it, wasn't it?'

'I signed the Secrets Act,' he said. 'I couldn't tell you and, daft as it sounds, I still can't – but I did search out the properties as a cover for my work, that bit was always genuine, and I can help you find good ones to renovate, but I don't want to be involved more than that. I think I might like to do market gardening... If we move to the country, we'll get some land...'

'Ryan!' Janet stared at him in surprise and then started laughing. 'Are you going to turn into a farmer? I can't see you getting up every morning to milk cows...'

'No, maybe that's a step too far,' he admitted with a wry smile. 'But market gardening is different – a thing of the future. We are getting more adventurous in what we eat these days, Janet. I might like to grow asparagus, peppers, tomatoes, lettuce and stuff like that... spend time just watching them grow and who knows. I'm not sure yet...'

'Well, let me know when you are,' she said. 'I shan't complain, Ryan. You have a perfect right to change things and I'll be glad if you're around more, for all our sakes. We'll make a good life for Jon – and a home for Maggie to come back to when she visits.'

'Yes, she'll be living in London for the foreseeable future,' Ryan agreed. 'Do you mind?'

'Not if it is what she wants,' Janet said and went to brush the dust from her hands. 'I'll leave this for now. We can go for a drink and a meal some-where if you like?'

'I'll help you get this done,' Ryan said. 'We'll go out this evening to that nice pub down the road.'

'I thought you didn't want to get involved?' Janet quizzed.

'Not in the business – that's yours and Pip's. I didn't say I wouldn't give you a hand now and then.' He smiled at her as he took off his jacket and began to roll up his sleeves. 'We've never done this together, have we? I was always too busy, but I liked what you did.'

'Yes, you've always been busy,' she agreed. 'I'm glad you won't be for much longer, Ryan. When do you give up your job?'

'I quit yesterday,' he told her. 'They were shocked. Offered me more money to stay on, but I refused. I want to get out into the fresh air and be able to just stand and stare at the sky before I'm too old to enjoy it – I might even be able to take you riding. I know you enjoy it...'

'Yes, it can be pleasant.' She looked at him and saw the man she loved. Janet had almost forgotten that she did love Ryan over the years, but it all came flooding back. 'It will be even better with you.' She gave a little squeal of joy and rushed to hug him. 'I'm so glad you've made the change, no matter what you do, Ryan. It will be fun starting new things together.'

'Yes, it will,' he said and hugged her before bending his head to kiss her long and hard on the mouth. 'Thank you for not giving up on me, darling. I must have been a real pain in the backside.'

'At times,' she admitted and giggled because all the doubts had fled. She was happy again. 'But you can be very nice too...'

'And so can you,' he said.

'Let's get this paintwork rubbed down, then you can spend some time playing cricket with Jon in the garden. You'll need to talk to him, Ryan, see if you can get him to tell you what's wrong – because if he is stealing there has to be a reason...'

* * *

'I just rang Mum,' Maggie said that evening when she and Fay were relaxing in their room. 'She had some surprising news. Ryan is giving up his job and going to take up market gardening.'

Fay looked astonished. 'Good grief. I thought he was a managing director for some kind of investment firm buying land and large properties all over the place?'

'He was and he earned a lot of money,' Maggie said and tossed her long hair back from her face. 'Good for him! He was working far too long hours and all he got was money.'

'All?' Fay cocked an eyebrow. 'Isn't that one of the reasons we want to be famous cooks?'

'Yes, but it isn't everything...' Maggie looked thoughtful. 'I knew Mum got fed up spending long evenings alone. I thought she might do something silly, but then we all went down to visit Uncle Pip and it was all right. She is happy doing that cottage up and she sounds excited about the future.'

'Did you think she might kill herself?' Fay stared at her in shock.

'No, she wasn't suicidal, but I thought she might be silly enough to have an affair with someone.'

'She wouldn't! Not your mum?'

'She didn't, I know that much,' Maggie said and smiled. 'Would you like me to brush your hair for you? It looks an awful mess at the back, all tangled like a bird's nest.'

'It's too fine,' Fay said. 'I suppose I should have it cut short.'

'No, don't do that, just give it a good brush and wear it back in a French pleat instead of letting it blow all over the place and getting tangled.'

'Will you put it up for me – so I can see what it would look like?'

'Yes, of course, I will,' Maggie said and smiled. 'You can paint my toenails with that pink varnish you bought in return.'

'All right,' Fay agreed happily and sat to have her hair brushed. 'I rang Freddie while you were talking to your mother on the other phone. He says he's received an offer to trial for a big football club, but he isn't sure whether to go or not.' There were three payphone booths in the reception for the use of guests and the people on the cooking course and another in the staff quarters.

'Surely he will? It would be wonderful for him.'

'He says he has to make a choice, because if he gives up his studies, he'll lose his chance to go to university and train as a teacher.'

'But he must take this chance now he has it,' Maggie said. 'He can always go back to university later in life as a mature student.'

'Can you do that?' Fay asked and grinned as Maggie nodded. 'I'll tell him you said so and then he'll listen. He doesn't always listen to me.'

'Jon never listens to me,' Maggie replied. 'My brother is a right little pain... he'll be trouble for Mum and Dad one of these days. They have no idea what he gets up to. I was forever rescuing him when I was at home.'

'What kind of trouble?' Fay asked, her attention caught.

'Fighting with other boys and... stealing.' Maggie frowned. 'I suppose I should have told Dad, but I didn't want to sneak. He stole some sweets from the local shop. They informed me when I went in and I paid for them. I warned him that I would tell Dad if he did it again, but I'm not sure he listened and perhaps I ought to have told Dad anyway...'

'I think you should have done,' Fay said. 'If Jon thinks he can get away with it, he might start to do worse. Stealing sweets seems a small thing, but there was a girl at school who used to steal our things – just a pencil or a rubber...' Fay jerked as Maggie hit a tangle. 'Ouch! Well, this girl was in the classroom one day when a policeman turned up and asked to see her. She was taken away, because she and others had robbed a small grocer's shop. I heard they sent her away to some sort of home where bad girls go...'

'Oh dear,' Maggie said. 'It might have been an asylum. They do send girls they consider bad to places like that sometimes. It is a pity someone didn't stop her stealing when it started...'

'That's what I mean,' Fay replied. 'If your dad knew what Jon had done, he would do or say something to stop him – but if he gets away with it, who knows what he will do next...'

'Yes, that's what worries me,' Maggie said. 'I think I was wrong not to tell then, but I can't now. It would seem vindictive.'

'You should talk to Jon then,' Fay suggested. 'Make sure he understands it is wrong, because if you don't, it may lead to more trouble for your parents.'

'Yes, I shall,' Maggie said. 'Next time I see him.'

22

'Hello, darling. It has been hot today. I've got a nice ham salad for tea – would you like a cool drink?' Maureen asked when Shirley got in that evening towards the end of August. It had been a hot sultry day but overcast and she had all the windows open.

'Yes, please. We've been busy all day and I think I'll have a nice cool bath after supper.' Shirley put down her bag with a sigh.

'Good idea, love.' Maureen hesitated for a moment, then, 'There was a phone call for you a few minutes ago. It was Ray?' There was a question in her voice.

'Oh, that's Mr Anderson – you remember, the consultant from the hospital in Durham. He came down and took me to dinner when he was giving a lecture at the Royal Society. I went to see it the next evening – it was brilliant.'

'Yes, I thought so.' Maureen lifted her eyebrows. 'He sounded very interested in how you were getting on in your job...'

Shirley sat down at the table and sipped the cool lemon barley her mother had made for her. 'Did he say why he'd rung?'

'No, just wants to talk to you... Perhaps I shouldn't ask – but when he was here, I thought he must be nearly forty...?' She looked dubious.

'Yes, I suppose he is something like that, late thirties anyway,' Shirley replied. 'I'm nearly twenty-five, mum. I'm not a little girl any more.'

'I know, but fourteen years is still a large age gap.'

'It's not that much.' Shirley shrugged carelessly.

Maureen looked into Shirley's face and nodded. 'You're in love with him, aren't you?'

'Yes, I am,' Shirley admitted with a sigh. 'I know it is daft. I do know there is the big age gap – and worse, there's the other gap... he comes from a different world. I suppose it is hopeless...'

'No, it isn't hopeless,' Maureen said, surprising her. 'It's just that one day he'll be old and you'll still be comparatively young – and then it may cause you a lot of grief. If you're prepared for that, the rest of it doesn't matter. You may have been born here in the East End, Shirley, but you're not set in concrete. You can move – and if it makes you happy, you should.'

Shirley stared at her. 'How could I? This is my life. I'm happy in my work – and there's you and Dad and Gordy...'

'And we shall manage just fine wherever you are. Besides, you can visit as you did when you were at college,' Maureen said firmly. 'We want your happiness and...' She took a deep breath, glancing over her shoulder to make certain Gordon wasn't listening at the door. 'If anything should happen, you can't stop it just by being here.'

'One day soon we'll be able to help patients like Dad more,' Shirley remarked. 'I don't think I could bear to leave even if...' She laughed suddenly. 'Ray hasn't said anything about being in love with me anyway, Mum. It's just that I've fallen for him.'

'Oh, he will,' Maureen said. 'I know by the way he was talking about you on the phone to me that he cares about you a lot. Promise me, Shirley. Promise me that if he asks you to marry him and to move back up there, you won't let us stand in your way.'

'I'll think about it if he asks,' Shirley replied honestly. 'I can't promise, Mum, because at the moment I just don't know.' She laughed. 'For years I didn't even like him! I respected his work and his skill, but I didn't like him... and now.'

'You love him so much it hurts when he isn't around?' Maureen nodded.

'I suspected something when you went out to dinner with him, but when we met, I thought he was too old.'

'You don't think so now?'

'I would probably have said so once, but I understand the value of love now,' Maureen told her. 'We can't help who we love, Shirley, and we can't stop loving someone just because it isn't suitable or doesn't fit in with our plans.' She paused. 'At one time, we thought you might go off to Africa with Keith...'

'Keith came along at a time when I needed something in my life, just after Richard let me down, and I still think of him as a good friend,' Shirley explained, 'but, if we'd loved each other, we would have got together long ago. Keith said he loved me, but it was just the idea of me being a doctor and working with him that he liked.'

'That's a little harsh, love.' Maureen looked at her quizzically.

'It is the truth, though.' Shirley shrugged. 'Did Ray say anything else?'

'He is coming down this weekend – but he said he would ring back later. You'd better have your tea. I made a cheese and onion flan with salad this evening. Your father loves cheese and I know he shouldn't have too much – and there's the pastry, too, but he asked for it and so I made it. He had a small piece and then went into the garden to snip the heads off the roses.'

'I'll just walk down and see if he is all right,' Shirley said. 'I know Dad likes things like that, Mum – but not too often.'

'I know...' Maureen sighed. 'You tell him there's a fresh pot of tea and I'll have it ready when you get back.'

Shirley nodded and went out of the back door.

*　*　*

Shirley saw her father just standing, staring at his roses and went up to him, putting an arm about his waist.

'All right, Dad?'

He seemed to come back from wherever he'd been and looked at her, smiling. 'Yes, I'm fine, love. I was just thinking that summer is almost over and how well the roses have done this year...'

'They have been lovely – they still are,' Shirley said and bent to smell one that she knew was Maureen's favourite because of its wonderful perfume. 'This one is perfect. Why don't you cut it and give it to Mum?'

Her father looked at her and nodded. 'Yes, I will. Did she tell you to fetch me?'

'No. I came because I wanted to – though there is a fresh pot of tea.'

He inclined his head again. 'Yes, there always is these days. It fills me up instead of cake...' His eyes moved to her face. 'That friend of yours rang earlier. Is he the one for you, Shirley?'

'He might be, Dad. He hasn't said, but I do rather like him.'

'I hope he is – he'll look after you,' her father said. 'You'll have a good life with him; he'll respect you and won't clip your wings – but you won't forget your mum and Gordy, will you? When I've gone, they will need to see you sometimes. Not all the time – Maureen has her own life, thank God – but sometimes...'

'Of course, I shan't, Dad,' Shirley said and watched as he carefully cut the dark red rose. 'I love her – she has been as good to me as any mother could be.'

'I was lucky to get her. She was a bit younger and had been in love with someone else, but he let her down. After I lost your mother, I didn't think I'd love again, but I did – more so, if the truth is told. She can manage. The business is in good shape and she'll be all right. Gordy needs a man to guide him, but Able will do that – he told me not to worry. I wish I could look after you all, but it seems a long life hasn't been granted to me...'

'Oh, Dad...' Shirley caught back a sob. 'I wish I could do something. All those years of training and there's nothing—'

'You keep working with that friend of yours and one day perhaps there will be.'

'I don't know whether I should go back to the hospital. I know Ray wants me on his team, but my work here is so important...'

'From what you told me about those homeless folk you treated any competent nurse could do that much – I thought you trained to be a doctor because you wanted to save lives?'

'I did – I do...'

'And how many lives have you saved since you've been home?'

'Well... none,' Shirley admitted. 'I've been treating routine illnesses and if anyone was seriously ill, we'd send them to the hospital.'

'Exactly.' Her father's eyes looked directly into hers. 'You might one day save a life by working in the practice – but working with a man like Ray Anderson you will probably help to save dozens. Think about it, Shirley. Think about the life you have here – and the one you could have...'

Shirley was stunned. She'd expected her father to want her to be around, but his straight talking had put a new perspective on things. 'Ray does save lives and says I'm wasted here and he wants me to go further and take up surgery.'

'I know. He told me,' Gordon said. 'He rang and gave me his phone number when he was here before and I had a long talk to him. He told me you were one of his best students and he believes you could be a good surgeon if you put your mind to it.' He laughed as she looked at him in surprise. 'Nice bloke – and he thinks a lot of you, Shirley. You should give it some thought.'

'It means I'll have to do more training,' Shirley said uncertainly.

'Under his guidance – so you'll be working together, as you should be. If you love him, you may be living together as man and wife too.'

'He hasn't asked me yet,' Shirley reminded him.

'No?' Gordon laughed softly. 'Well, he asked me if he could marry you if you were willing.'

Shirley stared in amazement. 'He didn't have to ask. I'm not under age.'

'No, but he knows that you are precious to us – and that he is older. He wanted to know if you would have our approval and I said that I'd be happy for you if it was what you want. It is a gentleman's way, Shirley, and I respect him for it.'

'Does Mum know he spoke to you like that?'

'No. I didn't tell her. I asked him about my prospects too...'

'He told you the truth, of course?'

'He said that he couldn't be sure as he hadn't examined me, but from what you'd been told, I was probably living on borrowed time and should make the most of it.'

'Yes, he would,' Shirley said. 'I'm sorry if he upset you, Dad. I used to think he was cruel when he told students brutally that they hadn't a hope of passing their exams unless they pulled themselves together. Some of the students were terrified of him and one man cried...'

'You didn't cry though?' her father said with a smile.

'No. I just glared at him and worked harder so he couldn't say rude things to me – he did sometimes, but not unless I deserved it. He always tells the truth, Dad.'

'That's why he's just about good enough for my girl.'

Shirley laughed. 'Mum thought I might marry Keith...'

'He wasn't nearly good enough for you,' Gordon replied. 'If you'd loved him, I wouldn't have said anything, but I was glad you didn't.'

Shirley laughed. 'Thank you. I love you too, Dad.'

'You're my daughter and want you to be happy always.'

She nodded, understanding. 'We'd better go up or the tea will spoil.' Shirley smiled, feeling very close to her father in that moment.

'Yes, all right.' Gordon walked just behind her and Maureen came to the back door just as they arrived.

'Ray is on the phone again,' she said. 'You're just in time.'

'Thanks.' Shirley ran past her into the house and snatched up the receiver. 'Ray... sorry I was in the garden with Dad...'

'No need to rush,' he said and his voice sent tingles down her spine. 'I'm coming down on Friday night and I'll be stopping until Tuesday evening.'

'Oh, that's lovely,' Shirley exclaimed, 'but I'm not sure I can get time off from work.' It would be too disappointing if she couldn't!

'Doesn't matter. I have something arranged,' he replied. 'I just wanted to be sure it was all right – you haven't arranged anything special for the weekend?'

'No. I was just going to watch TV or read a book,' she said. 'I sometimes go out with a friend, but she has her in-laws staying this weekend.'

'Ah.' She could hear the smile in his voice. 'I'll see you Friday evening then. How is work going?'

'Pretty good. I've got quite a following at the clinic now – they come to see me even if they just want a cup of tea and a biscuit.'

'You didn't train for years to hand out tea and biscuits,' he said sharply. 'Don't waste your talents, Shirley.'

'That's a harsh thing to say,' she retorted, forgetting that her father agreed with him. 'I'm doing a good job—'

'You're wasting your time,' Ray said. 'You're a damned fine doctor, Shirley, and I need you on my team. Think about it.'

It was on the tip of her tongue to say she would, but instead the doubts crept in and she said, 'Don't bully me, Ray. You know why I came home...'

'Your parents don't need you to nanny them, and your patients will be fine with any of the GPs in your practice. You need to be here with me.'

With that, he put the phone down on her, leaving Shirley to stare at it in annoyance. He was so damned high-handed! She'd been on the verge of telling him she was considering a return to hospital work, but his tone had made her furious. He was an impossible man and her life would not be half as easy and pleasant working with him as it was here. She would be mad even to think about going back and as for being his wife – whatever was she thinking?

Janet looked at the freshly plastered walls and felt a little kick of pleasure. The plaster had dried out and was ready for painting and the enlarged kitchen would look wonderful. Sheila's father had been delighted when he saw it.

'I'm not one for sitting in the front room,' he'd told her. 'I like to come into the kitchen from the garden and sit at the table or a chair by the stove when it is cold. This is big enough to have my armchair and a table and dining chairs round it. My oak dresser from at home will go just right on that wall. Sheila's mum loved that Welsh dresser...' He'd sighed and looked sad for a moment. 'I reckon she'd have liked it here – I know I do...'

Janet had had a new enamel sink put in with a wooden draining board each side, a cooker and a fridge, also a row of cupboards along one wall. It left room for other furniture, which exactly suited its new tenant. Sheila's father had told her to call him Bert and they'd got along really well as Janet painted walls and window frames, chatting away in the garden when she took a break and they shared a flask of tea or the sandwiches she brought with her. Jon spent some time with them most days, wandering in and out and giving Bert a hand in the garden. He seemed to like the older man and they talked about plants and the birds they saw.

'You'll be finished next week,' Bert said now, coming into the kitchen behind her and nodding. 'You've made a real nice job of this place, Janet, and I'll be happy to move into it.'

'I'm glad you like it,' Janet said. 'I was just thinking about what I'll do next. I've enjoyed renovating this for you, but the summer has flown and I shall have to return to Scotland for a while soon to sort things out before we move. Jon should be back at school, but I've let them know that he won't be back since we're moving. I'll have to find him a new school, but in the meantime, we'll give him lessons ourselves.'

'He's a bright lad – but where do you intend to settle?'

'Ryan and I were talking about it last night,' Janet said. 'We've decided to look for somewhere to rent in the area for the time being – just until we make up our minds where we want to live. Ryan is searching for a small-holding with a house that we can renovate.'

'You'll be busy then,' Bert said and looked round. He bent down to look under the sink.

'Have you lost something, Bert?' Janet asked, seeing that he was looking worried.

'I thought I put my watch on the draining board.' He shook his head. 'You haven't moved it?'

'No, it was definitely there earlier. I saw Jon pick it up to look at it when he came in for a few minutes...'

'Perhaps he put it somewhere safe,' Bert said. 'My Dorrie gave me that watch years ago. It means quite a lot to me.'

'Yes, it must do,' Janet said and frowned. Jon shouldn't have touched his watch and she would be asking him what he'd done with it as soon as she saw him.

* * *

'I didn't touch his watch,' Jon said defiantly when Janet asked her son later that day if he'd put it somewhere, but he looked so guilty that she knew he was hiding something.

'I saw you pick it up,' Janet said and looked at him hard. His flush made her suspicious. 'Did you take it? You did, didn't you? Where is it?'

He hung his head. 'I put it away for safety,' he replied, but he was lying and they both knew it.

'Where is it?' Janet repeated sternly.

'In my things,' he admitted reluctantly. 'I'll get it.'

'No, I'll come with you and you can show me where,' she insisted and followed him out to the caravan he was sharing with Chris now that Freddie had returned to London.

Jon's things were strewn over his bed, but there was a little cupboard beneath the bunk and he went to it, taking out a box. He tried to extract the watch without her seeing the rest of the contents, but she held out her hand, compelling him by her look to hand it over. Inside were several things she knew belonged to other people: a penknife that was Freddie's; it must have been left behind when Peggy, Able and Freddie returned to London, and Jon had found it and put it with his things. There was also a fountain pen that belonged to Pip and a key ring that belonged to Sheila – all little things that had disappeared recently, along with a compact that she knew was Peggy's and a coin purse that belonged to her. The compact was silver and a gift from Able. Janet knew her mother had missed it. She'd asked Sheila and Janet if they'd seen it, but of course, none of them had because Jon had found it first. There were also a few trinkets that she didn't recognise but knew were not Jon's and she gave him a reproachful stare.

'Where did these things come from, Jon – I know some of them, they belong to the family – but these others?'

'They're mine,' he said defensively, but she shook her head and he looked down before confessing. 'I took them at school – the other boys didn't want them. They just left them lying around... Why shouldn't I have them if people don't bother about their stuff?'

'Because it is wrong to steal, Jon,' Janet said. 'I don't understand why you've done it. If you wanted a penknife or a key ring, I would have got you one. Why take other people's property?'

Jon shrugged. 'I didn't think you would care. You never take any notice of me. Dad's always out and you only think about Maggie and your friends,' he said, accusation in his voice.

'That isn't true,' Janet replied, but she felt guilty. Had Jon been neglected? She'd considered herself a good mother and he'd never gone hungry or without anything he needed – but perhaps she hadn't spent enough time talking to him, asking him about school and his interests. When Maggie was growing up, Peggy had been around most of the time and she'd made friends quickly in Scotland, taking up riding and enjoying long walks in the woods. Both Janet and Ryan had spent lots of time with Maggie, but because Jon was a boy, he'd been allowed to go off on his own more. It seemed that he'd felt uncared for and that was her fault. 'We both love you very much, Jon. Surely you know how much your dad loves you?'

'I suppose so.' He shuffled his feet awkwardly. 'I get fed up – you're always busy and so is Dad. I want him to play football with me the way Grandad Able does – he and Granny Peggy are the only ones who ever notice me.'

'Now that's just silly,' Janet said, because it wasn't quite true, but he did have a point. Jon had been happy whenever he'd stayed with Granny Peggy and Grandad Able, running about in the sunshine and going on trips to the pictures or the zoo in London, but since they'd returned home, Janet had spent most of her time renovating the cottage. Jon had been with her some of the time, helping a bit and running in and out of the cottage as he pleased, but sometimes he'd gone off for long walks or a bike ride on his own. She'd thought he'd been happy doing it but now she realised that it might have seemed like disinterest to a child. 'I'm sorry you feel that your dad and I have neglected you, love – but I thought you were happy amusing yourself.'

'I am some of the time,' he admitted. 'But I get bored and then... I don't know why I do it. I didn't mean to take Bert's watch. I like him. I'm sorry, Mum.'

'You'll have to show me which things you took from your school so I can return them. I won't say anything about you, I'll just post them anonymously.'

Jon looked ashamed. 'Maggie threatened to tell you if I did it again.'

'Maggie knew?'

He nodded. 'I took some sweets from the shop. She paid for them, but she said if I did it again, she would tell, but she didn't and I haven't taken anything more from a shop. Just things people leave lying around.' He moved his feet again uncomfortably. 'Will they lock me up?'

Janet resisted the impulse to smile. 'No, I don't think so, not this time – but if you keep doing it, one day you will get into big trouble and then you'll go to prison. Do you really want to live that sort of life, Jon?'

'No…' Tears dripped down his cheeks. 'I'm glad we're not going back to Scotland, Mum. The boys hated me there – because I was English and they said I was a cissy. I took their things to punish them.'

She nodded, because she could understand that, but that didn't fit with the other things he'd taken. 'But Bert wasn't horrid to you,' Janet pointed out. 'This watch means a lot to him, you know.'

Jon looked ashamed. 'I wish I hadn't done it, Mum. Will he have to know?'

'I think you should tell him yourself and give it back,' Janet said.

'I'll tell him and say I'm sorry,' Jon replied in a small voice. 'He won't like me any more.'

'Sometimes you have to be brave and face up to what you've done, Jon.'

'Are you going to tell Dad?' he asked and looked scared.

'I think he should know,' Janet said. 'When he comes back this weekend, I think you should talk to him. Tell him what has been upsetting you and perhaps he will help you.'

'He won't love me any more…'

'Your father loves you more than anything in the world,' Janet said. 'We both love you all the time and this won't make us stop, Jon. It is because we love you that we have to stop you doing these things – because it could ruin your life.'

Jon rushed at her and she caught him in her arms as he sobbed. She held his little body to her, feeling that he was trembling, and tears came to her own eyes. What sort of a mother was she? She'd let her own boredom and problems blot out Jon's. Maggie had known what was going on – why hadn't she?

'It's all right, darling,' she said. 'I know you're not a bad boy, but I want you to promise you won't do it again.'

Jon promised, his head buried in her arms and his voice muffled with tears. She stroked his hair and berated herself for not being aware that he was unhappy. He wasn't short of anything in a material sense, but he'd felt unloved and excluded at school because the other boys teased and bullied him. She hadn't known that and she ought to have. That was her fault, hers and Ryan's. Hers because she'd been bored and searching for something new, Ryan's because he'd been too busy making money to spend time with his family. Well, Janet had found her new interest, but in future she would have to make sure that she gave Jon enough attention, make time to ask him what he felt about things. She wasn't sure what else she could do to break this unfortunate habit he'd got into, but somehow, she must find a way – find an interest for him. Something like Fay's skating that had consumed her time and kept her busy and happy.

'What do you want to do with yourself, Jon?' she asked now. 'We have a little while before you start school again – what would you really like to do?'

'There's a local cricket match on tomorrow afternoon,' Jon said. 'Will you take me?'

Janet had wanted to finish her painting that afternoon, but she knew it would have to wait. 'Yes, I'll take you,' she said. 'We'll ask Bert if he wants to come to make up for you *borrowing* his watch...'

* * *

Bert looked at him sorrowfully when Jon returned the watch and slipped it on his wrist. 'Well, that's all right, as long as it was safe with you,' he said. 'I thought I'd lost it in the garden and that would upset me – because my wife gave it to me many years ago.'

'I'm sorry,' Jon said. 'Do you hate me now?'

'No, lad. I don't. You're a brave boy to return it to me yourself. I think we can forgive it this once – as long as you don't make a habit of it.'

'I won't,' Jon promised. 'Mum says will you come to the cricket match with us this afternoon? We're going to take a picnic.'

'Well, that's lovely,' Bert said and smiled at him. 'Yes, I'll come – and thank you for returning my watch.'

Jon couldn't meet his eyes. He'd done what his mother had told him, because he had to, but he wasn't really sorry. He'd got into the habit of taking things at school – a lot of the older lads did it and they'd jeered at him because for a start he hadn't wanted to, calling him a coward. Jon had taken the sweets from a shop just because the bullies wouldn't leave him alone, but then he'd started stealing their things and found he got pleasure from it. It amused him to steal a pencil box from one of the bullies who had pushed him into stealing the sweets. He hated the school he was at, where they all ganged up on him because he was different. He couldn't tell on them because that would just have made them worse, so he'd got his own back by taking their things – but then it became a habit and he took other people's things. Jon had stolen from people he liked and, in a way, he was sorry that he'd upset Bert, but he shouldn't have left the watch lying around. And Bert had been the reason Jon's mother was busy all the time; when it was the school holidays and other mothers were taking their sons to cricket matches and the beach, she was working on the cottage. He felt a little surge of rebellion and resentment. His mother didn't care anyway. She was always too busy to notice him.

He'd got used to doing whatever he chose. Jon would have to be careful what he took in future and where he hid it, because his mother would check his pockets and under his bed. He smiled to himself. When they got to the farm or wherever they were going, he would find somewhere special – somewhere no one would ever find his treasures, because he didn't want to be punished, but he liked taking stuff. In his dreams, he was like one of those clever criminals in the movies and the books he read, and as long as he didn't get caught again, he would do it whenever he felt like it – though maybe not from his family or people he liked.

* * *

Ryan was shocked when Janet told him what their son had been up to. 'My God,' he exclaimed. 'I had no idea. I'm so sorry, Janet. I blame myself entirely for neglecting him.'

'I am as guilty as you,' she said. 'I was usually at home when he got in from school and I looked after him in a material sense, but I never realised that he was being bullied at school or the consequences. Apparently, Maggie knew he'd taken things but she never said anything.'

'Didn't want to split on him, I suppose,' Ryan said, frowning. 'I wish she had, though, because something like that needs to be nipped in the bud right at the start.'

'Well, I've talked to him, but I think you should, too,' Janet suggested. 'I wasn't sure whether to punish him or just try to make him understand it is wrong to steal.'

'He must know that already,' Ryan said. 'I think I'll take a firmer line with him, Janet. I shall warn him that if he does it again, I shall report him to the police and he will be put on remand somewhere.'

'You wouldn't!' Janet was shocked by Ryan's expression.

'Yes, I would,' he said firmly. 'He has to learn, Janet, otherwise he'll become a thief and it will never stop. Do you want your son to end up in prison?'

'No, of course not! That would be dreadful. I feel bad enough about what he has done now.' She hesitated, then, 'Don't be too harsh with him, Ryan. He is only eight years old, you know.'

'I'm angry,' Ryan admitted. 'As much with myself as with him, but I think I have to be firm, make him understand the consequences.'

Janet nodded. Her own inclination was to make more fuss of her son, make sure she spent time taking him wherever he wanted to go and show him that she did love him, and she feared that Ryan's tough stance might just convince Jon that his father didn't love him. 'I don't know what to do,' she said. 'I've never had to deal with anything like this before and I'm at a loss to know what to do for the best...'

'He has to learn, Janet. I've never hit him, but I think he deserves a few smacks on the back of his legs...'

'Please don't hit him,' Janet said. 'Talk to him, warn him if you like, Ryan, but don't hit him. I'm sure it won't do any good and it will probably turn him against us.'

Ryan looked at her for a long time in silence and then nodded. 'All right, I won't smack him this time – but if he does it again, I shall punish him. This is serious, Janet. The last thing we want is for our son to be a thief.'

'Perhaps when we're living on the farm and he's in a different school – away from the bullies – things will be better for him and he won't be tempted.'

'I can understand that bit of it – taking from bullies – but from his family and Sheila's father? No, Janet. It has to stop.'

* * *

Janet listened to the lecture Ryan gave Jon from outside the door. He'd refused to allow her to be present because he'd said she was too soft with the boy, but she shook her head as she heard the anger in Ryan's voice. Somehow, she felt it would make things worse. If Jon had started the stealing because he felt unloved, being angry with him wasn't going to help the situation – but what would?

Janet wasn't sure. She felt helpless and disappointed – and very guilty, because she'd been too wrapped up in her own concerns. If she'd thought more about Jon than herself, it might never have happened. Janet knew that if Jon didn't stop stealing and eventually ended up in trouble with the law, she would always blame herself – but Ryan wasn't helping. She could hear Jon crying as his father said some more cutting things and then, suddenly, he rushed out of the room and past her, out to the caravan.

It took all her willpower not to go after him and comfort him, because she knew if she did, Ryan would be furious with her – and she couldn't interfere when he'd been disciplining his son, but it hurt to see Jon so upset.

She went into the room where Ryan was standing alone. Pip and Sheila had stayed in the kitchen so as to keep out of it, looking at each other in distress when they understood what the fuss was about, though neither had spoken a word of condemnation. Ryan looked at her and she saw the doubt and pain in his eyes and knew it had cost him to punish Jon.

'Did I do right?' he asked and she knew he would suffer the same doubts and grief she was feeling right now. 'He looked so stricken...'

'Yes, I know,' she said. 'I don't know what the right thing is, Ryan. He did need to be punished and he does have to learn – to understand that what he did was wrong, but...' She shook her head. 'Perhaps he needs love more. I'm not sure...'

'Go to him,' Ryan said. 'Make sure he is all right.' He sighed. 'Why did this happen now – just when I thought things were going to be so much better?'

'Perhaps they will,' Janet said. 'When we move and start living a different life, perhaps he'll see that there are better things to do with his time.'

* * *

Alone in the caravan, Jon fought back the tears. He wasn't going to let it hurt him because his father was ashamed of him – what did he care? They didn't really love him anyway. He looked at the book on his bed; it was the story of Al Capone. Everyone had looked up to the gangster and respected him – feared him. Jon would win that respect and power for himself. Love didn't matter. No one cared for him so he wouldn't love anyone else...

As he heard his mother's voice at the door, asking if she could come in, Jon hid his book. She was softer than his father. He would act like a hurt little boy and she would comfort him and take him out somewhere – but it wouldn't change him. He'd made up his mind. No one was going to hurt him again...

Peggy tasted the sauce Maggie had just made to accompany the fish she'd grilled and smiled, licking every last drop from her finger.

'Did you learn that from your course?' she asked. In the background, Cliff Richard was singing his hit song 'Move it'. It had reached number two in the charts and was being played all the time on the radio. 'This sauce has a lovely lemon flavour, but it is delicate and creamy too.'

'I picked up the recipe in the kitchens in the hotel in Torquay,' Maggie said. 'I think I learned more there than on the actual course.'

'And do you still want to do all those things you spoke about before you went on the course?' Peggy asked. 'Work in the pub for now and then turn it into a high-class dining venue as time goes on?'

'Yes please, Granny,' Maggie said. 'If it is all right with you? I don't want to push you out – we can all do our own thing here. Some of the dishes you make are really good and we'll have them on the menu. Your shepherd's pie is always popular and your regulars would walk out if there was no apple pie, so it is sensible to keep them happy.'

'Yes, it is,' Peggy agreed. 'I've always thought it would be nice to provide a more adventurous menu, but I never had the time. For now, I'd like us to work together. Ryan is going to put up some of the money for the refurbishment and Able will do the rest so that you and Fay can go ahead with your plans for the shop and the catering business.'

'Yes, I know,' Maggie said happily. 'Fay didn't want to go back to school when the holidays ended, but I persuaded her that she should, at least until next spring – she can practise when she's home and it's going to take time to get things ready for her anyway. It is better for her to have her own kitchen for her cakes and the catering business, too... keep it separate from the pub.' She paused, then, 'I think she should take that course in France next summer, Granny. She really needs more experience and it's the best way to get it...'

'Yes, perhaps – I still tend to think of her as my little girl, but you're both so grown up now.' Peggy sighed. Children grew up so quickly!

'We know what we want in life,' Maggie said. 'That's a good thing, don't you think? Poor Jon doesn't know what he wants – and he's in so much trouble with Dad now. I am too. He was very cross with me for not telling him what Jon had done. He says the longer it goes unchecked the worse it becomes...'

'Perhaps he is making too much fuss over a small theft,' Peggy said. 'A lot of young lads do it, stealing sweets to be big – and then they grow up and stop.'

'That's what I thought,' Maggie replied, 'but he took that watch...'

'He's only a little boy,' Peggy said indulgently. 'We've all done naughty things when we were young. He'll grow out of it, I'm sure.'

'I hope he does,' Maggie agreed and looked thoughtful. 'I saw him reading a book about Al Capone.'

'Al Capone – that awful man?' Peggy said with a frown. 'I heard they were talking about making a film of his story – it's strange how a legend seems to have grown up around him since he died. He was just a nasty little gangster and if they glamorise him by making a Hollywood film, it will give boys the wrong idea...' She shook her head over it.

'That's just the kind of thing that sets young boys thinking it would be good to be like him...' She stared at Peggy. 'You don't think he does want to be like Al Capone... Jon, I mean. He couldn't think something like that...'

'Of course, he doesn't,' Peggy said. 'Your brother just needs a bit of love and attention that's all.' She looked at Maggie. 'Although, I was just thinking about Tom Barton's brother this morning. He got in with a bad lot and was looking for valuables on a bomb site when a bomb exploded and killed him. His mother never got over the death of her younger son...'

'At least we don't have any bomb sites now,' Maggie said and glanced at her sauce. 'This is ready. I'd better take it through or it will spoil.'

Peggy calmly watched her take her tray through to the bar, but she was concerned. The memory of Tom Barton's brother getting killed had sent a shiver down her spine. Tom had tried hard to stop his brother running wild with a gang of looters, but he hadn't been able to prevent the tragedy. She had a bad feeling about Janet's son all of a sudden. How was it that none of them had realised that Jon was unhappy at school and had turned to bad ways?

* * *

The radio presenter was talking about bad weather in the south-east, which had disrupted power and communications. She hoped they were all right down where Pip was. Janet and Ryan were staying there until the end of the month when they hoped to have a new home to move into and to have found a school for Jon. At the moment, he was doing the work his mother set him, in limbo really until they got settled. Not a particularly good thing for him.

Peggy shook her head over the forecast. This was only September. You didn't expect fierce storms this time of the year. Fortunately, as she listened, she realised it was nowhere near Pip and Sheila's place. As the latest Elvis Presley song began to fill the kitchen with his particular style of singing, Peggy's thoughts centred on her youngest grandson once more.

She wished that Jon was in London so that she could talk to him, try to make him understand that what he'd done was foolish but not the end of the world, to ensure he knew that he was loved and valued and whatever he did he always would be. She knew that Janet and Ryan were thinking of settling on a small farm about fifty miles from Pip and Sheila. It was a perfect distance for Janet and Pip in their new business and Ryan had determined that he was going to change all their lives for the better, but this business with Jon could blow up in their faces if they weren't careful.

Peggy knew that the shadow of his younger brother's death had never left Tom Barton. He'd blamed himself for it – and, if anything bad happened to Jon, Ryan and Janet would blame themselves too. Would it help at all if she offered to have her grandson living with her? Jon normally responded well to her, but that didn't mean to say she could stop him being silly. Sometimes young boys got it into their head it was clever to do something and when they did, there was no stopping them.

Maggie returned to the kitchen just as Peggy took a shepherd's pie from the oven. She smiled as she saw it. 'That smells good, Granny. I've just taken two orders for it and another for apple pie. At the moment, your dishes are still more popular than mine.'

'About even I would say,' Peggy said. 'Wait until you get the place looking as you want it, love – that's when your customers will start to outnumber mine.' And they would be different customers, newcomers. Peggy had already noticed them visiting now and then. London was changing and so was the world. Aeroplanes were making travel much easier and famous stars flew all over the place for concerts. The general public would soon take air travel for granted and expect to spend their holiday abroad rather than at the British seaside. Thankfully, her two were still thrilled to have a holiday in a caravan at the sea or a guest house on the front and Butlin's were opening more and more camps, too. Freddie had said he might like a holiday there and perhaps next year they would go together as a family. In a year or so, the twins would want to holiday with their friends rather than their parents.

Peggy frowned as she pondered the problem of Fay's cooking course in France. Maggie wouldn't have time to go with her, so would she be safe to go alone? Sighing, she went back to her pastry making. Children were a joy but they were also a constant worry, although she'd been lucky with all of hers. Peggy had never had a problem like Janet and Ryan were facing now...

* * *

Janet looked thoughtfully at Ryan after reading Peggy's letter. 'Mum has offered to have Jon to stay for a while – just until we get settled at the farm. What do you think?'

'It is typical of her to offer,' Ryan replied, putting down his newspaper to look at her. The headlines were still on about Britain's so-called 'Cod War' with Iceland that had broken out at the beginning of September and the Notting Hill race riots, which happened at the very end of August. 'But I don't think so, Janet. We have to sort this for ourselves. Your mother would probably spoil him to death and he has to learn his lesson. He is staying put at home for the time being and no treats until he shows some remorse for what he did.'

'He is only a small boy,' Janet reminded her husband. 'Don't be too harsh on him, Ryan.' Her plea seemed to fall on deaf ears.

'He's old enough to know right from wrong,' Ryan said. 'Don't make excuses for him, Janet. Jon knew he was taking things that didn't belong to him. Do you want your son to grow up to be an accomplished thief?'

'You know I don't,' Janet said, 'but he's been told and I think your disapproval is punishment enough. He was crying his eyes out the other night again.'

Ryan looked at her oddly. 'Do you imagine this is easy for me? Jon means the world to me – if anything happened to him, I don't know how I would bear it.'

Janet nodded. He'd lost his first wife and two sons in an air raid during the war. Ryan never spoke of it to her, but she knew it still haunted him at times. She sometimes thought he compared his present family to his first and found it lacking. 'I know. I'm not blaming you, Ryan. I'm his mother. I should have seen something – put it right before it got this far.'

'Maybe if you hadn't been fancying that bloke you went riding with, you would have,' Ryan snapped and then stared at her in horror. 'No, I didn't mean that, Janet. I'm sorry. It was a foul thing to say... but he used to look at you as if he could eat you.'

Janet took a deep breath. Since they were talking this way, it was best to be honest and open about it. 'You were always away on business, Ryan. That wasn't supposed to happen when we moved to Scotland. It was the reason for our move. Can you blame me if my thoughts wandered? But it was only ever in my thoughts...'

'I know. I blamed myself for leaving you all so often and I know I promised I wouldn't when we moved up there, but the firm offered more money and I wanted to give you all everything you wanted...' He shrugged. 'It isn't going to happen again. I might still have to work long hours, but I'll be home every night and Jon can help me on the farm. He won't have time to run with a bad gang.'

'I don't blame you for any of it,' Janet said and saw surprise in his eyes. 'I think Jon gets his difficult streak from me. I fell out with my father over my first marriage. I always regretted what happened after that – it broke my parents apart and I've always blamed myself.'

'For what?' Ryan asked. 'Peggy is happy and Able adores her. If she'd loved your father, it wouldn't have worked out so well. Their marriage was probably falling apart before you married Mike.'

'Yes, perhaps,' Janet said and changing the subject remarked, 'I can't wait to move to the farm – is the house decent?'

'It is solid and the roof doesn't leak, but you can do what you want with it,' Ryan replied. 'It will keep you busy while you look for another project to share with Pip.'

'Yes, I shall enjoy that,' she said and smiled. She was going to stick to her plans to renovate houses but would make sure she was there for Jon when he came out of school and at weekends. 'Are you sure you won't let Jon go and stay with his granny for a while?'

'I think we have to get through this first,' Ryan said. 'When he settles and stops being so resentful, then I'll think about it – perhaps at Christmas...'

Janet smiled. She knew that Jon was more obedient when Peggy was around; he listened to her. At the moment, his parents were persona non grata, as far as Jon was concerned.

* * *

Listening outside the door, Jon scowled as he heard his father refusing the request for him to stay with Granny Peggy. Of all his family, she was the only one who really loved him, he thought resentfully, and his father was punishing him, not allowing him to spend a little time with her. Well, he'd show him! One of these days he'd make him sorry. Not his mum so much, because Jon thought she did love him, even though she'd been too busy to pay much attention to him recently.

He made up his mind there and then. If he didn't like it on the farm, he would run away to Granny Peggy and beg her to let him live with her...

25

Shirley came out of the clinic where she worked in London's East End that evening to find Ray standing outside waiting for her. It was a few days since he'd put the phone down on her and she'd been in turmoil for most of it, her heart at odds with her head as she battled with her feelings.

He held a huge bunch of roses out to her and looked at her ruefully. 'My tongue says things I don't mean,' he said. 'Will you forgive me? You know I care about you?'

'Ray – you idiot!' she laughed in relief because she hadn't been sure he would still come. 'These must have cost a fortune.'

'Picked them up for a song on a market barrow,' he lied and she held them to her nose, inhaling the exquisite perfume.

'Oh, they smell gorgeous,' she said and smiled. 'Yes, you are forgiven – but we have to talk about the future, Ray.' He offered his arm and she took it. 'I hardly know anything about you... your family.'

'I just have a sister. Our parents died when we were both young – and she basically brought me up after that. She's ten years older, but it wasn't easy for her until I went away to college, using the money my father had left for me.'

'So you dedicated your life to medicine?' Shirley asked as they started to walk.

'More or less. I have plenty of friends, but I like my work – the combination of surgery and the chance to teach has been very fulfilling... and I wouldn't have met you if I hadn't done those lectures, would I?'

'Probably not,' Shirley said. 'I disliked you for a long time, did you know that?'

'It was pretty plain that I wasn't your number one person,' he said with a wry smile, 'but I think it made me notice you – and then, very gradually, I fell in love with the feisty young girl who looked as if she would like to slay me!'

'I didn't look like that!' She laughed but her heart raced. 'Well, maybe I did, but then I started to admire you for your work and to quite like you, but it wasn't until that party that I started to get to know you. I missed you a lot when I left the hospital.'

'I know...' He hesitated, then, 'I could come and work in London...'

Shirley stared at him in surprise. She hadn't expected that. 'Would you be willing to do that?' she asked. 'Give up your teaching and your work in the hospital in Durham?'

'Life-saving surgery could be done here at Great Ormond Street, just the same,' he said. 'It might be the solution, Shirley – if it makes you happier...'

She was tingling all over now, because the look in his eyes left her in no doubt that he was about to propose.

'I ought to do this over a bottle of good wine,' he said but took a little box and opened it to show her the beautiful, white diamond, solitaire ring nestling against a dark blue velvet bed. 'I love you more than I know how to express – will you marry me, Doctor Shirley, and spend your life with me?'

She gave a little gasp and closed her eyes for a moment, but when she opened them, he was still there and she was smiling. 'Yes, I will,' she said and looked up at him. 'I think we shall probably argue a lot, but I don't think I could live without you.'

'Thank you, darling. You've made me happier than I ever thought I could be,' Ray said and reached for her, pulling her in for a kiss.

Hearing a chuckle and some clapping behind her, Shirley looked round as he released her and saw Mitsy and her young escort standing there watching.

'Sorry to intrude, Doc,' she said, 'but we need your help for Billy. He's took a turn for the worse. I reckon he might be real bad this time...'

Shirley turned to Ray. 'I need to see Billy. He's my patient. If you come to the house this evening at half-past seven, I'll be home and ready – and you can give me the ring and flowers then.'

Ray put the box back in his inside pocket and took the flowers she thrust at him. 'Are you all right to go alone?' he asked. He nodded to Mitsy. 'Look after her for me, please?'

'We'll do that all right,' Mitsy said with a little cackle.

Shirley smiled at him and turned to follow Mitsy. She was fairly certain of her way now, though she had never attempted to visit the derelict warehouse alone. Although no further murders had taken place, two was enough to make her wary of the area, and although she felt safe with her escorts, she would not have felt as safe had she been alone.

'How long have you known him then, Doc?' Mitsy asked as they walked.

'Oh – for seven years or so,' Shirley replied with a little smile. 'He was one of my tutors when I was learning to be a doctor in Durham.'

'So will you be goin' back to Durham then?' Mitsy asked and there was an odd look in her face as she stared at Shirley.

'I'm not really sure what I shall do,' Shirley admitted. 'Never mind me, Mitsy – what is wrong with Billy? Is he in a lot of pain with his leg?'

'Ain't his leg,' Mitsy said and scowled. 'He is coughing and spitting blood and that's new...'

'It certainly is,' Shirley said. 'A very worrying change, Mitsy. It sounds as if he should be in hospital.'

'You know what Billy thinks to hospitals,' she replied doubtfully.

'Supposing I promise that I won't allow him to be put in a home?' Shirley suggested. 'It might be a question of life or death, Mitsy. Would you rather Billy went to hospital, recovered – or died in pain?'

'It ain't up to me,' Mitsy said. 'I'll tell him what you promised about making sure they don't put him away.'

'Yes, because if he is as ill as you say, he will need to be in hospital. If I can't help him myself, I will do all I can to make him comfortable, but I am not allowed to bring the medicines he may need with me – and he will probably need oxygen and perhaps an operation...'

Mitsy nodded. 'I trust you so I'll talk to him if he has to go and I'll go with him.'

'Yes, that would help. I could come, too, make sure he is settled.'

Mitsy grinned. 'Yeah, you go and I'll just see him off. That would be better, Doc. They might want ter keep me and give me a bath,' she chuckled with mirth at the idea.

* * *

Two hours later, Shirley rushed into the house to find Ray waiting for her. 'I'm sorry I'm late,' she said. 'I had to go to hospital with my patient and he was in great distress. It wasn't until they gave him something for the pain and he went to sleep that I was able to leave him.'

'One of your down-and-outs?' Ray nodded. 'Your father told me about them. Go up and get ready. I'll wait. Your mum just gave me a lovely cup of tea and a piece of apple pie.'

'I made it for Gordy,' Maureen said defensively as Shirley turned to her. 'Your dad didn't have any – he was very good.'

'It must be hard to resist,' Ray replied sympathetically as Shirley went upstairs. 'I hope that quite soon we'll have some tablets that will help – and before long there should be an operation. They are working on the possibilities.'

'If I live that long,' Gordon said ruefully. 'Shirley is doing her best to keep me on a strict regime, but I slip a little occasionally. I buy something – a small cake when I'm out...'

'Oh, Gordon,' Maureen reproached. 'Shirley would be so cross if she knew.'

'But we're not going to tell her,' he said and winked. 'I'm not stupid, Maureen. I don't overdo it, but I just can't keep to the rigid diet without a little something now and then.'

'So I might as well make what you like occasionally,' Maureen said and smiled at him. 'To be honest, I'm finding it hard, too, love.'

'Just keep it to a couple of times a week and it should be all right,' Ray told them and then looked up with a smile as Shirley entered the kitchen.

'That must be the quickest wash and change for a lady I've ever encountered. My sister takes hours in the bathroom.'

'Perhaps she has more time,' Shirley replied and laughed. 'I jumped in and splashed about a bit and then out. It was easy to dress and my hair's no trouble. I just put a brush through it.'

Shirley was lucky with her complexion, because she took the sun easily and, in the summer, had a faint golden sheen naturally to her skin. She'd used the merest dash of lipstick in a new peach shade, which went perfectly with her York tan silk blouse and suited her. The look in Ray's eyes told her that he approved of her pencil skirt and silk blouse, which she would top with a jaunty little jacket with pleats at the back. The colour of the skirt and jacket were a pale cream and looked as if they came from the West End, which was deceptive since one of Shirley's school friends had made them for her in her own little dressmaking establishment.

'You look beautiful,' Ray said and reached for her left hand. 'Shall we tell your parents?'

'Yes.' Shirley felt herself blushing as she looked at her father and saw his expectant expression. 'Ray asked me to marry him when I left work – but I had to dash off to a patient...'

'Not before she said yes – and I have witnesses,' Ray said and slipped the ring onto the third finger of her left hand. It fitted perfectly.

'Congratulations, Shirley and Ray,' Gordon beamed. 'I couldn't be more pleased – that is wonderful news.'

'I am delighted for both of you,' Maureen said and embraced them, receiving a bear hug from Ray.

'Perhaps news that will please you as much if not more is that I've been offered a job at Great Ormond Street and I have more or less accepted it. I just wanted to confirm with Shirley that it suited her.'

She looked up at him, searching his face. 'Are you perfectly sure you want to do this, Ray? I could commute or something if you'd rather...'

'I wouldn't,' he replied firmly. 'I shall be quite happy working in London. I have to find us somewhere to live and I thought perhaps a Christmas wedding – to allow for me to work my notice in Durham...'

'That is wonderful,' Maureen said. 'You will start your new job in the New Year.'

'I'm hoping to have a new assistant,' Ray said, 'but whether she will join my team or prefer to stay where she is, I'm not sure...'

'I might be able to do some volunteer work now and then at the clinic,' Shirley suggested and smiled. 'The main thing is I'd still be living and working in London – and that is a wonderful hospital, Ray. I think I'd like to work there.'

The look in his eyes told her that he would like it, too, but he just nodded. 'We ought to go or the restaurant will wonder if we're coming. I did ring and explain we would be late.'

'Yes, we must go.' She went to her father and hugged him.

He smiled and gave her a brief hug. 'Off you go and have a lovely time, both of you.'

Shirley nodded and they left. She held tight to Ray's arm as they went to the car. 'I can't believe you've changed your job for me.'

'If the mountain won't come,' he mocked and she laughed.

'I love you,' she said. 'I am so happy, Ray.'

'Me too,' he said, 'and this is just the beginning.'

* * *

Shirley looked at her ring before she took it off that evening and carefully placed it in its box on her dressing table. It was beautiful but not the kind of thing she could wear for work. The evening had been wonderful and if Shirley had had any doubts about the future, they were all gone. The age gap was there and it wouldn't go away, but they were both still young and for now it didn't matter. As Maureen had warned her, it was only in later years that it might – but life was unpredictable and there was no point dwelling on what might happen. With God's grace, they would have many happy years together.

Her thoughts went to someone she knew was close to the end of his life. Billy wasn't likely to recover from his illness this time. It was a serious chest infection and she thought his lungs were probably damaged by years of living rough and neglect of himself. Shirley felt sad to think that he might never leave hospital alive and knew she would have to tell Mitsy the news herself. The old woman cared for him and she would be deeply distressed.

So, the next afternoon, Shirley left the surgery at three o'clock, which gave her time to visit the derelict warehouse and tell Mitsy what had to be said. She had memorised the names of streets and lanes and so she found the warehouse without too much trouble. Mitsy was sitting outside on a chair, making tea in a can over a fire that someone had lit in an old oil drum and she looked up in surprise as Shirley approached. She'd brought a packet of tea, biscuits and a tin of condensed milk, as well as two rock cakes that Maureen had made for her lunch.

'You've come to tell me Billy is dead,' Mitsy said and glared at her.

'He isn't dead, but it is touch and go whether he will leave hospital again,' Shirley said. 'Billy has lived a hard life, Mitsy. He should really end his days in the comfort of a nice home…'

'You promised you wouldn't let that happen,' Mitsy said and her little body bristled with anger. 'If they force him, he'll die anyway – and he'll hate me for making him go to the hospital.'

'You only did what had to be done,' Shirley said and put her paper bag down beside Mitsy. 'I just said it would be better for him.' She hadn't said he must stay in hospital and, if he felt he needed to, she would help him to leave, though it would probably kill him.

Mitsy wouldn't be silenced. 'If they shut my Billy away, I'll never forgive you… You can take your things away and never come here again!'

With that, she jumped up and went back into the warehouse without looking at Shirley, refusing to let her speak or finish what she'd been going to say.

'If he wants to come back here to die, I'll help all I can…' she said to the empty air and then sighed. It was no use promising anything, because Billy might die before he could be released. The nurse hadn't been confident of his recovery when she'd telephoned before she came.

Sighing, Shirley left the package beside the oil drum. If Mitsy refused it, some of the others would take it. She walked away sadly, disappointed that the old lady hadn't trusted her to do the right thing. It was as she reached the end of the lane that she noticed how dark it had become suddenly. She glanced up at the gathering clouds and realised that it looked like a storm was coming and began to hasten her steps. She didn't have an umbrella and if it poured with rain, she would get soaked. Looking over her shoulder, she saw a dark shadow looming towards her and for the first time ever when in this area she was truly afraid.

* * *

Shirley had never walked home alone since that first night and she shivered as a man rushed at her. He smelled strongly of beer and his breath was foul.

'Little whore...' he muttered in a thick voice. 'I've seen yer lookin' fer trade – but yer won't no more. Filthy bitch.' He raised his hand to grab her.

'No,' Shirley screamed the word aloud. 'You've got it wrong. I'm a doctor. I'm not a whore.'

His hand was reaching for her throat and she saw a flash of silver. He had a knife and she felt its point at her throat and sensed that she was about to die. Kicking out at his shins, she fought desperately and, in the struggle, felt a sharp sting as his knife scored her throat and the bottom of her chin and then, suddenly, she heard a snarling sound and the attacker was torn off her and thrown to the ground.

What happened then was a fierce fight to the death, but Shirley was not aware of it. She was losing blood and unconscious when the ambulance arrived to take her to the hospital...

* * *

Maureen took the call at about nine that evening. She and Gordon had already phoned the police, because Shirley had never been this late and when the surgery said she'd left early to visit the vagrants in their warehouse, they were all very worried. Ray was with them, waiting anxiously for news, because he'd arrived earlier, expecting to take Shirley out when she got home

'She's been attacked,' Maureen gasped into the receiver. 'Is she badly hurt – dead?'

The voice was reassuring, though the news was shocking to Shirley's loving family and fiancé. Maureen repeated it aloud for their benefit.

'She was attacked and injured with a knife – a throat wound and a small

wound to her chin, but she's alive... Oh, thank God... Yes, go on...' Maureen
listened carefully, nodding all the time while the anxious listeners waited.
'When can we see her? Not until the morning – thank you so much for
letting us know...' She replaced the receiver with trembling hands and
blinked hard as the tears trickled from her eyes. 'Shirley was attacked and
her throat was cut but not deep enough to kill her. They've operated to sew
her up and they say she'll be all right, but she will likely have a nasty scar...'

'Oh my God!' Ray hid his face in his hands. 'I thought she must be
dying from the look in your eyes... thank God she is alive...'

'How did it happen?' Gordon asked hoarsely. 'Was it the same one as
murdered those other women?'

'He is dead,' Maureen said. 'They think it was the same one – the
method of his murders was never published in the paper to avoid copycats,
but it was the same, so they think it was him.'

'How did he die?' Ray was puzzled. 'Did the police get him?'

'No – they think it was one of the tramps. The doctor wasn't sure of all
the details. He says the police will be in touch with us—' She stopped as
the doorbell rang. 'Wouldn't you know it – they arrive just after the hospital
rings...'

She went to open the door and admitted the young constable. He apol-
ogised for not coming earlier. 'I was writing my report and then the sarge
said I should have come and told you straight away—'

'Well, now you're here, get on with it,' Ray said in clipped tones. 'What
happened to my fiancé?'

'She was attacked by a man with a knife,' the constable explained. 'She
very bravely fought back and that is probably what saved her life – that and
the arrival of a young man. He was invalided out of the Army a year ago
and has been living with the vagrants. Apparently, he's been looking after
Doctor Shirley, making sure she gets home safe, but he didn't know she'd
been to see them this evening and he was late arriving on the scene. He
fought Doctor Shirley's attacker and in the fight, the attacker was killed...
and he was injured. He is being cared for in the same hospital as Doctor
Hart.'

'If he needs a lawyer, I'll pay for it,' Ray said instantly. 'Please make sure

I have his details and I'll see that he gets rewarded for what he did. I hope you don't intend to prosecute? He should get a medal.'

'We think the same, but it isn't down to us,' the constable said. 'We just present the facts and the Crown Prosecutor decides.'

'Well, they had better decide the right way,' Ray said sharply. 'I'm going to the hospital, Maureen. I'll telephone later.'

'They said not until the morning,' Maureen replied, but he set his face.

'They will let me see her,' he said and she believed him.

'Yes, please go and tell us how she is? I know Shirley. She is a fighter. She won't give in—'

'She'd better not,' Ray said fiercely and left.

Maureen looked at the police officer. 'Would you like a cup of tea, young man? It sounds as if you were the first on the scene and it isn't often you have to witness something like that.'

'Thank you.' He took his helmet off and sat down as she poured it for him. 'I thought your daughter was dead at first, but then she made a sound, so I got the ambulance quick. The young man that saved her life was also injured pretty badly, but I think he will live.'

Gordon sat back in his chair and put a hand to his chest.

Maureen looked at him anxiously. 'Are you in pain, love?'

He shook his head. 'It's just the shock. Get me a little drop of brandy, Maureen, and have one yourself.'

Maureen got up to fetch it for him. She offered it to the young constable, but he shook his head. 'Better not – I'm still on duty, but this tea is very nice, hot and sweet, just the way I like it.'

She nodded, thinking it was a good thing Gordy was in bed and knew nothing about this. In the morning she would have to find a way to tell him without upsetting him too much. He thought the world of his big sister and would be devastated that she'd been attacked.

26

Shirley opened her eyes and a little moan issued from her lips as she felt the soreness in her throat. She blinked, because it was daylight and for a moment she couldn't focus or think what had happened to her. She wasn't at home in her own bed – so where was she?

'Shirley dearest – are you in pain?'

The voice and his face peering at her anxiously brought Shirley sharply back to awareness. 'Ray...' she croaked. 'I was attacked...'

'Yes, I know. Fortunately, you fought back until help arrived.' Ray reached for her hand and held it. 'I've spoken to the doctors and it seems no internal damage was done. You will have a little scar or two, but everything should heal and you'll be none the worse.' Shirley's eyes filled with tears. 'I might have died...' she said on a sob. 'If help hadn't come when it did... I was warned not to go to that place alone. Mitsy was angry with me because I couldn't tell her that Billy would come back and so she went off in a huff and I walked back alone...'

'But when someone else realised it, he must have followed and caught up with you. He fought your attacker and he won't be hurting another young woman – but your protector was wounded himself.'

'His name is Tim,' Shirley said, her voice little more than a croak. 'He never speaks to me, just follows us to make sure we're all right.'

'You shouldn't have been there alone,' Ray said. 'In future, make sure someone else goes with you – if it can't be me, take one of the nurses. That's if you go at all...'

Shirley nodded and wiped the tears from her cheeks with the sheet. 'I shan't have much time for the clinic if I'm working with you – perhaps one afternoon a week as a volunteer.'

'The streets should be safer for a while now that devil is dead, but there is always the chance of an unwanted attack or theft if you visit that kind of place after dark,' Ray said. 'I'm not scolding you, my darling – but I don't want to lose you...' The look in his eyes made her tears start again. 'Just when I've found you.'

'I don't want to die either,' Shirley said. 'I'll speak to the nurses at the clinic – see if any of them are prepared to come with me.'

'I'll make sure they are,' Ray said forcefully. 'My wife isn't going to take that sort of risk again.'

She gave a tearful chuckle and then gasped as it hurt. 'My throat hurts...'

'I am sure it does,' Ray agreed. 'You were lucky not to be more seriously injured – although it was your own bravery that saved you. By fighting him, you gained time and then your guardian angel arrived. I haven't thanked him yet, but as soon as he is well enough for visitors, I shall – and if he needs a job, I'll find him one.'

'Was he badly hurt defending me?'

'He received several stab wounds before he managed to turn the knife on the attacker, but none of them are life-threatening – he's just been sewn up and he will recover shortly.'

'Good – was the man that attacked me killed in the fight or did he die afterwards?'

'Apparently, he fell on the knife and died almost immediately – or that's what the police are saying. They are sure he's the murderer they've been searching for and are pretty glad to have him out of the way.'

'Poor man. I wonder what made him so unhappy that he needed to kill to avenge his pain.'

'He was probably just a deranged victim of life,' Ray agreed. 'He should have been in an institution receiving medical attention rather than roaming the streets.'

'Everyone has a story or a reason for what they do,' Shirley said. 'I can't hate him for what he did to me – but I was lucky...' She clung to Ray's hand, but her voice had dropped to a whisper and he looked at her in concern.

'Stop talking and rest, Shirley, or they will throw me out. You sound terrible, so just sleep, my darling.'

'I'd like that...' she whispered and closed her eyes.

When she opened them again, it was dark and the lights were on in her room.

A nurse entered and smiled at her. 'You're awake again. We've let you sleep, because we thought it best. Are you ready for something to drink, perhaps a little jelly and ice cream?'

'My throat is sore,' Shirley said. 'I'd like a drink and the jelly – you don't have a strawberry blancmange, do you?'

'Funnily enough, your mother brought one in for you this afternoon,' the nurse said. 'She sat with you for ages, but you didn't wake. She said the blancmange was your favourite.'

'It is.' Shirley smiled weakly. 'Was someone else here earlier? Or did I dream that?'

'Your fiancé was here all night. We sent him home to have a meal and a rest, but he is coming back later – during visiting hours.'

Shirley nodded. Her hospital experience had taught her how important that was, because of the routine that needed to be followed to keep things flowing smoothly on the wards. 'Can I have a wash – can I get up and go to the bathroom myself?'

'Doctor says you're to stay put for the moment,' the nurse told her. 'I'll bring you a drink and something to eat and then I'll wash you before your fiancé comes. If you need the toilet, I'll fetch a pan to you first.'

'Yes, please,' Shirley said. 'That would be best.'

She pushed herself up the bed in readiness and discovered it took more out of her than she'd thought. Clearly, she would need a few days in bed to get over her ordeal. It was the mental stress and trauma as much as the physical injuries, which she'd been fortunate to get away with lightly. The realisation that she might have died in the attack by the crazed knifeman made her understand just how lucky she'd been. It was her own fault for not listening to the advice she'd been given and she certainly wouldn't risk it happening again, because next time she might not be as lucky.

* * *

'Thank goodness she is feeling better,' Maureen said when Ray visited later that night. He'd returned with the good news and looking so relieved himself that she and Gordon were able to relax again. 'I honestly thought we might lose her.'

'If that knife had gone a little deeper, we would have done,' Ray told her honestly. 'She was within a whisker of dying, Maureen. Had her protector not arrived when he did, she couldn't have won the struggle alone.'

'Thank God he did arrive – do you know much about him?'

'Not much,' Ray replied with a frown. 'I visited him in hospital and thanked him. He looks a bit pale and shocked, but he'll live – and I've told him I can get him a job in the hospital. I need a porter on my team and he said he would consider it.'

'He can have a job in our shop if he'd rather,' Gordon said. 'I didn't feel up to visiting the hospital today, but I'll go tomorrow and I'll thank him myself. Not every young bloke would have done what he did.'

'No, they wouldn't – especially after the way he's been treated since his Army discharge. Couldn't get a job and left to walk the streets...' Ray shook his head. 'I deplore what happened to Shirley, but these people do need help – and if they refuse to visit the clinic, then we should go to them. I'm going to look into it, see what can be done to set up a proper visiting team. It should consist of at least one fit man as well as a doctor or a nurse.'

'Shirley isn't going to do it alone again,' Gordon said fiercely. 'I thought we'd lost her... and I couldn't stand that...'

'No, I think she has learned her lesson,' Ray agreed. 'She still feels it was the right thing to do, visiting them, but she needs an escort at the very least.'

'If what you say is right, it was the old woman that let her down.'

'Yes, she was upset and went off in a sulk but, fortunately, the young man she'd previously asked to escort Shirley was there and realised what had happened. He immediately set off after her. It was too late to save her being attacked, but he undoubtedly saved her life.'

It was a little miracle that he'd arrived in time and they all felt sobered by what might have happened to the young woman they loved. Maureen had warned Shirley to be careful, but she'd never really expected that her daughter would be attacked and the shock had thrown them all off balance.

'Do you know when she will be able to come home?' Maureen asked. 'Or haven't the doctors said yet?'

'They think at least a week in hospital and then probably another week at home,' Ray told her. 'I have to return to Durham on Tuesday, but I'll come down again at the weekend and I've arranged to take leave due to me, so I'll be relocated to London, thank goodness!'

'Yes, that will be much better for both of you.' Maureen smiled approvingly. 'I'm glad you decided to move down here rather than ask Shirley to come to you. It was thoughtful and kind.'

'My work will be much the same,' he said with a shrug. 'I may have even more research opportunities here, but I knew it would be too hard for her to leave London, so I really had no choice. I love her and that is what matters to me.'

'It seemed to happen so suddenly.'

'Not for me,' Ray said and his smile lit his face. 'I liked her when she first came to my class and, over the years, I learned to respect her determination and her dedication. I suppose it was when she was no longer around that I finally understood what she truly meant to me.'

'I'm so pleased that it has worked out well for both of you.'

He smiled. 'Shirley is a remarkable young woman. I consider myself fortunate that she likes me enough to trust her life to me.'

* * *

Maureen sat reflecting on her daughter's narrow escape and the ups and downs of fortunate or fate or whatever you liked to call it. Her own life had not been straightforward, but she'd been lucky to find Gordon and her marriage had been a happy one. If she'd married Robin's father, it would not have been, she knew that much. Peggy had been married for years to her first husband, but, although they'd got along all right most of the time, it was only when she met Able that she knew the happiness of being truly loved.

Rose Barton had lost a man she loved to the war, but Tom Barton adored her and her daughter by her first lover. Janet, too, had lost her first husband, because of a war wound, but she was happier now with Ryan – at least Maureen thought she was, though with Janet you could never quite be sure.

Maureen would go round and see Peggy in the morning. Her friend was always there for her, always the same, a steady presence in her life that she'd missed when Peggy lived on the coast for a while. It would be interesting to see how Maggie and Fay were getting on with the cooking and Peggy would want to hear her news.

'Mum – are you all right? Shirley isn't worse, is she?'

Maureen looked at her son, who was staring at her anxiously from the doorway. 'I'm fine, darling. Couldn't you sleep?'

'I keep thinking about our Shirley... she won't die, will she?'

'No, I promise she won't,' Maureen told him and held her hand out to him. He came and took it and she smiled at him. 'I'll tell her you asked after her when I visit. I'm sorry the hospital rules don't allow you to visit, love.'

'That's all right – as long as they look after her.'

'Yes.' She smiled at him. 'Would you like a piece of that cake I made and a cup of cocoa?'

'Yes, please, Mum.' He leaned forward and kissed her cheek. 'You're the best mum in the world. I love all of you – and one day I'm going to make lots of money and buy a big house where we can all live together...'

'How are you going to do that then?' she asked, cutting him a slice of the almond-flavoured cake he liked.

'I'm not sure,' he said and looked thoughtful. 'Maybe I'll write books...' He grinned at her. 'I don't know how – but I will be rich and I'll look after you and dad, Mum – and Shirley too.'

'Good – well, you go back to bed and I'll bring some cocoa up to you, love.' Maureen watched as he took his cake and left, munching as he went.

She smiled as she thought of the new generation at Mulberry Lane, continuing the tradition of friendship and working together. They didn't have a war to bind them together the way Maureen and Peggy had, but it appeared that Maggie was strong and she'd helped to set Fay's feet on the right path... and now it seemed that her Gordy had his own ideas. She would talk to him again about what he wanted, because if he wanted to go to college, she would make sure he did, whatever happened in the future.

Maureen looked at Gordon, asleep in his chair. He did that a lot in the evenings now. He was walking the two miles a day that Shirley had told him he needed to and she sometimes wondered if it was tiring him out, but perhaps it was just his illness.

He opened his eyes and smiled at her. 'Sorry, love. I think I'll go up to bed. Will you bring some cocoa up?'

'Yes, you get in bed and I'll make it,' Maureen said and her heart caught. She didn't know what she'd do if she lost him too soon. Gordy had been upset enough when she'd told him about the attack on Shirley. She didn't know how he would cope if his father died. It was all too upsetting. As long as Gordon lived, she would have hope.

27

Maggie picked up the letter and looked at it, feeling puzzled. She didn't recognise the handwriting and it had been posted in Hertfordshire. Who did she know that lived there?

Opening it, she read it through quickly and frowned. It was from Jason. He had come down from Scotland to England on business and thought he might like to stay in London for a few days. He was asking whether she would have time to show him some of the sights. Maggie shook her head and decided that she very definitely wouldn't. The last thing she wanted was Jason whispering suggestions in her ear. Maggie was interested in cooking, her family and the pub, which she now saw as her future. She liked the young artist, James, whom she'd visited just once, but so far, she hadn't got round to taking him more of her food, though she was considering it. Maureen had taken him food several times and told her that he'd asked after her, so perhaps she would soon – but what was she to do about Jason?

'You look cross?' Fay said curiously. 'Is it that letter?'

'Oh, it's from Jason – you know I told you about him,' Maggie replied carelessly.

'He made up to you one minute and your mum the next,' Fay said and giggled. 'Has he written to tell you that he's discovered he can't live without you?'

'He wants me to show him London.' Maggie gave a sigh of annoyance. 'I don't even know it that well myself. I was too young to go far on my own when we lived here years ago – and I don't have time anyway.'

'Poor Jason,' Fay said, laughing. 'I could take him round London if you like. I know all the sights.'

'I wouldn't expose you to his charm, Fay,' Maggie said and smiled. 'He would seduce you and take you off to his lair in the wilds of the Highlands, never more to be seen.'

'How thrilling,' Fay said and flopped back on Maggie's bed. 'Poor Jason has come all this way to see you, worn down with love, and you won't spare him the time...'

'Minx!' Maggie said loftily, immune to her cousin's teasing. Actually, their relationship was more complicated as Fay was, in truth, Maggie's aunt, but they'd always thought of themselves as cousins. 'I am glad we're together now, Fay. When you were small, I thought you were horrid.'

'And I hated you,' Fay said and smiled up at her from a pile of pillows she was lounging on. 'They say absence makes the heart grow fonder – that's why Jason wants to see you, poor man.' She gave an exaggerated lovelorn sigh. 'I can't believe you won't see him...'

'I shall see him for a short time if he comes here to the pub,' Maggie replied with a shrug. 'He is all right. I like him as a friend, but he made it so obvious what he wanted. I just think that sort of man is best avoided.'

'Live dangerously, go on a date with him,' Fay dared her, but Maggie shook her head. Fay left it and they turned to their favourite subjects, which included the latest pop music, jeans as opposed to pedal pushers, which were jeans but cut off mid-calf and cooking. Maggie liked to wear her jeans for working in, but Fay preferred her washed-blue pedal pushers.

'I've been asked to a rock 'n' roll dance.' Fay announced suddenly. 'Should I go?'

'Am I invited too?' Maggie asked, interested. 'Who asked you?'

'I don't think you know him – Steve Jensen went to the same school as me but was three years ahead of me. He actually plays part-time in a band, on the drums. He isn't hired to play at this dance, but says he might get asked to play a spot.' Fay looked up at her innocently. 'I'll get you an invite if *you* let me show your Jason the sights of London.'

'Oh, have it your way, but you've been warned,' Maggie replied with a sigh. 'I suppose I should come with you to protect you.'

Her answer was a pillow in the face.

* * *

When asked, Freddie said he would come to the dance, too, as Maggie's partner. 'You can go off and find someone else more interesting,' he told her. 'I'm not much of a dancer anyway, but I'm better than nothing.'

'As a matter of fact, I'd rather talk to you than most men I know – apart from Dad and Grandpa Able or Uncle Pip,' Maggie told him with a smile. 'I just love to dance and I can always dance by myself.'

'If you haven't got a partner, I'll do my best,' Freddie promised with his lazy smile. 'But I'd bet my chance to trial for Manchester United that you'll have more partners than you can dance with before we've been there five minutes.'

'Oh, Freddie! Have you got the confirmation letter at last?'

He grinned and nodded at her, shy for a moment, and then, bubbling over, 'I have to go next month and they will put me up with some other lads in a guest house. We'll all train alongside the team and then we'll play some five-a-side matches to show what we can do. I don't suppose I'll get in, but it will be fun just to try.'

'I'm so pleased. What do your parents say?'

'They were pleased but warned me not to be disappointed if I didn't get taken on when the trial is over.'

'You will – if you want to,' Maggie said. 'I haven't watched you play in ages, but I remember you were good the last year we were down for Christmas. Dad brought me to watch and I saw how much you contributed to the game.' She hesitated, then, 'But is it *really* what you want, Freddie?'

He looked at her and then inclined his head. 'I'm not certain, Maggie. Dad has always said I could play sport professionally but—' He hesitated, then, 'I love to play for fun, but I think perhaps I might prefer a different kind of life. Though I think I would like to try it for a while.'

'You would be a good physical fitness trainer,' Maggie said, 'Or a sports teacher. That's really what you want, isn't it?'

'I think it might be,' Freddie replied seriously. 'I'd enjoy teaching youngsters to love playing the way I do and—' he paused. 'You'll think me a cissy... but I'd rather like to work with handicapped kids if I can, even if I do that on a voluntary basis.'

'Freddie! I don't think you're a cissy, I think that is absolutely lovely,' Maggie exclaimed. 'It would suit you down to the ground. You've always had so much patience.'

Freddie coloured. 'I didn't say it because I want you to praise me, Maggie. I just feel kids that can't do everything we can, need more help. I've read a bit about it and they can play if you teach them how – so I'd like to be able to do that, at least part of the time and work at a normal school the rest,'

'You'll need to go to college for that,' Maggie said and he nodded. 'That makes it more difficult, Freddie. You can't play for the team for a year or two and then go back to school – or perhaps you can go on to college after a break?'

'I could go to college later, providing I get my higher exams. I'm not sure whether I would be able to keep studying if I played football on a regular basis. It's something I still have to discover.'

'Ask questions when you're on the trial,' Maggie advised, 'and don't be rushed into anything you don't want to do.'

'I shan't,' he said and laughed. 'Thanks for listening, Maggie – and thanks for the invite to the dance.'

* * *

When they arrived at the dance the following evening, a singer was crooning the Everly Brothers hit, 'All I Have to Do is Dream', and the young men and women on the floor were smooching to the number. Freddie looked at Maggie and she shook her head.

'I think we'll sit this one out. I have to hang up my coat anyway.'

'Thank goodness,' Freddie said with such evident relief that she laughed and went off to put her coat in the cloakroom, accepting Fay's

when she thrust it at her. When she came back, Fay and Steve were dancing, but the band was now playing an Elvis Presley song and Freddie
grinned at her.

'I can do a bit of what they're doing,' he said, nodding at his sister and
her partner. 'I'm not good at proper dancing though. I'd tread on your
feet...'

Maggie laughed. 'I'll remember that,' she said and took his hand.

They joined in the carefree dancing, waving their hands in the air and
grinning. Steve had just thrown Fay over his shoulder and caught her in a
fancy move that they didn't try to emulate.

Freddie shook his head at his sister as they all met for a drink after the
session ended. The band had played about six hit songs without stopping
and they were all hot and thirsty when it finished and someone put a softer
record on to give the band a rest – The Platters this time.

'You'll do yourself an injury if you let him throw you about like that,'
Freddie warned his sister and she laughed.

'We did it at the school end-of-term dance last year when Steve left. He
is very strong, Freddie. I trust him not to drop me.'

'But your skirt and petticoats went up and we could all see your knickers...' He gave her a big brother look of disapproval, but she ignored him as
Steve brought their drinks. 'What are you having?' he asked as Steve
handed her a glass. 'I hope that is just orange juice?' He gave Steve a hard
look.

'Yeah, sure,' Steve replied, but he winked at Fay.

'If there is gin in there, Dad will kill you,' Freddie said. 'I'm sticking to
orange juice and so is Maggie. If you have any sense, Fay, you'll do the
same.'

'Oh, don't be such a bore,' Fay retorted. 'Are you the same age as me,
Freddie, or fifty?'

Freddie coloured and turned his back on her. He'd warned her and it
would be her own fault if she felt ill in the morning.

Just as Freddie had predicted, Maggie was soon asked to dance by other
partners, and although she danced with Freddie again, she mixed her
dance partners all night, seeming to have fun. Freddie danced with a quiet,
shy, young girl who sat most of the dances out, but he didn't ask his sister to

dance. He was cross with her and although he didn't see her perform any further fancy tricks, she danced with Steve the whole time, refusing other offers. He saw her have two more drinks but thought she stuck to orange juice after the first.

When Steve was invited to play drums for a guest spot, Fay stood by the band and danced by herself. Freddie wondered if she'd fallen for her old school friend. He wouldn't have asked her, because it was something she would normally tell him when she was ready, but she hardly spoke to him that evening and he knew she was sulking because he'd told her not to drink alcohol.

'I shouldn't worry too much,' Maggie said quietly as she stood by his side. Freddie jumped, because he hadn't seen her approach. 'She's just having fun. Fay knows what she wants and marriage isn't on the horizon – at least not for years.'

'She is still innocent,' Freddie said. 'Fay has never had boyfriends – no time to go out with them because she was always training. Although, there was a skater she liked. He used to come and stay occasionally, but then he stopped. I don't think she's heard from Robin for years...'

Maggie nodded. 'I think I remember seeing him once when we came down... but it was a while ago.'

'At least four years,' Freddie replied. 'What do you think of Steve – is he good enough for her?'

'I don't know him well enough,' Maggie said with a smile. 'I think he seems nice, but he only asked me to dance once when Fay went to the cloakroom, so we've hardly talked.'

Freddie nodded. 'I suppose he is all right. I'm just protective of her. I know she is my twin, but she always seems younger.'

'Don't worry about it,' Maggie said. 'I doubt it is serious on either side; they just like each other.'

'Why are you so much more grown up than Fay?'

'I am a couple of years older,' she replied with a teasing look.

'No, it's more than that, you think about things more. Fay only had vague ideas about her cooking until you came along and now, she knows just what she wants.'

'I suppose I've been more inclined to think seriously. I didn't have a brother my age at home to talk to about things I liked. Mum and Dad were always busy.' She smiled at him. 'You two were lucky being twins. You always had someone to share with.'

Freddie looked at her thoughtfully. 'Mum and Dad were always around. They were busy, but they always made time for us. Poor old Mags...'

Maggie shook her head. 'I'm fine, Freddie. I'm doing what I want and now I have both of you for company... until you go away.'

'If I go,' he said and made a face. 'I'm nervous, Maggie. Supposing I'm not good enough? I'll always know...'

'You will also know that you tried,' she said. 'Dad always says that you should try, even if there isn't much chance that you'll succeed.'

* * *

Fay woke with a thumping headache and pulled a face. Steve had kept buying her gin and orange, disguising it as plain orange juice. He'd bought her three and she'd taken the last one to the cloakroom and poured it down the sink, because she didn't want to get drunk. After Freddie had warned her, she'd been annoyed but knew he was right and she'd told Steve to stick to orange juice, but he hadn't. He'd been hoping she would go outside with him for a kiss and goodness knows what else, but she'd managed to refuse, despite his persuasion.

She liked him and he was good fun to dance with, but she knew what she wanted and that didn't include starting something serious with Steve that might end up in a hasty marriage. Freddie hadn't needed to warn her, because Fay knew what she was doing, even if she did get a little carried away, but halfway through the second gin and orange she'd realised what was happening and stopped and she was pleased with herself – but she still had a headache this morning.

Next time she went to a dance like that with a bar, she would make sure she did stick to plain orange juice. She rolled over in bed and hid her head under the pillows as someone knocked at the door.

'Go away,' she moaned. 'I'm dying...'

'No, you're not, let me in,' Freddie said. 'Go on, Fay. I want to talk to you.'

'All right,' she groaned and rolled over to the side of the bed and then went to open her door. 'What's wrong – is the house on fire?'

'Are you still in a bad mood?' he asked, looking at her uncertainly.

'No, not with you,' she admitted. 'It's my own fault I have a headache. Drank almost two gin and oranges and Steve bought me a third, but I poured most of it down the cloakroom sink.'

'He shouldn't have done that,' Freddie said. 'Be careful of him if you go out with him alone, Fay.'

'He's all right,' she replied, 'but I doubt he'll ask again. I made it clear I wasn't going to be easy and that's what he's looking for, so he won't ask again.'

'Good...' Freddie looked at her. 'You don't care – do you?'

'No, not a bit,' she said and laughed. 'It was fun, Freddie. That's all I want for a while – don't you? Time to look for love when I'm older.'

'Yes,' he agreed. 'Fay – should I take that trial with Manchester United or tell them I've changed my mind? I'm not sure it's what I want.'

'Take it, enjoy it and have fun,' his sister told him. 'You can always come home when you've had enough.'

'It won't disappoint Dad if I don't get taken on?' Freddie looked anxiously at her.

Fay smiled and reassured him. 'Dad doesn't care what we do as long as we're happy, Freddie – just go and have fun.'

28

'What are you looking like that for?' Peggy asked, seeing her youngest daughter look furtive as she slipped something into her apron pocket a few days later. 'You're up to mischief – going to tell me?'

'It's nothing,' Fay said innocently. 'Honestly—'

Peggy hesitated. Fay wasn't going to tell her. 'I thought you were going to make a special cake this weekend?' she said to cover the small silence.

'I am,' Fay said. 'It will be coffee and walnut but like no other you've tasted. Francois showed us how to make it on the course.'

'We'll see,' Peggy said a little sceptical. She'd made the cake herself many times, but when Fay presented it to her triumphantly some hours later, she couldn't help exclaiming. There were four layers of sponge filled with fresh cream lightly flavoured with coffee and the icing on the top was delicately decorated with walnut pieces. 'When are we going to try that?' Peggy asked, feeling the anticipation immediately.

'Not until this evening so that everyone is here,' Fay told her. 'It is for Freddie because he's leaving in the morning for his trial with that football club.'

Peggy nodded and sighed inwardly, managing to keep her smile in place. She would miss her young son terribly, even though he would only be away for three weeks initially. If he was taken on as a young player by the club, of course, he would be living away from home. Able said they had to let him do what was best for him, but Peggy would have liked to keep him at home until he went to college. Able had assured her and Freddie that he would be given time to continue his studies.

'You'll probably have day release once a week to go to a school in Manchester and you'll need to do homework in the evenings.'

'That will save me from being bored or getting into mischief,' Freddie said with a grin.

Peggy thought that of all the children in her family Freddie was the one she would trust most to be sensible. She wasn't exactly worried about him getting into trouble, but she would miss him a lot. He was always around, cluttering up the place with his football and cricket gear and playing loud music on the radio or the new record player they'd bought him for his last birthday. His and Fay's laughter would ring out whenever they were together and although she wasn't demonstrative towards her twin, Fay was going to miss him as much as Peggy would – hence the special cake.

When Peggy at last got to taste it, she looked at Fay with respect. 'I have never tasted a sponge quite that light,' she said and laughed as Freddie took another huge slice. 'You'll be too heavy to play football if you eat all that...'

'I'm not going to get cake like this for weeks,' he said and grinned at his sister. 'Perhaps not ever – so I'm eating as much as I can of this one.'

'Oh, I might make you something nice now and then,' Fay replied and looked smug. 'I learned how to make quite a few special things on my course, and if I go to France next summer, I'll learn a lot more. One day our names will be up in lights, Freddie. You'll be football's latest star and I'll be cooking for the rich and famous at their posh parties.'

'I might hire you when I'm rich,' Freddie teased and her eyes sparked with a mixture of indignation and laughter.

After tea, the two of them went off to make sure that Freddie had everything packed that he needed. Peggy could hear their laughter and thumping as they jumped on and off Freddie's bed, clearly having a last play fight as they had regularly all their lives and pillows would be flying everywhere.

'I'll miss that,' Able said, glancing up at the ceiling. 'I hope he does well for his sake, but I don't mind if he decides it isn't for him.'

'He's been football-mad for years,' Peggy said. 'Surely he's going to jump at the chance to join their team if it is offered?'

'Freddie is very deep,' Able replied thoughtfully. 'I talk to him a lot about the future, but I'm still not certain what he wants to do and I don't think he is. Apparently, Fay told him to go and have fun and that's what he is planning on doing.'

'And his school have said he can catch up with his work by attending class once a week and then doing homework. They were very good about it – said it was excellent training for the future and would help him make up his mind whether he wants to play football professionally or teach.'

'Well, he's getting his chance, the same as Fay and Maggie...' Able frowned. 'Where is Maggie? She missed tea and the cake – that isn't like her?'

'Oh, a friend has come to London. Apparently, he has been attending to family business and now he wants a few days holiday before he returns to Scotland. She has gone to meet him at the station. He is staying at the boarding house for a few days and she and Fay are going to show him a bit of London this weekend.'

'Well, Fay knows it fairly well, but if it is Maggie's friend, won't she want to be alone with him?'

'Actually, she doesn't,' Peggy said. 'Maggie isn't that keen on him and was going to tell him she was too busy, but Fay persuaded her she should meet him. They're going to get up early to prepare food for the pub and the cake shop and then leave the cooking to me for once.'

Able smiled. 'Will you enjoy having your kitchen to yourself, love?'

'Actually, I love having them both around. Fay goes to school three days now and they've let her have two days off for her cooking as – and I quote – "work experience".' Peggy laughed softly. 'Once Fay leaves school, and I've agreed she can next spring, she'll work with us until she gets her own kitchen and they set their business up. Then, it will just be Maggie and me – with Fay popping in and out as she pleases.' Peggy sighed. 'I'm going to miss Freddie if he goes though...'

'We both will,' Able agreed. 'I wonder if this would be a good time to have Jon to stay? It might do him good to have new experiences.'

'I asked Janet and she is willing, but Ryan won't let him come to us,' Peggy said. 'He thinks we're too lenient with him.'

'Maybe I should ring Ryan and talk to him,' Able suggested. 'They will be moving to the farm – or smallholding, as he calls it – soon and Jon will need time to settle in. Perhaps if he had some time with us, it would help.'

'You try then,' Peggy agreed. 'Janet says he won't listen to her, because he is too angry.'

'Being angry with the boy isn't going to cure him,' Able said and frowned. 'Jon has always been a little bit insecure and lonely, I suppose. He needs to know that he is a loved member of the family and I believe you're the one to do that, hon. If he doesn't respond to you, he won't to anyone.'

'I think we might help him,' Peggy agreed. 'I understand Ryan being upset over what he's done, but I think he is handling it all wrong – he's just going to alienate his son and that won't help anything.'

'I'll ring this evening and see if he will listen to me,' Able smiled at her. 'We haven't seen half enough of him anyway and I like the boy. I think he just needs a little extra attention.'

Peggy looked at him gratefully. 'What did I do to get so lucky?' she asked. 'I hope he listens, Able.'

* * *

Jon listened to his father turn down Grandpa Able's invitation for him to spend time in London with them and scowled. It just wasn't fair. Maggie was there. His father hadn't turned down her request and he wasn't even her real father – but to Jon it seemed that she got all the attention. His father must hate him to punish him all the time. Well, that was all right. He hated him too... but it hurt inside his chest, even though he told himself it didn't matter and he would get back at his father one day.

'Thanks for offering,' Jon's father said into the phone. 'But Jon has to learn. Staying with you and Peggy is a treat and at the moment he doesn't deserve that. If I thought he was sorry for what he'd done, I'd let him come, but he isn't – he's defiant and insolent and that is what I have to break.'

Jon ran upstairs to his room as his father replaced the receiver and left the hall to go back into the living room. He flung himself on the bed and punched the pillow furiously. Just because he'd borrowed Bert's watch and taken things from bullies that deserved it, he was being punished! It wasn't fair.

Maggie was always doing nice things and she had a lovely future ahead of her. His father had given her what she wanted as soon as she asked and yet when Jon asked him to go to the football match last year, he'd said he was too busy and they would go another time – but he'd just forgotten about it. In Jon's mind that meant he loved Maggie because she was beautiful and he hated Jon because he was bad – so he would be bad... as bad as Al Capone had been. People looked up to him because he was powerful and clever – and Jon would be like that one day. Let his father just wait and see! He'd pay him back one day...

Maybe he didn't have to wait until he was grown up and rich to pay his father back... An idea crept into Jon's mind and he smiled. Maybe he would teach his father a lesson now and make him sorry for the way he'd turned his back on him...

* * *

Freddie felt nervous as he approached the stadium where he'd been told to present himself after leaving the bed and breakfast room he'd been taken to the previous afternoon. He'd been met from the train by a friendly woman who had taken him in her car to the small, clean and respectable lodging house that she ran. Three other boys were staying there and Freddie had talked to them in the evening. They'd gone out and bought fish and chips in a bag, eating them on the way back to the boarding house.

'Mrs Brown doesn't like us having them in our rooms,' a lad of Freddie's age named Kevin said. 'I do sometimes, but she turns up her nose...'

'Have you been here long?' Freddie asked.

'I got here three days ago,' Kevin confirmed. 'I came early because there was nothing much to do at home. Ma works all day – my dad died two years ago. I hope I get in, because otherwise it is the boot factory for me. Ma says she can't afford to keep me at school any longer and I've had to buy my football stuff on hire purchase. She says the restrictions on the never-never are easing now, so she's going to buy a new bed that way.'

Freddie nodded. It was easy to see that Kevin was less fortunate by his clothes and his much-worn football boots. Freddie had everything new when he needed it and knew he was lucky. It was another reminder to him that life wasn't always fair and something inside him kicked against that; he wanted to make things better for other kids – not Kevin, who was tough, but for kids that couldn't look out for themselves.

The other two lads staying at the boarding house were older than Freddie and their names were Gil and Brownie. He thought they might be pretty good at sport by the way they talked so confidently. They had arrived the same day as Freddie and they were all going to the stadium for their first practice session at the same time, but they kept their distance from Freddie and Kevin. Clearly, they thought themselves better than the two London boys.

That first morning was hard work. The trainer had them running round the field, doing exercises and physical stuff that made them all sweat. They didn't even get to touch a ball for the whole morning or to meet any players or even watch them train. All the new lads wanted to catch sight of the Busby Babes, as the survivors of the Munich air crash had been dubbed in the papers. Bobby Charlton and Harry Gregg, who had helped to save lives at that terrible disaster were on the field together with the manager, Matt Busby, but Freddie didn't get to speak to any of them that day, though he thought Kevin might have.

At lunchtime, they were taken to the canteen and told to choose what they wanted from the menu. The trainer watched them like a hawk and Freddie chose cold chicken, salad and a jacket potato. He resisted putting a lot of butter on it and received a nod of approval from the trainer. Some of the other lads had heaped their plates with chips and all manner of fatty foods.

After lunch, they had a lecture on the proper diet and were told to avoid eating things like fish and chips in the evenings.

'Two of you are old enough to drink beer – *don't*,' the trainer told them. 'If any of you turn up the worse for strong drink, you are off the trial instantly. The younger ones should drink water and an occasional fizzy drink – but avoid too much sugar and fat whenever you can. A part of getting fit enough to play professional football is to eat properly. Yes, it is a sacrifice, but if you want to play for us, that is what you do.'

Freddie listened and accepted that he should do what he was told but saw that Kevin looked dismayed. Freddie didn't say anything, but later that evening when he was asked if he wanted to go out and get some chips he refused.

'Mrs Brown did me some brown bread sandwiches – salad and egg and cress,' he said. 'I had a glass of milk with it. It's better than all the fat in fish and chips.'

'That's a load of rubbish,' Kevin said. 'I've always eaten them and I can play football as good as anyone – you watch me in the morning and you'll see.'

Freddie nodded but stayed home and did his homework regardless. He'd decided he would go out one night a week with Kevin and then he would eat whatever he fancied. If they went to a dance or the pictures, he'd have an ice cream or a fizzy drink, but the rest of the time he would stick to the diet the trainer had set them.

* * *

The next morning, they played five-a-side football with some of the lads who were already in the young players' team and Freddie saw that Kevin wasn't boasting. He ran rings round most of the players and Freddie felt pleased he was on his side. He himself was on the wing as usual – so the team had done their homework and placed him where he played best – and Kevin was at the centre. Kevin scored twice that morning against a more experienced set of players and he was full of it when they finished and went into lunch.

'What did I tell you?' he crowed as he helped himself to a large serving of beef and ale pie accompanied by chips again in the canteen at lunchtime.

'You're good,' Freddie said and grinned at him. 'They need players like you, Kevin – after that terrible plane crash.' A little shudder went through him as he imagined the devastation it had caused amongst a team who were friends as well as colleagues.

'Yeah, I know,' Kevin said and for a moment, the cocky grin was gone. 'That was bad – but they've got some decent young players coming on. You're not bad on the wing. It was your pass that enabled me to score my second goal. Gil isn't bad on the other side either – but Brownie was rubbish.'

Freddie nodded. The older boy had been sluggish and slow and he was almost sure he'd caught the smell of stale beer on his jacket, but he said nothing. They had been warned and he wasn't surprised when on the fourth day of the trial, Brownie was told he could go home.

He'd thrown a sour look at the trainer but left without a word. The trainer looked at the rest of them for a moment and then said, 'Brownie broke the rules. He was suffering from a hangover this morning. I warned him twice and then sent him home – make no mistake, get drunk and you're out...'

Freddie felt sorry for the youth who had so quickly lost his place, but it was his own fault. He should have stuck to the rules if he wanted to play for one of the best football teams in the country.

They got taken to one of the first-team's games the following Saturday and cheered them on to victory as they won. 'They haven't done as well since the crash,' Gil said, 'but that was a better performance today. I reckon they'll get back on top again soon.'

The boys all nodded and agreed. It was wonderful to see their heroes play and win after what had happened on that fatal flight and they all felt happier as they returned to their homes that night.

Freddie phoned his parents and told them about the match. His mother came on first and asked questions about the food and if he was all right and then his father asked about the training.

'Are you enjoying it, son?'

'It's great, Dad,' Freddie said. 'They make you feel like part of the team – and it was lovely watching them play. Best match I've seen live for ages.'

'So you're happy there then?'

'Yes, it's great,' Freddie said. 'I miss you and Mum – and Fay – but I'm having fun and getting fitter all the time, and I'm learning a lot.'

'What kind of things?'

'About proper diet, the right exercises and being part of a team,' Freddie replied. 'All the kinds of things that you need for, well, all sorts of things in life.'

'That's good,' Able said and Freddie could hear the approval in his voice. 'I'm glad. We'll see you when you come home after the trial – and ring whenever you like. You can reverse charges if you're short of money.'

'You gave me plenty. I haven't spent much. We're going to a rock 'n' roll session this evening – three of us from the new players – but I stay home most evenings and do my homework. My landlady gets me a proper meal. I pay her, but it is no more than Kevin pays for his fish and chips and much healthier.'

'You love fish and chips,' Able questioned. 'You're not starving yourself?'

'I'll have them tonight – once a week is plenty,' Freddie said. 'I'm fine, Dad. Don't worry.'

'I'm not,' Able said. 'Just have fun, Freddie. It doesn't have to be all work.'

'Mr Robinson wouldn't agree with that,' Freddie told him. 'He is dedicated to fitness and working hard all the time – he is our trainer and if anyone has too much to drink, he sends them home.'

'You don't drink too much I hope?' Able said teasingly and Freddie smiled to himself.

'I'm not that daft, Dad – and I'm not old enough to go to pubs yet. I know I could buy it from an off-licence and take it to my room, but I don't like beer that much.'

'Good. You stick to that and you won't go far wrong.'

'I'd prefer a nice glass of your best whisky or a fine wine,' Freddie said and laughed to himself. 'Goodnight, Dad.'

He heard his father laugh at the other end and went off feeling pleased with himself. He'd tasted his father's whisky at Christmas for the first time and did like it but was sensible enough to know it was best kept for celebrations. He liked the wine his mother sometimes served at lunch on a Sunday and would drink the small amount she allowed but wouldn't think of going out and buying it. One day he would like to know more about wine, but Freddie knew he would never be a big drinker – not like Brownie, who he'd seen hanging around outside the stadium a couple of times since he'd been let go. He'd been drunk and looked miserable and Freddie felt sorry that the youth had a problem that had caused him to lose his dream. He wondered how his friend from school had got on with his trial for Sheffield Rangers. It was odd that Bob hadn't been in touch. Freddie frowned. It wasn't like him not to come round and Freddie decided that he would pay him a visit when he got home.

Freddie wasn't yet sure what he would do if he was offered a place with the young players' team, but he knew he wouldn't waste the chances he might have by getting drunk.

29

Jon went to his father's jacket that was hanging in the hall and, after glancing over his shoulder to make sure no one saw him, took out the wallet. He extracted three one-pound notes and slipped them into his pocket. He wasn't going to that horrible place that his father had found. They'd taken him there and showed him the house that his mother was going to do up and he'd hated it – it was dark and old and there was nothing for miles around, not even a village within walking distance. Jon would have to catch a bus every day just to go to school and that meant he'd have no friends. He wanted to live with Grandma Peggy and Grandpa Able – and he was going to! So, he would run away and turn up in London. His grandparents wouldn't send him home and it would show his father what he thought of him – make him suffer the way he'd made Jon suffer.

If his father fetched him home, he would do it again and again until they got fed up with having to fetch him back. Jon smiled to himself. That would just show them. All he had to do was sneak out without them noticing. Once that would have been easy, but these days they always seemed to be watching – except just now when the phone had rung and his mother had fetched his father, who with his back to him had walked down the stairs and into the kitchen.

'I think it is the people Ryan worked for,' Janet said to Aunt Sheila as

Jon entered unnoticed and listened. 'I hope he doesn't decide to go back there after all.'

'He isn't likely to, is he?' Aunt Sheila asked and Jon sidled past them, picking up his jacket from the back of a chair.

'Where are you going, Jon?' his mother asked and he shrugged.

'Just outside to play ball.'

'Well don't go too far,' Janet told him. 'It will be dark in another hour or so and your father will be cross if he has to come looking for you.'

'He's always cross,' Jon muttered, but his mother didn't hear. She was talking to Aunt Sheila about the house his father had decided that he wanted to buy and, although he didn't stay around to hear very much, by the sound of it, his mother didn't like it much either.

'The house will be all right when I've done it up,' Jon's mother was saying as he closed the door softly behind him. 'But it's more than two miles to the village and I'm not sure how—'

He heard no more because he was running away from the house. His cousin, Christopher, called to him to come and kick a football around, but he ignored him and bolted while he could. It was a long walk to the railway station, but if he kept on going, he might manage to catch the last train to London. If he missed it, he would just have to hide out somewhere until the morning.

Jon shivered as a bird called from the hedgerow and he was aware that it was chilly. Not freezing cold, because it was only the beginning of October, but cooler than of late. He hoped he would be in time to catch that last train.

* * *

'There are just two places left,' Kevin told Freddie that Saturday morning. 'Most of the applicants already know whether they've been taken on and the others have either left or been sent home – except for Gil, you and me.'

Freddie looked at him thoughtfully. 'That means one of us will be sent home,' he said. 'I don't think it will be you, Kevin. You've been playing well the whole time.'

'I was ticked off for choosing chips again yesterday,' Kevin said and looked anxious. 'I am trying to stick to what he says – but I've always been used to getting chips for me tea. Mum just gave me a sixpence and told me to clear off when her friends came round... she called them my uncles, but they weren't...'

'That's rotten for you,' Freddie said. He couldn't imagine having a life like that and felt sympathy. 'Mine always makes sure we have proper food. We have a lot of nice things that Mr Robinson wouldn't approve of but plenty of healthy food too.'

Kevin nodded. Mr Robinson, their trainer, had told them to call him Boss and most of the lads obeyed, but Kevin was a rebel and knew that his selection was on a knife-edge and that was making him nervous. Even if he was the best player, it didn't mean he would be picked. He was a goalscorer and that should mean he would be an instant selection, but both Gil and Freddie were good overall players – and they both obeyed the rules.

Gil was summoned that morning after training. The others looked at him expectantly and, when he joined them at lunch, he was triumphant. He'd been confirmed as one of the young players' team.

'It's just between you two now,' Gil said. 'The Boss said he'd chosen me because I play well wherever he puts me – and I can score goals. I think he is looking for someone on the other side – that's you, Ronoscki. He hinted as much when he congratulated me on being selected.'

Freddie saw the flash of pain in Kevin's eyes and realised that his friend had nothing else but his hope of a place in the team. If he failed, he would return to an uncaring mother and a job in a factory. Freddie's thoughts crystalised in that moment and he knew what he wanted and, that afternoon, he played badly, missing a pass twice and not going for the ball as he normally did.

'What is wrong with you today?' Mr Robinson asked as he called him over later. 'Did you have a late night, last night?'

'No, sir,' Freddie said and looked him in the eyes. 'I'm sorry, but I've decided against making football my career. I have other things I want to do more.'

A look of annoyance flashed into the trainer's face. 'It's a bit late to tell me that, isn't it?' he asked harshly. 'I don't like people wasting my time, Ronoscki. Why didn't you tell me sooner?'

'I enjoyed the experience,' Freddie said truthfully. 'I made friends and I like playing with Kevin – he's a brilliant player and I think he'll be great one day, when he settles down to the routine...'

The trainer's eyes narrowed. 'You do, do you? And where does your knowledge come from, Ronoscki?'

'Just watching the brilliant footballers that you have on the team, sir. I still love football and it will still be my favourite team – I just have more important stuff to do.'

The trainer gave him a suspicious look. 'I was intending to select you – are you sure you want to turn the chance down?'

'Quite sure,' Freddie said firmly. 'I'm good enough to play for amateur teams, but I'm not good enough for yours, sir – and I'm going to university to be a sports teacher.'

'Made up your mind then,' the trainer nodded, seeming to come to a decision. 'Well, I can't say as I blame you – it is a steady job. Your friend Kevin does have the makings of a great player, but it depends on whether or not he can learn self-discipline.'

'Oh, he will, sir,' Freddie said earnestly. 'He hasn't had as good a family life as me – and this means the world to him...'

The trainer smiled. 'And you're a loyal friend. Loyalty is a good trait and it's one of the reasons I had you picked, Ronoscki – but maybe I'll take your advice...'

'I hope you do decide to give him a chance, sir, though it's not my business.'

'Go on then – you'd better pack your kit and get off home.'

'I'll ring my father this evening and travel in the morning, sir,' Freddie said. 'Thank you for all you've taught me – I shan't forget your lessons; they will come in useful in my future career.'

'Will they indeed?' The trainer hid a smile as he turned away. 'Kevin – I want to speak to you now...' His tone turned from indulgent to sharp.

Freddie left the field and went to collect his gear from the locker room. He was aware of a faint regret but knew that he'd done the right thing. He wasn't as good a footballer as Kevin and he'd never been certain that it was the life for him. At least he'd had the experience and it wouldn't stop him playing for local teams for fun. He turned as Kevin came into the locker room and the look on his face told him that he'd been given his chance.

'He's taken me on a six-month trial,' he told Freddie. 'He read me the riot act about sticking to the diet and following the regime all the time – and then said that I was in.' The smile faded from Kevin's face. 'You had a bad afternoon – is that why he sent you home?'

'I should think so,' Freddie lied with a smile on his lips, because he was happy for his friend and knew that it had been his own decision. The place in the team had been his if he'd truly wanted it. 'It means you'll have to keep on your toes, Kevin, but at least you've got your chance.'

'Yes, I have.' A look of relief had entered Kevin's eyes. 'I'm not sure what would have happened if I hadn't. Mum said I'd have to work in the factory where she works, but now I'll be getting a wage and I'll be independent.' The look on his face banished any lingering regrets Freddie might have had and he felt good inside. His decision was a good one for both of them.

'Just don't forget what he told you and stick to the rules.' Freddie offered his hand. 'Good luck. I hope it all goes well for you.'

'No hard feelings?' Kevin said and smiled when Freddie shook his head. 'I shall miss you – you're the only one who was truly my friend. I wish he'd taken us both on...'

'No, it isn't what I want after all,' Freddie replied truthfully. 'I've had a wonderful time, but it isn't the life for me. I'm glad you've got what you want, though, and I'll be watching for news of you. I shan't forget you.'

'Thanks – you'll keep in touch?'

'I'll be your biggest fan when you're playing for the first team,' Freddie promised and they shook hands solemnly. 'I'll give you my address and you can visit or write to me whenever it suits you.'

'And your Mum wouldn't mind if I just turned up?'

'Not a bit,' Freddie said blithely.

* * *

Freddie rang home that night and told his father he was coming home in the morning.

'I hope you're not too disappointed?' Freddie said

'Not for myself, only for you,' Able assured him.

'Then don't be, Dad. I was offered a place with the young players' team, but I turned it down.'

'Ah, that's all right then. As long as you know that's what you want?'

'Yes, I do,' Freddie said and, as Able told Peggy later, there was a new maturity in his voice. 'I'm going to university and I'm going to teach young boys to love sport the way I do – and, one day, I'm going to work with youngsters who have been less lucky at home than I have.'

'Then I'm proud,' Able said and sounded a bit croaky. 'Very proud. We'll speak to you when you get home.'

'I was so emotional I couldn't speak,' he told Peggy later. 'He's a lad we can rightly be proud of, hon.'

'Yes, he is,' Peggy agreed. She would have said more, but the telephone rang again and she answered it. The smile of pleasure left her face as she heard what Janet had to say. 'You say he ran away the night before last? Why didn't you let me know yesterday?'

The answer came back in a breathy voice as Janet struggled to control her tears, 'We looked everywhere for him, Mum, and then Ryan went to the police. They said Jon isn't classed as missing for at least a week. They think he will probably come home again – but I think he is more likely to come to you in London.'

'Does he have enough money?'

'He took about three pounds from Ryan's wallet,' Janet's voice had a suppressed sob in it. 'I thought he was just going out to play. Chris asked him to play football, but he just ran off.'

'Did you enquire at the railway station?' Peggy asked. 'They would surely have noticed a young lad travelling alone to London.'

'Ryan went there, but they said no young boys had bought a ticket. So, unless he boarded without one...'

'Where else would he go?' Peggy asked. 'Has he any friends – back in Scotland?'

'None that I know of in particular. I think that was partly the trouble, Mum. The boys at his school rejected him because he was English – or that's what he told me. He says that's why he took their things...'

'We'll keep a lookout for him,' Peggy said. 'We can only hope that he's heading here.'

* * *

Freddie arrived home the next day just before lunch. After greeting him with hugs and smiles, everyone seemed a bit quiet and when he asked what was wrong, they told him about Janet's phone call the previous evening. Freddie saw their anxious faces. His parents were concerned about his cousin, Jon – by birth he was actually Jon's uncle, but because he'd always thought of Maggie as a cousin, he'd treated her brother the same, as a younger friend rather than a nephew.

'Why would he run away, Mum?' Freddie was puzzled. 'I don't understand.'

'He's been in a bit of trouble with his father,' Peggy said. She hadn't told Fay or Freddie about the small thefts, because she'd hoped they would blow over and need never be more than a small problem for his parents – but taking money from his father's wallet and running off was more serious. 'I had hoped we could sort it out, but now I'm worried what might happen to him. He's only eight.'

'Jon is a bit... well, strange,' Freddie said. 'Both Chris and I tried to get him to play football with us, but often he just refused and went off on his own. I think he must be very unhappy, Mum.'

'Yes, I think you're right,' she replied. 'I wish I could do something...' she sighed. 'Are you very disappointed about your football, Freddie?'

'I told Dad last night. I decided against accepting a place, Mum. When I told Mr Robinson, he was a bit cross that I'd wasted his time, but he accepted it – said he had intended to select me, but would choose someone else.'

'That was lucky for whoever it was then,' Peggy said. 'As long as you're sure?'

'I'm sure, Mum.' Freddie would never tell his parents that he'd turned down the chance so that his friend would be chosen – he was actually feeling a bit relieved. The life of a star football player was never easy and it could be cut short by an accident or a drop in performance. He knew that what he'd decided to do instead would be rewarding and steady. If he worked hard at university, he would have a job for life and that suited Freddie. Perhaps it wasn't quite as exciting as the life he might have had, but he would find his enjoyment in other things and he would play football with his friends at weekends. He would pop round to his friend, Bob Travers' house and see how he'd got on with his trial. In the meantime, he'd keep an eye out for his cousin.

30

When Jon missed the last train to London, he'd been able to sneak into the waiting room and stay there until morning, when he'd ventured out in search of a toilet. When he'd seen his father at the local railway station, enquiring at the ticket office, he'd known that he dared not risk trying to buy a ticket. His father had his back towards him and Jon moved quickly away before they turned and saw him. The man in the office would be looking out for him now and he'd be detained and sent back home to face his father's anger. He'd set his face stubbornly. That wasn't going to happen. He was cold, tired and hungry but still determined to run away. If he couldn't get on a train here, he would find a bus going somewhere else and then go to another railway station, where they wouldn't be looking for him.

Jon knew where the bus shelter was down the road and he'd simply waited until one came along and then got on when it slowed to a halt. He'd paid his fare as far Exeter, which had been written on the bus itself and was one of the few places he'd heard of. When he'd got there, he'd felt hungry so he went to a shop selling snacks and bought a packet of egg and cress sandwiches and a can of fizzy orange. There was a bench on a small green and he'd sat down and eaten. Then he'd asked the next passer-by the way to the railway station. On arrival, he'd asked the price of the fare to London at the ticket office and bought a one-way ticket at the cost of a few shillings.

He'd had to wait for twenty minutes for the next train to arrive and discovered that he was hungry again, so he'd bought three bars of chocolate and sat and eaten them while he waited. Once he was on the train, he'd amused himself by playing I-spy until he fell asleep.

* * *

The next thing Jon knew, a hand was shaking his shoulder.

'You have to get off here, son,' a voice had said.

Jon had opened his eyes and saw the man smiling down at him.

'Are we in London?' he'd asked.

'Yes. You've been asleep for over an hour,' the man had said. 'Where are your things?' He'd looked around as if seeking a bag or suitcase.

'I didn't bring anything,' Jon had said and wriggled away, running down the aisle to jump off the train before the stranger became too inquisitive. As he'd approached the ticket collector at the gate, Jon had felt a bit nervous in case they were looking for him there too. Had his father informed the police? Would he be arrested?

He'd handed in his ticket and the man had hardly looked at him. Jon had breathed a sigh of relief. It had been far easier than he'd thought, apart from an uncomfortable night and a bit of time wasted on that bus journey – but he was here at last and he was free to do what he liked.

It was now mid-afternoon and Jon decided that he would have a wander round the streets before he caught a bus to Mulberry Lane. It would serve his parents right if they were worried about him, he thought. Perhaps they would miss him – and Granny Peggy would be so pleased to see him. She would give him a big hug and put her arms around him and she'd offer him a slice of apple pie. Thinking about his granny's apple pie made Jon feel hungry again. He saw a barrow selling fruit just across the road and decided he would buy some bananas, so he just ran across the road without thinking. His head was filled with his triumph at how easy it had all been and how clever he was and he just never saw the van that hit him...

* * *

Peggy smiled as Freddie settled down at the kitchen table and got his schoolwork out. Her son knew his own mind and she didn't have to worry about him. Despite the glamour of the past few weeks, he was looking forward to a return to his school and to taking his exams the next summer ready for going to university.

'I know what I want to do now, Mum,' he told her as he tucked into a large slice of her apple pie. He'd refused the custard she'd offered him, telling her that he intended to follow the diet that he'd learned about during his time with the prestigious football club. 'I shan't keep to it as rigidly as Mr Robinson would like his players to, but I shall stick to the idea – a sensible diet is good for us all, Mum.'

'I know,' Peggy agreed and she'd gone without her own customary dollop of custard. 'I am trying to lose a little bit of weight.'

'You don't need to,' Freddie told her with a loving smile. 'You are perfect as you are, Mum. I wouldn't want you to be any different.'

Peggy felt her eyes sting. Freddie had always been loving towards her, but he seemed even more so that day. 'That's lovely, darling.'

'Kevin's mother doesn't care what he does,' Freddie said, looking thoughtful. 'She just gave him sixpence and told him to buy some chips every night for his tea. He said he had lots of pretend uncles when he was a boy – and if he hadn't got onto the team, she would have forced him to work in the factory or just abandoned him.'

Peggy looked at him. 'She doesn't sound like a very nice person, Freddie.'

'I felt sorry for him. He is a fantastic footballer, Mum, much better than I am – he deserved the last place on the team.'

'Did he, darling?' Peggy was thoughtful. 'I'm glad he got it then.'

'I think it will be fun at uni,' Freddie said and smiled at her. 'I can't wait to go, Mum. There will be lots of sport and it will be exciting – don't you think?'

'Yes, I do,' Peggy replied. 'I think you'll have a wonderful time there...' She heard the phone ringing. 'I'd better answer that... Oh, it sounds as if your father has.'

'I think I'll get in all right,' Freddie said and looked anxious for a moment, but before he could say anything more, the thoughts were wiped from his head by his father's words from the doorway.

'That was the police,' Able said. 'They've found Jon... but it isn't good news, hon. He has been knocked down running across the road just outside Paddington Station.'

'No!' Peggy felt the colour drain from her face as she rose to her feet. 'Poor little Jon. Is he very badly hurt?'

'Yes, I am afraid he is,' Able replied, looking grave. 'He has several broken bones, some slight internal damage – but they don't know if he will be brain damaged because he took a knock to the head.'

Peggy sat back down heavily and the tears started to roll down her cheeks. 'Oh my God! That is terrible – but I don't understand – why did they ring us?'

'Apparently, Jon had a piece of paper with your name and telephone number on it. He had written Granny Peggy, Mulberry Lane and our number – so the police rang to ask if we had a young son. I told him our grandson was on his way to stay with us, which I am even more certain now that he was.'

Peggy wiped the tears from her cheeks. 'We have to let Janet and Ryan know – and then we have to get to the hospital. Will they let us see him?'

'I imagine they will, even if it is briefly,' Able said. 'It's an awful thing to have to tell your daughter, hon. Would you like me to do it for you while you get ready to visit him?'

'Yes. Yes please, Able,' Peggy said. 'I'll talk to Janet later...' She glanced at Freddie. 'You'll be all right here, love?'

'Yes, of course, I shall, Mum – I'm very sorry this has happened. If anything happens to Jon, Janet and Ryan will never forgive themselves...'

'Will they be able to forgive each other?' Peggy asked and shook her head as she hurried from the kitchen to change her working dress for something she could visit the hospital in. Freddie was right. Janet and Ryan would blame themselves for this – but they might also blame each other and that could mean the end of their marriage. Peggy had heard of it happening, where a tragedy to a child had resulted in the parents hating each other, blaming each other. It was Jon's own carelessness that had caused the accident. He must have run straight across the busy road without looking each way – but young children did that and Jon had never been out alone on the London streets. Always, he'd had someone with him, to hold him back and remind him that he had to be careful.

Somehow, he'd managed to get here by himself. The realisation that he'd been only a short distance from her and safety made her heart catch with pain. She loved Jon as she did all her grandchildren and the dread of his death and what it would mean to the whole family hung over her like a dark cloud.

Maggie and Fay came in together just as Peggy returned to the hall. They'd been planning the kitchen in the cake shop with Tom Barton and were talking excitedly until they saw the long faces.

'What's wrong?' Maggie asked, looking anxious. 'Is it Jon?'

'Yes, I'm afraid it is,' Able told her. 'He's had a nasty accident. We're on our way to the hospital now and your parents are coming up immediately.'

'Should I come to the hospital?' Maggie asked, her face white.

'It's probably best that we go this time,' Peggy said. 'I'm not even sure they will let us see him, darling. I'll tell you everything when we get back.'

Maggie nodded. 'I'll look after things here if you don't get back before opening time,' she offered. 'Just go and see how he is, please.' Her eyes were brimming with tears but she held them in check.

Peggy went to give her a little hug and she responded with a watery smile.

Fay was no longer bubbling over with excitement, the joy of her new kitchen overshadowed by the terrible news.

It wasn't just Jon's parents who would be affected by this, Peggy thought. They were a close-knit family and everyone was going to share the pain.

* * *

'He was hit up into the air,' the doctor said, 'and the injuries are bad. I am not going to lie to you, Mrs Ronoscki. It will be a miracle if your grandson lives and if he ever recovers to enjoy a normal life. This first couple of days are crucial and that is just the physical injuries. We can't know until he wakes up if he will be mentally impaired, so prepare yourself for the worst.'

Peggy closed her eyes. She'd been through this once before when Pip was injured in a car crash, but this was even worse in a way because Jon was only eight years old.

'What is your professional opinion of his chances, Doctor?' Able asked him. 'Does he stand a chance?'

'Seventy-thirty against him completely recovering,' he replied. 'I'm not sure how extensive the damage to his kidneys and liver is yet, but I know there is damage to his left leg, which is broken in two places, and possibly his spine. We're operating to repair the damage we find but...' He shrugged. 'In these cases, it is sometimes the trauma that kills.' He looked at them sympathetically. 'I am so sorry to be so brutal, but I have to prepare you and his parents.'

Able reached for Peggy and put his arm around her, supporting her as the tears ran unheeded down her cheeks. 'Thank you for being honest,' he said. 'We appreciate all you are doing for him.'

'May we see him?' Peggy asked tremulously.

'He is in theatre now,' the doctor said. 'If you wish to wait, you may see him briefly when he comes back from recovery – or visit this evening for a few minutes. He may not be conscious, but sometimes patients know the person they love is with them.'

'I'll come back later,' Peggy said.

She let Able take her away and summon a taxi. He sat with his arm around her, holding her as she wept all the way back to their home. It was only as she got there that she straightened up, her head lifting.

'Janet and Ryan are going to need us,' she said, 'and Maggie. We mustn't let this spoil things for her and Fay. We have to be strong, Able. We are the ones that have to keep the family together. Janet may never forgive Ryan for this – but we have to, because he is going to be in torment over it and blaming himself...'

Able nodded, because he understood what Peggy was trying to say and do. It was a difficult situation. Ryan had naturally been angry that his son had stolen things and he'd punished him, but sometimes children needed more subtle and understanding treatment and love, and now the finger of blame would point at Ryan. If anything happened to his son, he would be haunted for the rest of his life. They could only hope and pray that Jon recovered...

* * *

'I'm so sorry,' Fay told Maggie when they sat looking at each other across the kitchen table after seeing her parents rush out to the hospital. 'It is awful news.'

Maggie wiped a hand across her eyes and sniffed. 'Poor little kid,' she said. 'He must have had a rotten time to make him run away like that.'

Fay nodded in agreement. She couldn't imagine what that would be like and was suddenly very aware of how lucky she'd been. Her mother and father had given her everything they could, letting her have all those skating lessons and not even saying a word when she suddenly just gave it up. Freddie had told her they were lucky, but she'd just taken it for granted. 'I'll do the cooking for today,' she offered Maggie. 'You go and sit down or do whatever you want.'

'No, I'd rather work with you,' Maggie said. 'I'm glad Jason has gone back to Scotland. I wouldn't have wanted to see him this evening, but he made up his mind quickly. Do you know why?' She gave Fay a direct look.

'Yes, I think so.' Fay nodded and a look of mischief entered her eyes. 'He asked me to meet him the other evening – the day after we all went out together – said he wanted to talk to me alone because he'd never met anyone like me and I'd taken his breath away.' She tried to keep a straight face and failed, giving a naughty giggle. 'He told me that now his great-aunt has left him lots of money, he can restore his estate and marry the right girl...'

Maggie looked at her hard, dismissing Jason's revelations. 'The cheek of it! He hardly knows you. What did you say when he asked?'

'I told him I would—' Fay hesitated. 'I let him wait and then I didn't go – I thought it was funny, him being stood up, and I was going to tell you, but it doesn't seem so funny now.' She looked chastened. 'With Jon so ill...'

Maggie's mind was still on Jason. 'You just let him wait and you had no intention of meeting him?' she questioned.

'Well, he shouldn't have asked me,' Fay said. 'He's years older than me – and you'd warned me not to trust him, so...' She laughed. 'Don't you think it served him right? I can just picture him sitting there waiting and getting annoyed, can't you?'

'Yes – and he would have been so cross.' Maggie gave her a half-smile. 'Minx! I do think it served him right. I can just imagine what your mum would have said if she'd known what he'd asked you. She would've skinned him alive!'

The girls looked at each other for a moment and then burst out laughing as they pictured the scene. Poor Jason would have been reduced to a quivering mess once Peggy Ronoscki got going on him.

'Well, being stood up would have deflated his ego. No wonder he sent me that curt note saying he was going back to Scotland today.' Maggie shook her head at Fay. 'I saw him flirting with you and I was worried you might fall for him – and then you play a trick like that...' Maggie looked at Fay in wonder. There was more to her than met the eye – more of her mother than anyone yet guessed.

'I'm sorry. He's your friend. I shouldn't have done it.' Fay was apologetic.

'Oh, but you should,' Maggie said. 'He won't come here again in a hurry.' She reached for Fay and hugged her. 'Thanks, Fay. You've cheered me up. Normally, I'd be happy, laughing at the thought of his annoyance – but all I can think of just now is Jon.'

'He will be all right. I know he will,' Fay said and gave her a quick kiss on the cheek. 'He must know we all love him, surely he does?'

31

'Oh, Peggy, I am so sorry,' Maureen said when she went round to see her friend the next morning. 'I wish I could say or do something to help, but I know I can't. I know how awful it feels.'

'All we can do is pray and hope,' Peggy replied, looking anxious. 'Janet and Ryan are at the hospital now. Janet rang me when they got here and they were hoping to be able to spend a little time with him.'

Maureen nodded. 'I was feeling so pleased because Shirley is back home and seems none the worse for her ordeal. She has a nasty scar on her chin and her throat, but she says they will fade and doesn't seem very upset by them. Ray told her that they just make her more interesting and she was happy with that – they're planning a Christmas wedding, but now...' She looked sad. 'We do seem to get it, don't we?'

'I sometimes wonder what I've done that is so terrible I have to be punished,' Peggy said and swiped at the tears on her cheeks. 'I haven't been a wicked woman, have I?'

'Of course you haven't – and none of this is your fault,' Maureen said firmly. 'Come on, Peggy. You know better than that. Keep your chin up, love. We've both been through rotten times before.'

'I remember how devastated you were when you lost Robin. Jon isn't my son, but he's Janet's and she wanted him so much – and so did Ryan. I just can't understand what went wrong. Why did Jon start taking things that didn't belong to him? There must be something behind all this... something that made him unhappy.'

'Yes, I'm sure there was,' Maureen said. 'You told me Ryan refused to let him come and stay with you, perhaps that was why he ran away?'

'It may have been – but his father was adamant that he needed to learn discipline.'

'By the sound of it, I think Ryan must have just handled it badly – he was too angry to see what he was doing. Kids do things you don't approve of now and then, but getting angry and punishing them hard isn't always the right thing. I remember that woman on the farm hitting Shirley with a hairbrush. It upset her so much and I was so angry I could have hit her, but I just brought Shirley home and promised that whatever she did, I would never hit her because I loved her. She never caused me a moment's worry after that.'

'It never happened to any of mine,' Peggy said. 'Janet getting pregnant before she married Mike was about the worst and I didn't even mind that – it was just her father that caused the rift. I've always thought that if he'd accepted it... and yet if he had, I wouldn't have Able or my Freddie and Fay...'

'Life is strange at times,' Maureen said. 'In Shirley's case, she has learned not to take risks – and Ray is making sure that a proper service is set up for those poor devils who aren't on the doctors' lists – so good came from her pain.'

'I doubt anything good can come from this,' Peggy said and caught back a sob. 'Jon is too young to suffer like this, Maureen. I think his accident is going to cause trouble in that family, because Janet may blame Ryan and I'm not sure that things will ever go back to how they were if he does recover.'

'If Janet blames Ryan,' Maureen looked sad, 'it is bound to cause distress and perhaps a rift. I've always felt sorry for her after what happened with Mike. I don't think she ever quite got over it...'

'Ryan thinks the world of her,' Peggy reminded her.

'Yes, I know he does,' Maureen agreed, 'but she needs a strong hand and Ryan has been absent too often... and I think perhaps he's a bit selfish.

Maybe I'm wrong – but it has always been about what he wants. He wanted the job in Scotland and then he wanted this smallholding. Has he once asked Janet what she wants? Or Jon for that matter? Able would always consult you, wouldn't he? Just as Gordon always asks me what I think.'

Peggy was struck dumb because it hadn't occurred to her that Janet or Jon might not want to go along with Ryan's plans. Yet when she thought about it, Maureen was right. He did tend to present his ideas as an accomplished fact rather than a suggestion. 'You might be right,' Peggy said thoughtfully. 'I was surprised when Maggie said she wanted to live and work here in London with me – perhaps Jon feels the same. He might not want to live in the new house. Janet says it is a bit of a mess, though she has plans for it... But it didn't sound as if there was much to interest a young boy. I'll talk to them about it – but first of all, we have to see if Jon recovers from his injuries. We can't plan anything until then.'

* * *

'Why don't you go to your mother's?' Ryan said as Janet moved uncomfortably in her chair. 'They told us he probably won't wake for ages and there's no point in us both being here.'

'I'm not leaving him,' Janet said sharply. 'If you've had enough, you go and get something to eat.'

'I'll stay with him,' Ryan replied. 'You look exhausted, Janet. Please go, love. I don't want you ill too—'

'You should have thought about that when it mattered,' Janet snapped and he turned away, a shaft of pain in his eyes. Janet softened as she saw it and said: 'Sorry. I'm just out of my mind with worry. It isn't your fault.'

'We both know it is my fault,' Ryan said in a flat tone that told her he was struggling to control his feelings. 'I handled him all wrong. You told me not to be too hard on him and I didn't listen. I was so angry and ashamed that a son of mine could take that watch.'

'It was a shock,' Janet agreed. 'I didn't like it any more than you did, Ryan, but we need to talk to him, to understand why – and we should have let him come to Mum. Brought him up ourselves. She would have sorted him out...'

'He's our son – it's our mess… or mine,' Ryan said and looked utterly miserable. 'I know I am the one who should have seen it coming. It's because I was never at home. When I took you to Scotland, I promised I would be around and then I let you down.'

'It's not all your fault…' And yet in her heart, she blamed him. Her son was lying in a bed, pale and unmoving, fighting for his life, and she knew that if Ryan had been kinder, more understanding, it wouldn't have happened. She didn't want to blame him. A part of her kept saying it was an accident that no one could have foreseen – but the other half of her screamed that if Ryan had listened to her, it would not have turned out like this.

'We both know it is the truth,' he said heavily. 'I shall blame myself for the rest of my life if—' He left the words they both dreaded unsaid, because it was unthinkable that they could lose the son they both loved so much.

'If I hadn't been busy doing Pip's house up – if I'd spent more time with him, taking him places…'

'You did take him to a cricket match and to the beach. He was with the family – Pip, Sheila, Sarah and Chris – and he came with you to the cottage some of the time,' Ryan said. 'He needed his father and I wasn't there – I was too busy earning money.' The bitterness was in his voice and his soul. 'I'm a damned fool, Janet, and I know nothing I do will ever make up for what…' He choked and then bent his head and wept.

Janet got up and went to put her arms around him, holding him as he sobbed. She knew that if Jon died, in the future she *would* blame Ryan and she would never truly forgive him, but for now he was suffering just as she was.

* * *

'I'll telephone and ask to speak to the doctor looking after Jon, if you like, Mum,' Shirley said. 'Better still, I could ask Ray to do it – you know he specialises in this kind of thing. He understands head traumas as much as any other doctor. If he speaks to them, they will tell him the truth.'

Maureen hesitated for a moment, then, 'Peggy had a call from Janet.

She says the hospital doctors are concerned because he hasn't come out of the coma yet...'

'Well, it is early days, Mum. You know that from your own experience as a nurse. Sometimes the body just needs to rest after a terrible accident. We just have to wait and see, because all we can do is help the body to heal – it does that little miracle all by itself sometimes.'

'Yes, I know,' Maureen said and smiled at her. 'We saw that often enough in the war. Some of the men – their injuries were so bad you couldn't see how they would ever recover, but they did in time, with good nursing and medicines.'

'It often looks and sounds worse than it is at first,' Shirley said hesitantly. 'Even if the worst happens and Jon is damaged in some way, he is still their son and they will still love him.'

'Yes, but...' Maureen shook her head. 'I hate to think of that happening to Janet, love. She has suffered enough.'

'What if it happened to Gordy?'

'Don't!' Maureen shuddered. 'It doesn't bear thinking of...'

'But if he was so badly injured that he was in a wheelchair – would you put him in a home of some sort or bring him home?'

'You know I would bring him home.' Maureen's reply was instant, unthinking.

'Then Janet and Ryan will do the same,' Shirley said. 'I know it is horrid, Mum, but it happens. They will learn to cope with it, just like everyone else who suffers something of the sort.'

'That's *if* he lives...'

Shirley looked thoughtful. 'I would say he has probably come through the critical stage,' she said. 'If he's made it thus far, he will probably live – but he may be damaged.'

Maureen sighed. 'Peggy went through all this once before, when Pip was injured. It doesn't seem fair it should happen again.'

'It wasn't fair that we lost Robin. There is no rhyme nor reason for accidents and sickness, Mum, we just have to cope,' Shirley said gently. 'Ray will find out all he can for us. He said he would ring me this evening and I'll talk to him then.'

'He'll be living here in London soon,' Maureen said and smiled at her. 'I haven't forgotten your wedding, love. We'll have to start planning for it.'

'Ray is looking for a flat for us to live in when we're married,' Shirley nodded, looking thoughtful. 'I wondered if we should just have a quiet wedding, Mum, and have it as soon as Ray gets somewhere to live down here – for Dad's sake.'

Maureen stared at her and then inclined her head. 'You've noticed it too...' She closed her eyes as she saw the answer in Shirley's face. 'He seems to be tired more often these days.'

'Yes, he is,' Shirley agreed. 'I've told him not to do as much exercise for a while.'

'Yes, probably wise,' Maureen agreed. 'Perhaps he's been doing too much.' She made the suggestion, but, in her heart, she didn't believe it. Gordon's health was slowly deteriorating and that was why Shirley wanted to get married sooner rather than later – in case he wasn't around by Christmas. Maureen blocked her desire to cry. She wouldn't let herself think about that possibility.

'Yes, I expect it is that,' Shirley said but Maureen knew she didn't believe it either. They reached for each other's hands and held them briefly, united in love.

* * *

After Shirley had gone to work, Maureen did some cooking. She made some extra sausage rolls and two casseroles, so that she could take one to James. It was several days since she'd visited and she knew he would probably be living out of tins.

His door was open despite the touch of frost in the air and she knocked, but when there was no answer, she just walked in. He turned with a look of hope and expectation in his eyes, which faded as he saw her.

'I just brought you some food, James,' she told him. 'Were you expecting someone?'

'I thought it might be her – the beautiful girl who came once before,' he replied. 'I think she said her name was Maggie. She said she would come back, but she didn't...'

'Maggie has been busy,' Maureen replied and told him why. He listened to her story with interest and his face clouded with concern when she came to the bit about Maggie's younger brother. 'I expect she'll come when she can,' she finished.

'I shan't be here for the next three weeks,' James told her. 'I'm flying on that new Comet jet aircraft BOAC that has started to take passengers across the Atlantic. My London show was such a success that they want me to exhibit in America...' He hesitated and then turned a canvas round so that Maureen could see it. 'Do you think it looks a bit like her?' he asked shyly.

Maureen stared at the portrait. It was Maggie and yet it wasn't – he'd made her represent the Lady of the Lake. She smiled and nodded. 'It is like her, James, but it isn't Maggie. She is so much more than this – but that is a lovely picture.'

'Yes, she is more – but I need her here to paint her properly,' he said. 'Will you ask her, Maureen? Tell her I'll be back in a month and ask if she can find time to let me paint her – please?'

'Well, I'll ask,' Maureen said, 'but I know she is busy...'

'I can't get her out of my head,' James said, shaking it. 'I need her to sit for me. She doesn't have to cook anything for me – though it would be nice if she did...'

'Did you get paid anything from your London show then?' Maureen asked, realising that they were going to lose their delivery driver.

'I shall do when they send the cheque,' James said vaguely. 'Oh, I'll still do the deliveries when I get back.' He smiled at her. 'I hope you can manage while I'm gone. How is Gordon now?'

'I've got a new assistant now for the shop, so I'll send Ginger on his bike with the deliveries,' Maureen said and sighed. 'Gordon is as well as I can expect. I will tell Maggie, James, but I can guarantee she will do it.'

'Just an hour or so now and then – in the evenings, if she's less busy...'

'I promise I'll speak to her,' Maureen said and he nodded.

'Thanks – and thanks for all the lovely food you keep giving me. I do appreciate it, even though I might not always remember to say.' James flashed her a winning smile and Maureen nodded. He could be very charming when he remembered. He just spent most of his life wrapped up in his work.

32

Ryan was alone in his son's hospital room when Jon finally opened his eyes. He'd managed to persuade Janet to go to her mother to get washed, changed and rest for a while, promising to let her know the moment Jon woke. The doctors wanted Jon kept quiet for a few days, away from the bustle of a busy children's ward so it was best if only one person was there at a time.

Jon's eyes flickered a few times and then he was staring at Ryan, but there was no hint of recognition, no feeling of either hate or love or anything else and Ryan's heart sank. If his son was permanently damaged, he would never forgive himself.

'Jon – son, I'm sorry I was upset with you,' Ryan said and held the small hand in his. 'I shouldn't have been angry. I was wrong and we'll sort it out between us when you're better. I promise.'

Jon's eyes closed, but his features relaxed into a smile and, when the nurse came in a few minutes later to check up on him, she nodded and took his pulse.

'He seems much better,' she said. 'I think he is going to pull through – and all you can do is keep giving him the love and attention he needs. He is going to be a sick little boy for quite a while, but it looks as if he may be through the worst of it.'

'Thank God – and you people here,' Ryan said, voice throbbing with emotion. 'I would never forgive myself if anything...' He broke off and gave a little sob. 'He means so much to us all. I don't think he realises how important he is to his mother and me... We waited a long time for him and, well, you know how it is...'

The nurse nodded sympathetically. 'Yes, I do. My little brother is about his age and I can just imagine how my parents would feel if anything like this happened to him.'

'I blame myself entirely for what happened,' Ryan said.

'You weren't there. It was an accident – and the police say the driver had been drinking whisky. Not much but enough that it slowed his reactions. Jon just ran straight across the road and the driver didn't see him until it was too late.' The nurse patted his arm. 'It was a terrible accident, that's all.'

'But if he'd been at home where he ought to have been, he wouldn't have run across that road,' Ryan said. 'I'd been cross with him – more than I should have – and he ran off because he was so unhappy. I can't forgive myself for that—'

'Don't blame yourself too much,' the nurse said kindly. 'Children do these things for all sorts of reasons.'

Ryan nodded and she went off on her rounds. She was being kind, but he knew that his son was lying here in this bed because he'd been too harsh. Janet had been right. He should have talked to Jon about what he'd done instead of going in with a heavy hand and laying down the law. Yes, Jon had done wrong, but he was only a little boy and he needed help not punishment. He felt his son stir and looked down at him.

'Dad...' the word was only a whisper, but Ryan heard it and leaned down to touch his son's face. 'Where am I?'

'You're in hospital,' Ryan said. 'You had an accident. You ran across the road and a van hit you...'

'Am I going to die?' Jon looked frightened and Ryan's heart twisted with pain. 'It hurts all over...'

'No, son. You'll feel unwell for a while though. I'm so sorry,' Ryan choked out the words. 'Can you forgive me?'

'Forgive you?' Jon blinked at him. 'What did you do?'

'I was cross with you and you ran away.' Ryan looked at him. 'Don't you remember that you got on a train and came to London by yourself?'

'No. I just know it hurts,' Jon whimpered and a tear trickled down his cheek. 'Will I get better, Dad?' He clung to his father's hand as Ryan took it.

'Yes, you will,' Ryan answered positively. 'You will be sick for a while, but we'll get you better, I promise. I'm going to look after you. I'll be spending lots of time with you, Jon. I'll make sure that you have all you need.' He could feel the tears on his cheeks. Ryan had been given a second chance and he wouldn't mess up this time. In future, his son would be his first concern.

'Can we live in London with Granny Peggy and Grandpa Able?' Jon said in a small voice that trembled. 'I don't want to go back to Scotland. I don't like that school – they bully me and call me names because I'm English...'

'You never told me that, Jon?' Ryan looked at him. 'I would have taken you away from there if I'd known.'

'You were never home,' Jon said and shut his eyes again.

Ryan stared down at his son. He said he didn't remember running across the road in front of that van and yet he remembered the bullies at school. It seemed strange, but he would ask the doctors about it. The main thing was that Jon had pulled through. He was going to live and if caring and love could do it, Ryan would get him over this terrible accident. At least, he'd seemed not to have the damage to his brain the doctors had been concerned about. Now that Jon was resting, he would take a few minutes to ring Janet and let her know that he'd woken.

* * *

'There was some swelling in his head we weren't sure about,' the doctor confirmed when he visited Jon later that evening. 'It seems to have subsided and, as you witnessed yourself, he isn't badly damaged mentally.'

'He didn't recall the accident – is that a sign of damage?' Ryan asked, still fearful.

'Not necessarily. It happens sometimes, because of the trauma,' the doctor replied. 'His memory may be patchy – he will recall some things and others he may not, some people or places – we can't be sure. However, most of his vital signs are good. His bones will heal and the internal damage wasn't as bad as first feared – so Jon has every chance of making a good physical recovery. He will need patience and care as he recovers. He will need a wheelchair for a while when he leaves here – and there may be some lasting injuries to limbs that will never quite be the same, but we have to give it time and see.'

'And when can he leave hospital?' Ryan asked.

'He'll need another couple of weeks at least. There is just a small chance that because of the damage to his spleen an infection could flare up and we might need to operate, but we shan't unless we have to because it can be detrimental to the blood count. If we'd taken it out in the first place, he might have needed to take iron tablets for life, because of the risk of anaemia.'

'Yes, I understand,' Ryan said, feeling relieved. 'But you think he'll be able to live a normal life – once his injuries are better?'

'I hope so, yes,' the doctor replied. 'I can't tell you that your son is fine, because after an accident like this – well, things can develop suddenly. I can only say that the signs are good and I believe he will make a good recovery.'

It was a cautious reply, which meant they weren't certain Jon was completely out of the woods yet. 'He was complaining of pain earlier...'

'Yes, I expect so,' the doctor nodded. 'We are giving him some painkilling medicine, but we don't want to use anything too strong. I'm afraid he will feel a bit miserable for a while yet. Just talk to him, take his mind off it if you can. What kind of books does he like? Bring him something he's interested in to help him through the next few days or so.'

Ryan thanked him and, later, when Janet got back to the hospital, he telephoned Maggie with the news. 'He's getting on as well as can be expected,' he said. 'He asked me where he was and seemed to understand but didn't remember the accident. The doctor said he needs something to keep him busy – do you know what kind of books he likes or puzzles?'

'You didn't bring anything up with you?'

'No – we just came out in our coats and left everything...'

'Well, I'll see if Freddie has a few books that he no longer uses. If not, I'll buy him some magazines and puzzles.'

'Yes, that sounds like a good plan. Maggie...' Ryan hesitated. 'Are you getting on all right? I'm sorry if I was annoyed with you for not mentioning what your brother was up to.'

'No, you were right. I should have told you – I feel it's my fault Jon ran away and had the accident.'

'No, never,' he said. 'It was my fault for handling it badly, but I'll do better now. You do know I love you?'

'Yes, thanks, Dad,' she replied and laughed softly. 'I've never doubted it. I'd like to visit Jon when I can.'

'Perhaps tomorrow,' Ryan suggested. 'Most of the time he just sleeps at the moment, but he is improving. He woke up properly that once and again when your mother arrived. She kissed him and he smiled and she told him she loved him and he said he loved her – and then went back to sleep.'

'Are you coming home? Granny says there's a bed here for you – or at the boarding house if you prefer?'

'I can't leave yet,' Ryan said. 'Once I've seen him awake for long enough to sit up and eat, I'll rest, but until then...'

'You made Mum come home and have a rest,' Maggie said. 'You should, too, Dad. If you're ill, you can't look after him – and he will need that.'

'I know – but I daren't leave him. He already thinks I don't love him. Imagine if he wakes and I'm not here.'

'You'll need to show him how much you care when he's better.'

'Yes, I know. He wants to live in London near Peggy and Able. I'd got the papers to sign for the land I was going to buy, but if Jon wants to be here...' he sighed. 'At the moment, I don't know whether I'm coming or going, Maggie.'

'Have you asked Mum and Jon whether *they* want to live on that farm?'

'No... I just thought it would be best for us all.' Ryan's spine prickled. 'Has Janet mentioned it to you?'

'I don't think she was very keen. She says it is too far for Jon to go into school by himself every day and he will have no one to play with or anywhere to go. If you haven't signed, I wouldn't – get something nearer to a village so they have a bit of life, or better still come here. There are parts of London where you could get a big enough garden to do what you want and you can add more land once your business gets going. I've been researching it and I can give you a few hints as to what you should be growing for the restaurant market. If you can secure good London customers, you can do well growing specialities for them.'

'Thank you. I'll think over what you say.'

'It's time you thought of yourself *and* Mum and Jon. Don't worry about work too much; it will come right.'

'You have a wise head on your shoulders, Maggie.'

'I've thought about what I want for years...'

'You wanted to live here...' Ryan hesitated, then, 'Did you hate it in Scotland too?'

'Me?' Maggie sounded surprised. 'No, I loved it – but it wasn't suitable for what I want to do. I'll be going back for holidays with friends sometimes.'

'Jon hated his school apparently.' Ryan sighed.

'I think he got in with a bad crowd,' Maggie said. 'There were some bullies that gave him a hard time. I wanted to sort it out for him, but he said it would only make things worse.'

'I'd have moved him somewhere else if I'd known.'

'Yes, I should have told you but...' She hesitated and he knew what she was unwilling to say.

'I was never around?'

'Well, not enough to have a long talk. I thought you and Mum had enough to cope with – but I didn't realise how unhappy Jon must have been.'

'Poor kid,' Ryan said. 'I didn't understand what my long hours were doing to the family, Maggie. Wherever we settle in future that mustn't happen again.'

'Can't you please find something nearer to London so that Jon can visit often – or just let him live with us and you and Mum visit as often as you can?'

Ryan was thoughtful as he replaced the receiver after reminding Maggie to look for the books for Jon. He'd never thought of himself as a selfish man. His long hours had been to provide a good life for his family and his reaction of leaving his job and looking for a farm had been instinctive, but he hadn't thought to ask Jon or Janet whether it was what they wanted. Obviously, he would need to cancel the contract he'd been about to sign and next time he would have to make sure that the whole family was happy before he decided to buy a home.

33

'I am so glad Jon is starting to get better,' Maureen said when she visited Peggy a couple of days later. 'I was very worried about him. Shirley's fiancé says that his doctors are very hopeful that he has no permanent damage.'

'He still wanders in his mind a bit,' Peggy said with a relieved look. 'He knew me and Able straight away but doesn't remember what happened or why he was in London on his own. He can remember bits of his holiday but not after we came back to London – that all seems to have vanished... and perhaps it is a good thing.'

'Yes, I'm sure it is,' Maureen agreed. 'Anyway, as long as he is getting better, that's all that matters. Now, the reason I came round today is to invite you all to a wedding. Shirley is getting married in three weeks. It is in church, but it will be a quiet affair. I know she said Christmas, but they've brought it forward to November. She doesn't want a big do and she's asked to have just a few friends. Your family are all invited and a couple of her hospital friends and one school friend. Ray doesn't have anyone much of his own, so he's just inviting his sister, an uncle and three colleagues from his old hospital.'

'A nice intimate gathering,' Peggy said with a smile. 'Just what we could all do with, Maureen. I don't think any of us would have felt like attending a big do – but is Shirley sure that's what she wants?'

'Yes, quite sure. I think it is for her father's sake, Peggy. She says a big wedding would be too much stress for him.'

'Yes, perhaps it might,' Peggy agreed. 'What can we buy her as a wedding gift?'

'I think something silver or porcelain,' Maureen said. 'Ray is used to nice things so we're getting them a silver tea and coffee service – some cutlery would be good or a porcelain tea or dinner service?'

Peggy nodded and smiled. 'I'll go and buy it in Harpers. They have lovely things there.'

'Yes,' Maureen nodded. 'There was a rumour last year that they were closing, but they didn't thank goodness. I'm going to buy a new dress and coat there for the wedding – navy and pink I'd like.'

'That will suit you,' Peggy replied. 'Oh, isn't it lovely to have something nice to talk about again? What with Shirley's attack and Jon's accident – it has been awful. Gordon too – how is he, Maureen?'

'Not good,' Maureen said and a shadow passed over her face. 'He has been a bit quiet and that's never a good sign with him.'

'I'm so sorry, love,' Peggy said. 'If there is ever anything I can do...'

'I know.' Maureen smiled at her. 'Let's think about the wedding for now, Peggy. One thing I do know is that Gordon is looking forward to it. He is thrilled that Shirley is marrying Ray – such a lovely man and so clever. Gordon says he couldn't have picked better himself. I thought he might worry about the age gap, but he says it doesn't matter because they are very much in love – and they are. You can see it in the way they look at each other.'

'Lovely.' Peggy hugged her impulsively. 'I'm always here for you, whenever.'

'I know,' Maureen replied. She hugged Peggy back. Their friendship was the thing that kept her going whenever she felt like breaking down. She was the person Maureen headed to when she had good news or bad.

* * *

'They're going to put the opening of Parliament on television,' Able said from behind his newspaper that evening. 'That should be interesting – and they've awarded a life peerage to a female for the first time. What do you think of that, hon?'

'Good for her,' Peggy said and sat down next to him. 'It will be nice having a wedding again.' He laid down his newspaper, which was headlining Mike Hawthorn's fantastic achievement in becoming Britain's first driver to win the Formula One championship in motor racing. 'I rang Pip and Sheila and they are going to come up for it – so we'll have all the family here.'

'Will Jon be out of hospital in time?' Able asked, frowning. 'I'm not sure Janet and Ryan will feel like a wedding celebration if he isn't...'

'I think he should be, even if he is still in plaster,' Peggy said. 'If not – well, it can't be helped. We'll still all be together in London and we'll manage a bit of time in each other's company somehow.'

'Yes, we'll do that,' Able said and looked pleased. 'Fay is excited because Shirley has asked her and Maggie to do their catering. Fay says she'll make them the best wedding cake ever and Maggie is busy planning a nice, simple but delicious menu. Shirley said she wants it to be something that we will all enjoy rather than fancy stuff.'

'Fay will be in her element making that cake, but I wonder what Maggie will come up with,' Peggy said with a smile. 'I know what I would have done for a family party like this.'

'I thought she might have asked you?' Able suggested. 'You're not upset that she didn't?'

'No, this is their chance to shine,' Peggy replied and held out her hand to him. 'It is a new time, Able – a new dawn at Mulberry Lane. The young ones are getting into their stride and this is a chance for them to show what they can do.'

'What would you have done?'

'I think I'd have had a nice prawn cocktail for starters, a lovely shepherd's pie with vegetables, followed by—'

'Apple pie and cream?' Able said hopefully.

'Well, apple pie and cream or sherry trifle – so people can choose,' Peggy agreed and laughed.

34

'Have you decided on the menu for your wedding?' Maureen asked when Shirley told her that Fay and Maggie were to do the catering. 'Having it at the Pig & Whistle is a lovely idea. It keeps it in the family and makes it more cosy. Is Fay excited about making the cake?'

'Yes, she has all kinds of ideas, but I told her just a simple two-tier cake. I knew you would understand about having the reception at the pub,' Shirley said. 'Ray said I could have whatever I wanted – he would have paid for a reception at the Ritz if it was what I asked for, but this is what I feel comfortable with – and it will get Fay and Maggie started.'

'Yes, it will,' Maureen agreed. 'So what are you having then?'

'Maggie is going to do a nice tomato soup with crusty rolls for starters, Peggy's special shepherd's pie for main course and apple pie with cream or strawberry blancmange with fruit and cream as the sweet course.' Shirley laughed as she saw Maureen's face. 'She says the men in her family all love the apple pie and she knows strawberry blancmange is my favourite.'

'Considering that most caterers can't think of anything better than cold tongue, ham and salad, followed by fruit trifle as the wedding breakfast, I think that sounds lovely,' Maureen said with a smile. 'But I thought Maggie would want to do something fancier?'

Shirley nodded. 'She suggested a lobster and prawn mousse followed by Beef Wellington and sauteed potatoes with a lemon souffle to finish, but I told her that was too fancy for me.' She smiled. 'Besides, it is their first go at catering for several people apart from the pub meals, and I don't want them to get flustered and worried. This way they can prepare it all earlier and enjoy the wedding. They are my friends as well as my caterers.'

'That was thoughtful of you,' Maureen approved. 'But are you happy with it?'

'It is one of my favourite menus,' Shirley said and smiled. 'You know how much I love tomato soup and Peggy's shepherd's pie is always delicious – and they are going to ask her to make that but do the rest themselves. I think you'll find that the soup will be the best you've ever tasted and the rest will all be delicious.'

'I'm sure it will.' Maureen laughed. Peggy would be surprised to be asked to prepare the main course, but it would make her feel a part of it all. Shirley had thought it all through, the way she always did, telling Gordy that he was to be her attendant and hold her bouquet, because if she'd suggested a page boy outfit he would have been horrified. He was going to wear a grown-up suit with long trousers and that had pleased him no end. Maureen felt a sense of pride in her daughter. Who would have thought that a selfish spoiled little girl of seven would turn into this considerate young woman? The first time she'd visited Maureen's home, she'd been rude and naughty, but ever since Maureen had taken her in as her daughter, her true loving nature had shone through. 'And you've bought your dress,' Maureen said, smiling at her. 'It was the nicest one we saw, Shirley. There were lots of fancier ones, but I like what you've chosen. It looks wonderful on you.'

Shirley had picked a simple, white velvet dress that fitted her slender figure. It reached her ankles and had long sleeves with a point that lay over her hand and looked a little medieval, simple and pure. With it she had a short veil of heavy lace and a little coronet of pearls. She looked like a princess out of a fairy tale to Maureen's mind, and beautiful.

'I knew as soon as I saw it,' Shirley said and smiled at her. 'We were lucky to find you a lovely outfit, too, Mum.'

The shop had specialised in weddings, catering not only for the bride and bridesmaids, but also for the mothers of the bride. Maureen had bought a nice two-piece with a dress and a three-quarter length coat in navy blue, fine wool and she'd found a pillbox hat in shocking pink with lots of veiling that looked good on her. Gordon had a smart, navy blue pinstripe suit in the wardrobe that he planned to wear and Maureen had bought him a pale blue shirt with a dark blue tie to go with it.

'So what do you think Ray will make of it all?' Maureen asked her. 'Have you told him what we're having at the reception?'

'No...' Shirley gave her a smile filled with mischief. 'He'll get a surprise and it will be fun to see what he makes of the menu – and all of us.' Ray had met her family and Maggie so far.

Maureen nodded, amused by her daughter's expression. 'He will take it all in his stride, Shirley. I doubt if much bothers Ray.'

'I'm so lucky that he decided to come to London to work,' Shirley said. 'I'm not sure what I would have done if he hadn't...'

'You would have gone back to Durham,' Maureen told her firmly. 'But Ray didn't force you to make that choice – and that's why I like him so much. He put you first.'

Shirley nodded happily. 'Yes, he did, Mum, and that shows he loves me. I asked him if he was certain he wanted to change his life so much and he assured me he was quite happy. I know he admires Great Ormond Street for the wonderful work they do and he says he's proud to be a part of their team, so perhaps it was all meant to be.'

'Yes, I'm sure it was,' Maureen agreed. She looked round as Gordon entered the kitchen. He'd been upstairs having a lie-down. She smiled at him. 'Are you ready for a cup of tea, love?'

'Yes, please,' Gordon replied. 'Are you all set for the wedding, Shirley? Nothing more you need?'

'Just your blessing, Dad,' she said and went to put her arms around his neck and kiss his cheek.

'Well, you have that always,' he said and smiled.

'I'm going to pop round to see Maggie and Fay,' Shirley said. 'They want to show me something to do with the wedding.'

'Off you go then,' he replied and watched as she put her coat on and left.

* * *

'Where are you going for your honeymoon?' Maggie asked as she, Fay and Shirley sat drinking coffee and eating a slice of Fay's coffee cake. 'Has Ray said anything?'

'He says it will be a surprise – but I think we're going to France. I know he sometimes borrows a house out there from a friend, so I think he'll take me there to show me all the places he loves.'

'I'm going to a chateau in France next summer,' Fay said confidently. 'For a cookery course I want to take.'

'If Granny Peggy lets you,' Maggie reminded her.

'Oh, she will next year,' Fay replied. 'I'm grown up now and very sensible.'

'Huh,' Maggie said and made a face at her. 'I'm not sure Jason would think so – playing tricks on him that way.'

Fay giggled and reached for another slice of cake. 'This is scrumptious, even though I say so.'

'Eat too much of it and you'll get fat,' Maggie teased, though Fay was willow-slim and she probably wouldn't get fat if she ate the whole thing.

'Well, I am going to love you and leave you,' Shirley told them after they'd finished their coffee and the cake. 'Is there anything else you need to know for Saturday?'

'No – and don't worry it will all be perfect,' Maggie said. 'We're really looking forward to doing this for you, Shirley.'

'So am I,' she replied and looked round as Freddie entered the kitchen. 'We've eaten all the cake, Freddie, sorry there's none left for you...'

'That's OK, I had some earlier,' he said and smiled. 'It was a good film, Fay. You should have come with us. Bob would have liked that.'

'I don't like cowboy films,' Fay said ungraciously. 'Besides, I don't like him much...'

'Oh, well, your loss,' he shrugged and went into the pantry, emerging with his mother's cake tin, which he opened. 'Ah, coconut twists, great!'

'I thought you didn't want any cake?' Fay remarked.

'I'm hungry,' Freddie said and took two of the coconut biscuits from the tin. 'Goodnight all.'

He went out again, busily munching. Fay and Maggie looked at each other and laughed.

'He came back from his football trial with his head filled with his special diets, but he's back to the old Freddie again,' Maggie explained.

'Just the way we like him,' Fay said. 'We need him to experiment on – try out all the food. When he tells us we shouldn't eat this or that, it just spoils things.'

'He's right though,' Shirley replied. 'A balanced diet is better for everyone.'

'Boring,' Fay said and Maggie laughed.

'Yes, absolutely,' Shirley said. 'I'd better go. I have some more packing to do. Ray is coming down tomorrow and I'm moving my stuff into the new apartment.'

'Oh yes, you're going to be posh now – living the other side of the river...'

'I'll still visit as often as I can,' Shirley said. 'I like the apartment Ray chose for us and it is convenient for work – but I shall miss being just round the corner from you two when I'm married...'

'No, you won't,' Fay replied. 'You'll be with Ray and it will be lovely – and we'll see you when you visit Maureen and your dad.'

'Yes, you will.' Shirley got up and they laughed and then had a quick hug all round. 'See you on Saturday then... and it had better be good...'

'It will be,' they chorused as she went out.

Maggie looked at Fay as the door closed behind her a little doubtfully. 'I hope she will be pleased with what we've done. I'm not sure we should have changed the menu, Fay. Shirley was quite certain she wanted Peggy's shepherd's pie...'

'It is too boring for the wedding of a special friend,' Fay insisted. 'We're making a shepherd's pie anyway – or Mum is – but the other is a surprise. So everyone can choose which dish they want.'

* * *

Freddie hadn't said a word to his twin about Bob's experience, but Bob had told him he was doing well until the man who had recruited him made suggestions he didn't like. Bob had kicked him in the shins and run off, locking himself in his room. The next morning, he'd been told to go home because he wasn't good enough.

'I was better than any of the others,' Bob said and Freddie knew it wasn't a boast, 'But I knew what you'd told me and I wasn't having any of that.'

'I'm glad you didn't stay if that's how it was,' Freddie told him. 'Have you spoken to your father?'

'I can't tell him,' Bob said and made a face. 'Mum isn't going to get better – the hospital said the illness has gone too far. Dad is too upset about her and so am I. They were just glad I was home'

'I'm sorry.' Bob shook his head and Freddie nodded, understanding that he didn't want to talk about it. 'So what will you do in the future?'

'I'm good at maths,' Bob replied. 'I'll probably train as an accountant – boring but steady, my father says.'

Freddie agreed, feeling sad for his friend and then he laughed. 'Knowing Maggie and my sister they'll have no idea about bookkeeping – you will have to offer to sort the accounts for them when they get into a mess, and they will...'

Bob's face lit up. 'It would be worth taking it up just for that,' he said. 'I really do like your sister, Freddie.'

'Well, maybe one day she'll have the sense to like you,' Freddie said and gave him a brotherly push. 'She's busy with this wedding at the moment, but when it's over, I'll see if she will go out with you. We're mates you and me, Bob. I'd like you as my brother-in-law one day and you'll be around now rather than playing football all over the place.'

'Yeah.' Bob grinned at him. 'I'd rather be back home with you, Freddie. We can still play football for the local lads, can't we?'

'Run rings round them,' Freddie said and laughed. 'We'll watch that new sports programme *Grandstand* together. I haven't seen it yet, but Dad saw the first three and says they were good.' He gave Bob a friendly punch in the arm. 'I'm glad you kicked that so-and-so in the shins. If you told your dad and he spoke to the boss at Sheffield Rangers they would sack him.'

'Nah, not worth it. He'd only say I was lying. It's over and I'll forget it.'

Freddie inclined his head. Bob was probably right. They talked some more and Freddie invited him to come round after the wedding was over on Saturday.

'It's friends of ours and Mum will be busy, but she won't mind you coming round – you could stop the night if you want and, on Sunday, we can go to the match together.'

* * *

That Saturday in November was fine and sunny, even though it had the chill of a winter day. Shirley got up early and went for a walk round the garden before breakfast. When she came in, Maureen had prepared a special breakfast of muffins and honey and they ate it in a leisurely way before Gordon ventured down. He had toast and honey and they all sat over a cup of coffee before Shirley went up to have her bath and prepare.

Rose Barton came round at mid-morning with a large box wrapped in pretty paper and stayed for half an hour talking to Maureen and Shirley. Shirley was wearing her dressing gown and slippers and had her hair in rollers. The scar on her neck was still there, but the angry red had faded to pink and the neckline of her wedding dress would soften and conceal most of it. Maureen knew that Shirley had accepted it and all that mattered was that she'd recovered well from her ordeal. After chatting over a cup of tea, Rose went off home to her husband and children.

'That was nice of Rose and Tom,' Maureen said and Shirley looked at her.

'I never thought – should I have asked Rose and Tom to the wedding, Mum?'

'If you'd been having a bigger wedding, yes, but Rose understands. I spoke to her and she wasn't offended at not being asked – she knows it is just family.'

'Rose is a bit like family, though,' Shirley said. 'I suppose I should have asked.'

'You can ask them to tea when you're settled in the flat,' Maureen suggested and smiled. 'Don't worry about it, Shirley. Rose isn't upset, I promise you.'

Shirley nodded. 'I'd hate to offend her. I just didn't think...'

'I know, darling.' Maureen looked up as Gordon entered with his son. Both of them were wearing their suits and clearly ready.

Gordon's brows rose. 'Hadn't you two better be getting ready? It is a quarter to twelve. We don't want to be late to the church...'

'Gosh, the time flies.' Maureen jumped up. 'It won't take me ten minutes – but let's get you dressed, Shirley.'

'Yes, my hair is dry now.' Shirley smiled at her father. 'Good thing we've got you to keep us right, Dad, or we'd never get there.'

'He'll wait for you, Shirley,' Gordy said and grinned at her. 'Can I have a bit of cake, Mum?'

'Yes, help yourself,' Maureen said, 'but don't get your shirt dirty – and leave room to eat something later.'

* * *

They were at the church exactly on time. The bride didn't use her prerogative to keep the groom and guests waiting and the ceremony was conducted. The bride and groom looked so happy and more than a few tears slipped down cheeks as the handful of guests watched.

Afterwards, they paused in the winter sunshine for photographs to be taken and then everyone piled into the hired cars to go back to the Pig & Whistle. The bar had been closed for the day and it was decorated in white, silver and turquoise, the tables covered in pristine cloths and set with Peggy's best dinner service and cutlery.

The menus were handwritten and decorated with tasteful, silver swirls and more extensive than even the bride had expected.

Spicy Mediterranean tomato soup

Or

Prawn and salmon mousse

***

Peggy's special shepherd's pie with beans

Or

Beef Wellington with creamed potatoes and buttered cabbage à la Maggie

***

Apple pie with cream

Or

Strawberry blancmange with fruit and cream

***

Fay's Special Wedding Cake

Coffee and liqueurs with home-made truffles

'Oh, my word,' Maureen said as she looked at the menu. 'Those two must have been up all night by the looks of this.' She shook her head as she read it again. 'I'm sure Shirley doesn't know they've gone to all this trouble.'

'Well, I think it's lovely of them,' Gordon said and looked pleased. 'I think I'll have the mousse followed by the Beef Wellington – and maybe just a little of the apple pie.'

'I think I'll stick to the soup and the shepherd's pie,' Maureen said, a little doubtful that the girls had managed to pull off such an ambitious menu all by themselves – though, of course, they'd have had Peggy's help.

The guests were spoiled for choice and, after some deliberation, the men in general went for the soup and the Beef Wellington, while most of the ladies had the mousse and the shepherd's pie.

'You missed a treat,' Gordon told his wife after he'd eaten his two courses. 'Those girls certainly know how to cook.'

'I liked mine, thanks,' Maureen said but knew she'd chosen the pie out of loyalty to her friend. Shirley, Sheila and Janet had done the same, she was almost sure, but all the men had tucked into the Beef Wellington and were looking very pleased with themselves. The children mostly went for the shepherd's pie, though Jon looked pale sitting quietly in his wheelchair next to Ryan, and ate hardly any of his meal. He'd been allowed out for a few hours and would return to hospital later that evening to finish his treatment. For now, he was sitting between his father and Granny Peggy, who had managed to make him smile a few times. Peggy had chosen the Beef Wellington and seemed very happy when she tasted it. When it came to the sweet, all the men went for apple pie, while the ladies were split. Shirley enjoyed her favourite dessert and Sheila's daughter, Sarah, tucked into it, too, and asked for more.

The cake, coffee and liqueurs were enjoyed by all but the youngest children, who were not offered the alcohol, and when the bride and groom had been toasted, Maggie and Fay were called in to be applauded at the groom's insistence.

'I have been to a couple of posh weddings in my life, but I don't think I've ever enjoyed the meal as much as this one,' Ray said. 'I salute you, young ladies, and I thank you for a wonderful surprise.'

'You shouldn't have gone to so much trouble,' Shirley said, 'But it was wonderful and we all loved it – thank you.'

Maggie looked a little shy, but Fay beamed and curtsied, grinning like a Cheshire cat, as her twin told her later.

And then the toasts and speeches were all over and the bride and groom were leaving, being showered with confetti. Shirley gave her beautiful bouquet of roses to Maureen.

'I want you to enjoy these, Mum,' she said. 'Put them in water where you can see them.'

'Thank you, darling,' Maureen replied and kissed her. 'Have a lovely time – and a wonderful life. I don't have to tell you to be happy, because I know you will.'

'I'll be back soon,' Shirley said and hugged her. 'Take care of yourselves – you and Dad and Gordy. He looked so grown up today. I was proud of him.'

'He is quiet sometimes and very thoughtful, but, like you, he knows what he likes and what he wants. Have a lovely time.' Maureen kissed her cheek and then waved to her as the car drove off to start their honeymoon, Shirley waving out of the window. Maureen felt Gordon's arm go around her waist. 'Didn't she look beautiful – and so happy,' Maureen said.

'She has every reason to be,' he replied and smiled at her. 'Just as I have.'

'Me too,' Maureen said, looking at him with love. 'Shall we go home?'

'Yes, please. I'm a bit tired.'

'I'll just say goodbye.'

Maureen went and hugged Peggy, smiled at Able and thanked everyone for being there. She told Maggie and Fay how much she'd enjoyed their meal and saw the pleasure in their faces.

'I shall never forget the look on Shirley's face when she saw what you'd done for her – she meant it to be an easy trial run for you two and then you went to all that trouble. I don't know how you managed it.'

'It was easy,' Maggie said. 'We did the blancmange last night and made the pastry first thing, then prepared the vegetables and the soup – and then the fancy stuff. Fay made her cake a week ago and iced it yesterday.'

'The cake would have been even better if I'd made it a few weeks ago,' Fay said. 'I didn't have enough notice to the right amount of brandy.'

'It was delicious anyway,' Maureen said. 'Everything was, thank you.'

'Ray is going to recommend us to his friends,' Maggie said. 'It should get us started.'

'Yes, I imagine it will,' Maureen replied. 'Gordon loved his mousse and the Beef Wellington. I've never made that, Maggie. You must tell me how you did it another day.'

'Come round and I'll show you,' Maggie offered. 'But it has to be for a special occasion – when there are enough people to share it.'

'Yes, I imagine it is quite a lot of trouble to make,' Maureen agreed, smiling. 'And very expensive.'

'But special,' Fay said and glanced at Maggie. 'We had to cook it three times before today to make certain we got it right.'

'Good gracious.' Maureen stared at them in amazement. 'I don't think I could have done that – whatever did Peggy say?'

'She said as long as she got to eat it once a month in future she wouldn't complain.' Maggie laughed. 'We tried it out on the pub customers and some of them said they preferred Peggy's shepherd's pie. I don't think they realised what it was.'

'Well, good luck, girls. I have to go.'

'I'll be round in the morning,' Peggy said and hugged her friend. 'Your Shirley looked wonderful, Maureen. You must be so proud of her.'

'We are,' Maureen agreed. 'Just as you will be of Fay and Maggie when the time comes for them.'

'Neither of them wants to get married for years.' Peggy smiled. 'They are very modern young women, Maureen. All we ever thought of was getting married, but they want to set the world on fire with their cooking – not literally, of course.'

Maureen laughed. 'No, that wouldn't be a good idea – but I think they will, you know. Did you see all the men had the beef? I felt sure they would go for the shepherd's pie.'

'Why should they when they can have Maggie's signature dish? I know which one I like.' Peggy laughed. 'Don't look so shocked, Maureen. Once upon a time we were lucky to get shepherd's pie and we knew it, but it is a new time, love. A new dawn, and things are improving for most of us. We have to take what we can and hold it, enjoy it. If that means I can eat the kind of food that my clever granddaughter makes, then I'll drink to that.'

Maureen looked and saw that Gordy and her husband were talking to Freddie and Able and laughing. It was good to see everyone so happy, though she knew that Ryan had taken Jon upstairs to rest. Janet had told them that Jon had wanted to come to see them off but was tired and needed to be quiet for a while, before returning to the hospital. Yet they were lucky that he had survived his accident without lasting damage and would continue to improve, when it could have been so much worse. 'It was lovely food.' Maureen smiled at her friend. 'And I had the shepherd's pie because I like it and, also, I didn't want to offend you...'

Peggy smiled. 'I know and I love you for it, Maureen. In future, choose whatever Maggie makes. You missed a treat.'

'Yes, well, there's always next time,' Maureen said with a laugh.

35

Gordon was looking tired when they got home. Maureen felt a spasm of concern as he sat in his chair and closed his eyes for a moment.

'I'll make you a cup of tea,' she offered, but he caught her hand and asked her to sit down. She did so, her heart racing as she saw his serious expression.

'I have something to tell you,' Gordon said and she drew a shaky breath, fearful that he was about to tell her he felt very ill, but his next words surprised her. 'When Ray returns from their honeymoon, he is going to book me into a private clinic and he will operate on me himself. He has seen my X-rays and the results of my tests and he thinks my chances are much better than that doctor told us. Ray says that if he does it, he's certain he can give me several years – and by then, there will be other treatments that will prolong my life even further.'

'Oh, Gordon.' Maureen was surprised, overwhelmed by a sweeping relief and tears pricked her eyes. 'You refused it earlier this year,' was all she could say. 'What changed your mind?'

'Ray will do it himself and there's the difference,' he said. 'He is a brilliant surgeon and I trust him, Maureen, and I know that he will bring me through. He told me that if he wasn't certain, he wouldn't attempt it, because Shirley would never forgive him – so if he is that confident, so am I.'

'Then I'm glad,' she said and the tears just rolled unchecked down her cheeks. She'd been so fearful of losing him. 'I'm so glad, my darling.'

Gordon smiled and squeezed her hand. 'I reckon the odds are in my favour with Ray doing it himself, don't you?'

'Yes, I do,' she agreed. 'I know he regularly saves the lives of children, so why shouldn't he save yours?'

* * *

Peggy just smiled and hugged her when she told her the news. 'I'm so glad,' she said. 'I know how worried you've been and Ray is the very best; if he says Gordon will be all right, he will. It's been hard for both of us recently, but you will be fine now; we'll all be fine. Jon will soon be out of hospital. He was tired after the wedding, but he is gradually getting stronger and Ryan says he can stay with us for a while when he comes home – just until he finds somewhere to live and work not too far away so they can visit regularly. This time Janet is looking with him and she wants to live closer to us so that they can see more of us. Hopefully, that will help them all get over the trauma of his accident. It looks as if things will be better all round.'

'If anyone can sort that lad out, it's you, Peggy,' Maureen said and brushed away her tears. They were happy ones, because Peggy was right: she would be all right now for a while. 'You said it was a new time and perhaps it is – perhaps this is the start of the good times. Not just for us and our families but for poor old Britain, too. It has taken us a while and a lot of struggles to get over the damage that last war did, but perhaps now things will change for the better. Just like Supermac said.' She laughed at the nickname people had given the Prime Minister.

Only just over a year earlier, the Prime Minister, Mr Harold Macmillan, had told them in a radio broadcast that Britons had never had it so good and the two friends had shrugged their shoulders and doubted his words. Now, however, with their personal lives looking brighter than they had for a long time, both felt that perhaps he was right. Perhaps a new era was on its way – and they were both still here, able and eager to share it with the younger generation who would make it happen.

'It is a time for the young ones,' Peggy said. 'Don't you feel it, Maureen? I do. The new music and dancing, even the fashions are for youngsters with lots of energy, and the world is bursting with new ideas and new hopes. There are jet planes flying across the Atlantic and look at the way Donald Campbell set that water speed record! Everything is changing, getting faster, bigger, better in a way we would never have dreamed it could. Yes, it is surely a new beginning – and it's about time too...'

MORE FROM ROSIE CLARKE

We hope you enjoyed reading *A New Dawn Over Mulberry Lane*. If you did, please leave a review.

If you'd like to gift a copy, this book is also available as an ebook, digital audio download and audiobook CD.

Sign up to Rosie Clarke's mailing list for news, competitions and updates on future books.

http://bit.ly/RosieClarkeNewsletter

Why not explore the *Welcome to Harpers Emporium* series, another bestselling series from Rosie Clarke!

ABOUT THE AUTHOR

Rosie Clarke is a #1 bestselling saga writer whose most recent books include *The Shop Girls of Harpers* and *The Mulberry Lane* series. She has written over 100 novels under different pseudonyms and is a RNA Award winner. She lives in Cambridgeshire.

Visit Rosie Clarke's website: http://www.rosieclarke.co.uk

Follow Rosie on social media:

 twitter.com/AnneHerries

bookbub.com/authors/rosie-clarke

facebook.com/Rosie-clarke-119457351778432

ABOUT BOLDWOOD BOOKS

Boldwood Books is a fiction publishing company seeking out the best stories from around the world.

Find out more at www.boldwoodbooks.com

Sign up to the Book and Tonic newsletter for news, offers and competitions from Boldwood Books!

http://www.bit.ly/bookandtonic

We'd love to hear from you, follow us on social media:

facebook.com/BookandTonic
twitter.com/BoldwoodBooks
instagram.com/BookandTonic

Lightning Source UK Ltd.
Milton Keynes UK
UKHW042040280222
399365UK00001B/8